I0527739

No Senator's Son

RJ Huddy

A PEACE CORPS WRITERS Bc

To Patty, my sister

Acknowledgments

My deepest gratitude goes to James Burgett, Harvey Kline, Garry Lingerfelt, Anthony Martin, and Tom Sumner for generously lending their invaluable knowledge and expertise to this project.

The comments of Hannah Arendt are taken from The Jewish Writings by Hannah Arendt, edited by Jerome Kohn and Ron Feldman, Schocken Books, March 2007.

Cover design by James Burgett
Cover graphics modified from images available at www. shutterstock.com, www.letmecolor.com (Frank de Kleine), and http://etc.usf.edu/.

A Peace Corps Writers Book.
An imprint of Peace Corps Worldwide.

First Peace Corps Writers Edition, October 2011.

No Senator's Son. Copyright © 2011 by RJ Huddy.

ISBN 978-1-935925-17-0

Some folks inherit star spangled eyes,
They send you down to war, Lord,
And when you ask them, how much should we give,
Oh, they only answer, more, more, more.

It ain't me, it ain't me,
I ain't no senator's son.

—John Fogerty, Creedence Clearwater Revival

BOOK ONE

Sons of a Congressman

1

THE SECRET CONFERENCE TO CREATE A NEW WORLD, 1959

WALTER HEARD VOICES beyond the far doors—superior tones from noses held high. He almost laughed out loud. Wait until these so-called geniuses saw what he had in store for them. These worthies. This nobility. Taking America down the road to ruin. Senators, congressmen, financiers—people with power to draw a line on a map and say, *You! Out!* They had no idea what was about to hit them. Let them crowd together out there. Let them think they're walking into a normal conference where they can put on airs and act like lords. That's what made it so funny. Walter would lift his cup, the doors would open, and a new world would grow from the carcasses of the high-and-mighty.

From his carcass, too. He could never get away with it. They would take him down with them—he understood that. He saw that just as clearly as he saw America's ruin. But screw it, he thought. I will change the world before I go. When you know the future already, what's the point of living it?

He looked down at his cup. If he wanted to change his mind, it had to be now. After this there would be no turning back. Lift the cup, destroy one world, create another.

He held it to his nose, closed his eyes, and inhaled the dark, pungent aroma, dank and peaty, well-aged but still alive; carbon life forms decaying back to basics. God it smelled good. For one moment he lost himself in it. He took a sip, let the taste linger on his tongue, swallowed, and opened his eyes.

The great ballroom was nearly empty. The chandeliers gleamed; the chairs sat in perfect order. Across the room Jimmy stood with his back pressed to the big green baize doors, the voices growing louder behind him. He watched Walter for a sign. Roxanne busied herself checking a list of names on a clipboard. She pretended not to watch Walter from the corner of her eye. At the back of the hall

5

three Mexican bartenders in uniforms stood almost to attention behind a long table of bottles and glassware.

Record all this, Walter reminded himself.

Aged only thirty-two, yet the next raised cup would close out his second existence. His first existence had been the son of a Texas dirt farmer. That one veered into instability when he won a scholarship to Texas Tech. It was blown to smithereens when the Ammenstar field shot a column of oil two hundred feet into the sky. His memory held that transformation like a vivid dream never to be erased: a low approaching roar followed by a dirty black fountain rising from the dry Texas earth. Dirt farm kid to oil baron; took about five seconds.

This one would take one raising of a coffee cup. Dirt farm kid to oil baron to . . . to what? What would they call him after this? Statesman? Visionary? Maniac?

For a moment Walter Sisler was no longer a young wildcatter, but a five-year-old boy holding his mother's hand as she gave ground against the sheriff and an auctioneer and a crowd of men in straw hats. All those white short-sleeved shirts with bright neckties coming through their paddock gate, not even closing it behind them, then big black trucks and their diesel smoke following them and spreading out till the warm smell of dirt wasn't even a memory. The crowds kept on filing through the gate like they owned the place, which, before the sun went down, they did. All the while Dow Sisler squatted with his back to the cinder block wall of the smokehouse, his head bowed between his knees, and spat tobacco juice on his shoes.

Walter said aloud, "This here is Texas. You're in *my* country now."

Roxanne looked around at him. Jimmy had been staring at him already, and the Mexicans didn't budge.

Roxanne hurried over to Jimmy. "You hear him talking to himself? That's whisky he's drinking from that coffee cup. It's for his nerves, the sneak. He's worried about what we're doing."

"You're crazy. Walter's never been afraid of anything in his life. Maybe you're the one scared. They'll get you too, you know."

"It's worth the sacrifice," Roxanne told him. "And it's not like

6

my life was going much of anywhere anyhow." She smiled sadly at him, then turned and headed for Walter.

"High muckety-mucks," Walter was saying. "Pushing people around like a herd of cows." It was the whisky talking, but he didn't care. Let the whole stinking world get its nose out of joint. He knew the road America was on. He didn't just guess at the future, with all its blood and massacres and whole civilizations in upheaval. He didn't just guess at it—he saw it; saw it in numbers clearer than soothsayers can see it in tea leaves, and a damn sight clearer than those so-called geniuses could see it in their theories and models and in—god help us all—their articles in *Foreign Affairs*. He'd run the numbers many times and every time what came out would pin their ears back. He knew the kind of men in control of the Arabian oil fields, and the kind of people they ruled and who in turn ruled them and what kind of people they were and . . . he couldn't complete the thought. It made his blood run cold. For that very reason he intended to run some cold blood through these so-called geniuses who ran this country and a whole bunch of other countries too, and who right now could be heard as a low rumble behind Jimmy and his doors. They wanted at that table of booze.

"When I get done with them they'll know a thing or two."

Walter saw Roxanne heading his way, so he abruptly raised his cup. "Fling wide the green doors, Jimbo! And don't let the so-called geniuses trample you to death while you're at it."

Roxanne swirled by and deftly plucked the coffee cup from his hand. "Let me just freshen this up for you, chief." Without slowing down she scurried into the little kitchenette off to Walter's right and emerged with a different cup, this one with real coffee in it.

Walter sipped, and said "Jesus, woman! You might at least put some sugar in it."

Without taking the cup, Roxanne slipped back into the kitchen and came out with a small handful of sugar cubes, which she let slide into his coffee. "Stir it with your finger, tough guy."

The attendees were filing in. For the past week Roxanne and Jimmy had been meeting them in dribs and drabs at the train station in San Vitores, about forty dust-clogged miles away, as the

7

crow flies, which, as they said in these parts, no crow would even consider, lessen it was payday.

The grand ballroom was but one part of a resort complex that in its contrast to the surrounding high plains must have constituted a near mirage of wonderment. Young Walter Sisler's run of luck was already trade lore in the oil drilling business. And even when he didn't strike oil, what did he find? A dry hole? Nope. He found thermal pools. So he built Asclepius Waters, named for the Greek god of healing, which turned out to be a kind of oil well, or maybe gold mine, of its own.

Driving in from San Vitores, after miles of arid and barren Texas plain, the visitor gradually realizes that up ahead, through the haze, the vision of an oasis is materializing. A green hue starts to penetrate the dusty air as a canopy of trees appears. Red-roofed buildings take shape, and outlines of stands of eucalyptus and palmetto. There are the beginnings of a vineyard and an olive grove, along with garden paths overhung by flame trees, so that in early summer when they drop their flowers, visitors walk through gardens on a carpet of crimson petals.

The whole thing happened suddenly in space and suddenly in time. Five years earlier the place had been just another parcel of shortgrass prairie. It was as hallucinatory as oil and water mixing, and with so satisfying a symmetry: the miracle of oil money had built it; the miracle of water sustained it.

"See that guy there?" Walter said to Roxanne. "That's Senator Goldwater of Arizona."

"His father was Jewish. I guess you knew that."

"No, I didn't."

"The family name was Goldwasser. I think his principle motive for being here is politicking. He hopes to out-maneuver Nixon and Rockefeller."

"There's Eleanor Roosevelt. Couldn't miss her ugly mug. Who's that she's with?"

"Her Jewish doctor friend, a Dr. David Gurewitsch. They're inseparable. These days she even lives with him and his wife. People say that before she met him she was a normal upper class anti-Semite."

8

"Now she's Israel's best friend. She and Golda Meir should make horror movies together."

"Like you're some big prize yourself."

"I wasn't talking about their looks. Is it too late for me to fire you?"

"I didn't say you were dumb. See the man standing alone by the bar? He's Zev Rotem, an Irgun member, one of the men who helped Menachem Begin blow up the King David Hotel in Jerusalem. He's due to talk about that on tomorrow's program. That smallish man in the plaid sports jacket—see him by the door? That's Ellison Saunders, top assistant to Breckenridge Long, who headed FDR's immigration section during the war, and who single-handedly barred entry to the U.S. of thousands of Jews trying to flee Germany. It'll be interesting to see if Eleanor reacts to him, since her husband could have replaced him at any time, but never did. Look over there. See the guy in the yellow vest? He's a reporter from *Le Figaro*, based in Washington. Name's Marius de Clèves. He's going to speak on the Dreyfus Affair. I think he's also prepared a paper on the mess the French have made in Algeria. He won't quite admit it. It's amazing how frightened he is of that topic. Beside him is the Palestinian poet Akram Khouri."

"That guy's Palestinian? He looks like he just stepped off the dance floor of American Bandstand."

"Very westernized, now teaching at the University of Chicago. A Christian. Jimmy and I played tennis with him and Zev Rotem this morning."

"My god, a breakthrough for humanity."

"I don't think either of them knew who the other was. We needed a fourth and he was just strolling by so I handed him a racket. They took the set from Jimmy and me."

"Ask for a rematch."

"Yeah, revenge is sweet." She looked at Walter to make sure he'd got it.

"Sweet as sugar." He smiled, a little residue of the whisky still in his eyes. For an instant he considered hugging her and telling her that her passion was the backbone of this entire scheme, this secret-within-a-secret conference to create a new world.

9

Her passion, his nerve, Jimmy's desire to please them both, yet wrapping all that up somehow was her flip refusal to admit that the whole of the human condition merited anything more than a good swift kick up the backside. If they'd been alone he might have revealed all that to Roxanne, but the room was filling fast, and in a moment the coffee would take the last of the sentiment from him.

"The guy with the two boys is Congressman Joe Hatling from Kentucky's seventh district."

"Him I know from the Energy Commission. He's here for the free booze. And probably to see if that big, tall boy of his can get lucky with one of *las masajistas*."

There were three other congressmen there; the only senator other than Goldwater was the freshman senator from Minnesota, Eugene McCarthy. Of all the foreign delegates, none was connected with his government.

She pointed out a professor emeritus at Stanford, Dr. Evan Grogan, who would talk about Gesya Gelfman and the Russian pogroms that followed the assassination of Tsar Alexander II. Ibrahim Mousa al Mur wore a kaffiya with his Jermyn Street suit. He would present on the massacre of Deir Yassin. Dr. Philip Nelkin of Columbia would speak about the Zionist Lehi's assassination of UN envoy Count Bernedotte in Jerusalem. Roxanne had attempted to persuade Eleanor Roosevelt to do it, as it would conflict within Mrs. Roosevelt two of her great public causes, the UN and Israel. The tension implied by the exposure of that dichotomy might have made for a great speech, Roxy reasoned, but Mrs. Roosevelt had declined, pleading reasons of health.

"Is that Hannah Arendt with Jimbo?" Jimmy was showing a woman to the front row.

"Yep. You'll introduce her as the opening speaker. Have you got your remarks ready?" Walter patted the breast pocket of his jacket to indicate the folded papers safely tucked away there. "Then what say we get started? Let's mingle a minute or two while the canapé trays circulate, and then get everybody settled in."

Several more Mexican waiters made their rounds through the ballroom with assortments of those pretty diversions the Asclepius chef took such pride in: canapés of hickory nut paste on toast; kufta and mint on biscuit rounds, salsa moutabel on celery sticks; chopped chicken liver and chow chow on rye crackers. The stuff sure smelled good. Walter vaguely wished he could ask for another whisky to wash down that chicken liver, but Roxy was right.

He weaved his way to the front row where Hannah Arendt sat alone, by all evidence at complete ease with whatever was to come. "Mrs. Arendt, please allow me to introduce myself. No, please don't stand. I'll just plop myself down here beside you if you don't mind."

She smiled as if to say, This really is Texas, isn't it?

She declined a drink, assured the Mexican whom Walter had summoned that she was still quite satisfied from her ample lunch, and said she would not require a pitcher of water, as she would be brief in her opening remarks.

Given this, Walter mounted to the lectern and made a couple of soft clicks against the microphone, both to test that the mike was live and to indicate that it was time to settle in. He was well suited to the lectern; he seemed at ease up there. Even his blocky shape was lectern-like, as if a light down front had cast the shadow of the lectern on the wall behind, with a big, round, ruddy-complexioned head stuck on it.

"First of all, I'd like to welcome you with my deepest sincerity to Asclepius Waters. I hope all of you have received your personalized health regimen for the week and that you are following it scrupulously." Some people flexed and arm or a leg, gave out a fake, or maybe not so fake, groan.

"Glad to hear it! As the ancients said, A healthy mind in a healthy body. So now that we're turning our attention from the body to the mind, let me start by reminding you that this is a gathering completely devoid of publicity. Even the journalists among us have agreed that this is all on deep background. The only information that will go beyond these walls is what you choose to tell people, and your word, implicitly given by your agreement to be here under these ground rules, that you will use nothing you hear this week to further your career at the expense of anyone else's, means we can all speak in total candor. This Secret Conference to

Create a New World, as we so modestly bill it, . . . " he waited for the polite chuckles to die away, "is in my opinion as important as any you have ever attended in your, in some cases long, and in all cases eminent, careers. It has become a cliché to say that we live in an uncertain world. We don't know what the Russians are going to do with all those bombs. We don't know what threat this new fellow Fidel Castro poses just off our shores. We don't even know who will replace Ike as the leader of the free world."

At this Sen. Goldwater good-naturedly raised his hand. People near him laughed and when Walter pointed to him and said, "Oh, I see we have a volunteer," more people looked around at him and joined in.

"Since Lyndon isn't here," the senator said, "maybe I can even carry his home state."

"No Kennedy or Nixon here either. We've given you a wide open field."

"No doubt one of the Rockefellers is here in disguise." Again many in the crowd laughed.

"The uncertainties just keep piling up," Walter got back to his theme. "But while it is true that there are many things we can't predict, that is not the underlying message of this conference. That is not why I asked all of you here. As smart and perceptive and wise as you may be"—he was now very glad Roxy had taken him off the whisky, or he would have laughed out loud at these words— "No matter how prominent you are in your fields, you cannot see into the future. I didn't ask you here to enlighten us with your vision of the world to come. I asked you here so *I* could enlighten *you*."

A nervous shuffle of feet and rearranging of postures went through the great ballroom. "Because in my field I *can* see the future. My field is the oil field. As soon as I finished college I started roaming the earth, scouring the research, poring over the magnetic surveys, talking to experts who have been at it a lot longer than I have, and calculating, always calculating."

He saw Jimmy respond to something at the door, through which emerged not a latecomer but just an arm holding a piece of paper. Jimmy read it and looked up toward the podium. Jimmy quickly passed it on to Roxanne, who glanced at it, then seemed to

12

read it more carefully. Walter had broken off his speech to watch these proceedings, and now the crowd caught on and shifted its attention as well. Roxy proceeded in an unhurried yet purposeful march toward Walter. When she reached him she said quietly, not really concerned whether the microphone caught it or not, "Maybe you should announce this."

Walter read the note. "Umm, ladies and gentlemen, some of our security guards in the main office have the radio on, and they tell me that according to Mutual station KKUT in San Vitores, the Kremlin has just announced that late last night Premier Nikita Khrushchev was taken ill and has at least temporarily been removed from any position of authority in the Politburo."

A real buzz went around the hall this time. Everyone talked excitedly in their little groups. Walter gave them a minute to collect their thoughts, and then said, "I know we'd all like to know more, but apparently that's the entire news release. I'll have my assistant monitor the situation carefully." He asked Jimmy to go out and keep an ear to the radio, which was about the only media access they had.

"Well . . . I don't know how much this news will affect what you have to say at this conference. It's not really our topic, although this Cold War means that in some ways everything touches everything else. Of course Russia has lots of oil too, which is more to the point. More and more uncertainties. But back to my original point,"— he straightened the papers of his prepared address—"there is at least one certainty that I want you to consider: the world's supply of oil is finite. As people around here say about land, 'They ain't makin' it anymore.' I have calculated all the variables, again and again, and allowing for the probability that even vast reserves are out there to be discovered, *even* allowing for that, my numbers tell me that our great-grandchildren will live in a world depleted of oil. That's not even a matter of debate. When those boys of yours have grandchildren," he looked at Congressman Hatling of Kentucky, "they can tell them to get used to the idea: they will have to survive in a world without oil. Or maybe not survive. I don't know how they'll manage. I just know they'll have to manage somehow, or else the whole human race will drown in blood.

"Furthermore, within our own lifetimes the demand for oil will grow to the point where the countries that have most of the oil will be able to form a cartel and make it stick. Yes, ladies and gentlemen, I said *and make it stick.* They might be able to do it right now, if they only knew it. I won't tell them, and I don't want you to tell them, but they're smart people and pretty soon they'll come to the conclusion that if they can get together and squeeze supply while the world's requirement for energy just keeps rising and rising, they could raise the price by a factor of five hundred to one thousand percent. Yes, you heard right. Yesterday when we drove you to Asclepius Waters from San Vitores, it cost us twenty cents a gallon. If the world's oil producers, especially in the Middle East, could get their act together this very day, by the end of the weekend it would cost us as much as two dollars a gallon to drive you back."

Walter paused here, hoping for, and, as the ramifications of this prediction set in, soon receiving, a groundswell of nervous chatter. "Now don't you worry," he said, with his comic relief chuckle, "I happen to own a couple of oil wells, so we'll manage to drive you back all right. But do consider this over the long term: What happens when enormous amounts of cash flow into a civilization that for the last few centuries has suffered some pretty hard times, but before that was a dominant force, *the* dominant force, towering in wealth and achievement even over Europe? And don't think they've forgotten that golden age, either. As a culture they still hold dear the age of the caliphs, the triumphs of Saladin, the glories of Baghdad and Cordoba. They think that was their time, their true destiny flourishing as it should. They believe that was their rightful place in the world. Furthermore, they think they'll return to it one day.

"I've worked and traveled among these people. They've opened up to me not only their homes and hospitality, but their hopes and dreams. So what happens when people who dream of a lost golden age, suddenly attain vast wealth? They devote themselves to restoring that golden age.

"And what feature of their life is the vector of their lost and longed for glory? What is the most important thing in the world

14

to those folks? What unified and sustained them through the centuries of power and the centuries of collapse? Their religion: Islam. If you think maybe I'm talking through my hat, when we split off into break-out sessions, ask any of our distinguished Muslim guests."

They didn't really have to wait to ask the question. Many of those guests in attendance were already nodding agreement.

"Much of that new wealth will fund new mosques and religious schools all over the world. And make no mistake, the teaching of these centers will reflect the hard-shell fundamentalists who control most of the Arabian peninsula. They're called Salafis, and they have most of the oil.

"Consider this: religion follows wealth and influence. Does anyone here really believe that Christianity became the world's most populous religion because everybody from Aztecs to Hottentots to Filipinos to Eskimos suddenly fell blinded on the road to Damascus? Or was it because the warriors who brought the concept of a god raised from the dead also brought wealth, and military might, making conversion to their religion seem like a pretty smart thing to do? And for those Christians who saw their nations triumph over weaker peoples, did they say, 'We did this by strength of arms and ruthless exploitation and by the pure blind luck of carrying within us microbes for which those natives, dying off at the ratio of nine in ten, possessed no antibodies?' Or did they say, 'Kneel before the cross of our Lord, Who commands us to rule over you.'?

"And will the Salafis say, 'We just got lucky with all that oil.' Or will they say, 'It is the will of Allah.'?"

"So my message to you is that in all your influential acts and in all your votes or decisions, consider that global power will inevitably shift to the Middle East. Inevitably. People can try to ignore it because they don't like it, but it's coming. It may not be in the stars, but it's in the numbers.

"And what is the one principal issue that can galvanize and incite all the holders of that increasing power? When they try to explain to themselves why they've been in decline all these years, they will look to outside forces. That's how humans work, especially humans who feel they have received into their supremely providential midst the revealed word of God. So who will they blame? Us, that's who. For modern Muslims, Muhammad's wars with the Jews of Medina in the 620s, and the Christian Crusades a few centuries later, are not forgotten pages in some moldy old history book. These are current events. These are today's headlines. Their old foe, Christendom, has teamed up with their truly original foes, the Jews, to bring them to their knees. That's the devil's alliance that has humiliated them. Conspiracy theories sell like hotcakes on the Arab street, and this one sells best of all. And what proof do they have for what to us may seem like such a cockamamie idea? Israel. The state which they believe colonialist forces stole from under the feet of their brothers in Palestine. That's what we're here to talk about."

Jimmy walked back into the room and took his accustomed position by the green baize doors. Walter looked up at him. "Any news on this Khrushchev thing?" Jimmy shrugged his shoulders: nothing.

"All right. In that case, let's just get on with it. I'm very pleased and proud to introduce our first speaker. She was born in Hanover, Germany, in a year that I won't specify." He looked at her and saw that she was smiling up at him.

"1906," she put in. "A bloody poor choice of a year to be born a Jew in Germany."

"But she slipped Hitler's clutches and made it to France. She was there for the Fall of France in 1940, whereupon the Vichy French tried to pen her up in a concentration camp in Aquitaine. Did I pronounce that right?"

Arendt shrugged, made a mouth. Didn't know, perhaps, or didn't care.

"They couldn't contain her any better than Hitler had. She managed to escape from there and found her way, after many way stations, to Princeton University. And I'm very pleased that she managed to escape from Princeton for the far more stimulating environment of Asclepius Waters. She is the author of *The Origins of Totalitarianism* and *The Human Condition*. Ladies and gentlemen, please welcome, Hannah Arendt."

She was received cordially, even enthusiastically. Apparently a lot of the guests knew of her only by her bio-sketch: German Jew concentration camp survivor. She spoke for about ten minutes on the theme of a bi-national, non-religious state in Palestine. She flatly called Menachen Begin a fascist. When she concluded her remarks, the applause was thin, barely polite.

After Hannah Arendt, the presentations went in chronological order by topic. An Oxford Fellow by the name of Julian Rea spoke of the Jews murdered during Europe's Black Death in the years 1347-1360. Dr. Grogan narrated the events following Tsar Alexander II's assassination in 1881 by a group called The People's Will, which included but one Jew, a woman named Gesya Gelfman, the girlfriend of one of the assassins. According to Grogan, the Russian government was so reluctant to admit that the Tsar's own people had killed him that they used Miss Gelfman as a scapegoat and sent out accusations that it was a Jewish plot, thus setting off pogroms throughout Russia that killed hundreds and sent thousands seeking shelter in, among other places, Palestine. It was the first big Jewish influx into ancient Israel in hundreds of years, and started the movement that eventually led to the creation of modern Israel.

There were no more outside interruptions. When Walter closed the evening session he could announce that Mutual news was simply repeating the Khrushchev story without further amplification or analysis. He read a summation from his notepad: President Eisenhower made a statement wishing his opposite number a speedy recovery. A reporter asked him whether the military was on heightened alert. The President said no, no more than usual in these situations. Secretary of State Herter said the State Department was keeping its ear to the ground, but really they didn't know any more than what TASS was telling everybody.

But by the next morning there was more news. Walter was able to tell the gathered delegates that a triumvirate of military chiefs was now in control of the Politburo. "Please forgive my Russian pronunciation—remember I'm just guessing at the spelling of this from the radio—but as best I can tell they are: Dimitri Pichtchenko from the army; Lubomir Vasiliev from the navy; and Valenti Suslov from the air force. Do those names ring a bell with anybody here?"

He looked out over the hall. Nobody volunteered any knowledge. "No Russian experts out there? Of course, according to Senator Goldwater, Senator McCarthy probably has secret cables from these guys about three times a week, but we won't go into that now, will we?"

McCarthy, the liberal freshman senator from Minnesota, didn't take the bait, but Goldwater chipped in, "I've been introducing him to these fat steaks we serve down here in cowboy country. I think he's starting to go soft on capitalism."

Even at this point nothing seemed terribly ominous. What really got the attention of the delegates was when Walter informed them that station KKUT would air a special half-hour news bulletin at noon that day. He said he could have his technicians patch it through the speaker system in the cafeteria and they could listen to it over lunch if they wanted. He asked for a show of hands. It was nearly unanimous. Akram Khouri, the Palestinian poet, didn't care one way or the other—he had a lunchtime tennis date with Roxanne—but the news filled everybody else with unease. If Mutual News was devoting a half-hour to the story, and on a Saturday right before the Michigan State-Notre Dame game at that—it had to be important.

The lunchroom was silent. The loudspeakers had sufficient volume, but even so people placed their cutlery gently on their plates and no one spoke above a whisper. A newsman was detailing the item-by-item criticism leveled by the new Soviet leadership against Khrushchev, all of which formed an indictment that he had been lax in his diligence against the West. It was clear that the once-feared Premier was not ill, but ousted, probably by now in Lubianka prison.

By extension the target of the criticism was the U.S. The accusations focused on Khrushchev's inability to prevent or then respond adequately to that oldest of Russian fears: being surrounded by hostile states. Only now the new enemies were armed "to the teeth," as the reporter phrased it, with nuclear weaponry. There were U.S. missiles in Turkey "aimed at the Russian heart." They had uncovered a plot to convert Israel's supposed Atoms for Peace reactor at Dimona to military use. Britain, France, Norway and the U.S. were implicated. The CIA was plotting to overthrow the new ruler of Cuba and restore a puppet regime controlled by the mafia. Likewise in Mexico, American *agents provocateurs* fomented violent struggle by trade unionists in order to provoke a heavy-handed crackdown by Mexican forces. The U.S. was sending military advisors to Vietnam to carry on French imperialism under a new regime. Imperialist forces within the U.S. itself had fired into peaceful demonstrations by Negroes and American Indians who merely demanded equal rights. They had assassinated Patrice Lumumba in the Congo in a vain attempt to stop a worldwide movement for black man's freedom from white domination.

The list went on and on. Some of the charges were clearly preposterous: When was the last time Indians had been massacred in the streets of America? Had any black man from El Paso to Galveston ever even heard the name Patrice Lumumba? Roundhouse accusations such as these denoted a leadership riddled with paranoia, or shots of straight vodka, or maybe both— true heirs to their Stalinist ancestry.

The afternoon's review of the Dreyfus Affair went by about as expected, but the description of the British trying to pick the corpses of their soldiers from the rubble of the King David Hotel, and of Israeli soldiers depopulating the village of Deir Yassin, with, according to the UN report, wanton murder and rape, and by extension the whole execution of Plan Dalet, whereby enough Arabs would be slaughtered to scare the rest off their land, all this blood and malice seemed to bring an extra urgency with it, as though the cries of the infants and the entreaties of the terrorized were not so many thousand miles away, and not so long ago.

People didn't sleep so well that night. No matter that the *masajistas* were well-trained at relaxation therapy, that the tennis courts were smooth and well-lighted, that the thermal pools were steamy and the towels fleecy; nobody slept well. All credit due to Walter Sisler and company, but these Asclepius Waters had been poisoned by threats from afar. They would be glad to go home on Monday.

At least the Sunday morning sun broke onto a gorgeous day. Walking through these lush gardens surrounded by mile after mile of crackling bush was almost enough to make you forget that madmen controlled the fate of millions. When they gathered for breakfast, Roxanne and Jimmy shared the duty of passing from table to table and in a manner as genuinely cheerful as they could fake, and telling them that the phone lines were still down. No, it doesn't mean a thing. They're prone to do that a couple of times a month. Usually they get repaired within hours, but with today being Sunday, who knows. Most of the repairmen are probably in church anyway.

Asclepius Waters in fact had a church of its own, along with a sort of ecumenical pastor who was expert at obfuscating on the subject of his denomination. Some of the delegates attended the service there. Some slept late. Some took their health and exercise regimes seriously. The Frenchman Marius de Clèves polished his report on Algeria—he would give it after all. The Christian Palestinian poet twirled his tennis racket in his hand, hoping— vainly, as it turned out—that Roxanne would pass his way.

Radio station KKUT went off the air just before noon. The loudspeakers in the lunchroom had been switched on in time to catch the noon report, but all they got was static. Was it a coincidence that the phones were out too? Some guessed that, yes, these short-outs occur often enough out here in the middle of nowhere. Back in civilization we just don't hear about it. Some figured that there had been a common cause—a big electrical blackout, say. But the electricity was fine at Asclepius Waters, and no, Walter said, although they had their own generators, they weren't using them right now.

It was during Monsieur de Clèves explanation of the Algerian situation that the great ballroom went dark. Apparently this too was a common enough occurrence, for swiftly and in a practiced fashion several Mexicans began lighting candles in wall sconces that up to this point most people, if they'd noticed them at all, had taken to be decorative. But no, now a low but useful illumination bordered the hall.

Jimmy was quickly on the walkie-talkie. Soon he announced—

20

shouted really—that the generators would be fired up within minutes.

Within the hall, now filled with silent tension, you could hear a faint diesel pulse as the engines started up, and you could almost sense electricity as a flow of fresh blood moving through arteries of cables into the illuminating brain of the chandeliers. The room was dimmer than before, and more orange, but the relief after the darkness made it seem almost cinematic. There was the temptation to feel jolly again with one another.

The mike was live again, so Walter urged de Clèves to take up where he'd left off on Algeria. His description of the nighttime raids, the brutal annihilation of whole clans in house to house slaughter, with white Frenchmen who called themselves Algerians, and Arab Algerians fighting among themselves, urged by the *pied noir* French to settle old scores under the impunity of civil war; these descriptions gave to the commotion that started in the bar area at the back of the hall an aspect of sound effects to underscore the Frenchman's drama.

The shouts, however, were in Spanish, and the gunshots brought real plaster falling from the ceiling. The three Mexican barmen had reached under the tablecloths and brought out Russian-made automatic weapons. Roxanne saw them moving toward the stage so she rushed toward M. de Clèves and ushered him down to his chair.

One of the Mexicans, still in his waiter's uniform, commanded the vacant lectern. He lifted his rifle in a sort of demonstration that doubled for a victory salute. "My name is Comandante Tejas," he said. "Do not be alarmed, for if you do nothing foolish you are safe here. But . . . look around you!" he ordered. That's when people started to realize that the room was ringed with Mexicans, all the waiters, the *masajistas*, the pool boys, everyone, it seems, who had been so kind over the past few days, was now brandishing the rifle that the man at the lectern called a Kalashnikov, or AK-47, which he assured them was the world's finest assault rifle and which he and all his comrades would be perfectly happy to use on any enemy of the people who dared challenge him.

Roxy did dare challenge him. She rushed at him, her arms

21

out wide, pleading. "You have no right . . . " she began, but his two bartending colleagues grabbed her and forced her onto the floor.

"We have every right. You are in Mexico now."

Next Walter charged the stage. "Don't you lay a hand on her," he warned. His was a true bull-rush at the so-called Comandante Tejas. He would have flattened him, but both bodyguards lifted their rifles and fired. He fell hard to the stage floor. Even over the echoes of gunfire, people could hear his head slam against the floor.

After that there was silence, until Comandante Tejas said something in Spanish to the Mexicans nearest him, and called something else to those by the doors. Two Mexicans grabbed an ankle each and dragged Walter's body down the side aisle and into the kitchenette, leaving long streaks of blood on the shining parquet floor.

Roxy hadn't seen the shooting; she'd been held face down on the floor. When she turned to see the two men dragging Walter away, she shrieked and tried to break free. Trapped, she put her face in her hands and cried, "Why? Why?"

The instructions to the man by the door had apparently concerned the radio, for now it came on, first time today, patched through the ballroom's speakers. A man was reading the news, as usual, but it was a different voice than the twangy Texan one they'd come to know. This was a Mexican voice, absolutely fluent in English, but polished and studied. His message was simple and short. It seemed that it fell to him to repeat the same communiqué again and again.

He started each script with *Bienvenidos a Mexico! Ha llegado el día de la revancha por fin!* Then he switched to English. "Today the combined forces of the Soviet Union, the Democratic Republic of Cuba, and the Revolutionary Council of Mexico, have launched a defensive strike against the imperialist forces of the United States of America. Fraternal forces controlling secret installations of missiles carrying nuclear warheads on the island of Cuba are poised to strike at all major cities on the American east coast. Advanced Soviet T-55 tanks have already crossed the Rio Grande and have captured large parts of Texas. The will of the

Revolutionary Council of Mexico is as follows:

"We will retake the lands that were stolen from us during a war not of our making, a war begun under lies and false pretenses by the United States government. For more than one hundred years these foreign occupiers have illegally held our land and our citizens hostage in their rapacious grasp. We will take back Tejas, Nuevo Mexico, Arizona, Nevada, California, and Colorado. Those are our demands. If they are not granted within a period of twelve hours, the entire eastern half of the United States will disappear.

"When our demands are met, U.S. citizens now residing in those parts of Mexico stolen from us during the War of 1846 will be allowed to leave, without fear, to take up residence in any other U.S. state they choose. Their fixed possessions will be accepted by the Revolutionary Council of Mexico in lieu of reparations for the damages suffered during that infamous and unjust war.

"These demands are not negotiable. *VIVA LA REVOLUCIÓN!*"

Then there would be a silence of about ten minutes, followed by, *Bienvenidos a Mexico!*

El comandante sent his soldiers around the room with forms. They were very short and simple: name, address, position, family details. The collected forms were separated into two piles: residents of the reacquired Mexican lands, and everybody else. Eighteen of the delegates, including Senator Goldwater, were removed from the others in order to give more detailed information: type of real estate owned; square footage of houses; acreage of land; furniture and valuables; estimated value of all holdings. It was all quite businesslike. Nobody got rough. They were all scared, even the soldiers. Frightened soldiers often lead to atrocities, but el comandante kept them all on a leash.

This went on for exactly two hours. That was the length of time Roxy and Walter had agreed on. She actually wanted it longer. She wanted to keep them penned up all night, but Walter cut her back to two hours.

He checked his watch and at two hours on the dot he walked from his kitchenette straight down the middle aisle and onto the stage. He still had his pig-blood stained shirt on. The blood and bruise on his head were genuine: he really had cracked his noggin

23

on that floor. Roxy had warned him to practice falling, but he figured, What kind of idiot can't fall down? Now he knew.

"Switch off that radio," he told Jimmy. "God-DAMN I'm tired of listening to Manny going on and on. I'm sure you all are too. Tell him he did fine and to go get a beer for his throat."

The Mexicans quietly filed out of the room. Comandante Tejas and his comrades returned to their posts behind the bar. "You guys were great!" Walter called out. "Really convincing. Next stop for you—Hollywood."

The at-first stunned silence erupted into, "What the hell is this all about?" and "You son-of-a-bitch!"

"Yes!" Walter said. "Yes, you're angry, aren't you? Woo-hoo! Hell yes, you're madder'n a hornet's nest!"

"It's prison for you, Sisler! You'll be lucky if you ever get out!"

"Absolutely the right reaction. Now you see how it feels? Feels pretty lousy, doesn't it, getting invaded and kicked out of your homes. Yet . . . "

There were so many catcalls that for a while he just let them burn themselves out. Eventually the voices started to modulate. He raised his hands to ask for quiet.

"Yet . . . " he continued, "your captivity lasted only two hours. The loss of your homes was just a threat, hardly a real prospect. Even so, look how incensed you are. And damn right, too! Burning anger is the normal response!"

"You're the one going to burn! We'll all see to that!"

"No doubt you will. I took my chances. I'll pay my dues. But while you're being so powerful and high-minded, at least one little part of your life has now been touched by injustice, and you have experienced how it feels. To a tiny degree; a very small degree compared to those whose lives you control. You didn't see any sisters raped, no sons mowed down. You didn't actually have to walk across that desert carrying whatever you could of your belongings, and look back to see some foreigners already moving in to your house."

He could hardly believe it, but they were actually quiet for a moment; at least a lot of them were.

"So just remember this when you decide on people's lives.

Drawing a line on a map in some palace somewhere seems nice and easy, then everybody goes out for a drink. But maybe now you'll know how it felt when the guns were raised. Maybe now you can put some heart and soul into what you do."

Roxy was still quietly weeping, in her corner. After cowering there in pretense for the whole show, she remained in position, lingering in self-confinement, her fake tears now unanticipatedly real. Her chest hurt from the jolt of her earlier melodramatic sobs, but now there was a fresh pain, nearer the heart, the ache that means to stay. This was the finest man she'd ever known, at his finest moment, and he would be going to jail. She would too, of course, but him . . . that's what hurt.

"So now," Walter advised the delegates, "let's call it a day. Let's go take the waters, go for a swim, a bike ride. Have dinner, have a drink. We can all still be friends. Or we'll drive any of you back tonight to San Vitores, if you really want to leave so soon."

"Your ass is in a sling, pal. The police will be here for you shortly, and you'll never see daylight again."

"Well, send them for me when you get to San Vitores. The phone lines here really are out. That wasn't part of the play."

He left the stage, walked to Roxanne's corner, put down a hand to help her up. It occurred to him to give her a sportsmanlike pat on the butt, good teammates to the last, but thought better of it. Instead he used his thumbs to smooth away the tears on her cheeks. She smiled up into his round, sunny face, saw it layered in color, the pink flush of success, rusty streaks of dried blood leading from a nasty purple contusion, but this sunset only brought her a run of fresh tears, which she contented herself by pressing into the lapel of his ruined jacket before she pulled away from him.

As the guests were filing out—many, in fact, for the pools or gardens, the dining room, the bar—that tall boy, the older son of Kentucky Seven, swung wide of the crowd and spoke to Walter.

"Don't worry, sir. My father will help you. He's a lawyer and a U.S. congressman."

2

WHEN PROMINENT PIKEVILLE attorney and City Commissioner Joe Hatling's first child turned out to be a son, Commissioner Hatling, as a sort of joke but sort of not, made sure that a basketball goal was nailed up over the garage door to welcome mother and baby home from the hospital. And twelve years later when U.S. Congressman Joe Hatling realized that this son was already as tall as he was, and on top of that showed every sign of moving with athletic grace right through the famously awkward years of adolescence, he had the same company that laid down outdoor basketball courts for the Pike County schools come by his house and fit a smooth half-court in the back yard between the swimming pool and the forsythia strip that bordered the conservatory. The congressman paid standard rates for this installation. If he ever got voted out of office it wasn't going to be for some petty corruption that would draw sniggers from county court clerks. In fact, his main campaign strategy over all his re-election bids could be summed up by the formula: "Joe Hatling may be *(insert any manner of criticism)*, but you've got to admit he's an honorable man."

When he could escape Washington to spend a few nights at home in Pikeville, it became his custom to announce his availability for family time by pounding a basketball hard onto the pressed-dirt basketball floor. At the sound, both boys would come bounding out of the house. Even Barbara, who was generally in the conservatory—really more of a small hexagonal library with big windows and a few plants—would soon take her place on a bench beside the court. The extent of her athletic involvement was to put out a foot if the ball happened to bounce her way. She had lightning reflexes. She claimed to have been the kickball queen of her high school P-E classes, and often advised her men to include in their nightly prayers a petition that she never be moved to get up off her bench and take up basketball, because, she predicted, she would wipe up the court with the three of them.

But tonight she didn't join them. If the three players happened to glance over the border of forsythia they could see her, sitting in her favorite reading chair within the bright, uncurtained conservatory. She held a book in her lap. It was a warm evening, for the time of year. The window beside her was open. She was listening more than reading. People said of Barbara Hatling that she didn't miss much, and when she did miss something it was because she was busy catching something else more important.

Joe thrust the ball at Clark and Clark slammed it back just as hard. "Are you going to help Mr. Sisler, Dad?"

"Help him how?"

"Defend him in court. I reckon he's in big trouble."

"That man can afford a hundred lawyers."

"But wouldn't it be much better if his lawyer had actually been there on the scene, one of the captives? And a U.S. congressman on top of that?"

"Oh, sure. Sure I'll represent him. And then I'll take up a full time position as the most ridiculed attorney in Eastern Kentucky. What kind of knucklehead question is that?"

"I just don't think he was being . . . "

"You just don't think, period. Sometimes I wonder about you, boy." The congressman hit him with a pass that stung his hands.

Clark started to say something about this being America, but that was Joe's territory. He held the ball out from his body but looked down at his feet. He was stuck.

Jerry sprinted toward the basket and called, "Lay up!"

Clark caught him right in stride. Jerry was always doing stuff like that. His timing was impeccable. He missed the lay up by two feet, but that didn't detract from the brilliance of his move.

Clark asked his father, "Why is it crazy to think that a man who really believes in something should have decent legal counsel, even if he went a little overboard?"

"A little overboard? Listen here little buddy, Walter Sisler pitched straight off the deck into the belly of a whale."

"Ha, Pops! Good one," said Jerry.

"But still," Clark placed a wary foot forward, "this is America."

The light in the conservatory went off; the forsythia seemed to disappear.

"Listen son, let me lay out a home truth or two for you. I've told you many a time that this congressional seat will be yours for the taking one day. That's because our voters aren't so much party loyal as man loyal. And they're clan loyal. I win every election by big majorities, not because I'm some second coming of our fellow Kentuckian Abe Lincoln—who by the by got the socks beat off him for not being warlike enough against Mexico. Ironic, to say the least, that right before his baleful eyes over a half a million Americans would die. I win because I'm what we call a constituent's congressman. It's not what I do about taxes or war or anything else that wins votes for me. It's because if a town in eastern Kentucky fears flooding, I get them a floodwall. If a coal hauler gets fined because his trucks are too heavy, I get him an exemption. If a soldier from Prestonsburg stationed in Okinawa wants to marry a Japanese girl, I get her a visa. If a man has worked in the mines for thirty years, then he automatically gets black lung benefits, even if he's been smoking two packs of Camels a day since he was nine, and can still run a marathon. Do you get me, son?"

"I get that part, but . . . "

"Then get the rest of it. For the big questions, I follow the party. That's the simple answer to all my problems. If the leadership thinks taxes are too high, I vote to lower. If they want more taxes, I vote to raise taxes. Same thing with foreign policy. If the party thinks Israel needs all the friends it can get, then I'm a friend of Israel. And if Walter Sisler is a horse's ass, then I let him get what's coming to him."

"HORSE!" shouted Jerry. He fired one from thirty feet, almost hitting his father in the back of the head.

"Horse's ass, I said!"

But Jerry laughed. "Horse's ass, then!" You couldn't make him mad no matter how hard you tried. He flipped one backwards over his head. Incredibly—not incredibly for Jerry, who couldn't drop a pop bottle straight into a garbage can, yet who routinely hit these wild shots—but incredibly for most people, it swished straight through. "Let's see you do that, Pops!"

"Jerry, go sit on that bench and behave yourself while I set your brother . . . no, you piddle around here with your trick shots. Me and Clark are going to sit on that bench and clear up some things."

"In that case I consider you an H by forfeit." Jerry drop-kicked one from half-court that rattled off the backboard.

The bench was darker now without the light from the conservatory, but it was turning into the kind of conversation that darkness abetted, one where when it was over somebody was going to be left alone to contemplate what had been said.

"Clarkie, do you know why I took you to Texas?"

"Because we don't spend enough time together, you said."

"Yes, that's part of it. But then too I'm thinking it's time you got your feet wet, politically speaking. I've been thinking about this for a while, and here are my ideas. Anything you don't like, you just say so, but first try to trust me. I know what I've built up here and how to pass it on to you. Do you trust me to lead you straight, son?"

"Of course I do."

"Okay, here's what I've been thinking. You know I didn't take you to live in D.C. with me permanently because I wanted you to grow up here and be a local kid. I wanted you to talk like District Seven voters and understand them. It wasn't because I didn't want you with me. You know that, don't you?"

Clark nodded warily. He didn't really know where this was leading.

From the court Jerry called, "You couldn't face coming home every night and getting your butt kicked in HORSE."

"None of your lip!" Joe said.

If they could have looked over the forsythia bush and through the now-darkened window of the conservatory, they would have seen that Barbara had pressed her book to her face to stifle a laugh.

"As I was trying to say," he looked up and smiled at Jerry, who was still mugging at him, then turned his attention back to Clark, "you're not an uppity kid and we didn't bring you up to be one. So when you finish high school, go straight to UK. Don't mess around applying for Ivy League schools. Just go to UK and let that be that. They all use the same books anyhow, and this way you won't look

29

snooty. Then at UK, go out for the basketball team. Voters here don't really trust college men, but if you play for Adolf Rupp you'll be all right. Not scholarship, of course. Just walk-on. You'll get to play the last thirty seconds against teams like Georgia, when we're already ahead by twenty points. But you'll practice hard, make good friends, be a crowd favorite. Take a pre-law degree, probably poly-sci.

"While you're there find yourself a sorority girl, maybe a Kappa Kappa Gamma or Alpha Gamma Delta, but not a snob, and marry her as soon as you graduate, before law school. People respect a man who'll both support a family and try to better himself. Pick as a mate somebody who looks good in family photos, whose idea of a successful life is to serve carrot cake and coffee to anybody and everybody, from the DAR to the wives of coal miners. I'm not saying to marry a ninny. A congressman's wife needs lots of class. Class but no sass, if you know what I mean."

Understanding crept over Clark, like the physical response to a threat he'd known was there but had let surprise him anyway. Suddenly he sensed not only the danger, but felt stupid on top of it. This wasn't what he wanted to talk about, not now. Jesus, Dad, he thought. Which sorority my wife comes out of? All he could think of was poor Mr. Sisler cracking his head, not knowing how to fall.

"But Dad, all I asked was for you to defend a guy I didn't think..."

"There you go thinking again. Defend Walter Sisler? Son, do the math. I won the last election by almost 70,000 votes. Amongst the upstanding citizenry of these mountains, 120,000 voted for me, lord love 'em, and 50,000 voted for Ned Sutherland, may they all rot in hell."

"Say 'hades' Dad," Jerry scolded. "Mom's sitting just over there."

"She knows I'm not serious about that. Anyway she's gone to bed, so you just clam up and shoot buckets, okay? Now Clark, can you guess how many votes I pick up for even hinting that the Palestinians might just perhaps have the tiniest little hint of a beef? Take a guess."

"Not many, I guess."

"Not many is generous. Try zero."

"There must be some ..."

"No, there's not. Not one. Maybe a dozen KKK types will get all excited if they think I've turned Jew-hater, but then when they think it through they'll figure out they hate Arabs just as much as they hate Jews, so there go my twelve KKK votes. Other than that there's not a man, woman or eighteen-year-old kid from the Tug River border of West Virginia to the central Bluegrass who decides his or her vote on the issue of Palestine. Any anti-Semites left over from the thirties don't consider it a live issue. Our Baptists haven't even figured out that Jews tossed Christians out of their homes in the Holy Land. Don't ask me why the Palestinians haven't thumped that tub to high heaven, but they haven't. In fact, they've done diddly squat to help their case in Congress. They have got to be the worst PR people on earth. See, in politics it's not whose cause is wrong or right. Don't let your civics teacher snow you on that. Usually there's no wrong or right anyway. Most of the time it's point of view. To my chances of being reelected it doesn't matter whether their cause is just or not. What counts is votes. And the result is I pick up how many votes by defending a man who defends Palestinians?"

"Approximately zero."

"No. Precisely zero."

"And how many do you lose?" asked Jerry, who was now preparing a set-shot while sitting in the dirt.

"Let's not even think about it. When AIPAC decides you're on the wrong side, you don't last long in politics. People say *Don't mess with Texas*, but the lesson you need to heed right now, Clarkie boy, is *Don't mess with Israel*. Not if you want to inherit your old daddy's mantle of greatness."

Jerry fell in step with the changed tone and said, "So let's play some hoops! It's already HORSE'S AS on both of you. I gave you the apostrophe free for me being such a little kid."

"No, bud. You two go ahead and play. I think I'll retire while I'm a HORSE'S AS." They both rose from the bench but Clark looked weary. In silhouette he seemed the older man. Joe left them

31

alone on the half-court. "Don't stay out too long," he said. "School tomorrow."

When his father had gone, Jerry pushed a pass to Clark, who sent a soft jump shot through its true arc to the basket from twenty feet. Jerry said, "H on me, for sure," then, out of nowhere, added, "You're thinking about Toody, aren't you?"

"About Toody?" But come to think of it, he was, among a hundred other things.

"'Cause he couldn't play with you at UK. Not unless Rupp lets Negroes on the team."

Clark dribbled the ball a couple of times and then just let it bounce away to wherever it wanted. "Man oh man, Jer—things are all messed up." He went back to the bench and sat down.

Jerry sensed that HORSE was over for the night, so he hurried over to retrieve the ball from under a bush, stuck it coolly under an arm, and started for the house. Ever since he was a toddler he had put his toys away. As he disappeared into the mudroom he offered his summation of the evening's turn: "Play the last thirty seconds against Georgia, my eye. You and Toody are already the best backcourt combination in Pike County."

Inside the darkened conservatory, her book long since closed in her lap, Barbara Hatling decided it was time to bake some chocolate chip cookies and some pecan sandies; maybe even a German chocolate cake.

Clark opened the kitchen cabinet and reached straight for the jade green Depression glass bowl he'd always used when he was little. Barbara started to warn him to be careful with it because it was a remnant of her own cookie-baking childhood, bartered for in the '30s with wrappers of Octagon soap that her mother had carefully laid aside, but he hadn't broken it when he was six, or seven, or eight, or nine, or ten, so why should he break it now? Let his own now great spanning hands add to the wear on the green glaze and therefore onto the history of that bowl, as had Barbara's tiny, then later adult, hands, and as had his grandmother's knotty, arthritic hands, and before that her tough mountain woman's hands that had stirred cornbread batter in that bowl, then gone

32

out to hoe the corn that would provide next year's bread.

"Saturday was always supposed to be baking day. Can you believe it's been five years since you and I baked together?" One third of his life; one-eighth of hers. But computations such as those meant nothing to a teenager. "I wonder why we stopped?"

"I think it was when we all voted that we liked Little Debbie's oatmeal cakes better than your chocolate chips."

She bopped him on the back of his head with a spatula. "You never voted any such a thing."

He rubbed the back of his head as though it had really hurt. "No, maybe not. Maybe it was Oreos."

"Oreos can only dream about coming out of my oven. Anyway, thanks for getting up early to help. It's a good chance for us to spend some time together. Your dad left late last night for Washington; Jerry will sleep half the day."

"Do you reckon Frank Ramsey's mom made him get up at the crack of dawn to help with the baking?"

"As a matter of fact, she did. That's what gave me the idea. I just read a story about it in *Look* magazine."

"Don't give me that."

"His mom said he could mix cake batter every bit as well as he could dribble a basketball."

"You're making this up as you go along, aren't you."

"That's for me to know and you to find out. Did you have any big plans for the morning?"

"Toody's coming over about ten o'clock."

"Then he'll have plenty of baked goodies waiting for him when he gets here. Is he coming for ball or study or what?"

"Little of both, I guess. We have a history exam on Monday. Mostly for hoops, though. That's usually how it works."

He was sifting flour, always his favorite part. At age six he would laugh and say, *Look Mom it's snowing!*

"Here's what I could never figure out about history," Barbara said. "Why is being alive so interesting, but studying about people who used to be alive so boring?"

"Wow, I was just having that same thought at the conference. But it was more like, Why is classroom history so boring, when

33

really, Mom, during those lectures I never lost concentration, not for one minute. I don't know why."

"Maybe you figured that you were part of it and it was part of you. Now put a cup and a half of sugar in with the flour."

Clark measured carefully, as though a half-teaspoon more or less would ruin everything, then began to stir, slowly, contemplatively. "Mom, did you know that in 1347 a ship pulled into port in Sicily carrying rats infected with a bacteria which killed them, and when they died their fleas would move to some other creature, looking I guess for a live body to take blood from, but at the same time some of the rat's blood that it carried would go into its new host, which in just a couple of days would get sick and die? All the while these fleas were reproducing and jumping from one host to another. Do you know what happened?"

"Lots of people died."

"Maybe half of Europe, in four years. The Black Death. Half of everybody was just gone. Not to mention horses and dogs and whatever else. But you know what was even worse?"

"Can't really imagine much worse, unless you beat my cake batter to death."

"The worst part was nobody knew about the fleas and bacteria and so on. They only figured that out this century. Back then they thought God was so mad He just started slaughtering people by the millions."

"Now why would the Good Lord want to go and do a thing like that?"

Clark's voice rose. "But that's just it—they stopped believing in a gentle God and went back to the Old Testament God of floods and plagues and stuff."

"So this conference was about what? Disease control?"

"No, it was about the crisis in the Middle East." Clark had to laugh when Barbara looked at him, dumbfounded. "Oh yeah, that was just background. The point was that the Christians started killing Jews. They said Jews must be poisoning wells all over Europe, so they started rounding them up and burning them in big town squares. And the pope, even the pope himself said 'Don't do that!' I forget his name—I have it in my notes. I took notes throughout this whole conference. Anyway he was the pope and he wrote a bull—I swear, that's what they call it." She was mugging at him, just like Jerry. "Don't make fun of me."

"What do you mean, the pope rode a bull?"

"He *wrote* a bull. Don't get me started laughing!"

"The pope wrote a bunch of bull?"

Just as when he was an infant, when Clark laughed he would lean way over. One of the most magical moments of her entire life was the first time he got so tickled in his high chair that he just laid his forehead against the tray and surrendered to helpless laughter. Jerry laughed at least as much as Clark did, but he would look you right in the face and let fly. Clark seemed slightly embarrassed for the world that it was so ridiculously funny.

"He didn't write a bunch of bull, Mom! That's the word for some kind of official decree, like 'You listen up or it's excommunication for you, Sid'."

That was his and Toody's new word. Now everybody was Sid.

"All right, I'll be serious. So what did His Popeness say?"

"He said, 'Look here now! Don't be stupid!' Okay, I remember two points. He said, the Jews are dying just like we are, so how can it be a Jewish plot? Do you think they're killing themselves just to cover up? And he said, There aren't any Jews in England and they're dying there like flies. Only, he probably didn't say like flies."

"Maybe he said like fleas ."

"Stop it, Mom!" Again he pitched forward in laughter, his face almost in the bowl.

"So did the killing stop?"

"No, it didn't stop! See, the thing was, it was the bigwigs egging this on, because you know why?"

"Because they were scared out of their minds?"

"Maybe so, but mainly because—get this—they owed money to these Jews and by murdering them they not only cancelled their loans, but they confiscated their property on top of that."

Up to that point Barbara had been leading him on, but at this revelation she was genuinely taken aback. She laid down her spatula, wiped her hands on a dishtowel, clasped them and brought them to her mouth, a favorite thinking posture of hers. "Now I'm

35

starting to follow you. Jews were the bankers and money-lenders. Because back then Christians couldn't charge interest on a loan. So it's far better to kill your banker than to pay off your loan."

"Sure. Then grab his bank to boot."

"And what does this have to do with the Middle East?"

"Beats me. I didn't follow all of it. I guess when the UN gave them a country, why didn't they give them land from the people who'd been trying to wipe them out instead of people who hadn't."

"I wanted to talk to you about the conference. I didn't even know you were being held captive until it was all over, so I can't pretend I was beside myself with worry. But a couple of nights ago I heard you talking with your dad. You were going to say something about Walter Sisler but Dad cut you off before you finished. Do you remember what it was?" He thought about it, drew a blank. "You were asking Daddy to defend him because you didn't think Mr. Sisler was being . . . what?"

"Oh, I don't know exactly . . . being mean, I guess. Immoral. *Guilty* maybe is more like it. Obviously he had people all scared and everything, and kept us . . . I don't know . . . kidnapped or whatever they'll call it. It just seems to me like even though he did illegally detain us, he's not guilty of it."

"Why do you say that?"

"Maybe because I wasn't scared."

"Were other people scared?"

"I guess so." He thought back over the scene, and had to admit, "Oh sure, I saw some women crying, people looked pretty shook up. But to me it was more like watching a play, you know? There we were sitting all in rows, like at a movie theater, watching stuff happen up there on a stage. The lights were dimmer than normal. I was just real calm. I can't explain it."

"What about Jerry? Did he cry?"

"Not a chance! He was bug-eyed! I think he enjoyed it. Dad kept patting us on the knee and saying not to worry, we'd get out of this just fine, but Jerry was like, Out of what?"

"Listen Clarkie, I know your dad has these big high hopes of you following in his footsteps."

"Yeah, so?"

"What do you think about that?" He withdrew into silence. She waited, finally gave in. "Well, here's all I want to say. If you have any doubts at all about his plan, don't worry about it. You be your own man."

"But he seems to be counting on me so much. He'll be really disappointed."

"He may have it all wrong. I know both my sons better than he does. I'm with you all the time. He's part-time. It's not his fault, exactly, but that's the way it worked out. He thinks you'll be a great politician because you're tall and good-looking and bright. You started getting your picture in the paper since you were about ten."

"Only because of basketball."

"And honor rolls, and county tests, essay competitions. You're the star. And you're the first born."

"That's not really my accomplishment, is it?"

"No, exactly right. But one day he'll figure out that the real candidate is waiting in the wings."

"You mean Jerry?" He hadn't meant for it to come out with such force.

"That's the very one. I've noticed it since he was a whelp. Even at age four or five in his playgroup, give him ten minutes and he was organizing a new game, smoothing over troubles, keeping everybody happy. So don't put too much pressure on yourself. Daddy doesn't know it yet, but he's got a Plan B."

Barbara Hatling carried a tray of cookies and iced tea past the basketball court and placed it on the picnic table beside the now-covered swimming pool, watching Clark and Toody exert themselves into sweat and exhaustion under the noontime sun of an Indian summer day. She let her eye follow the fierce bounce of the ball, which seemed to foreshadow a springing up of legs and a reaching out of arms, all sudden flex and extension. She noticed the almost violent jerks and directional adjustments they required to evade the obstacle to their goal, or to prevent the other's success, and she wondered if her son's future would also take such abrupt turns, these bounding advances and retreats, if he followed her admonishment to be his own man, to allow his life to follow a

37

trail made up of small victories or mistakes along the way. Or would he—shouldn't he?—choose his father's packaged success to a possibly fulfilling and certainly prominent life?

When she said, "Why don't you boys take a break and have some tea and a bite to eat?" did she mean she wanted them not to have to struggle so with what the future would bring, or did she just want them to stop jumping for a while and rest? Later, she might have read more into it than what was there originally, but at the time she couldn't know that one day Toody Baker, by that time Frank Baker, wearing Boston Celtic green, would tell reporters that the best point guard he'd ever played with was his best friend in high school, Clark Hatling.

And she couldn't know then that Joe Hatling would never accept that his laughing, trick-shot, second son was his natural heir. Clark was the "electable son." Couldn't she see that? And standing there with her tray of refreshments she had no way of knowing that just before Christmas following his senior year and a state championship, with Toody at the University of Cincinnati, and Clark on the all-white Kentucky freshman squad, that Clark would skip practice one day and walk downtown to the Army recruiting office in Lexington. He just thought that he could use a couple more years to resolve things, and why not do it in a new place a million miles from home, in a country that nobody much had ever heard of: Vietnam.

He wired his decision to his father. Joe didn't respond immediately, but after a day's reflection he wired back: *Great idea, son. Voters love a military man.*

3

HISTORY RUNS IN THE FAMILY

WALTER PUT DOWN his pen and paused to consider what he had written. "I love my country. I am proud to call myself a patriotic American. I am as proud of our flag and what we stand for as is any member of this jury. I love America so much that I was prepared to commit an outrageous act in order to steer the course of our history away from a huge national mistake."

He needed a moment to think about how he would phrase the huge national mistake that he wanted to avert. He needed to put it in such a way that the jurors wouldn't take him for a crackpot, yet leave his lawyers room to argue that they should find him not guilty, him being such a crackpot and all. He decided he would have a nice swim as he worked through that. He phoned Jimmy's office in the sports complex to see if the pool cleaners had finished. This was Monday morning, slowest time of the week at Asclepius Waters, and time for the week's major pool cleaning. Jimmy's line was busy, so Walter decided to walk to the pool. If it was open, fine; if not maybe the walk would turn out to be an equally effective way to clarify his thoughts.

He found himself in surprisingly high spirits for a man preparing a plea that had little chance of keeping him out of jail. The day itself was lovely, with blue skies washed clear of dust by last night's rare autumn rainstorm. The last of the scarlet petals of the flame trees were gone. The rain had also cleaned them off the walking paths, marking a new season in the cycle.

Beyond that, his attorneys assured him that while the Feds could get involved, since he'd set up the conference using interstate communication, most of the plaintiffs would only be embarrassed by a trial, and the bigger the name the more embarrassed they would be. Also, a trial would allow him to showcase his opinions, so AIPAC mainstreamers would be just as happy to let the idea of any public proceedings die a quiet death.

Something to make his walk this morning a bright affair: he might not go to jail. On the other hand, if he did go to trial it would give him the chance to present before the court, and probably before the world thanks to the media, the very *I love my country* speech he was in the middle of preparing right now. It was hard to tell which way he wanted it to go. The best outcome would be for the jurors to break down in tears, set him free, and then set off as disciples to roam the highways and byways of America preaching an even-handed approach to the Palestinians in exile. He was having a private little chuckle about that—twelve jurors, twelve disciples—when he looked up and saw Jimmy turning the corner of the tennis courts and running toward him in long, loping strides.

"Oh, sir, I couldn't reach you. I was coming to get you."

"Hold on and catch your breath Jimbo. What on earth . . . "

"It's your father, sir. On TV."

No man in Texas was less likely to be on TV than old Dow Sisler. Unlike Walter, who had grown up on that desolate five hundred acre sandbox only because his parents had dragged him there, Dow Sisler had actively sought it out, paid for it with what was left of his auction money and quit the road crew way back in East Texas to move there. Dow was only at peace when he was alone with his cattle, and in his worst moods he'd been known to stare down a cow, asking, "The fuck you thank you lookin' at?"

By the time it was on TV, it was all over. A reporter from the Dallas CBS station had discovered the farm where Walter grew up, and found that his father was still living there, so he and a cameraman turned up just about breakfast time in search of a new angle on the now-infamous Walter Sisler. They naturally went straight for the front door of the nice white brick ranch house that Walter had built for his old man, not knowing, as even Walter did not know, that Dow continued to live out in the plank-and-tarpaper cabin that had been his home now for almost thirty years. From here Dow saw the men walking from window to window of the brick house, camera and microphone in hand. When they gave up on finding anyone over there, they came straight for the cabin, where Dow was waiting with his old bolt-action Remington

.30/06. The reporter went down at once. The cameraman leapt behind an old truck body that was rusting away in the yard. His film shows Dow leaving the cabin to check out the body of the fallen man. At this point he looks disoriented. He walks around the body, kicking at tufts of grass. He seems to have forgotten all about the other intruder. He drops the rifle beside the dead reporter, ambles into the cabin, and a few seconds later he returns to the porch with a handgun. The camera caught, although TV stations didn't run, the single shot to his right temple.

If anything, Walter's star rose even brighter in the public imagination. It was seen that he was from pure Texas stock. What was more Texan than shooting an intruder, then, when upon reflection you realize you have sinned in hot-headed haste, doing the right thing with a pistol on the front porch? Walter wept at the reporter's funeral. He asked the man's wife, "Please find it in your heart to forgive him. He got insaner and insaner as time went by." She said she would try. She said she hoped it didn't run in the family. Walter said he did too.

At his father's funeral in San Vitores he sat dry-eyed through the hymns and the Bible reading at the Bethel Baptist Church. Roxanne took his hand as they stood before the closed casket.

"You know Roxy, I think he's happier right now at this moment than he ever was in life." He didn't mean that in some state-of-grace, right-hand-of-God sense. He meant as he lay there now all closed up, with no electrical charges in his brain ever to fire again, the fever conquered, a pile of dust in process.

Probably none of this mattered to the outcome of the prosecutorial discussion. The charge of false imprisonment was dropped; conspiracy was dropped. Only fraud remained. The indictment was secret and by grand jury. Defense counsel obtained a compromise whereby prosecution would be deferred for three years—equaling the statute of limitations—providing Walter agreed to restrict his activities to normal business practices and remain resident in the state of Texas.

So he didn't get to give his *I love my country* speech, but as they left the courtroom there were smiles and handshakes all around. The dignitaries wouldn't be embarrassed; the government had

41

asserted its primacy; defense had kept their man out of prison. If you'd just spotted the lot of them along the corridor you might think they'd all just returned from a jolly lunch at the country club.

Only one man looked grim. He approached the group from within the shadows of a doorway and walked straight up to Walter. "I'll need a few minutes of your time, Mr. Sisler. I'm from the Internal Revenue Service."

4

NO SOUL CAREENS in turmoil like the soul of the adolescent male. The evil vapor descends heavily, thoroughly, with neither trigger nor announcement, then lifts, evacuates, evaporates, an ephemera on a whim. Suddenly it's back, blacker than ever, wrestling and pinning like some underwater creature enjoying every element of advantage, while the adolescent male struggles for movement, breath, purchase. Toody put an amiable shoulder into his chest, slammed him against his locker. Clark faded with it, heard the metal door shudder, felt the lump of his combination lock rub against his spine, not hurting much. Didn't help.

He had felt, rather than considered, the position of Walter Sisler; made his impetuous and daring stand, declared himself. His dad was the answer. His dad would step in and save the poor intrepid fool. But, no—a stupid idea, inspiring only a father's ridicule.

Toody slugged him in his hard stomach, called him a queer. Didn't help.

Later that evening, in a gym packed with opposition fans sensing a huge upset and baying for blood, Clark threaded the ball through the lane, past three defenders, hit Toody in stride for a lay-up to beat Prestonsburg at the buzzer. Within the dancing embrace of his teammates and the thin cheers of Pikeville supporters, Clark threw himself over the cliff into the happy void of oblivion, but even minutes later, as he showered in that stinking visitor's locker room, as he gently soaped a knot on his cheekbone put there by the deliberate elbow of Prestonsburg's big oaf of a center, he remembered Walter's bloody forehead, and, without warning, the cold, crawly admission of a betrayal by innocence settled over him.

It had to be done. He wrote to Walter in care of Ammenstar Oil to apologize that he could not deliver on his offer of his father's help. Walter responded almost immediately, and in his own handwriting, that Clark shouldn't worry, that his own lawyers were competent, if not quite up to the standards of Pikeville, Ky. Considering only the written words, this letter might have seemed a roundhouse insult, and a totally unwarranted one at that, but on the contrary it lifted Clark's spirits no end. There were a couple of reasons for that. The quickness of the response, for one thing. How many superrich oilmen staring prison in the face would make a priority of answering a courtesy letter from a high school kid? For another, Walter had ended the sentence containing the slur about the standards of Pikeville, Ky. with a big exclamation point. Clark interpreted Walter's punctuation not, as his grammar books had taught him, as added emphasis, but as a kind of written elbow in the ribs, a wink, the inside joke of a couple of yokels who know they are much smarter than they look.

The thing that put the seal on this letter as a special bond, however, was the short note added as a p.s., in an assured, floating, feminine script:

You are one nice kid. You be sure to keep in touch, okay?
Roxanne

So Clark did keep in touch. When he heard news reports of Dow Sisler's end he sent Walter a sympathy card. It was a sappy one from his church, with a Bible verse and praying hands, but he figured, What the hell. With his letter following the Panthers' state single-A basketball title, he included a newspaper article and a photograph of him and Toody hugging at the final buzzer. He didn't write during his few weeks at the University of Kentucky, but did from the Presidio of Monterey, where the army assigned him to study Vietnamese. He explained, in a shorthand version, that he had left college because he felt he needed "seasoning," as he put it, before he charted out his real future. He wrote them from Saigon about the sidewalk cafés with their baguettes and plates of two-dollar chateaubriand and duck a l'orange. Later, when the VC bombing started, he wrote them about the sand bags and barbed wire, about the end of street cafés and the beginning of dark bars

44

with Bière 33 and weightless girls dancing.

He wrote them from Georgetown to let them know he had made it out of Vietnam and was back in the States. He told them that he'd decided to major in History, and that in some way that he hadn't quite pieced together this decision went back to the conference at Asclepius Waters. He added, cheekily perhaps, but with an exclamation point, that the Conference to Change the World had certainly worked, "at least in my case!"

To all previous letters, Walter and Roxanne had replied promptly. The first letter he'd received from them in Vietnam ended with Roxanne's customary p.s., but this time she'd signed it "Roxy Sisler." Clark followed this with a note of congratulations attached to a small lacquered box filled with packets of lotus tea. The thank you note arrived almost by return mail.

For some time, though, the letter from Georgetown brought nothing. He didn't think they would have taken offense to the wisecrack about Asclepius Waters. Maybe they didn't like it that he'd chosen Georgetown in order to live near his father, after having had the guts to reject his prescribed route through UK. Could that be why they didn't write back? They thought that in some psychologically complex way he'd sold out? Maybe the marriage didn't work out and they were already divorced or something, and replying to people like Clark was no longer a joint venture, so it could be ignored. After a month had passed with no word, he chastised himself for assuming that an acquaintance as incidental as his with the Sislers would survive the years.

The postmark explained the delay: Beirut.

The letter explained Beirut.

Dear Clark:

Don't be shocked by the strange stamps, because yes, it's true—we are in Lebanon. I can only explain this by saying that the U.S. government tax people are a cussed bunch and guess what? I am every bit as cussed as they are. After months extended into years of tussle and negotiations, the IRS still insisted that I sign over to them everything short of my first-born son, and him too if I had one. I was afraid one of them

45

sons-a-bitches was going to try to seduce Roxy just to insure I had a firstborn son to get title to, seeing as how I haven't produced one for them yet.

No joking now for a minute: I didn't mind one bit admitting that I'd planned the whole conference to shock all those self-important people into considering how they'd feel if somebody muscled in and ran them off their property. I was prepared to go to jail for my just desserts. But I never cheated the government out of a penny, and I'm not going to play like I did. They didn't have the guts to charge me with my real crime, so they tried to strip me of my assets as a backhanded way of prosecuting me for what they were too chicken to charge me with.

So I got out as many assets as I could, and anyway a lot of my wealth was in foreign holdings to begin with. I can look after my so-called empire just fine from here. Of course I can't go back home until all this blows over, but I'll make my peace with that. The real oil money will be in the Middle East now anyway.

Beirut is a blast. "The Paris of the East," they like to call it. It's not all hidebound and hardshell religious like those Arabs in the Gulf, but it's Arab anyhow and we're both treated well here. I've always had a connection with these folks.

I have a big suggestion you might consider. If you're majoring in History, why not make it Middle East History, and come over here to study? The American University of Beirut is a fine old institution. There's even a basketball team. I bet between me and your daddy you could get in (!)

The food here is great, there are some delicious local beers, and the girls will buckle your knees. We have a huge house (they call it a villa here) and you'd be more than welcome to bunk here, or if you prefer a dorm, nobody would argue with that. Just give it some thought.

Yours,
Walter Sisler

p.s. Darling, just let me clear up a couple little—let's call

46

them misconceptions—that Brother Walter has left you with. First of all, he doesn't know if there's a basketball team at AUB or not. That's just him being a lying-through-his-teeth salesman. Second of all, he doesn't know if the girls here are beautiful or not because I don't let him out of the house without a blindfold. (Because I'll say you bet they're gorgeous!) That's it! Everything else is the God's own truth: you'd be more than welcome here, so think it over.

Love,

Roxy

Barbara and the boys joined the Congressman in D.C. for the first part of the summer following Clark's freshman year at Georgetown, then when Congress adjourned they went back to Pikeville for a good couple of weeks of family basketball and politicking. Joe was up for reelection in November.

Barbara was crocheting on the bench by the court while the three men had a shoot-around. Clark had saved his announcement for the basketball court, where discussions never seemed to get as out of hand as they might in more formal settings.

"I've made a pretty big decision about my major. I'm going to specialize in Middle East History. How does that strike anybody?"

"Definitely an important and timely subject," Barbara said.

"Are you two crazy?" asked Joe. "Think how that will look to voters. You'll seem like some sort of fruitcake."

"Aw, on campaign literature ol' Clarkie's going to list it as *Holy Land Studies*, aren't you big brother?"

"That might work," Joe said.

"You can say anything you want," Jerry added, "as long as you thump a Bible while you say it."

"Who told you that?"

"You did, Dad! Ha!"

"Well you can't say that, Bible thumping or no Bible thumping."

"You see," Clark said, "that's exactly why I'll never be as good at politics as you are, Dad. Even if I know something to be absolutely true or false, I've still got to watch my mouth because voters might not like it. I don't know how you do it. You've got to censor every

47

word you say, constantly be on guard. You even show up at church every time you come home."

"And he always manages to have a photographer waiting for him on the church steps. That's the key, huh Dad."

"No, Jerry," Clark intruded, "that's not the key. The key is believing it's all true. If at church you sing, *He watches over the sparrow, so I know He watches me*, and then you drive home and find the cat eating a sparrow on your front porch, you can't allow your mind to connect those two events."

"Ha! He's watching over the cat now, right Dad?"

Barbara looked up from her handwork, her crochet hook continuing its intricate movement. "Listen, boys," she said. "It's normal to have doubts as you grow into adults, but soon enough you'll see that the church is full of good people who will be there to help you through thick and thin. It's a place where you don't feel alone in the world."

Joe added, "And on top of that it's a star-spangled vote winner. You'll get the hang of it as you mature."

"But I don't want to mature into a hypocrite. That's my point."

"You'll never be a hypocrite, Clark. I know my son well enough to know that."

Joe stared at Barbara but didn't say anything.

Jerry fired a shot past the backboard and had to crawl under the bare forsythia bushes to retrieve the ball. He came out muddy, with sticks in his hair and when everybody laughed he said, "What?" When they laughed at that, he said, "You wanted the ball back, didn't you?" and they laughed some more. He threw the ball to Clark, who danced the ball to behind the circle as though fighting off two defenders, wheeled and sank one from twenty-five. He decided to continue his confessions.

"I should tell you that another part of my plan is next year I'll take my junior year abroad at the American University of Beirut."

This time Jerry was the one who looked at him like he was nuts. "You're going to be the Georgetown starting guard as a sophomore, and as a junior you'll give that up to go study a million miles away?"

"Some things matter more than basketball," Clark said, but Jerry wasn't interested.

48

"Plus I'll need to learn Arabic."

"Oh, my lord. Kentucky Seven will have a calf."

"I'll need two languages, so I'll study Hebrew too."

"That'll help. Tell church groups you want to read the Bible in its original."

"Actually the Bible was written in Greek, Dad."

Joe stopped and looked at him. "No. I don't believe that."

"I'm talking about the New Testament. Most of the Old Testament was written in Hebrew, but the New was in Greek."

"Jesus spoke Greek?" Joe took the pass from Jerry and put the ball under his arm.

"No, he spoke Aramaic. None of the disciples spoke Greek. Only the educated class could read and write, and when they learned to write, it was Greek they learned."

"So how did Matthew write the book of Matthew?"

"He didn't. The gospels were written decades later, and nobody knows who wrote them. They got their names later. It was branding, like your Caddie. Chief Cadillac didn't design your car. It's just a name that sounds good."

"Is this the stuff they teach you at Georgetown?"

"Hey, it's a Catholic school. They can't go too far wrong."

Jerry piped up, "They're the ones who came up with the Inquisition."

That stopped the conversation for a moment. Clark looked at Jerry; Jerry shrugged. The congressman looked at his wife, who raised her eyebrows at him, as if to say, "I told you he was more than a loveable clown," before returning to her crocheting.

Clark said, "And the Jesuits were the educators of the Enlightenment. Not that they meant to be."

"I'm not buying any of this. Barbara knows a lot of this stuff." She looked up again from her work. "Barbara, what language was the New Testament written in?"

"English. I've got one in the house to prove it."

"Don't be humorous."

"If you'd open yours more often, you'd see for yourself."

"Talking to this family is like talking to inmates in the loony bin."

"Hey, it's all Greek to me!" Jerry chipped in, proudly.

49

"Let's hope to God no voters ever hear this conversation or any like it coming out of the mouth of anybody in this family. I'm going to have to ship all of you off to Beirut—or better yet Outer Mongolia—until after the next election."

"Dad," Jerry said, "you won last time by 35,000 votes."

"The time before that it was 55,000."

Jerry said, "That was the year Clarkie won the state championship."

"Yeah right," Clark said, "like it was a one-man show."

"He's got a point, though," Joe said. "Your name was out there."

"And last time was mid-term," Jerry added, not putting it all down to Clark. "The in-party always loses votes in mid-term elections."

"And your point is?"

"Relax, Dad. You're safe as Fort Knox."

"Well, maybe so." Joe put in a compact twenty-foot jumper over Jerry's waving arms. "Okay Clark, you've got my qualified blessing for this plan of yours, but here's the bottom line. Do not—UNDER ANY CIRCUMSTANCES—fall in love over there. You understand me? You marry one of those girls and you kiss your future goodbye. You find yourself a Kentucky girl. You got that?"

"Yes Dad, you've made your point."

"You go over there, you don't even look at a woman."

"Right, right."

"I'm serious now. This is non-negotiable."

"Yes, Dad."

"I'll disown you. I swear to God I will."

Just over a year later, high up in the mountains outside Beirut, at a Halloween ball in the Sislers' ornately tiled villa in Beit Mery, while Walter and Roxy, dressed as Batman and Catwoman, jitterbugged within a crowd of revelers to the Colman Hawkins version of *Go L'il Liza*, Clark took refuge in the corner of a spacious terrace and gazed out over an inlet to the Mediterranean and the mountains beyond. While his thoughts effervesced into the beauty of that view, and then completely dissipated inside a consideration of just what the hell he was doing in this breathtakingly alien land, a hennaed hand was creeping its way along the wrought iron railing and toward his own. He felt a warm grip on his wrist, and suddenly a nun was pulling him toward the dance floor. She was in full habit—white scapular, white coronet and all. He'd seen plenty of nuns at Georgetown, but none had ever started to do a sort of slow-motion Lebanese version of the twist right in front of him. She announced, "I'm Aziza the Flying Nun—and you're going to dance with me."

5

ALL MICHELINE FOSSARD ever wanted to do was paint pictures, but her father insisted on a secretarial course as a back-up plan, which is why, as France started to reassert control over its empire following World War Two, she found herself in Beirut, sitting in a row of both French and Lebanese typists in the Office of Trade Licensing. Native-born French women of any station were in short supply in late-1940s Lebanon, so Micheline had to withstand a barrage of bids from stolid French bureaucrats who found one excuse after another to pass by her desk, requesting this form or that form, giving tips on life in the East, offering a cigarette, lunch, drinks, or a night out. Yet one Friday she left for lunch a half-hour early, in search of a new hat, simply because a dapper Palestinian silk merchant in a loose brown business suit, wide tie and two-toned shoes had asked her, "You like art galleries?"

Hassin Aruri was a salesman with an eye for pattern and color, and, he assured her, he was moving up. He took her to *La Galerie de la Paix* on the *rue André Chénier*, where his company promoted its silk business with displays of serigraphy from its own designers and artists. He offered to teach her the entire process, if she was interested. She was.

She was also interested in Hassin Aruri. He had a lively face that demanded a portrait. The following weekend when he picked her up she was carrying a sketchpad and pencils. She agreed to accompany him to his small apartment along the *corniche*, where he produced a carton of unfiltered *Gitanes* and the bottle of Armagnac he'd brought back from his most recent trip to France. Lighting her cigarette and pouring drinks forbidden by his religion, he assured her that although he had been born into a Palestinian Muslim family, he considered the whole idea of religion the relic of a dying era. Micheline said that this opinion had been widespread in France for many years, but she hadn't expected to encounter it here.

"Nor did you expect to encounter Hassin Aruri, I think."

She smiled, surveyed his kitchen for composition, and moved a chair. "Sit down here. I will draw you," she told him, "and you will tell me exactly what I've found."

What she'd found was a husband; a secular, free-thinking son of Palestinian Muslims who considered religion to be fine in its place—that place being perhaps the last five minutes of one's life, on the chance there really was a heaven. Soon she'd also found a black-haired, blue-eyed daughter. They named her Aziza.

Aziza grew up in Marseilles and in Brooklyn, where her father managed textile outlets, and in Beirut, where he oversaw exports of finished clothing. Aziza often spent hours with her mother at her gallery exhibitions. One day Roxanne Sisler walked in to buy a painting, and the three of them became instant best friends.

Hassin had enough of being an employee, even at vice-presidential level, and decided to start his own firm, so he did not attend that year's Halloween party at Walter and Roxanne Sislers' new villa in the mountains north of Beirut. Aziza was dressed as a nun, Micheline in the nineteenth-century artist's get-up of floppy beret and cape. She carried her easel and a box of paints. In fact, it was not all costume—she planned to paint.

A lot of the guests had already arrived. The terrace was crowded with dancers. After greeting Roxy, Micheline weaved her way through to the corner and began to set up her canvas.

Alone with Roxy now, Aziza asked, "Is he here?"

Roxy pulled her to the edge of an arched doorway, from where she could see the people at the far edge of the terrace. "That's him over there—that tall boy."

Aziza saw Clark standing against the railing in the corner opposite her mother. He was not watching the dancers, but looked out over the cliffs to the sea. He was slender, good-looking, at least in profile, with straight brown hair gone shaggy, but not hippy-long. His only effort at a costume seemed to be a pair of empty eyeglass frames and a shoe-polish moustache. Even immobile he looked an athlete. Aziza turned to Roxy and said, "He even *stands* gracefully." She wondered what he was thinking about, with his gaze directed elsewhere.

"Honey, he's got a heart of gold. Go on over. He'll stand there all day if you don't."

Clark didn't see her coming. Aziza grabbed his wrist and said, "I'm Aziza the Flying Nun—and you're going to dance with me."

Clark thought, Why not? He was a good dancer. The Vietnamese women had taken giggling delight in teaching him, and he was a natural athlete. Like most men he wasn't an avid dancer, but unlike most he was good at it. He couldn't understand why other men didn't see how attractive a fine male dancer was to women.

"You don't have to ask me twice." One of Joe's lines Clark trotted out when he was stuck.

"Who are you, anyway?"

"Clark Hatling."

"Clark Hatling? Who the hell's Clark Hatling?"

"Um, the guy you asked to dance?"

"I didn't ask your name, *idiot*." She pronounced it the French way: *ee-dee-o* "And I didn't ask you to dance. Not technically."

"In that case *who are you anyway* means . . . oh, my costume. Groucho. I'm Groucho Marx."

"Then it's not fair. You should be smoking a cigar."

He had no ready retort for that. It seemed a conversation closer. He was too caught up in the contrast of blue eyes and black hair, which her coronet did not quite properly cover; by her nose, which, with its graceful round tip protruding ever so slightly further into his space than he might have expected, indicated that it might be more supple than most human noses, and could twitch, or pivot, to explore its environment. Later he would come to think of it as a Phoenician nose, but even at the time, on their first meeting, he had the immediate sense that to bite down softly on its spongy tip would offer unaccounted-for pleasure.

He didn't want the conversation to stop with him needing a cigar, but he was stymied. Aziza, though, said, "Let's see what we can do about that." She reached into her purse and produced one. It was a handmade Cuban brand, unavailable in the U.S., a *Romeo y Julieta* in a metal tube. He had no idea if that was some sort of karmic fate, or whether *Romeo y Julietas* were as common in Lebanese purses as were, say, Salems, or Spearmint gum, in American ones. Much later he would learn that Roxy had set it up with Aziza, knowing he would come as Groucho, but was unlikely to smoke.

"Look at the little Girl Scout."

"I think I should probably resent that remark."

"Sorry. Always prepared, I mean. Boy Scouts, anyway. I don't actually know if Girl Scouts are always prepared or not."

"You make it sound like carrying a condom in your wallet."

"Jesus. I though Arab girls were shy and retiring. Where did you learn to talk like that?"

"Brooklyn. I grew up there, mostly. And in France. *Où c'est un préservatif, si on parle français.*"

"Sorry?"

"Never mind. You can learn Arabic instead. All spies need to know Arabic."

"Why do you say that?"

"I tricked you. I know who you are."

"This is a very puzzling conversation. One thing I do know, we can't dance with this thing on your head. It looks like an albatross or something." He uncovered her head and flipped the coronet over the balcony railing. They watched it catch the breeze over the tops of the cedars and sail out over the sea, finally landing deftly to float on the surface. To Clark at that moment it seemed his own white-winged heart had caught the wind and made a seabird landing on the quiet waves.

A slower song began. She led him into the cluster of dancers. He put his arm around her. The top of her head fit right under his chin. He wished he had the nerve to pull her head close to his chest and feel her warm hair against his throat.

"I knew you were Clark Hatling all along. Your reputation precedes you. Is it true you are already a sports star, a war hero, and a spy?"

He decided to play her game. He tightened his grip around

55

her waist, closing all space between them. He could feel her breasts lift against him as she breathed. "You understand, don't you, that's a question where if I answer *yes*, then you know it's a lie, and if I answer *no*, it might be true, or it might still be a lie."

"So what's your answer?"

"No."

"Oh, good. International man of mystery; maybe honest, maybe not."

"And why did you pretend you didn't know who I was?"

"I was toying with you. That's what women do in this part of the world." She eased her head back to watch his response.

"It's what everybody does everywhere. In the beginning."

She said, "You seem annoyed."

"Not one bit. As long as it doesn't go on too long."

"And how long does it go on? Where you come from, I mean."

"Ideally," he told her, "about three minutes."

She pressed the side of her face against his chest, and he felt her warm hair against his throat. Within the circle of his arms he felt her permanency, as though he'd been molded to receive her, but he quickly reminded himself that this was an illusion. How much time could they really have together before he had to return to Georgetown? One year, his junior year abroad. No, he remembered—by now not even a full year. He counted the Beirut months left to him. Nine. The impact of that number caused a pause in his steps. Aziza pulled back and looked up at his face, as if to ask why he had stopped dancing. He resumed the rhythm, but repeated to himself: Nine months. The gestation period of a human being. Time enough to be born, but not enough to survive on your own.

After this meeting, Clark could sustain only one consideration: how to fit Aziza into his future. His internal dialogue gave up all pretense of civility and broke into a brawl, which soon escalated into all-out civil war. Over and over he heard his father's admonition that marriage to a foreigner, any foreigner, much less a non-Christian one, was toxic to the voters of Kentucky Seven. Clark wasn't at all sure he cared about that, but didn't want to close

56

off the option, not yet, not before he'd even finished college.

Not only that, but by marrying a Muslim, might he not endanger even his father's own seat in Congress? Would Joe be forced to respond publicly to any such marriage? Reporters would ask him about it, wouldn't they? Of course they would. They were all just scandal diggers anyway. And if reporters didn't ask, the Republicans sure would. Somebody would stick a microphone in his face and ask him what he thought of a son who married outside the faith. Would Joe say, "He can marry who he wants. He's my son, I love him, and I'll love his chosen bride." Or would he grab the microphone and denounce: *apostate!*

As if that weren't enough, Clark's own voice kicked in, echoing every coach, sports writer and scout he'd ever come across, reminding him that by leaving the Kentucky team once, and now Georgetown, the NBA already saw him as a lukewarm prospect. The voice warned him to get his ass back to Washington for a monster senior season if he didn't want his future as a basketball player to mean Greece or Turkey at five hundred bucks a month.

However . . . this woman. Now he realized he'd never loved anyone before. Only here, in Beirut, with this woman, had he finally fallen in love, and this was what it meant. He thought about her all the time. The moment they parted he started to plan how to see her again. What did the future matter—Congress, the NBA, any of it—if she wasn't there to share it with him?

He alternated wildly between *I cannot have her* to *I must have her.* He was like one of those sub-atomic particles that can shift between two different places without moving through intervening space. I must. I can't. I must. I can't.

The best he could do was to devise a stalling tactic. He decided that he should tell her frankly that his time in Beirut would end next August, when he had to return to Georgetown for his final year of college. He would put that out there in the open, leave no doubt about it. We have a deadline here, my dear. Let's just live for the moment, not wasting a precious day of our time together.

This plan would allow him to control his own fate. If by next August he still wanted to keep his options open, he could leave Aziza with a wistful tear but a clean conscience. If, though—and

57

this was the beauty of it—if by then he had decided that their love transcended everything else, he could always change his mind. A reversal of this kind would be unlikely to trigger anger and tears. She would be unlikely to say, You mean you let me spend months thinking I wasn't good enough for your family? That I was a convenient sex partner for your big Lebanese escapade, but a real millstone for your hotshot future?

No. In fact, such a change of heart would flatter her. She would think, All his hopes, his plans, his dreams; the censure of his family; even the threat to his father's position—all those mean nothing next to his love for me.

The first part of the plan needed to be dealt with quickly. He would tell her that August was the deadline, the end point, the final whistle. Kiss me farewell at the airport, and then we're both free as birds.

He had to tell her, and he had to tell her now. He had no idea how she would react. But really, did it matter very much? Not in the long run. She'd be hurt for the moment, maybe pissed off, but tomorrow the air would clear. His options would remain open, and he would have achieved a few months' time to think them through.

He told her at the tiny two-chair kitchen table in his flat, where she'd come by even before he got home from basketball practice to cook for him. Not, as he'd expected, some Lebanese feast, but a dish she'd learned from her mother, a cassoulet of lamb with white beans.

He tasted it and said, "You know, if we pretend this is a ham hock in here, this could be eastern Kentucky, where I come from."

She smiled, seeming to sense an approving closeness in this observation, a meeting of her background with his, and a suggestion of home in the overlap. She poured them each a shot of arak into a glass of water. They sat quietly as they watched it go cloudy, then she added chips of ice.

He tasted it. "Well, there goes eastern Kentucky."

"*Poof*," she said.

Neither said anything else for a long time. They ate silently and sipped slowly, allowing the flavors to blend and the arak to

58

soften thought.

Clark wiped his plate with a wedge of baguette, took his glass in hand, leaned back to look at her. He opened by saying simply, "*Ya Azizati*," which happily meant both "my Aziza" and "my dear."

She looked up, smiled at his use of Arabic, and answered, formally, "*Na'am, habibi?*"

"You know how much I care for you, don't you?"

Her smile disappeared.

"Love, even. I don't know why I shy away from the word."

Her eyes followed his hand as he lifted his glass to finish off his arak, but still she didn't speak.

"But you and I both know what happens, come August."

"No. But it appears you're going to tell me."

"I head back to D.C. Back to the real world."

She snapped her head to look away from him. Her black hair caught the light as it flipped around. "Don't kid yourself," she said, apparently to the kitchen sink, before looking back at Clark to finish. "You're just a fling for me too."

He congratulated himself on how smoothly it had gone. Just one sharp remark, no remonstrations, not a single tear. They continued to see each other just as much as before. They made love—which in their lovers' code became "making history"—just as often, and with no less intensity.

When not "making history" they discussed history—real history this time—and why they'd chosen to major in it. Clark told her about the Secret Conference to Change the World, how he'd sat there captive under the bullet-pocked ceiling of a Texas ballroom and felt history flow through him.

Aziza told him about the ever-inventive Miss Gillanders, a history teacher at William McKinley in Bay Ridge, Brooklyn, and her most influential teacher ever. She told him of the "Myself in History" lessons, when once a week a pupil would stand up for three minutes to tell what they knew of their family's past, and what events had led their forebears to leave the ancestral home. Then Miss Gillanders would devote one class period to precisely that topic. Aziza had told the class the story of her father's

59

fortuitous birth year of 1920, so Miss Gillanders talked about the end of the line for the Ottomans, the hundreds of thousands of Christians and Muslims who had been forced to move from Turkey to Greece, or from Greece to Turkey. She explained the secret French and English agreement to divide ancient Palestine after World War One, the creation of Israel in 1948, and the presence of refugee camps.

So they talked about history, studied history together, wrote their papers together, "made history" together, right through to final exams in May. Clark delayed leaving Beirut, even though he had completed his courses. Into the heat of June and July they spent more time together than apart. He still hadn't figured out what to do about her. More delay, he supposed, was about all he could do. Maybe he could come back next summer? It was an idea worth considering.

Things seemed on a course to remain unchanged right through to his August departure, until one stifling evening when Clark answered the door to find not Aziza standing there, but her mother, Micheline.

She had something to say. Could she come in for a moment? It was perhaps unfortunate, but it had to be said.

Her preface was a tortured account of her husband's failed business venture, and the mountain of debt he'd amassed in the process. They were ruined. They would soon be beyond poor.

Her main point was simple. The collapse of his enterprise had forced them to accept a decision that was as unpalatable to them as it would have been to any modern European family. Clark was not, she insisted, to see this as a retreat into some barbaric practice. The idea of an arranged marriage was anathema to her and Hassin personally, just as much as it was to Aziza herself. But Aziza was a fine and dutiful daughter, and had agreed. Before the year was out she would marry a man named Yousuf Hatoum. His father was the director of the *Banque du Moyen-Orient pour Liban.*

Micheline rose, walked to the door, turned and kissed him on both cheeks. When she pulled away, he saw tears in her eyes. "Believe me," she said, "I know what I am asking. But if you love Aziza, never attempt to see her again."

60

6

FREAK FLAG

FOR HIS SOPHOMORE year at the University of Kentucky in Lexington, Jerry and a few friends rented an old house on Linden Walk, a street of sycamores and sagging front porches in the freak district just off campus. The only phone in the house was located in about the worst possible place anybody could have chosen: on the wall right in front of the entrance to the common room, where, when the music was blaring, which was almost all the time, you couldn't hear it ringing, and if you did happen to hear it, between songs on an album, say, you sure couldn't hear to hold a conversation. A common sight at the Linden Walk house was the phone cord stretched across the hallway and into a closed closet. But on that cold November morning Hubbard had on his headphones and Marcy was up early, frying bacon and cooking oatmeal in the kitchen. Sometimes big things hinge on little things, like Hubbard's headphones and Marcy's breakfast.

Jerry heard the rap on his door and Marcy's fluted *"Jerry, telephone—Washington."* He rose unsteadily from his futon and was careful to distinguish sprawling limbs from bunched up bits of sleeping bag as he stepped over Lisa and onto the hardwood floor. *Christ* the room was freezing, so he threw on track suit bottoms and a UK sweatshirt, and slipped his feet into a pair of tennis shoes. Lisa hadn't moved. The only parts of her he could see were her autumn red hair on a pillow, and the perfect nub of a kneecap sticking out from under the sleeping bag. It looked blue from the chill, and the cold teeth of the bag's zipper rested against her bare skin. He bent to cover it before he left the room. He wanted to kiss it while he was down there, but he feared he wouldn't stop with a single kiss, and she would waken and sigh, or moan, or perhaps even raise that knee. Though he'd only known Lisa for a week, one thing he knew for sure was that at that point he could forget all about the call from Washington, so he gently tucked the covers around her exposed knee and went downstairs.

The phone dangled down the wall on its cord. Jerry heard a distant buzz of music which he at first took to be coming from the phone itself, until he heard its accompanying sound, the gurgle of a bong. He smelled weed, looked up and saw Hubbard holding the hose of the water pipe to his lips. It was the intricately ornate *arghile* that Clark had brought back from Beirut, more as a souvenir than a working pipe, he supposed. Although with Clark you could never tell. Hubbard gestured with the pipe, his offer to share, but Jerry waved him off and pointed to the phone. Hubbard relaxed into his music and his smoke. Jerry could just make out the song: *Almost Cut My Hair*.

On the other end of the line he didn't hear the voice of his father, but of Sandy, Joe's trusted secretary since his days as a junior partner in Pikeville. When Joe was elected to Congress he said he needed her in Washington because when any Kentucky Seven voter phoned his office he wanted the first voice that voter heard to be not some city voice, but a voice from back home. Sandy had completely pulled up stakes and relocated to Washington.

"Hello Jerry honey, this is Sandy, sweetheart. How's my boy?" She had at one time been in charge of the nursery at their church, and still thought of him as a three-year-old.

"I'm great, Sandy. But it's freezing here. I think our heat is off or something."

"We've had snow flurries here. How about you there?"

"I haven't actually looked out the window yet."

"Don't you have class today?"

"Not until one o'clock. Then rehearsal this evening."

"Well you just sleep in while you can, baby, 'cause the day's coming when you'll have to get up with the chickens like the rest of us. What are you rehearsing this time?"

"More Mark Twain stand-up. Like last time, but with new material."

"Your daddy put that picture of you from the newspaper in his scrapbook. You looked so cute in that big bushy mustache and that wig."

Well, actually it wasn't a wig, but Sandy didn't have to know everything.

"So by the way, what is the current scrapbook count between me and Clark?"

"Oh, I reckon you're holding your own, with your stagecraft and forensic clubs and all."

"In other words, Clark is ahead about five to one."

"I'd guess something like that."

"Soon to be nine or ten to one, now that he's going to be a Boston Celtic."

"Maybe so, but a million jump shots won't buy him your dimples, doll baby."

"That's right, Sandy. Let him eat his heart out."

"Anyway you old pretty thing, maybe you can skip school and rehearsal today, because I already booked you on the 12:30 flight from Lexington to National. Your daddy wants to see you about something that can't wait."

The matter that couldn't wait was sitting on top of the day's stack of newspapers in Joe Hatling's office in the Longworth. Joe had a subscription to all the daily and weekly newspapers from Kentucky's seventh district, along with Kentucky's two largest dailies, the *Lexington Herald* and the Louisville *Courier-Journal*, and one from Williamson, WV, which was the hometown newspaper for his easternmost constituents along the Tug River border. Today was Tuesday, meaning the fresh papers that arrived in the morning mail were the Sunday editions. The one that topped the stack was the *Lexington Herald*, whose front-page, above-the-fold, photo showed a group of UK students marching in an anti-war demonstration the previous day, Saturday. Hundreds of such demonstrations had taken place all across the country that Saturday. Hundreds of the nation's newspapers ran similar photos. This one made the *Herald* only because it was local.

About two seconds after Jerry entered the office and sat down, Joe picked up the *Sunday Herald* from the stack and flipped it into his lap. Initially Jerry couldn't figure out what was going on. He hadn't even seen the paper; didn't know his picture was on the front page. But there he was in the front rank of that column of demonstrating students, holding up one of two poles that stretched aloft a banner reading: *Hey, Hey, LBJ! How many kids did you kill*

63

today? They were just entering the little tunnel that led past the Engineering Building. That tunnel always incited the wind, and sure enough in this photo Jerry's long hair was whipping wildly.

"Oh, good. Another one for your scrapbook, Dad."

Joe glared at him. "Explain that."

"*Me* explain it? You explain to me why you're now bombing Laos and Cambodia."

Joe didn't have to explain anything to him. "Look, I fought in the Philippines against the Japs. No more ruthless an enemy ever roamed the earth. So don't come lecturing me on the horrors of war."

"This war is not like that one. In fact, if you want a Philippines' comparison, it's more like when we invaded the Philippines in 1898. Just a grab for colonial power."

"Don't feed me that line. Just tell me why you're trying to wreck my career."

"Hey, it's not personal. I'm trying to stop this war. What do you suggest—that I write a letter to my congressman?"

"If the voters back home learn about this . . . do you know how many votes it will cost me?"

Jerry looked at the caption beneath the photograph. His name wasn't there. Just *a group of UK students.*

"This war stinks, Dad. The whole country's turning against it."

"Maybe they are out there in Hippyville, but in Kentucky Seven they're not."

"They would if they knew the truth."

"Oh? So you're the truth expert, are you? What do you know about the truth?"

"For one thing I know that the whole of Johnson's authority is based on the Gulf of Tonkin Resolution. Without that he'd have no legal right to be fighting this insane war. And guess what? I know the whole resolution was based on a lie. We were not attacked. They just made that up because they needed an excuse to invade."

"To listen to you, you know more than anybody about everything."

"I know it because Clark told me." Joe's face lost its color. He turned from Jerry, went to sit behind his desk. "Clark heard internal VC communication. That was his job. You think I don't know he was ASA? That he had Top Secret clearance? He was a voice intercept at Tan Son Nhut airport. He listened in and read code."

"We can debate the technicalities another time. What I want to know is ..."

"No you don't, Dad! You can't sidetrack this one. This is not some press conference in Whitesburg. It was your idea to bring me here and put me on the hot seat, so you listen up. I know the resolution was a lie, and what's more I know that you know it was a lie. Clark told you too, didn't he?"

"Oh sure—when it was too late."

"Don't give me that. He wired you the very day."

"I don't know when he wired me, but I know when it got here. I've got it filed here somewhere, if you want to see it."

"I'd love to see it. I think you're lying right along with the whole U.S. government. It's like if Roosevelt had told the nation, 'The Japanese have bombed Pearl Harbor!' but they really hadn't. And Congress got up on its hind legs, baying for war. How would you have felt about that as you slogged through Luzon, if it was all built on a lie?"

"I'll find the Telex for you. I remember it well. It was stamped "Received August 8, 1964." Clear as anything. I'll show it to you if it'll shut you up." Joe was looking through his desk drawers.

"Show it to me, right now. Unless you're part of this whole goddamn cover-up. And from your own son, too. Your favorite son."

"That's not fair, Jer. You know that. Not my favorite son. My *electable* son. I love you both the same, always have."

"Your *electable* son sent you incredibly valuable information, which you ignored, and then you voted to send young men off to kill and to die."

"Don't you try to turn this into some kind of sibling contest."

"That's bullshit, Dad. The siblings here are in total agreement."

When the language turned ugly, Joe tried to tone it down. He quietly closed his desk drawer, leaned back in his chair. "Son, listen. I can't find that damn Telex right now. I'll have to ask Sandy

65

to help locate it. But trust me—I remember it all too well, and here's how it went. The first incident with the *Maddox* took place on August 2. Two days later there was another. Congress voted on August 7. Maybe Clark wired me immediately but the telegram reached me the day after the vote. It just got held up somewhere. Communications are tricky so far away. Things like that happen. At the time, I didn't know; none of us knew. We were kept in the dark just as everybody else was. The House voted 416-0. Only two senators opposed—both are now out of office, by the way. As far as we were concerned it was open and shut."

"Even if you got the telegram too late, you've had years to figure out that this war is a crime."

"Crime is a legal term. It's not a crime unless it breaks a law. You never used to go over the top like this."

"This war has put me over the top. Nobody can be a moderate anymore, not with this *moral crime* going on."

"How do you know it's a moral crime? You're still wet behind the ears."

"To the people of Vietnam it's not a war against the Big Bad Commies. They just want to be rid of invaders."

"Wow! Everybody listen to the great social philosopher! How do you know what they want? How many actual Vietnamese do you know?"

"I'm a human and I can understand . . . "

"Humans can feel all sorts of things. How do you know what they want? You know what you and your hippy friends want—with their deferments depending on college enrolment when they don't even bother going to class. It's pure self-interest. That's what you need to learn: right and wrong in this cock-eyed world depends purely on self-interest."

The confusion engendered by this role reversal stopped the argument for a time. Shouldn't it be the good Baptist father stumping for absolutes, with moral relativism going to the young rebel? They sat quietly and mulled over this murky turn. Finally Joe stood up, looked at his watch, put some ice in a glass and poured himself a shot of bourbon—something he had never, ever done at home in Pikeville, or indeed in front of Jerry anywhere. "I

66

guess I should offer you one. You're of age now."

"No thanks, Dad. I don't drink." He didn't say, Roll us up a big B-52 and let's burn it down.

"Your mother must be so proud."

Jerry couldn't tell if he meant that sarcastically or not.

"Anyway, son, listen . . . " He stretched out the thought, sat back in his big leather chair, swirled his drink to make that pretty, bell-like clinking sound. "Even if you don't feel compelled to consider my re-election position, you've got to think about your brother's reputation. You've really let him down this time."

Jerry was stunned. Where did that one come from? It was like a sucker punch in a street fight: you don't see it until you regain consciousness, and then you see it over and over, a thousand times, for the rest of your life.

"Let Clark down? What the hell are you talking about? Do the Boston Celtics ask the politics of their players' families?"

"You know full well that he plans to contest for my seat in a few years, whenever I retire."

"No, I don't know that. I don't think he has any such a plan."

"That's because I know him better than you do. Why do you think he came back to Georgetown?"

"You told him to go to UK!"

Joe ignored him. "To the center of government, where I could show him the ropes, introduce him to influential people. Why do you think he went to those meetings with me? And those parties?"

Jerry had no answer for that.

"And who's he been dating ever since he got back from Beirut? A Virginia girl, that's who. Explain that."

"He was living in Virginia when he met her! And anyway you told him to marry a Kentucky girl."

"Close enough. Good wholesome southern girl."

Yeah, right. One who walks past in a miniskirt and most men in the room can't stand up normally for a few minutes. "Dad, you don't understand Clark."

"*You* don't understand Clark. And if you don't tone down your ways you're going to reflect badly on him and destroy all his dreams. You don't want to do that, do you?"

67

"No, of course not. Not if ... "

"Exactly right. Start by getting a haircut."

Jerry remembered Hubbard and the music from that morning, that cozy, freezing, long-ago morning of possible snow, of frying bacon, of Lisa's smooth, protruding knee, the offer of a high. "It's called a freak flag," he told his father. "I intend to let it fly."

"Well, you think about it. Now let's go get some supper."

Sandy called him precious on his way out, and said she sure did wish her hair would curl up like that, instead of hanging as straight as spaghetti, and wasn't it the height of injustice when boys got the pretty locks and girls got strings?

On his way to the airport the next morning his taxi driver was a young black dude who had recently returned from Nam. When questioned he insisted that Jerry *really* did not want to know what was going on over there, and when Jerry gave him a nice tip he amiably called out, *Peace, brother.*

He thought about all this on the flight back to Lexington. While his father was dead wrong on just about every count, the one thing that stuck in his head was where his father was right: *How many actual Vietnamese do you know?* Let's face it, he told himself, you know absolutely fuck-all about how they live. If possible, you know even less about how they think and feel. One monk pours gas on himself and burns himself alive. What does that mean? Did he stand for a lot of people? Were there others who did the same? Or was he just one wacko monk? And those fighting on the side of the Americans—what kind of country did they want? Did they even think about what their new society should be like, or were they just backing the favorite?

In the freezing parking lot at the Lexington airport he rocked his little Datsun back and forth until the tires crunched and pulled loose from the iced-over asphalt. His heater fan blew a blast of white wind at him; the defroster didn't work either. He used an ice scraper to clear the inside of his windshield. Little flakes of ice fell on the back of his hand. On the radio Creedence Clearwater Revival was singing: *It ain't me. It ain't me. I ain't no senator's son.* He turned it up and sang along, as loud as he could.

He was driving toward the campus and the big house with

the bare, snow-trimmed trees on Linden Walk, but it felt as if he were returning to a sun-warmed world that would from now on shine brightly in his life, a world he would cling to and cherish as a beloved wife, but in nostalgia only, as a widower must, for his life there was now as dear to him, as finite, and as irrelevant, as a marriage ended by death. So he turned left down Lime and made his way to the Army Recruiting Office, on the same streets that Clark had taken at the beginning of the decade, a century ago.

The recruiting officer at the desk smiled and rose from his chair when Jerry hesitated at the door. Jerry walked in out of the cold wind.

He noticed. Plenty warm in here.

"I need a haircut," Jerry said.

"This ain't a barbershop, son."

"I know that, sir. But it'll do."

7

JERRY PROVED TO be an avid correspondent. Short letters, long ones—Jerry did them all. He didn't wait for responses; he just wrote more letters no matter what. During the basketball season Clark often returned from short road trips to find two or three envelopes in his mailbox. After a long road trip that included Portland and San Diego he would find a little packet of letters, dutifully banded by someone in the Celtics' front office in a way that seemed to say a brother's letters from Vietnam shouldn't just get tossed into a mailbox any old way.

Off season was trickier. Jerry sent all his correspondence to his father's office in the Longworth, and then Sandy would forward Clark's to him wherever he happened to be. Home base was Pikeville, where he and Frank Baker, once again Toody for the summer, kept in shape by running the steep hills and practicing in Clark's backyard, as they had done, it now seemed, since the beginning of time.

Saigon, July 6, 1971

Hey Big Bro:
You seem to feel that you somehow led me to make this goofy decision. Nope, forget that. I did it all by myself, so don't take any credit or any blame. I don't even know why I did it. Just to be ornery, I guess. I really wasn't thinking how you did the same thing. So far, I suppose I did the right thing. If I ever do decide to go into politics, the only reason would be to try to do some good in this world, to vote to stop ridiculous wars like this one. In case I did that, it would carry more weight if I'd been here myself, not just protested it from Lexington.

Do you really want Dad's seat one day? He thinks you do. I say you don't. Who knows you best?

FUCK it's hot here. It even rains hot water. I'll never complain about another Kentucky summer again.

Saigon, July 7, 1971

Thanks for saying that I'd make a much better congressman than you, but Dad was right about your chances. You're more electable than I'll ever be. I wouldn't want to run against you. So let's make a deal: I'll stay out of the NBA if you'll stay out of Congress.

Things here must be really different than during your tour. We're really restricted about where we can venture out to. It's clear to everybody we're losing the war. Locals are nervous as cats, trying to figure out just the right moment to jump sides. Troop morale stinks, even here in comfy old supply dump. Well, what did they expect? Stupid ass war.

Saigon, Sept 4, 1971

I guess Dad pulled some strings that ended me up in the safety of supplies. But it sort of drives me stir crazy. I'm sure that every upcountry grunt would kill to be in my place, but I just feel penned in. I mean that literally. There's barbed wire around almost everywhere we can legally go.

I guess you're into pre-season by now. How's the knee? Tell Toody I can still beat him at HORSE, at least if we stick to Wilt Chamberlain-style free throws from about 40 feet. Tell Red I'll send him a Thai-stick cigar the first game he lets you start.

Saigon, September 20, 1971

Hi Clark:

I'm starting to create strings of my own to pull. Soon I hope to be out of this city. Don't you dare tell Dad. Speaking of him, don't feel you need to defend him to me. It's true we've had plenty of problems in the past, both public and private, if I can put it like that. From the time you told me you'd notified him ahead of the Tonkin vote, to this very second, a part of me

71

hates him—yes, HATES him—for not standing up. Even that old fuddy-duddy preacher Eugene Deskins in Kentucky Eight had the balls to oppose it. I've often wondered if Dad showed him your telegram. Why else would the only opposition to it in the whole of the U.S. Congress come from next door in Kentucky Eight? Dad maintains that he got the telegram after August 7, and that the vote was unanimous. But it was a fake unanimity, because Deskins was out sick and they paired his vote, meaning that instead of 417-1 it goes down as 416-0.

But your point is a good one. Dad has done a lot of good things for the poor people of our area, and he voted with the Kennedy Democrats and against the southerners on civil rights. He cooled things off on school integration. Plus even though it was Mom who said we could invite Toody and all our friends over to hang out, Dad never said a word against it. I recently asked Mom about that and she said he agreed one hundred percent.

So, as I say ... no need to defend him. In a way I'm more like him than you are.

Saigon, October 7, 1971

I saw the most amazing thing today. You know, I can still remember the time we were playing ping pong down in the rec room, when you said (more like announced) that you were going to start reading the Bible again, but this time not as the word of God, but as a historical artifact. (Stick with me—I'll get to my point eventually. In my own sweet time, as Mom says. I too now think of time as something sweet, a dessert following an infinity of non-existence.) You said it was a collection of writing from the eastern Roman Empire of about nineteen centuries ago, and you were going to read it as you might read ... I can't remember who you said. Maybe Cicero. Whoever. So now, me too. I'm trying to figure out what I believe, if anything, and how much I'll have to fake if I go political.

So, I was saying that today I saw the most amazing thing. Right smack in the middle of Tu Do Street there was this raggedy looking guy walking barefoot, carrying a homemade sign that said, in both *tiếng Việt* and English, THE WORLD WILL END ON OCTOBER 31. He may be right—we'll find out in about three weeks—but here's why it's so amazing. In this new Bible reading of mine, can you guess what I read just last night? I bet you could guess. If I gave you three or four guesses, you would nail it for sure. It was Mark chapter nine, where Jesus tells a bunch of people that the Kingdom of God will arrive while some of them are still alive. So okay, Jesus gave himself a few years to play with while this short-sighted Vietnamese prophet only gives himself three more weeks, but still. People in our church think that way too. What is it that makes people want to believe the end is near? Is life really so bad that they'd push the plunger on the whole thing?

It just occurred to me that a lot of our dear Baptist friends would say that the coincidence of seeing an apocalyptic Vietnamese lunatic the very day after I read Mark 9:1 was no coincidence at all, but the machinations of our old friend Lucifer. Is this the kind of thing I'll have to pretend to consider reasonable if I'm going to get enough Kentucky Seven voters to send me to Congress?

You seem capable of thinking, Wow, these people are so fucked up, I'm outta here. But to me . . . I don't know. Maybe the power to prevent these mass slaughters is worth a little harmless pandering.

Saigon, November 1, 1971

Surprise! The world didn't end yesterday. Or am I celebrating too soon? It could still happen, Pacific time.

You may be right when you say the slaughter is of my own soul, but look: even Lincoln, Sainted Son of Kentucky, and as close to an atheist as any president this side of Jefferson, invoked the name of God all the time. Why did he do that? He knew no God was paying the least bit of attention, but lucky for us all he knew a few million Protestant voters were. Does that make him just another ambitious hypocrite? Well, yes, it does, but aren't we all grateful that instead of hiding in some

73

office somewhere writing honest treatises for freethinkers, he was faking Christianity and writing the Emancipation Proclamation?

Saigon, Nov 12, 1971

Forget politics and religion. I've met a girl! And she's not a hooker! Well, she might be an off-duty hooker. By day she runs a little street-side food stand selling duck *pho*. By night she's mine all mine, as far as I know. Thanks to you I already knew a few words of *tiếng Việt*, and have been studying here on my own. Not on my own any more! HA!

I just had a funny thought. You know how Dad always says if we marry a foreign woman our goose is cooked, politically. If I marry Nhu Le, my duck will be cooked, professionally. HA! Is that a good one?

Saigon, Nov 22, 1971

Yes, I have been smoking during most of these letters. What did you think? That I had suddenly gone far out philosophical? In fact, I recommend you toke up before you read them. Are there team rules against weed? I don't suppose you'd be so inclined to pound the Knicks senseless if all of you were stoned.

Hey, thanks for the books on the Apocalypse. That whole idea intrigues me no end. And talk about something to read stoned—man, read that shit any way BUT stoned and you just won't get it. I had no idea that the whole end-of-time thing was political, did you? What God supposedly promised the ancient Hebrews was land, in this world, not some future paradise, so when Joshua captured Canaan, in the process killing every man, woman and child in Jericho, that was God coming good on his promise. They didn't even expect a heaven, much less the End of Days. You just lived in the Promised Land, and then you died in the Promised Land. And that was cool. For hundreds of years Jews didn't even have a concept of heaven. But then when the Babylonians drove them out of Israel, the only way they could deal with this great injustice

74

was to believe that the great justice giver Himself would swoop down and settle up.

Even though I know it's pure fantasy, I'm still drawn to it. It works! The whole concept is a way of turning the tables on whoever is in control, and I'm enjoying the shit out of it. I roll me a big B-52 and read about it, only in my head I see LBJ and McNamara and Nixon and Kissinger being trampled by the Four Horsemen. And, uh-oh, there goes Dad! All the while, people like Nhu Le and me ride high and witness the gore. You can't even feel bad for the defeated as they wail and gnash, because it's God spraying the napalm, and who can question His morality? Besides you, maybe. But then you're a hell-bound apostate so TOUGH SHIT BIG BROTHER!

Saigon, December 2, 1971

I just found out (from Mom) that Aziza married that rich guy. I wonder how this news affected you. Not that you're likely to tell me, or anybody else. Maybe you shouldn't keep shit so bottled up inside. But still I'll tell you what I think. When I visited you that Christmas vacation . . . man, that was so great. Mr. and Mrs. Sisler were perfect hosts, and hanging out with you and Aziza, and even her mom . . . wow, so much fun. I'll remember that Christmas as long as I live. I thought Aziza was wonderful. I knew you were thinking about a future with her and I have to say I wouldn't have minded having her for a sister-in-law. Not minded it one little bit. But still . . . listen to me . . . you know what I'm going to say! You did the right thing! Yes, you absolutely did. If you have any desire for politics at all—which you say you don't but Dad says you do, and he has evidence to back it up—if you even think that maybe you'll ever want to run for any office at all, you had to leave her. Even forgetting for the moment that her father needed way more money than we have to keep his silly ass out of the poorhouse, you did the right thing, for yourself. Kentucky Seven voters would never dream of electing a man with a foreign wife, much less a Muslim. They might even vote dad out.

75

For you Aziza was a wonderful vacation from reality, just like my Christmas. There was no way to make it permanent. Anyway you've got Wanda (who might give lesser men than your brother wicked thoughts.) AND you're a Boston Celtic. You're doing just fine.

Saigon, December 19, 1971

Man I'm telling you, one of the coolest things ever happened last night. AFRS carried the Celts-Bullets game, and you were the starting guard. You know—I'd never mentioned to anybody in my unit that my brother plays for the Celtics. (Or that Dad is a congressman, for that matter.) So when the game came on the radio, a group of us were sitting back in one of the godowns, just waiting around—this was late afternoon. Most of the day's orders had been dispatched. We weren't stoned yet. At least I wasn't. So we just listened a while and bullshitted a while. Then somebody said, I ain't never heard of no Hatling before you and there's another one. Somebody else said, Yeah, he played for Georgetown. Then the announcer said it was your first starting assignment and you were the son of a congressman from Kentucky. Then somebody said, You motherfucker, you from Kentucky too, right? I just said, Yep, I was born and bred in the GREAT state of Kentucky— you know, like politicians always say their states. Then you fed the ball to Toody, he slammed it home, and I heard for the first time words that —no joke—sent my arm hair standing straight up: *Hatling to Baker—TWO!!!* The announcer then explained that no team had been seriously interested in you because first you'd quit the team at UK and joined the army, then left Georgetown your junior year to study abroad, but that you and "Baker" had been high school teammates, and that "Baker" had told Coach Auerbach that the best point guard he'd ever played with was his high school teammate, and his best friend. He told him that you'd left UK because you didn't want to play for a racist organization. And before the announcer could get all this out, guess what? *Hatling to Baker—TWO!!!*

76

All the guys were saying, No shit, he's your brother? And I'm playing it cool, like, oh yeah, me and Clark and Frank—we call him Toody. And they go, Frank Baker's got the nickname Toody? I say, sure, all his friends call him that. You know what he calls me? What? Runt! hahaha! Who ever thought I'd be taking pride in being called Runt?

Hatling to Baker—TWO!!! That's got to go down in the history of sports radio. Anyway, that game—those friends, sitting in that hot, dirty godown in Saigon—has got to be one of the greatest moments of my life.

But later that night there was an even better one. AFRS replayed the game late at night. I guess for them it was a time-filler, but for me it was like coming home from school and smelling cornbread in the oven. I was spending the night with Nhu Le in her airless little room. We had the ceiling fan on, all the covers kicked off. I just lay there sweating and listening to her breathe. She does the cutest little *bbbffff-bbbffff* with her lips as she sleeps. It was so dark I could just barely see her from the VD Clinic sign across the street reflecting off the blades of the fan. I had my transistor radio with me in bed, and my earphone plugged in. I listened to fifteen thousand people cheering for you, but this time I didn't listen for the excitement. Now it was me and you and Toody, in our back yard in Pikeville. It was brothers and friends and mom and cocoa, daydreaming on a cold Saturday morning in the fall. Playing our hearts out for no reason in this world, except that's where the happiness is. It was pure innocence. I felt like I was a part of your success, even a part of that game, although all I ever really did was get in the way. And on your case. I thought, *Hatling to Baker—THREE!!!* Counting me, of course.

January 1, 1972

Happy (???) 1972!

Mom told me you bought Wanda a diamond ring for Xmas. Assuming that went off as planned I hereby extend my congratulations to The Happy Couple. (Or if she turned you down I extend my congratulations to her. HA!)

Everybody's jumpy here because with the troop drawdown we expect the NVA to launch some New Year's fireworks of their own. One-way flights still take off as usual from your old Tan Son Nhut runways, but with one big difference: these one-way flights are planned that way. The U.S. is making its grand exit. Even Dad wants us out, or at least he voted for the second Cooper-Church Amendment. I'd like to think this was because I blew my stack at him, but I'm sure it's more because Cooper is from Pulaski County and offered him political cover, even if Cooper is a Republican. Anyway, the country wants us out and if ARVN can't hold its own, then they're dead ducks.

Speaking of dead ducks—I planned this!—let me bore you for the next hour with stories of Nhu Le. I told you she runs a little restaurant downstairs from our apartment where she sells duck cooked several ways. I'll tell you, man . . . she has changed my life. You may not even know this, but I was becoming harsh, ill-tempered, irritable; basically the exact kind of person I like least. But Nhu Le has brought me back to the self I like most, and even extended that self into new areas. She's so calm, so eager for each moment to arrive, but perfectly content if it arrives empty-handed. I think you could call it an expectant tranquility. I don't know if that part of her makeup comes from her Buddhist heritage, from her family or whether she was simply born that way.

An incident from early this morning will show you what I mean. She had a big vat of soup boiling, a sort of creek-water brown mixture, with boiled eggs, cinnamon, tofu, and I don't know what all. She had cleaned a duck and was laying it out on a wooden board to chop it up before adding it to the pot. But what happened was—you know how greasy a duck is—it slipped from her hands and splashed headlong into that vat of soup. At this point a lot of people would say *Shit! I dropped the goddamn duck look at my blouse all messed up and soup all over everywhere blah blah.* Right? Maybe me too. A few months ago, that's exactly how I would have reacted. But not Nhu Le. She squatted down to pick it out, and at that instant she looked up at me with this big round bright glow of delight on her face, and burst out laughing, just as I did, one split second after she did. The thing was, that duck was bobbing ass-up in the soup, just as if it were in a lake diving for food. Without her, I would have missed that moment. What I've learned from her is that moments matter. They matter a hell of a lot.

God, if this war takes her away from me, I can't imagine how I'll survive. I know it happens to other people, so it must be possible to put one foot in front of the other and keep moving on. But I can't see how.

Groundhog Day, 1972

January was very quiet. It's almost harder to endure the lull than it was the pressure. Half of the people you talk to say the big push is coming and it's coming hard. The other half say it's all over, that now we're in for a long, Korea-style stability. Me? I identify with the poor old Millerites of 1844 who had marked October 22 on their calendars as "Apocalypse Day." Then when it didn't happen they called it "The Great Disappointment." Like, *A billion people didn't get slaughtered today. I'm so friggin' bummed.* The difference is that since my prediction didn't come true, I'm feeling pretty bouncy about it.

Hey! Thanks for not warning me off getting closer to Nhu Le. I knew I could count on you. Don't you dare tell Dad. If the relationship keeps going, I'll deal with him somehow. Do you really think voters would go Republican just because I had a Vietnamese wife? It's not like she was VC. We were allies, for god's sake. But then—she is a Buddhist. Finessing that might take some fancy footwork.

Speaking of footwork—it looks like you're going to the playoffs. I foresee it! HA!

March 28, 1972

Your suggestion to teach Nhu Le that the American pronunciation of *Buddhist* is *Baptist* is brilliant! The best I could come up with was to cough on that first syllable. Like, "My wife? Yeah, she's a *Bahhkkdist*. Oh, yes indeed. A dyed-in-the-wool *Bahhkkdist.*" But then voters might not elect me on account of my weak lungs.

Congratulations on making the playoffs. I got that forecast right! But my predicted 1972 NVA offensive hasn't happened, not yet anyway. Maybe Melv-the-Pelv Laird was right when he said the NVA had more sense than to launch a major offensive against built-up ARVN forces. But on to happier topics, like … ta-da! … Armageddon.

I've finished reading that stack of books you sent me, and now my mind is on poor Isaac Newton. Who would have believed that this genius, a guy I always thought of as taking us out of the darkness of superstition into the light of reason, would spend his last years doing alchemy and using the Book of Daniel to predict the End of Time? The alchemy bit, I can understand, because nobody had any theory that made it impossible to make your own gold. But the Book of Daniel? Hell, I could tell that was bullshit even before I learned it was a hoax. Did you know about that? (I assume you read these books, too???) In case not: the Book of Daniel, which used to turn Pastor Couch's eyeballs into red hot coals, purported to predict future events from the vantage point of about 600 BC. But in fact it was written about 150 BC, so these "future events" were, in fact, historical events. Even then he got some of them wrong.

Scholars have been aware of this for a century. Maybe Isaac Newton's preacher didn't know that, but why didn't Pastor Couch tell us? He studied in some seminary somewhere. You think they didn't tell him? And why didn't he tell us that 666 was Hebrew numerology for Nero? Isn't Christianity supposed to stand for honesty? Isn't the truth supposed to set us free?

Sign of the Beast my ass. What kind of people try to terrify little children with this stuff?

See, I've got my own theory (two, actually; both of them so far out of the mainstream that they have to be one hundred percent correct.)

One: No matter how many predicted apocalypses don't materialize, people have to cling like crazy to the idea, because they don't really believe in heaven. They want to see Jesus coming right here and now because their deepest fear is to die like a normal person dies and during those final five minutes they won't be able to hang on to the make-believe. The end gets closer and closer, the fantasy pops, and they're forced to live out their last minutes with the sure and certain terror that there's nothing else out there, and then . . . nothing.

It's got to be this fear of losing their grip on the heaven-fantasy that makes them so eager for the Apocalypse. Otherwise, why don't they just get on with life? We all have our own little personal apocalypse coming. It'll all be over in the blink of an eye, then the believers will be sitting on the right hand of God. Or will they? They're scared shitless they won't.

If they really believe that paradise is just an instant away, why do they take medicine to ward off a natural death? Okay, I see why they can't commit suicide. That could be a sin that sends them to hell instead. But surely a ninety year old woman, mostly blind and deaf, with every pain and discomfort in the book, would opt for a nice natural end to this world of torment if an instant later she would be with the angels, right? I mean, if she really believed that was the deal. But let her doctor tell her that her cholesterol is up and she'll give up eggs and every bite of red meat—maybe her one single joy left on earth, a nice breakfast of eggs and bacon, of biscuits and butter, maybe a bowl of sausage gravy—she'll forego that one final pleasure and beg the doctor to prescribe a tablet that will give her a few more months on this earth. Surely eating an omelet wouldn't be suicide. On the other hand, taking a pill that would interfere with God's methods—now that might count as a sin. Right? That's the theologically dicey choice. But she'll take that chance in order to . . . to what? Watch one more episode of *The Guiding Light*? To lay awake all night because her knees ache so? No, because she can't hide her darkest secret from herself: she knows there's nothing after. She knows that after she's gone she'll be just exactly where she was before she ever came into this world—nowhere.

81

Whew! If you ever want to sabotage my political career, just save these letters.

My second theory? The Bible is absolutely right. Armageddon is going to happen in Israel, right there at the Har Megiddo, where its name came from. Israel has got nuclear weapons, and surely someday Egypt or one of the other rejectionists will get them too, and then they'll all get up on their hind legs and try to out-bluster each other, until somebody lets fly. And here come the U.S. and the Russians. And we're all a pile of ashes. It's got nothing to do with God. It's all about us.

Of course if I happened to be president at the time, I'd cast my spirit onto the face of the waters, and say, Let there be light. And there would be light. And other world leaders would say, Man, how did he do that? That guy's amazing!

Enough nonsense for now. The real news is that I'm nervous as a cat because I've got a week's pass starting tomorrow, and I've bribed a friend to chopper me and Nhu Le into her village of Loc Ninh—to meet her folks! Big step! It's about eighty miles from here, near the city of An Loc. Maybe you've heard of it?

The bribe? A basketball autographed by "Frank" Baker. Sorry about that. You can sign too, of course.

8   PRACTICE MAKES PERFECT

JERRY'S PROPHESIED NEW Year's Offensive turned out to be the Easter Offensive, when the North Vietnamese threw everything they had behind a three-theater push into South Vietnam: from the DMZ south into Quang Tri; across from Laos and Cambodia into the Central Highlands; and, further south, through Cambodia to An Loc, in an attempt to threaten Saigon itself. The road to An Loc ran straight through the small town of Loc Ninh. Thus Jerry's predicted "little personal apocalypse" came when a barrage of NVA rockets reduced to splinters every one of the plank houses in the neighborhood where Nhu Le had grown up, and where Jerry had been received as an honored guest, and potential son-in-law.

He wasn't the last American to die in Vietnam. In fact he may have been the first to die after everyone finally knew for certain that the war was lost. The South Vietnamese regime would survive another three years, but the lack of gumption that characterized ARVN officers during the Easter Offensive notified the world that this war would end in no Korean standoff.

Nhu Le, her family, and the citizens of Loc Ninh, however, were far from the last Vietnamese to die. She died with Jerry, with all her family, beneath the stilted house that offered a mere symbolic shelter from falling rockets. He'd only met them the previous evening; hadn't even learned all their names yet. Nhu Le and Jerry had just come in from the alley where they'd shared a laugh with an ice peddler as he took up a long-handled pick and laid into a block of ice. Nhu Le's father had twelve cans of Jerry's Pabst Blue Ribbon neatly arranged in a plastic bucket for Jerry to dump the ice over. They'd just settled onto a reed mat laid over the rough-board floor of her house, and were dipping lettuce-wrapped shrimp cakes into a sweet chili sauce, when the first tank shell exploded. Nhu Le's father thought to grab the beer before they ran down the ladder and crawled under the house. Everyone must

83

have known that hiding under a popsicle-stick house was a futile gesture, but there was nowhere else. And, to all but Jerry, this was home. As the shelling grew closer they all smiled at each other, sad smiles that said, What an odd end. Jerry wondered vaguely why some Vietnamese wanted other Vietnamese dead, but he understood that it wasn't meant to be taken personally. The NVA simply wanted the land, and they preferred it empty.

Nhu Le was too correct to take him in her arms, not with her parents present. At this stage such conduct would have been indecorous. She was holding his hand as they died.

Funeral services were held at the First Baptist Church of Pikeville, where the preacher, the rotund, dour and oddly named Jolly Couch, laid out an absolutely by-the-book Baptist funeral. This was as it should be, indeed as Congressman Hatling had requested, for in death, as in rural politics, nobody was one bit better than anybody else. If the deceased had ever reached any elevation, whether by birth or attainment, it died with them. All were brought level at the moment of death. Each had to approach the bench of the Lord with book in hand, its covers clasped and locked, its seals breakable only by the Ultimate Judge, who, without prejudice or favor, would open that book with a, "Well, let's see what we've got here," and then brother you were on your own.

Preacher Couch wasn't much to look at, nor was he exactly the life force of any church social, beyond his taciturn willingness to sample every single dessert on any picnic table. In the arena of Biblical scholarship he knew no more than was seemly for a Southern Baptist minister. But behind the pulpit the man knew what to do with his voice. At funerals his voice cracked at just the right moments. He intoned verses so predictable that they had transcended their own exhaustion, to be reborn as icons, possessing an almost material quality, as though they were no longer a string of sound waves unsettling the air, but hammered-out works of art, treasured not because they could be eaten or drunk or worn against the weather, or accomplish anything useful whatsoever, but because everybody agreed they were beyond price. His voice knew where to soar, where to pause, where to descend to a whisper that quieted even the children in the congregation. He could insert that

84

little catch in his throat, and mourners understood that while their hearts were breaking, his heart was breaking too, and, by extension, the Lord's own heart was breaking. They were all in this together.

There was nothing phony about it, even during funerals for the most obscure, lapsed, backslid and forgotten member of the church. Today, though, that was little Jerry Hatling lying there under the flag, and the pain flowed from deep down inside the well of human grief. It filled the church as once Jerry's cheerful spirit had done. The closed coffin right in front of Jolly Couch's pulpit held a dead hero whose infant footsteps had once stirred the dust from between the planks of these pinewood floors. His voice had squeaked from the choir. For those in the congregation who had been part of that church for the past several years, it was Jerry's laughter sounding through the halls that would be their lasting memory of him. When Preacher Couch's voice faltered, that remembered laughter filled the pauses, and many in the overflowing church wept openly.

Another tribute to Jerry, one that everyone noticed but no one spoke of, was that a good quarter of the faces in the congregation were black. Toody had come down from Boston with Clark, and all his relatives had known Runt Hatling ever since he was big enough to trail along after him and Clark. It was the largest collection of black people ever gathered in the First Baptist Church of Pikeville, brought there, perhaps to no one's surprise, by a little colorblind joker who never met a stranger.

More surprising still was the presence of Jerry's freaks from Lexington, friends who had trouble believing Jerry had volunteered for Vietnam in the first place. Jolly Couch had never seen such a collection of tie-dyed shirts, long hair, love beads and peace medallions filling his pews. But that was Jerry. If anyone present had entered the church unaware of the architecture of Jerry's life, they knew it now. Jolly Couch acknowledged it by ending his sermon, "With all our differences, our brother Jerry Hatling loved each and every one of us, just as much as we loved him. We all wish he'd lived a longer life; but no one could wish for a finer life."

After the funeral, a private plane flew the casket and the immediate family to Andrews Air Force base outside Washington,

85

where a hearse drove them to Arlington National Cemetery. Waiting at the cemetery entrance was a six-man honor guard, along with a four-horse team hitched to a caisson. Two of the horses were riderless. The honor guard placed the casket on the caisson for the final leg of Jerry's long journey home. Joe and Barbara were already in place before the bier that would hold their son's flag-covered casket. They sat on wooden folding chairs at the front of a small selection of local friends and invited dignitaries. Clark, Wanda, Toody, and Sandy sat up front with them. Sandy kept her head bowed into a handkerchief. Wanda was somber in elegant black. She did not wear a hat. Her blond hair seemed to announce that she would not be cowed by the follies of man.

Joe looked up as a film crew moved into place for a shot of Wanda flanked by the two young athletes, one white, one black. It occurred to him that the photographer was interested in the New America image of that scene. The message was that the country would yet prevail over its tragedies and would emerge from its confusion into a better world. Joe leaned forward to look past Barbara and Clark, and knew that the courage in Wanda's bearing, in the defiant hair surrounding her young, pained, and breathtakingly beautiful face, would be worth at least a thousand votes. No stranger tuning in would ever imagine she'd met Jerry exactly once in her life.

It was then that Joe had a thought. It was a thought he wasn't proud of. He wished he'd never had it; wished he were the kind of man incapable of thinking it. But think it he did, and he knew it was true. By losing Jerry, he would never lose Kentucky Seven. It was his for life, and he could probably pass it on to Clark.

Barbara, too, noticed the newsmen setting up. "Joe, can't you get rid of them?"

"Honey, we may not like it, but there's nothing we can do. This is national news."

She just stared at him. She reminded herself that one way to cope with grief was to distract yourself with petty irritants. Earlier that day she'd snapped at a florist. So this time she let it go, but she was pretty sure she recognized one face in that group, and it sure as blazes wasn't Walter Cronkite. It was the anchorman

86

from a Lexington station. She wondered who had paid his way to Arlington.

The day itself was lovely, a forerunner of spring, and no day for a burial. Frisbee weather, more like it. Barbara imagined Jerry bounding after one. The cemetery lawns still hadn't fully recovered from winter, but the sun brought a sharp green response, and the smell of patches of exposed earth produced thoughts of fertility and renewal. Cherry blossoms were everywhere. It seemed Jerry's burial day was a warning: Look around you. You've got this all wrong.

The honor guard placed Jerry's casket on the bier. The horses pulled the caisson away. With their lightened burden they too seemed to notice that spring was in the air. They tossed their great heads in recognition of the sunshine, quivered their muscled necks and snorted as they clopped away. The breeze across their backs carried the clean smell of straw and sweated hay across the congregants.

Joe delivered a controlled eulogy while Barbara sat there entertaining ideas as black as the clothes she wore. Clark gave a talk that, in concept, should have been a moving rephrasing of Jerry's pacifist inclinations, but which, in execution, skated close to being an anti-war diatribe. Toody came closer than any of them to getting at the essence of Jerry when he reminded them that what Jerry would be saying if he had the stage was that if you brought laughter and happiness to everyone around you, every minute of your life, then no matter how short your life was, it was a worthy one.

He said, "Listen to this typical Jerry story, you'll see what I mean. One Saturday afternoon—I'd say Jerry was about nine or ten years old—he came over to my house to pitch horseshoes. He loved horseshoes, and he got good at it. The thing was, I wasn't at home; nor was anyone else at the time. Just my mother, who wasn't feeling well. She got the pleurisy a lot; at times it nearly killed her. She was upstairs asleep in her bedroom. So Jerry got to the door—I'm guessing about this part—I suppose he knocked on the door and nobody came to let him in. But back where I grew up we didn't bother locking doors, and friends would just

87

stick their head in the door, ask is anybody home. That's mountain ways. So Jerry poked around downstairs, didn't find a soul. Why he went on upstairs we'll never know. It probably sounds suspicious to outsiders, maybe like he was up to some meanness, but if you knew Jerry, then you know that's just him being normal. Normal for him, I mean. You and I both know that what was normal for Runt Hatling wasn't what the rest of us call normal. And to my mind, that's a great pity. That beautiful young man lying under that flag there should be a lesson in normal for all of us."

Toody had to stop, get himself in hand. "This was supposed to be a funny story, and now I'm making my own self cry." Now some people laughed quietly, as did Toody, wiping his eyes. "So then Jerry looked around upstairs and found the room where Mama was asleep. I only heard this story from her, so let me tell it the way she did. She said she'd been running a high fever and every breath hurt her, so she took some of her medicine and went to bed. She had no idea how long she'd been asleep. Then from somewhere far away, through her fever and confusion, it seemed like she could hear the voice of the Good Lord talking to her. Then gradually she came to. She said, 'It seemed like I could see a little white angel way off in the distance, talking the words of Jesus to me.' She said, 'I thought, Praise the Lord! I'm cured of the pleurisy and gone to heaven. I just laid there and listened to that voice. Then pretty soon I woke up enough to where I could see it was nobody but little Jerry Hatling sitting over in the corner and reading me the Bible. He just found me sick and picked up the Bible from my nightstand and started reading it out loud to me in my sleep.' She would tell us that story and we'd all laugh till we cried. She'd say, 'I'm a-tellin' you the God's truth—I thought I'd died in my sleep and woke up beyond them pearly gates, with my own little angel reading to me.' And now we know what the little angel of my mama's vision was up to: he was practicing. Jerry Hatling will make a fine angel—he's been practicing for it all his life."

After the twenty-one guns had been fired, and the lone bugler over the hill had played *Taps*, Clark and Toody said goodbye to Joe and Barbara right there at the cemetery and went straight to the airport. They had a playoff game in New York that night. Wanda lived only a couple of miles away, in Alexandria. She drove herself home. Joe and Barbara would be alone in their house in Georgetown for the first time since learning about Jerry's death.

Barbara had to get through this day somehow. Through this minute. Then another and another. When she thought about the void once filled by Jerry, it seemed to her that the womb where she'd carried him was a vast cavern inside her, that it had collapsed and she was falling into the vacuum of herself, a foul and airless void. It smothered her, locked her chest, led her to believe that someone was strangling her, had sealed her face like a mummy's. It was as though she had doubled in on herself and was watching herself as she fell and suffocated, the wrapping on her face a clear plastic that pinned her eyes open to witness that the blackness through which she fell wasn't her own blindness, nothing as personal as that, but the pervading darkness of all things. She struggled for breath with her son as he lay paralyzed by earth, first in Loc Ninh, and now in Arlington.

The sensation of smothering was not a fantasy. She had simply forgotten to breathe. She had to remind her lungs to expand. She sat on the cold grass in her back garden, poking seeds into the ground. Into the ground where Jerry was. If these flowers ever escaped their grave, would she see them as light and color fighting back, as a memorial? Or would she resent them their life, and take a pair of scissors to slice them off at ground level?

As dusk settled she went inside to do something, anything. Tidying up might at least give her a false sense of control. But what she found was a spotless house. Somebody had already done her work. Some kind person, no doubt. She heard Joe walking upstairs, and then heard the sound of the little television he had in his office. Was it even possible that he was checking to see if the funeral had made the news? She went upstairs to find out.

He had it tuned to NBC. David Brinkley was describing the return of U.S. air power from Guam and Japan to Tan Son Nhut, the response to the Easter Offensive.

"You are! This is just too much, Joe."

"I just put it on for a distraction, Barbara."

"You don't fool me. You put it on to see how you came off in your eulogy."

"That's not fair."

89

"Is it fair that you hired a Lexington news crew to cover my baby's funeral?"

"That's a lie! Where did you get that idea?"

"Because I know the kind of man you are." She couldn't look at him. She turned her back to him. Now facing the wall of bookshelves, the name *Jerry* seemed to leap out at her. It was written on the spine of a scrapbook album. A single scrapbook, penned into the corner by a half-dozen other scrapbooks marked *Clark*.

"Barbara, I miss him as much as you do."

"Don't make me laugh." How dare he? Who had raised him, single-handedly most of the time? Who had made him feel special and loved while Joe was doting on Clark, his 'electable' son?

"We're both too distraught to have this conversation." He stood and walked over to her, put his hands on her shoulders and turned her to face him.

"Don't you touch me!" She twisted out of his grasp.

"Maybe we should take a quiet walk, just around the neighborhood. Maybe stop for a drink."

She turned on him and hissed, "What a brilliant idea. Let's go pour some liquor over your guilty conscience."

"Hold it right there! What are you . . . ?"

"You killed him! You know you did!" She knew she was going to break down soon, so she sat down in a corner chair while she still had the strength to move.

"Barbara, how can you possibly say . . . "

"He was always . . . always . . . trying to rise in your estimation. You never saw it. You never even recognized what a treasure you had in him."

"I always loved him deeply."

"My beautiful, laughing boy. You killed him."

"You're hysterical."

"You bring him all the way to Washington to berate him for his beliefs on this war, and he goes straight to the army."

"I didn't say a word about joining up! Jesus!"

"I bet you mentioned that's what Clark did."

"Not true, not one bit. You turn things every which way. I just

90

told him to lay low in his protests."

"He would do anything for your approval. If you loved Clark for basketball, Jerry would play basketball. He practiced all the time. You didn't even know it, because you weren't there. He practiced more than Clark did."

"I didn't ask him to be Clark."

"You don't think so? That just shows how blind you are. Look at that bookshelf. If you need it laid out for you nice and simple, just look at that bookshelf."

"What the hell are you talking about? I think we need to phone a doctor for you, Barb."

"Look at that shelf of scrapbooks! It's like a graph of your love for your two sons."

"Not love . . . "

"*Esteem* then. Appreciation. Admiration. Call it what . . . "

"Hey, I just pasted in what the newspapers printed. Is it my fault Jerry wasn't as newsworthy as Clark?"

"See! You're saying the words but you still don't get it!"

"Then suppose you tell me what I don't get."

"For you it's all about what's newsworthy. And somebody else says what's newsworthy and what's not."

"So?"

"So? So why didn't you fill his scrapbooks with other stuff? Why didn't you put one of his poems in there? Did you even know he wrote poems for his high school magazine? Why didn't you put his report cards in? Why didn't you let him draw pictures you could put in? Why didn't you ask Toody to write up that wonderful little incident he talked about today—reading the Bible to his sleeping mother? Everybody back home has a story like that. Did you know that when Myrt Ratliff broke her hip, Jerry got up at five every morning to teach her dog to fetch the newspaper for her? Then when the dog finally got the trick, Myrt looked out on her porch and found about thirty newspapers lying there? The dog had fetched every newspaper up and down the street. Jerry loved to tell that story, how he had to redeliver the papers until her hip healed. Why didn't you ask him to write it for your scrapbook?"

"Why didn't you tell me this before?"

"Oh, that's rich! Turn it back on me. Shame on you."

"Barbara. That's not what I meant and you know it." He carried a box of tissues to her, cupped the back of her head in his hand.

She shook it off. "I said don't touch me. Murderer."

"Actually I think the North Vietnamese had a little something to do with that."

"It was your war! You and all the other warmongers making money off of it."

"I didn't make . . . "

"The price of coal shot up. Don't take me for one of your idiot voters."

"The Communists have to be stopped. It's as simple as that. But that doesn't make it my war."

"You voted for it." Without any warning, her bitterness was transformed into a sense of calm understanding. Everything had finally started to make sense. This man had killed her son and many other mothers' sons. It felt good to say so at last.

"Honey, I'm only one of over four hundred. What good would one 'no' vote have done?"

"It would have made you a man of principle. Like Eugene Deskins."

"It would also have made me an ex-congressman. Like Eugene Deskins."

"You knew, didn't you?"

"Knew what?"

"That the Tonkin Gulf Resolution was based on a lie."

"Oh, for chrissake. Here we go." He sighed, and eased his way into a chair facing hers. "You know about that, do you?"

"Clark told me."

"When?"

"Today."

"Jesus."

"How could you still vote 'yes'? Why didn't you stand up in front of the House and tell the country the truth?"

"Okay. Let's talk this out."

"You talk it out. I already know the truth—you didn't have the courage."

92

"That's not the way it was. Clark's telegram arrived the day after the vote. I remember it clearly. The vote was August 7. The telegram reached my desk on August 8. The joint resolution had already passed."

"Yeah, right. I suppose Sandy took the most important telegram in years and stuck it in her purse for three days."

"Not Sandy. I don't know who held it up. But I didn't see it until it was too late. Furthermore, even if it had arrived on time, how could I have acted on it?"

"Just like I said. Stand up in front . . . "

"And explain that my son had leaked top secret information? That's a criminal offense. In time of war it's a hanging offense."

"Even if that's true, don't you think Clark considered that? His conscience forced him to act, even at the potential cost of his own life. You could have prevented this horrible war, and exposed the criminals who started it."

"Don't be naïve. Johnson and the entire power structure would have simply refuted it as the statement of a traitor. Clark would have been arrested and executed before we could even launch a full investigation."

"I don't believe you."

"Believe what you want." He rested his hands in his lap, allowed his body to go slack. "I'm exhausted."

Barbara stood up. "And I'm leaving."

"Where are you going?"

"Back to Pikeville."

"Don't be ridiculous, Barb. You can't fly back tonight."

"No. But I can drive."

She left him sitting there. He heard her moving a few things around, heard her walk down the stairs. He had no idea what to do, and no strength to do it with. He heard the back door shut, then the car door slam. He heard the engine start up. He finally got out of his chair and walked over to the window. She was just sitting in the car with the motor running. Was she letting the engine warm up? Or perhaps she still hadn't quite made up her mind. She stayed that way so long he actually looked for a hose running from the exhaust pipe. She'd seemed about that crazy. But

93

then the headlights came on, she put it in gear, and she was gone.

Joe took a jar from his desk, flicked paper clips aside and removed the key to a lockbox that he kept behind a case of cassette tapes in the stereo cabinet. From that lockbox he took a yellow envelope marked Western Union. He unfolded the cracked, graying paper inside, and read:

I WAS ON DUTY STOP THERE WAS NO TONKIN INCIDENT STOP
LBJ LIED STOP VOTE NO STOP TELL EVERYBODY STOP

Sandy's date stamp on the envelope was still legible: 5 AUG 1964.

Joe took Jerry's single scrapbook from the shelf and carried it to his desk. Only a few pages had been used. There were the high school honor roll notices from the *News-Courier*, his picture with the debate team after their regional win in Morehead; in the cast of *The Book of Job* at Pine Mountain; a group photo of the Honor Society; as Mark Twain.

With a bottle of glue he kept there in a drawer, Joe pasted the telegram onto the last page of the scrapbook, closed it, and placed it back on the shelf.

He went downstairs and turned on the big TV. Clark's playoff game would start in about ten minutes.

BOOK TWO

The Run for the Presidency:

Children of History

*If you want the present to be
different from the past, study the past.*

—Baruch Spinoza

The past is not dead. In fact, it's not even past.

—William Faulkner

*When an Arab and an Israeli dispute 'Mine's
longer than yours,' they mean history.*

—Mordechaj Warski

9

RED WATTLED LAPWING

WHEN THAT OLD renegade-from-justice Walter Sisler offers you a whopping consultancy fee for a two-week working holiday at his home in Dubai, you might reasonably expect princely accommodation at his beachfront villa, exquisite meals prepared perhaps by a young *Cordon Bleu* graduate, wine selected and shipped to him by some unlisted fussbudget agent in Bordeaux. A chauffeured Maybach, or at least a 7 Series BMW. With Sirius and NFL coverage. Maybe even your own personal butler to hop back to the villa for fresh towels and a whisky sour while you dabble your exhausted toes in the diffident surf of the Arabian Gulf.

Such were the expectations playing in the sleep-addled head of Cole Gibson as the exit doors finally opened after a fourteen-hour Emirates flight from New York. Add to that the flight from Tallahassee and the airport delays, and he was now into his twenty-third hour of travel. His watch said it was yesterday evening, his body clock had no clue, but the announcement on the plane said it was 4:30 a.m. in Dubai. He fervently wished for, and half-expected, a plain-clothes security man to whisk him away through the VIP gate and instantly, somehow, tuck him into the most comfortable bed he'd ever known.

None of that happened. What happened was something he'd never even dreamt of: amidst the jammed rope line of yellow-clad Filipina transit assistants and the white-shirted Indian drivers from the big hotels, there stood Walter Sisler himself, grinning like an ape under a cheap Panama hat with a green plastic front visor, holding up a big hand-lettered sign: COLE GIBSON. Even more surprising was that right beside him sat Roxanne Sisler in her wheelchair. Her gray hair had been twisted into a braid that flowed out the back end of an old Boston Celtics cap. She too smiled chimp-like. The old couple seemed to have caught some kind of grinning disease.

Cole Gibson was (according to a website that in absolutely no particular indicated it was under the aegis of one Danielle Gibson) the finest political consultant south of the Mason Dixon Line, or pretty much any other line you care to draw. The Sislers greeted him enthusiastically, though he was a stranger to them both. He tried not to wince—was pretty sure he succeeded—when Roxanne offered him a twisted hand, its fingers braided nearly as tightly as her hair. Walter took Cole's carry-on bag, a padded backpack with his laptop in it, stuffed it into a sort of luggage compartment fitted onto the back of the wheelchair, and pushed off into the growing wake of exiting passengers.

"Can I help you push that?" Cole asked.

"Naw, son. It's my lot in life. My punishment for not purchasing prostitutes even though I had the dough. Pre-AIDS and everything. Talk about *carpe diem*."

"I might still leave you yet, you old goon."

"Well, that would make pushing this chair a hell of a lot lighter, I'll say that much."

"I, for one, would like to thank Mr. Gibson for rolling in here during the wee hours. A girl needs to see the dawn from the other end occasionally."

Such insider banter accompanied him through the VIP fast-track passport counter; through the baggage area, where a teenaged-looking customs officer called out "Mr. Walter!" and hurried over to greet him by asking, "Are you fine?"; around three enormous lines for apparently scarce taxis; across pavement still wet from a rare rain shower and to a car that was not—*obviously not*, the slow-witted Cole scolded himself—the Maybach he had still been hoping for, nor even the BMW—but a large van with a wheelchair lift.

"Why don't I sit in the wheelchair and you push me a while?" Walter asked his wife. "It just doesn't seem fair. After all, I'm the oldest one here." Then, turning to include Cole in their nonsense, he said, "She's a stubborn little filly but I reckon I'll break her yet."

Roxanne winked at Cole. "That'll be the day."

It sent him into a deeper layer of weariness to be included in a dialogue that wasn't so much a conversation as the acting out

98

of a ritual, a script to mark the passage of one more night, the prelude to one more day, of happy marriage, of a marriage that works, not because, as marriage counselors liked to say—he knew the spiel all too well by now—not because good marriages take a lot of work, but simply because both husband and wife take such great pleasure at being together. Before starting this junket he had convinced himself that the vast distance between Tallahassee and Dubai would more or less automatically decouple his mind from thoughts like these, yet here he was, something like eight thousand frequent flyer points away from Danielle, not even out of the airport parking lot, and she was eating at him. These two old coots, in their odd, antiquarian idiom, had seeded in him the prefiguring of a nostalgia, a sort of reverse nostalgia, a homesickness for a future past he would never have.

The driver took Cole's bags from the trolley, allowing himself a hidden smile that said, "Don't worry. They're always at each other like that." Making it all the worse.

With the motion of the van his weariness slid into a state of half-sleep. A miniature mock-up of a city skyline, its futuristic buildings formed by jagged lines and irregular curves, blinking insistently in white and red points, bound together with strips of bright lights in blue and orange, all of it burning as with all the electricity in the world, seemed to spring up in a tight clump from a field of spinach. He saw that the glass-domed clock from atop his grandmother's fireplace had grown colossal and now was sitting in the middle of a traffic circle. Traffic was already heavy. Irritated drivers honked, flashed, gestured, roared past them in a blur. They drove through miles of construction sites, through a bewildering maze of traffic cones that only took him further into unreality.

Someone touched his knee—it was Roxanne—and he realized that they had passed the city and were into the desert. The van had stopped. The sun was just starting to rise.

Roxy said, "I know it's horribly cruel to wake you just now, Mr. Gibson, but that little rain cleaned the air of dust and the sunrise will show through these few clouds. I'm sure it would be more cruel to allow you to sleep through it."

The driver had positioned the van so that the rising sun would perfectly split the two minarets of a mosque the same shade of tan as the desert it sat in. The red sunlight gradually spread through low haze on the horizon, pinking as though the heart had awakened, the blood supply become sufficient once more.

"Don't let her fool you. She wanted to see it herself so she keeps the rest of us out here way past our bed-times."

"I absolutely did want to see it. Look at it, Mr. Gibson. Look how the desert goes red while the mosque stays the same shade of beige. Surely you didn't want to miss it. Your first Arabian sunrise. We usually don't get pretty ones. Just a blinding sun rising in a dusty sky."

"I wouldn't have missed it for the world. And why doesn't everybody just call me Cole."

"And I'm Walter. She's Roxy. The driver is Mushtaq, but we usually just call him 'knucklehead'."

"And maybe you will teach me the English word, sir, for a man who hires a knucklehead to be his driver."

They all looked at Cole, the driver via his rear-view mirror. "Oh, you're asking me? Well, let's see. I don't know . . . when I was a kid in Florida we might have called him a doofus."

That seemed to go over well. Mushtaq the driver had an infectious, wheezing laugh; Roxy a cackle. Walter's was more of a sarcastic ha-ha-ha. Those combined sounds, along with the red glow of the desert and the science fiction rocket shape of the minarets, played through Cole's head as he at long last reached the ultimate rung of his earlier fantasy—one that finally came good— the most comfortable bed he'd ever slept in in his entire life.

When he woke up he had a faint recollection of where he was and no idea how long he'd been there. He turned over and noticed a note leaning against a bedside lamp, propped up at its base by a cell phone. The note said, "Whenever you awaken kindly please press and hold number two on this phone. I will presently knock your door and render you all services you require." It was signed, Satish. He vaguely hoped that "Satish" was Arabic for "incredible hot young thing of your dreams," but the number two, when pressed and held, brought to his door a middle-aged Indian man.

He was holding, however, the incredible fresh pot of hot coffee of his dreams, which at the moment was at least as welcome.

Satish told him that the day's main meal would be served in about an hour, at 2:00, but suggested that if he had awakened hungry he could have fruit and yogurt or some pastries, or indeed anything he pleased, brought to his room. Cole assured him that the coffee would see him through, so Satish showed him where to find a bathrobe, towels and toiletries, then set about unpacking his things for him. Cole sat with his coffee at a small writing table that looked out through balcony doors to a few palm trees on a wide beach and on to where the aquamarine-covered shoal bled into the turquoise waters of the Gulf. A curious set of metal tracks ran in parallel down the beach, extending from the house, right into the sea. He leaned as far toward the window as he could, trying to make out where those tracks led from. Apparently it only now occurred to Satish that the balcony might be the perfect place to enjoy coffee, as when he saw Cole at the window he hustled over, slid back the doors, and hastily dusted off the outdoor table and two chairs. He said, "Moment," and left Cole standing there.

A fresh sea breeze penetrated the bedroom, prompting Cole to notice, belatedly, what earlier he'd been most looking forward to: a glorious early summer day in late November. Summers in northern Florida were pretty bad; winters were worse. But this—this cloudless day of moderate heat and low humidity, with the sound of the surf reaching his room, and the clacking palm fronds—now this was what a summer day should be. He heard a sharp bird call and looked down at some large species of plover prancing on its spindly legs in the sand beside some low palmettos. Instantly Danielle filled his thoughts. She knew all these birds, probably had a picture of this very species in a field guide on the bookshelf out on their summer porch. He could see her buying it, *Birds of Arabia*, with no intention of ever going there, but just to feel better knowing they had birds there, and what they looked like.

She should have come along. She should be here with him right now. Hey, you know—you marry a political consultant, you better be prepared to spend some time alone with the kids. But now the furor of the election season was behind him. This was the perfect time to get away. No doubt that's why Walter had scheduled it for late November; that, plus the onset of nice weather in Dubai. Cole had tried to entice her with every attraction from gold souks to desert wildflowers. He had pressed her to join him, stopping somewhere between beseeching and begging; but no. His mom would have been glad to spend a couple of weeks in Tallahassee and get the boys off to school; but no. No. The time apart would do them good. Clear their heads. Allow each of them to form some well-considered decisions.

Hell, who knew? Maybe she was right. He really was feeling better now. Beyond the balcony rail there was the surf; inside the room Satish was singing some trembly Indian song. The coffee was exquisite. On his own he could find out what bloody species that fucking plover was.

Satish brought cushions for both chairs. Cole wondered if the other chair was for somebody in particular, or if it was just a matter of form. Maybe sitting out there in the company of an empty but comfortable chair seemed expectant, inviting, while sitting there with a cushionless iron frame seemed forlorn.

In any case, now Cole could sit comfortably and peer over the balcony and down to where those little railroad tracks met the wall of the house. There was a hook and cable contraption there, and it finally dawned on him that all this could be rigged up to a wheelchair to somehow allow Roxanne Sisler to enjoy a swim independently of care givers. Perhaps in the salty Gulf water she was buoyant enough to move around on her own. He hoped to go for a swim with her. Maybe her buoyancy was contagious.

As Satish led him down the stairs, the sharp aroma of chili peppers directed him toward the dining room. "Whoa!" he said.

"Yes. One of the cooks is from Thailand. The food here is consistently perfect."

"I guess perfection would make it consistent, then."

"One day per week I am cooking. Vegetarian food from south India. Do you know?"

"No, I'm afraid not."

"Masala dosa, uttapham, idli. Or a full thali. You will see."

"I look forward to it."

"My day is Thursday. Do not leave before Thursday."

"I'll make a note."

"Of course you can buy in town for fifteen dirhams, but not like mine."

"I'm sure."

"Boss may being one rich man in world but he says good food being not always expensive and expensive food being not always good."

"Actually I thought the villa would be more like a mansion."

"Is having seven bedrooms only. And nine bathrooms only."

"Well, pretty big then."

"Not like some. You won't believe. Okay—dining room in that door."

If Cole was prepared for the aroma of masaman curry and of kale sautéed in oyster sauce, with rice and noodles and god knew what else, all laid out neatly on a Chinese lacquered lazy susan, he was decidedly unprepared for the extra three white, male faces he saw at the table. Their faces registered just what his did: *Yeah, well we didn't expect to find you here either.*

Walter was the ready emcee: "I know the four of you are all in the same business, but I don't know if you are acquainted. Do political consultants from all over the country know one another?"

"At our level, we do," Cole said.

"Well, then just for form's sake, Roxy, would you . . . ?"

"You fellas may be more used to hunting alone, like tigers, but this week you're working as a team. Allow me to present Team Sisler: Simon Angelo, Albert Tollson, Jeremy Allenberg and Cole Gibson."

"Let's dig into the grub while I explain in a few words what this is all about. As you are well aware, Roxy and I have a lot more money than we have time left on this earth to spend it all in. Some few years ago . . ."

"Try decades, Waldo . . ."

"I was trying to be polite and not make you feel like such an old bitty. But have it your way. A long, *long* time ago, in a country far, far away, we held a conference meant to dramatize how it felt

103

to be, let's say, a Polish Jew in the early 1940s, or a Palestinian in the late '40s. Or basically anybody who's ever been driven out of their homes and off their land by a more powerful force. The world's most powerful nations assuaged Europe's guilt toward the Jews by knocking the problem on to Palestine. At the time of our conference we didn't even predict the ethnic cleansing of Kosovo or Rwanda or any of those. What we did predict was that if the world's most powerful nations didn't find a way to play fair with the Palestinians, there would be a backlash. With all the oil money that was bound to flow into this part of the world—and where money flows in, power follows right behind—and with Israel sitting there in the middle of everything like some festering sore, trouble had to follow. Lord knows we've seen plenty of it already, but I fear the worst is yet to come. Guerilla warfare and terrorism are just too easy to do, and too hard to prevent. Even the most successful ethnic cleansing of all, the takeover of North America by Europeans—imagine if the Indians had had access to car bombs, airplanes, anthrax, plastic explosives, dirty nuclear devices, even simple AK 47s. Well, nobody can say what would have happened, but it wouldn't have been a cakewalk. Add to that so many of the world's Muslims living in dire poverty, not taking part at all in this oilfield boom you'll see around you, where local people whiz around in BMWs and Range Rovers and don't do a lick of work, just hire Indians and Filipinos and so on at the grand salary of $200 a month. Outside this oil field there are millions of young Muslims with no hope of a future, unless you count the future of a life after death, which is all they have to cling to for any chance of happiness. Rich Gulf fundamentalists pay families to send their sons to Islamic training schools, promise them more money if the son is martyred. This is a holy mission, righting some horrible wrong, protecting the godly against the satanic. These trainees can easily be convinced that glory for them and their families is just around the corner. All they have to do is bring it about as a result of a *jihad*. You see where I'm going with this?"

Cole was the one to answer. "Well, yes, sort of. But I don't see our part in it."

Roxy broke in. "We've been sitting on our duffs making tons

of money and hoping that world leaders would tackle the problem. But they've only made things worse. We know that on a planet of billions of young people full of piss and vinegar, we're nothing but two old people. But—*BUT*—we're two very wealthy old people. Wealthy enough to turn our whims into reality. We want you four—the four best political consultants in America, bar none— to put your heads together and broadly sketch out a campaign strategy, along with a short list of presidential candidates who would be favorable to a genuine solution for the Palestinians."

Cole broke in, "You want us to solve the crisis in the Middle East? You've got to be pulling our dicks. Sorry . . . do they know what that means?" He indicated the domestic staff.

Roxy answered, "They probably think it means literally pulling your dicks. So lock your doors tonight. They take requests from guests very seriously."

"No," Walter said. "You are not here to solve the problems of the Middle East. That's the job of the president along with a whole lot of other people. Your job is to tell us who that president will be. After dinner I'll show you up to your office. There's a nice-sized meeting room upstairs, with four phone lines and four broadband, unblocked, Internet connections. Here they block certain sites related to Israel, so I've used my *wasta*, my clout, to get them unblocked. Of course that means you can look at porn too, but what can I say?"

"And what are our ground rules?"

"Hardly any at all. You're here for two weeks. You can brainstorm anywhere you like—in the office, in your room, on the beach, together, separately. You're professionals. Each of you will also have a car and driver at your disposal. At the end of the first week, we expect a list of the four to five politicians in America who have some empathy for fixing the mess that this region, in fact the world, is in. During this week all we ask is that you stay more or less sober and especially don't go out sampling the hookers that Dubai is famous for. While it's true that I am something of a big wheeler-dealer around here, we live here on sufferance and, as our guests, if you soil your reputations you also soil ours."

"Save that for week two."

"Yes, indeedy. At the end of Week One you will give us our list and then shift to the Hotel Grand Marrakesh. Then you're on pure vacation. Your accommodations, food, drinks, the whole wad, is on us. The Middle East won't implode in the next two weeks, so enjoy it while you can."

For six days they mostly swam, sunbathed, drummed pencils on desks, clacked keyboards, tapped touchpads, scratched their heads, and groaned. They could have saved Ammenstar Oil a bundle if they'd simply spoken up with the truth at that first dinner: Your short list is so short it's blank. There ain't nobody on the horizon who can do what you want. But, professional politicos don't stay on top by being too cozy with the truth. Walter and Roxy wanted a list of at least four names, and a list of four names they would get.

They handed it over, official-like, in an envelope, at Satish's Thursday thali luncheon. He laid out the full set: puri, rice, three chutneys (coconut, coriander and tomato), potato curry, sambar, raita, and a sweet cream dessert with noodles floating around. The four politicos gorged themselves guiltlessly after a bad job badly done.

Politely, Walter and Roxy delayed the unveiling until they were alone that evening.

1. William Ellis, Lt. Governor of South Dakota
2. Mohamed Khalifa al-Suwaidi, mayor of Dearborn, MI.
3. Rashid Lewis, U.S. Congressman, New York
4. Ibrahim Teeves, District Attorney, Philadelphia

"Jesus Christ, Roxy, that's a sad looking bunch."

"I can't believe they left off Abdulla the Dogcatcher from Corpus Christi."

"Who the fuck are these people? Ibrahim Teeves? Are these names even real?" He went to find his laptop, but came back with Cole, who had been sitting in the dark on the back patio.

"Yep, they're real. The last two are Louis Farrakhan types, representing overwhelmingly African-American districts. Absolutely no chance ever to become president. The mayor of Dearborn is really popular—apparently gets those snowplows out onto the streets at the first frost. That counts big in Michigan. He became mayor after all the white people left Dearborn and the Yemenis moved in."

"And his chance of ever being president?"

"Zero."

"So why is he on the list?"

"You paid us for four names."

"And this Ellis guy?"

"His wife is a Lebanese Maronite Christian or something like that."

"His chances?"

"Well, you know he's held in high regard locally. Could be the next governor. Or even senator. Remember George McGovern."

"Good God."

"South Dakota, Walter. Birthplace of greatness. It could happen."

"But when?"

"Not overnight, I guess."

"Maybe I should have been more specific: I'm looking for a name who could become president in my lifetime."

"In that case you'd better take your statins and light a fire under Mr. Ellis. And even then. . . . "

"What?"

"Look Walter, I'm going to go ahead and be perfectly frank with you. You and Roxy have been wonderful hosts, and as much as I've enjoyed myself here, and as much as we're all looking forward to abusing your hospitality at the Marrakesh, I have to be honest: we're here on a fool's errand. It's a pipe dream."

"No way, José?"

"None at all."

"With essentially a bottomless well of funding to draw . . . ?"

"Dead in the water."

"Well, Cole, I appreciate your honesty. I know it's not your fault, and you don't need to worry. You'll get your luxury week at the Marrakesh. All four of you have done the best job you could with the task we laid out for you. You can't produce votes where there are none."

"Actually I can. That's my job. But I can't produce millions."

"Point taken. As it stands, you still owe me one day. I'll grab a bottle of whisky and send someone to round up the other three guys. I have one last job for you."

When they were all gathered around the conference table Walter said, "I have one name for you. All I ask is that you spend tomorrow devising a strategy that could lead him to the White House. Congressman Hatling of Kentucky."

America's four finest political strategists looked at each other. "I've heard of him, of course," said Albert Tollson.

"I guess that's a start. That's tomorrow's assignment. The next day—the Grand Marrakesh. Perhaps the finest hotel in Dubai. Makes the so-called seven-star Burj al Arab look like a kid's Etch-a-Sketch design. We own it, by the way. So don't break the beds."

Before Mushtaq pulled the van around to take America's foremost political consultants for their free luxury week, Cole laid the fruits of their last day's labor on the table by the back door. That meant it was bad news.

Hatling, Dem, Kentucky Five. Once safe seat now iffy. Lost margin with redistricting of old Kentucky Seven in 1993. Reputation as clean if unenergetic.

Personal History:
- (1963) Left Univ of Kenucky freshman year to serve in Vietnam (1964-65).
- (1966-67, 1969-70) College at Georgetown, Washington, star student, star basketball player. Took junior year abroad at American Univ. of Beirut (1968-69).
- (1970) Married Wanda Simmons. He was 25 y/o, she 19
- (1970-1975) Professional basketball player (Boston Celtics). Career cut short by knee injury.
- (1979) PhD in Middle Eastern History from London School of Economics.
- (1980–1983) Returned to Beirut as AUB history professor.
- (1984–1989) Georgetown U history professor.

· 1990 to Present, U.S. Congress.

Plus Points:

· Maintained ties to Southern Baptist Church—could steal Repub votes in South.
· Reasonable name recognition from championship Celtic teams—could help in New Hampshire.
· Looks the part.

Minus Points:

· No name recognition outside New England and Kentucky
· Presence of local candidate Elise Torsvik will prevent Iowa caucus surprise.

Voting Record:

· Moderate on taxes and spending.
· Supports policy on Israel.
· No record at all of support for Palestinians.

Odds v. anticipated Dem candidates:

· Sen Laverty, Pennsylvania 99-1 against.
· Former VP Foreman: 50-1 against.
· Gov Holmes, Oregon 30-1 against.

"So Rox, who's it going to be: No-Chance Ellis or No-Chance Hatling?"

"I think Cole was right—we're going to have to light a fire under somebody."

"Or else we're going to die in this God-infested desert."

The four men had little to say on their way back to the airport. Over the two weeks they had been chummy enough, but mostly had explored the area on their own and in their own way. The general feeling that they had been paid a great deal for undertaking a trivial mission seemed to bind them together, yet the tie was in some odd way a shameful one, making silence the preferred medium for expressing it. Cole passed the clock tower, noticed that it looked very little like his grandmother's prized German clock. The scale model cityscape in the spinach patch turned out to be the skyscrapers along Sheikh Zayed Road, backgrounded against the date palms and cassia trees of Zabeel Park. There were some striking white birds stepping gingerly on the lawn outside the park. Cattle egrets. He remembered that one. He never did find out the name of the plover one. He would ask Danielle about it, tell her how one had dive-bombed him when she thought her eggs were at risk. That would be a good place to start.

The Sislers saw their guests off at the hotel, then went into one of the little private rooms of the Grand Marrakesh's Korean restaurant for their dinner. It had been Roxy's idea to install a Korean restaurant in a Moroccan-themed hotel, and it wasn't really much of a success, but it more or less paid its way.

"Do you know why I love eating here?" she asked him.

"Because you like the privacy?"

"Yes, but there's more."

"Because *bulgogi* and *bibimbop* are two of the funniest food words in the world?"

"That too. But mainly because it reminds me so much of our visit to Korea."

"When that fraud of a stem cell doctor took us for a cool million?"

"Naw, before that. When we sat down in that little restaurant in Seoul and they started bringing us those teeny-tiny dishes of smelly this and stinky that. Do you know what I felt? I felt we were in a totally different reality, that's what; playing with a whole 'nother set of rules. Because if people could take such putrid gunk and say, Hey! Let's try eating this shit!, and it turns out they actually enjoy it . . . "

"You are so cute." He intertwined his fingers into hers.

"And can you guess what came to me then in those little-bitty dishes in that whole new reality?"

"A little-bitty premonition that the next day we would lose a cool million to a snake oil salesman?"

"No, silly. Hope! Little bowls of hope. And even now the memory of that hope returns with the smell of *kimchee* and, as you say, pronouncing the word *bibimbop*."

"We've still got hope."

"Bullshit. We've got the memory of hope. That'll have to do."

"Even when you cuss, you're cute."

She looked down at their embracing hands. "Waldo, how do you feel when you take my twisted-up hands in yours? Really. Tell me honestly."

He took a moment to consider the best way to put it. His gaze wandered from her face, up to the traditional wall hangings of pretty Korean girls in billowy silk *chimas,* and to the watercolor of white swans in a green bamboo thicket. He suspected Roxy thought of her hands as talons.

"Remember when we were first married and after we'd made love you'd throw a leg over mine and then I'd throw one over yours, and you'd top that with your other leg? They all fit just right and it seemed so perfect and peaceful that I felt I was floating off on a cloud into paradise? That's exactly how it feels."

Her eyes began to go teary, and she started to cover that with an "Oh boy, you are good," but just then Kim approached to light the gas grill. On his tray was a sealed manila envelope from Imran, the head of security at the Grand Marrakesh.

"Oh goody!" Roxy disentangled their fingers and rubbed her hands together. "Let's see what we've got."

"Roxy, does it disturb you to be so . . . like we are."

"You mean devious?"

"I guess that's the word."

"It's exactly the word. But I've never been devious with you, Waldo. Not even once. If that's what you're thinking."

"No, I just mean in general. Like we didn't tell them that what we also want is a president beholden to us, one who will give us a pardon to return home on our own terms. Or like this." He held up the manila envelope.

"No, it doesn't trouble me at all. It's who we are. We play the cards we're dealt."

"And we play them very well."

"Say hey, do we ever! Show us what you got, buster!"

Walter unsealed the envelope and removed a stack of 8x10

color photographs. What at first glance looked like bad porn was in fact worth a small museum packed with art treasures. Here were a dozen pictures of Simon Angelo *in flagrante* with a Chinese hooker he'd imported from downtown.

"Cheap bastard," Walter said.

"Ha! Cristina nailed Jeremy Allenberg. Leave it to the girls from eastern Europe."

"My word. Are all Romanian women gymnasts? Get a load of that!"

"Easy now."

"How can she possibly get her leg up there without . . . "

"Hey! Look at Tollson!"

Albert Tollson was with Eduardo, the Filipino from the barbershop.

"I knew it!" Walter said. "My gaydar synched right in on him."

"Would you look at that! You wouldn't think such a little shrimp of a Filipino barber would have such a....You think I need a haircut?"

"Your hair looks fine."

"Oh, shoot. What about Cole Gibson. We really need something on him."

He peered down into the envelope. "Nope, not a thing. Here's Imran's written report:

Mr. Gibson had no guests. As instructed, I asked Natalya at the front desk to be very attentive to him. Alexandra left signals as well. Every night at 11:00 he watched a half-hour newscast (Al Jazeera English) while drinking one beer (Leffe 75cl), and went to bed alone.

Yesterday afternoon I thought we would have success, as he phoned for Natalya to come to his room. She notified me and I activated the camera. She reports that she found the door open and Mr. Gibson on the balcony, where she joined him. She reports that he leaned close to her, and appeared to have been drinking. But all he wanted was to learn the name of one species of bird that lives in our gardens, the one with the long legs and the red stripe across its face. He said it had attacked him as he walked through the garden. She apologized for that, and for not knowing its name. She could only tell him that when this bird has eggs it is very protective. She feared he would raise a complaint about the attack, but he was not angry or upset. He told Natalya he would ask his wife about this bird, and indicated that she could leave.

Roxy said, "He should have asked me. I know a red-wattled lapwing when I see one."

Walter didn't reply. But he thought, And I know a loose cannon when I see one.

They both sat quietly, listening to the hiss and crackle of the gas grill heating up, waiting for Kim to bring their raw beef and the fork Roxy would require in place of chopsticks.

At length Roxy said what Walter had been thinking on his own. "Looks like we're down to one last hold card."

Walter didn't have to ask what she meant. "Our ace in the hole."

"Shall we play it? It's the equivalent of a political murder. It would destroy him utterly. And it's straight up blackmail—you realize that."

"Do you want to spend your last days back home, and then lie forever under rich Texas dirt?"

"Yes, Waldo, I do. I want that very much."

"All right—you've twisted my arm. I reckon our buddy the congressman would jump through a few hoops before he'd let us go public with that little bombshell."

The document was in fact a single page of lecture notes, probably the only such copy in existence, written years ago in Congressman Hatling's own hand. It began: *If the world had known in 1948 what we know now, the state of Israel as now constituted would not exist.*

10

WWW.FINDLOVE4LIFE.COM

BY NOW CONGRESSMAN Clark Hatling knew all the wi-fi coffee shops in the District and northern Virginia. He varied his choice of venues on the off chance that somebody would figure out that a U.S. congressman frequented one particular shop, or that Wanda would be driving by, spot his car outside, come swanning through the door. He knew which tables were private in the sense that no one could see the screen of his laptop. He clicked onto a dating site that seemed to be dedicated mostly to Asian women eager to meet western men. He'd learned about this site, indeed about the very existence of such introduction mechanisms, from a constituent who was having trouble getting a fiancée visa for his cyber-sweetheart.

The home page opened promptly: photos of three pretty, happy young women. To an experienced customer who looked closely enough it was clear that each woman represented a different country. One was a Filipina, one a Chinese, one maybe Thai. A truly discerning customer would have known that all three women were models, not clients. But the congressman had no idea about that.

He logged in: Danny Davies.

He loved being Danny Davies. University Professor. Of Milwaukee, Wisconsin. The girls never knew where that was. "It's on a beautiful blue lake," he would tell them, "where I love to go sailing." Then while the girls daydreamed of being with him in a sailboat on that lake, he would add, "But in winter the temperature can be -20 Celsius." *So cold!*, they would say. He knew they'd never even imagined that a thermometer had so low a setting. Most of these women didn't even own a sweater, didn't need one. He would tell them, "We'll have to find some way to keep warm." They would respond, *LOL*.

He checked out the faces of the women online today, and

clicked on a woman with a high membership number. That meant she was new to the site. Age: 18. Her round face was more cute than beautiful, with evidence of enduring baby fat. It was a studio photo. Everything looked misted over. Instinctively he scrolled down to the entry for the age brackets she was interested in: the defaults, 18-80. He scrolled back up to her address and thought, I knew it: Ormac. Girls who at least in theory would marry an 80-year-old dodderer were almost always from Ormac or Misamas Oriental or Lanao del Norte, or some other place nobody had ever heard of. She had been educated, she said, through vocational school. He didn't bother. She would type broken English about her broken life, and soon ask him for money.

A highly stylized pose of a thirty-something woman almost always indicated a Chinese divorcee with children. In Agriculture Committee meetings he'd heard plenty about Chinese demographics, but the statistics all said there was a shortage of women in the country. No one had mentioned all the divorced women wanting to get the hell out, but here they were by the boatload. He clicked on one who called herself Lizping, and went back to the photos.

Here was a Vietnamese called Candy who listed herself as a businesswoman from Ho Chi Minh City, with a B.A. and no religion. He loved that about these Communist beauties: no religion. In her photo she wore a red satin blouse with the traditional rounded collar buttoned high up at her throat. Her hair was parted on the side and swept behind her ears. She wore two simple pearl earrings. No religion, but the modesty of a Sunday School teacher. According to her profile she was sweety, honesty, romantic. He clicked the chat icon and typed: *Xin chào.* Vietnamese women always responded to their own language.

Her reply popped up almost immediately.

—*You no Vietnam?*

—*Mostly I've forgotten. Rat han hanh.*

—*Nice to met u too. Anh co knoe khlong?*

—*Tam tam. And you?*

—*OK too.*

With Vietnamese women he could reminisce a bit, talk about

Saigon as it had been. He asked if they still sold Bière ba-ba. She said it was now Bière ba-ba-ba, LOL. He asked if there was any resentment about the war. She said, no, so much suffering, ok now.

He thought, No religion, is it? Scratch a no-religion Commie and find a Buddhist hiding in there every time.

Someone signaled him; he accepted. As usual, it was a Filipina; pretty, 25 years old. Her username was Mara. Five foot seven, it said—tall for a Filipina. Her hair was short, almost boyish. He hoped it wasn't a shemale. As usual he checked her age parameters: 18–60. He'd listed Danny Davies as 50.

—*Hello*

—*How are you?*

—*How's ur search?*

—*Still looking for the perfect woman.*

—*LOL Ur eyes are so nice.*

He thanked her, had yet another laugh at how surprised the real owner of the eyes in the photograph would be to know how often and how warmly they'd been appraised across Asia. The photo he'd uploaded to his profile page was of Wayne Redmon of Jenkins, KY, and it was perfect. He was handsome enough to incite responses, would never in a million years be spotted on an Asian dating site, and even if he was, he was so distantly acquainted with the congressman that no connection would ever be made. It was from a random snapshot taken during one of Wanda's garden parties. In it Wayne had big, shining eyes and a wide smile. Wanda had probably just said something catty about his wife.

—*Thank you. The better to see you with, my dear.* Knowing she would never get it, but she said,

—*LOL Big bad wolf.*

He checked her profile more closely. Of herself she had written simply, "*If you get me out of here I will love you like you've never been loved before.*" Well, that wouldn't be all that hard. She might have set the bar higher than that.

The man I'm looking for: Funny, generous, educated, honest. So, I nailed three out of four of those.

Dislikes: Smoking, big noses, wife-beating. He thought he might just squeak through on those three.

116

Likes: Movies, cooking, basketball. That was one thing about Filipinas—many of them loved basketball. The cooking part was pure invention. He'd visited the Philippines for R&R, and had never had a bad lay or a good meal. They couldn't cook for shit, but they were enthusiastic in bed and loved basketball.

Religion: Catholic

Occupation: Caregiver.

He asked her:

—*What's a caregiver?*

—*It's like a nurse for people not sick enough for the hospital.*

—*Who do you take care of?*

—*An old Jewish bitch and her husband.*

Jewish? In the Philippines? Then he checked her data page again. Nationality was Filipina, but Location: Tiberias, Israel.

—*My God, you're in Israel?*

—*Yup!*

Just the sight of the word as he typed it onto the screen sent an electrical field of fear skittering across his skin. He recalled his father's repeated warnings that Israel was the third rail of American politics, advice that had started out as simple campaign wisdom but had, by the time Old Joe retired, become an obsession, and by his death more of a psychosis. Had his father's heated rants impaired his own perception of reality? As Joe sank into dementia and an almost Protocol-of-the-Elders-of-Zion-level conviction that Jews ran the world, did he impart some of that madness to his son, who watched and listened as Joe struggled to maintain a slipping grip on everything he'd ever known? Certainly now his first impulse was to exit that website and get the hell out of that coffee shop; maybe set a dumpster on fire and toss his laptop into it on his way home.

But he reasoned with himself. Does this woman look like an Israeli spy? He checked her membership number: it was lower than his, meaning she'd already been a member when he joined. Nobody was out there trying to track him down. Get a grip, Mr. Danny Davies, with the killer eyes of Wayne Redmon. If you're going to worry about getting caught, better to keep an eye on the door where Wanda might burst through. That's where the danger lay, not with the bloody Mossad.

—*Where did you study to be a caregiver?*

—*St Augustine's in Batangas.*

Quickly he googled it.

—*Does she have Alzheimer's?*

—*Who?*

—*Your employer. Is that why she's a bitch?*

St. Augustine's came up, and yes, a campus in Batangas. It was a six-month course.

—*She's not my patient. I take care of her husband.*

—*Oh, I see. My father had Alzheimer's and was kind of mean.*

—*Especially in the evening, right?*

—*Yes. You know about it.*

—*We studied it. Sundowner's syndrome.*

—*How long do you have to study to be a caregiver?*

—*Six months.*

—*OK.*

—*The old man is nice. He's just crippled.*

—*So you help him get dressed and everything.*

—*Yup. And I push him around in his chair and keep him company.*

—*Did he have an accident?*

—*A Palestinian bus bomb tore off his legs and shattered his spine.*

—*Oh wow, I'm sorry.*

—*Yeah, he's nice.*

—*Does he hate them?*

—*No, I said he's nice.*

—*Well, I mean . . . nice people might hate somebody who paralyzed them.*

—*The attacker's dead. It was a suicide bomb.*

—*Why is your job so bad?*

—*The old woman rules like a queen. She has this big house and now only the two of them live here, plus me. She treats me like a servant.*

—*Not like a health care professional?*

—*Sometimes me and Morty—he's my patient—we make up ways to kill her.*

—*Not really?*

—*Just for a joke. The funniest was to take her to Gaza and leave her on a street corner.*

—Ouch.

—But I told him we have to be careful.

—Or you'll get caught?

—No, or she might order everybody to clean that place up and then make them go home to prepare gifilte fish and some latkes.

—HAHAHA! But you still want to get out of there?

—Yes! I'm serious. Take me to America and I will love you forever. This I promise you.

Soon he checked his watch, told Mara he had to log off for now. She promised to send him some pix. He gave her his Danny Davies email address, finished his coffee, and left.

As he drove home he asked himself, Even if many of these women are only in it for the scam, why do you tease them with dreams of America? What's the point of all this?

Is this some kind of pathetic cry for help? Aren't you in fact hoping to get caught and go down in flames? As America's first ever politician ensnared in an Internet sex scandal you could kill off both your charade of a marriage and your miserable political career. Way down deep in your nasty little soul, is that what you want?

Or is it merely a response to growing old? Can you convince yourself that one last hurrah with some pretty young thing in a beach villa on Luzon would restore some of the lost years?

Just what precisely is the bloody fucking point, Congressman? He'd often asked himself this question, and the answer was always: One life isn't enough. Isn't that why everybody does such strange things? Why we leave job after job, spouse after spouse, replicate ourselves with kid after kid? I want to overthrow the tyranny of clock and calendar, rewind the whole damn reel and start again. I want to be somebody else. I am a fugitive from myself.

11   WWW.MANCHESTERUNION.COM

THE OLD SHEIKH slowly reached forward to touch the bowed head of young Amin Yousuf Hatoum, nineteen-year-old son of Yousuf and Aziza Hatoum. The Sheikh cupped the young man's head in his dry, gray hands, as for an anointing. Both men wore loose garments and skullcaps, and the old man had a long, proud beard, while young Amin had a decent start on one. A padded backpack for carrying a laptop was hanging from the back of a heavy wooden desk chair; on the desk lay a cell phone and a camera. Dominating the wall behind the desk was a large sign that said, in English, *There Is No God But Allah.* Despite the fact that *Allah* is simply the Arabic word for God, any poster writer who made the logically identical statement by reversing the order of the two terms into *There Is No Allah But God* would have earned himself a quick beheading, so it's a lucky thing for this one that he got it the right way round.

After three months at the training camp, Amin was meeting the Sheikh for the first time. In fact this little ceremony signaled the death of Amin Yousuf Hatoum, for the process of his rebirth was near its culmination. In a moment the Sheikh would bestow upon him a benediction, a new name, and then an assignment. The wasted nineteen years of Amin's past life would drop away as the molted skin of a death adder, and he would emerge as . . . who? Now, at long last, he would learn who he was.

The moment of revelation, of his resurrection into . . . what? . . . made him feel both light-headed and heavy-limbed. A sour effluence rose from his stomach and settled on the back of his tongue. Briefly he worried that he would be sick down the front of his new white *dishdasha*, but the touch of the old man's hands to his head sent an infusing peace throughout his body. He felt those hands vibrate as sensory devices rounding his forehead, touching the edge of his skullcap, feeling their way down to his ears and fluttering over his eyes, his nose, even his lips. He sensed the connection to the divine that God transmitted through those fingers. He looked into the old, white eyes, to the distant, transcendent vision that their blindness merely intensified. The eyes swept across his face as beacons of warning, as searchlights of rescue, not receiving light but transmitting it, as the ancients believed the human eye to operate, by casting visible rays on dark objects, only these bright double moons shone with rays from beyond this world, from the heavens, from the mind of God. For a long moment Amin stood transfixed, staring into those eyes, absorbing the light, then once more bowed his head into the old man's touch, his transmission of farewell, his legacy, his *baraka*.

"You are now a soldier of the *jihad*. From today I will call you Ibn Burak."

At the sound of his new name, a miraculous force field seemed to encase his whole body, for he knew that the *burak* was the small but powerful winged horse that had carried the Prophet, peace and mercy be upon him, from Mecca to Jerusalem, in less time than it takes to pray. He was no longer Amin Yousuf Hatoum, famed for his Beiruti playboy cool. The generalized disdain for the world that he had once sported as a fashion accessory now had a focus: the Jews who had stolen Palestine.

An enemy had robbed him of his patrimony, by right his natural home, that place where an idealized childhood lasts a lifetime. At last he knew why he'd always felt so out of place. After years of wrestling with it, the explanation was right there in his face. He felt out of place because he *was* out of place. His people, who had once ruled the earth in every way, from military might to science and mathematics to the most exquisite arts, had seen their greatness stripped from them by a demonic force, displacing him and all like him, leaving his culture prostrate and scorned. It was intolerable. God would not long endure such monstrous injustice. The rebirth of Amin Yousuf Hatoum as Ibn Burak was an earthly sign that God's patience had given way to God's vengeance. The hour of redemption was at hand. From this moment forward he had a *nom de guerre:* he was Ibn Burak. He was directed; he was tough. He was a *jihadi* whose strong back and swift feet would carry his people home to Palestine.

"Ibn Burak, you are a young man of God, but inside a devil's skin. That is why you have a special place in the *jihad*."

"I have tried to shed my old ways, *ya Sheikh*."

"That is your mistake. You must continue to wear your devil's skin. Wear it so that those who knew you before will not suspect that underneath you have become a man of God."

"But I want to be an example to my old friends and my family, sinners who don't yet follow the true path."

"You are not destined to be an example in this world, Ibn Burak, but from the next. When you become a martyr, multitudes of the faithful will overflow the streets of our great cities and towns. Even in the smallest villages women will ululate and men will chant your name. People the world round will see your face proudly displayed on placards, framed in lines from the Holy Qur'an. Poets yet unborn will write verses to your bravery. For seventy generations fathers will tell their children of your sacrifice. When your wayward loved-ones learn that you have been received into paradise, they will find God through your courage and your piety."

Amin thought, You don't know my family of whores.

The old Sheikh added, "Especially the women."

Ibn Burak's eyes filled with tears. He was still at the acolyte stage, not yet thinking out strategies or picking out his own possible targets, just delivering himself into the warm embracing arms that shelter the newly sanctified believer, the frightened apostate who, after a bitter struggle, has yielded up his volition, abandoned the terrifying high wire act of individuality, to find refuge in the wisdom of his elders. They had long ago been shown the pitfalls, the roped-off snares. They would guide him down the paths of righteousness. All he had to do now was hold fast to his trust.

"I'll do anything for the one true faith."

"Do not suffer, *walidi*. We have a plan for you. Return to your home and the life you led before. That will be your most perfect disguise. Within our faith you are now Ibn Burak, but to the world you must be Amin Hatoum. That is your special value. Most of the recruits here cannot mix in your circle. They are peasant boys, or children of the slums. Their parents were too busy striving for bread to educate them properly. They speak broken English, beggar's French, street Arabic. They are suspicious of boys like you who are at home in the villas of Beit Mery and Achrafieh, in the halls of a university. Go back there; let your family and friends think that you have returned to them. You will receive your instructions at the al-Omari mosque, the great symbol of our power, for the Crusader *faranji* dogs built it for the Prophet Yahya, the beheaded. But thanks be to Allah, the Almighty made it a mosque, ours now for eight hundred years. Go there for *fajr* prayers, but only on days when you are notified. Other than that, live your old life; even commit your old sins if necessary to maintain security. But be at peace; your day is prophesied. Your martyrdom will come at a level most *mujahideen* can only dream about."

Back home in Beirut, after a night in his comfortable bed, he walked into his spacious bathroom with its bright lights and big mirror, its shelf of lotions and scents, its musky, woody aroma of *oud* resin, saffron, rose. There sat his shaver. He'd intended to rid himself of all this three months ago, before he left for training, but now it was convenient to find it all there waiting for him. It seemed a sign.

One last time he looked at his new face, his real face, the face of Ibn Burak. He was glad the Sheikh had instructed his assistant to take his photo this way—presumably for the placards that people would display in the streets after his martyrdom. His beard was just starting to make a statement, but it had to go. He clicked on the shaver—the battery still worked. Clumps of long black curls fell into the basin. He inserted the drain plug. Better clean this out by hand. Don't want to destroy Mom's plumbing my first day back.

As his old face—his dead face—reappeared, it surprised him that it was still back there, ready to pounce. It was almost disconcerting the way Amin Yousuf Hatoum had lain in wait for him. It was all part of God's plan, though.

He used his shaver's No. 1 setting to restore his old goatee. His friends had called it the "padlock" look because of its shape. He found a *No Fear* t-shirt and an old favorite pair of jeans. They were loose in the waist after his three months of training, but they would do. He'd phone Marwan and maybe Essa and Majid. They were always up for a trip to the mall. They'd be thrilled to help him pick out some new jeans. And his mom would be more than willing to lay out a few thousand lira to see him back to his old self.

He shut off the shaver and took a long look at his new old self. Still a pretty good-looking guy, he had to admit. His padlock still looked manly. The girls used to say it scratched them just right. He noticed that the razor had exposed an untanned portion of his face. Might have to put in some beach time to take care of that. Beach time would also put in front of him a parade of female flesh. Luckily, part of the martyrdom bargain is that an instant before you die all your sins are forgiven. You arrive before God undefiled, with a purified soul, a soul as white as bleached linen. He need not fear the whores on the beach.

"*Ouf!*" he heard his mom shout from the dining room. "Amin! Come here!"

"What is it?"

"Stupid *Terranet!*"

Amin could see that she was one step short of smashing her laptop against the wall. "What's the problem?"

"*Terranet* connection. It almost acted like it knew what it was doing, then just as I got to a really important page it all froze and went blank."

"Let me take a look. Maybe it's your computer and not *Terranet.*"

"I hope they taught you a little something useful at this course you've been doing, because I'm ready to spit blood."

"Let your techno-superior son have a go at it." He noticed that her finger trembled as she directed her threats toward her laptop, so he tried to remain preternaturally calm. Beyond technology his course had taught him a few other tricks. One of them was that the calmest head in any tense situation can control events. This was a good chance to practice. "Let's see what we have here."

Aziza observed her son's deft manner as he clicked and tapped through his diagnostic steps. He seemed at home with technology, while it just made her anxious. It wasn't merely the broken

124

connection that had her in such a state; more than anything it was the headline of the article in the *Manchester Union* newspaper. She'd been allowed the briefest glimpse before it shut down. She was pretty sure the headline read "Hatling Hat in New Hampshire Ring?"

Occasionally she googled *Hatling*, just to "keep in touch," as she explained it to herself, but she'd never clicked through to such a piece of news as this. She thought back to her school days in America and seemed to remember that throwing in a hat meant to join in a contest, and throwing in a towel meant to resign from it. Or was it the other way around? She was more certain that New Hampshire held key significance for something—maybe the presidency? Or was it a totally different Hatling running for— or indeed withdrawing from—some miniscule New Hampshire state office? Was it even about politics? Maybe a sports story? And why would a newspaper headline end in a question mark? She needed to know these things and she needed to know them now. She could learn the answers in seconds if only the damn Internet would work, yet here sat Amin, patiently clicking through her connection settings and recovery options.

To curb her runaway imagination, Aziza left him alone and walked out the back door and into her garden, where a birdcall and the scent of blossoms caused her to look up into the orange tree. She spotted a laughing dove inflating its dappled red throat to sound . . . not laughter, she thought, nor anything in the least mirthful, but grief. A song to the pain of her mislaid life, it gave voice to her own quiet sacrifice. Her stomach ached with the missed opportunity that so many years ago had suddenly changed the hopeful and daring young Aziza into the one-day-at-a-time toiler she was today. She had to remind herself that it would be silly to cry over a cryptic newspaper headline, or even to let herself mourn the years she'd lost with the young man who had left Beirut, alone, so long ago. For a few moments she let the dove in the orange tree do her mourning for her, and then walked back into the house.

Amin asked her, "Are you interested in soccer, mom?"

"What a strange question. Can't you work a little faster?"

"It shows your last site was for Manchester United. That's an English football team."

"I know who Manchester . . . oh wait . . . you've misread it. It was a newspaper in Manchester, New Hampshire."

"Oh," he said, looking up from the keyboard. "I thought it was weird that with dad gone you were finally becoming a sports fan."

"Ha! Not likely." She finally noticed that he'd shaved that horrid beard and was wearing a t-shirt. She had so completely blotted out his Caliph of Baghdad look that she'd altogether missed his return to normal. The sight of him helped her to calm herself. "It's good to see your face again. You got your *mémère's* big blue eyes, you know. Like me. She always said you were the handsomest boy in the family."

"Yeah, well, I thought it was time for a change."

"Maybe that school did you some good after all. Did your papa pay for it all?"

"Yup. All paid up. I'm afraid it hasn't taught me how to fix this thing, though."

"In that case I'm off to Starbuck's. You want to come along?"

"I think I'll work with this a while then go do some shopping with Marwan. Can I borrow some money?"

She called "Aliya! Want to come to Starbucks with me?" and went upstairs. When she returned she had traded her housedress for jeans and an AUB jersey. Aliya followed her, wearing a short beige woolen dress, with tights a shade darker, and ankle boots. It was a shameful style Amin noticed everywhere these days. Every woman on the street seemed to be for sale.

Aliya pointed a warning finger at him. "Not one word, little brother."

He gave her an innocent look, hurt and unjustly accused.

"He's finished with that phase, now. And he's certainly not going to warn us about headscarves anymore. Are you, dear?"

"Never." He held up his hands, empty palms toward them, as if to show he was unarmed. But he thought, Go ahead and walk the streets like prostitutes. Your time is coming.

She handed him some cash. "Is this enough?"

"Looks like it."

"Sure I can't drive you and Marwan to the mall?"

"I haven't even contacted him yet."

"Sorry I can't wait. I'm dying to read that article."

"What's all the excitement, anyway?"

"From what little I saw, it's possible I know personally a man who is running for president of the U.S." Then, realizing how that had come out and how Amin might take it, she added, "He was a History Department colleague."

Aliya said, "Really, Mom?"

"You met him, too. You were just a little girl."

"How old was I?"

"I'd guess three or four, because he was here when Amin arrived."

"Think he remembers us?"

"I'm sure he does. He played with Amin like a babydoll."

"No way!"

"You didn't know your old *maman* knew people in high places, did you?"

Amin smiled at her, thinking, You probably fucked him, you old whore.

She smiled back at him. It comforted her to remember him so small and uncomplicated. She felt herself rising above the hollow lament of the laughing dove in the garden. And why shouldn't she? She'd raised a splendid daughter. Her son was turning his life around. Her ex-husband was exiled in Saudi Arabia, and deserved every minute of it. As for the young man who had left her behind so that she would drain away no votes in his rise to power; she just might phone him up one of these days to congratulate him on his foresight and his victory.

"So you see," she told her children, "you be nice to me and maybe someday I'll take you to the White House and introduce you to the President of the United States."

127

12

WWW.FINDLOVE4LIFE.COM

CLARK WAITED IN the short line for his coffee, took it to the table where he'd already set up his laptop, and typed, *Hi Mara. r u there?* He waited a couple of minutes, checked the Yahoo address of Danny Davies, sipped his coffee. There were a handful of subject lines that read, "Someone is interested in YOU!" with an emphasis that the website designers no doubt believed would incite a wave of high excitement, but which in effect said, "We can't believe someone is interested in a LOSER like you!" At the moment he wasn't interested in who was interested in him. His eyes scanned the inbox for one from Mara. He was hoping for a photo.

—*Hi! Danny! How r u?*

—*Fine now that you're here.*

—*WOW! I'm flattered. lol*

—*I'm serious.*

—*Every man says that. But some are liars.*

—*Probably many women too.*

—*Not me.*

—*Good. Hey, I found an email from you.*

—*Did you open it yet?*

—*I'm just now online. Did you include a pic?*

—*Yah. You didn't send me one.*

—*DAMN! I've been so busy I forgot to look. I'm not all that wonderful to look at anyway.*

In fact he was debating whether he looked enough like Wayne Redmon to fool Mara with a real photo of himself. Just the previous evening, while Wanda was out "with the girls," as she said—her gray-haired "girls"—he had flipped through her stack of Kentucky photo albums looking for another shot of Wayne, but the old hound dog was always surrounded by women.

—*Doesn't matter. I don't care about that. I know you have a kind face.*

128

—Can I have a minute to open yours?

—sure

—k brb

—k

The download was slow, revealing itself in thin strips of color. It excited him. It was seductive, like an unveiling, better than a striptease. It seemed to add to his image of her, made her seem playful, the kind of woman who would toy with a guy, use her power, establish herself as the one in control of the visual department of any sexual encounter.

Finally her face was completed, her eyes both bright and dark, looking at him from an angle, as though just taking a peek at his face before she returned her gaze to something else. Her lips were moist and parted. Her bare shoulders came into view, giving him the impression that she had sent him a frankly carnal pose, that this new relationship needed to be sharply redefined into one of those webcam porn-for-a-fee things. Luckily—or, as the congressman himself thought, not so luckily—a few more rows of pixels showed that she was wearing a pink tank top that covered, perhaps even emphasized, full breasts, not little Asian ones, more like some tropical fruits that when seen ripe on market stands make you want to purchase them not for food, not for nourishment, but for the perfume, for the syrupy juices that will drip out, for the way you almost have to laugh as you wipe your chin and let your sense of taste recover from the explosion.

—Wow. You really are lovely.

—ty I hope you like it.

—Wait. It's still downloading.

Now it became clear why her lips were parted: she was eating. She was sitting at an outdoor restaurant, holding up a tangled strand of noodles, not from chopsticks, as his time in Vietnam had taught him to expect, but from a fork. The rich fat from the chicken broth had put that shine on her lips. A photographer wanting to depict the partaking of life's small pleasures could do worse than shoot an Asian woman eating a bowl of noodles. He wondered how she would be in bed.

—Where did you take this pic? In Israel?

—*No, in Batangas.*
—*Who took it?*
—*My friend.*
—*Your bf? lol*
—*I don't have.*
—*Come on, be honest.*
—*Before, but he was a liar.*
—*Did you give him your virginity?*

Sicko, he thought, then assured himself that half the men on the Internet were just like him—middle-aged men seeking to turn back the clock, call mulligan, get one more spontaneous erection, beat the locked system of one life, one lifetime. You can be in your twenties for ten years, pal, not a day over. Ah yes, but the world holds many unfortunate young women who will play fantasy with me.

—*Bad boy.*
—*Sorry. I just want to know you better.*
—*k*

He wanted to ask her if married men, content with the course of their lives, ever signed on to say simply that lifelong happiness was possible, that good men were out there, just be skeptical and don't fall for jerks—but he couldn't. He needed a reciprocated fantasy. Otherwise he could just phone up a sex line.

—*So how is Morty?*
—*He's doing ok.*
—*And the battleaxe?*
—*???*
—*battleaxe means something like a bitch*
—*oh. she's still a battleaxe! lol*
—*You know what I'd like?*
—*no, what?*

What he wanted was a photo of her that showed her body, especially her legs, but he couldn't say: I'm a true leg-man. Your face and boobs are fine, but can you show me some leg? No, that wouldn't do. He struggled to find a way.

—*Do you like to go to the beach?*
—*sure. u must be romantic*

—*Why do you say that?*

—*Beaches are romantic places.*

—*A walk at sunset would be nice.*

—*I accept! lol*

—*Ha!*

—*When can you come over?*

—*???*

—*You must get a vacation. Come here and I will walk with you, hold your hand, be your best friend.*

—*I will try.*

—*I'm serious. If I love a man I will stay, thick or thin. You seem like a nice man. I'm not playing games.*

Soon after this he told her he needed to sign off and get to a meeting, or else he'd lose his job and she would have to support him. She said she would be happy to, lol, and asked him to come online at the same time tomorrow, if possible. He told her not to chat with any more men that session. She assented, but of course, he told himself, she would be nuts to follow through. He never did manage to ask for a picture of her legs, fat or skinny. He kept thinking, thick or thin, you bastard.

13

THERE WAS ALMOST no one at the Mosque of Omar for the Friday *fajr* prayers. It was still dark—on the way there Amin had used the headlight on his Vespa. For the midday *dhuhr* prayer it would be packed, but right now he found himself alone at the ablution fountain. A man appeared on his right, removed his black skullcap, and went through the same time-honored procedure.

"*Salaam*," the stranger said, making quick work of the formalities.

"*Wa alaikum salaam*," Amin responded.

"Listen carefully. As I enter the mosque, I will leave this bag at the door beside my sandals. Inside there is a packet, a set of delivery instructions, and a black jacket. Take the bag and make the delivery immediately. You have a car?"

"A Vespa."

"You're going to Yaroun, on the enemy border."

"I can get a car."

"Take the bag and go. Be sure to wear the jacket."

They prayed side by side but the stranger spoke no more, except as they parted on the mosque's portico, when he said, "Go in peace." Amin supposed this wasn't meant to be taken literally.

He borrowed his mom's car, telling her he was spending the day at the beach with some friends. That was the kind of activity that in her sluttish value system merited the loan of a car, and predictably she had a big smile on her face as she handed over the keys.

It really did drive well, her shiny little C-class Mercedes. He supposed it had come with the divorce. She sure couldn't afford it on a professor's salary. It made him laugh! Her and her silk and her make-up and her gold bangles jingling like the bells on some brothel-keeper's entryway. Take the settlement away and she'd soon be wearing thrift shop clothes and riding the bus.

The further south he got the crazier the roads got. Drivers were even more brazen, roads even more pot-holed. Hundreds of people seemed to be out trying to flag down a ride. He became so used to people waving from almost directly in the path of his car that at the first instant he didn't realize that those waving men up ahead were armed with handguns. One man fired into the air and took aim directly at his windshield as Amin hit the brakes and skidded.

They weren't brutal with him as they shoved him into the back of a Ford Explorer. They were just businesslike, matter-of-fact. One even protected the top of his head while he cleared the door frame, as in American cop shows. American training methods, perhaps? That's when he really got scared.

The blindfold was a store-bought one, not an improvised rag. In camp he had been taught that while being transported blind you should try to keep track of the time by counting your heartbeats, and you should sense left and right turns in the lean of your body. He was also told that these techniques were of almost no practical value at all, but they kept your mind occupied and gave you some psychological control. Even so, he estimated that they drove for an hour at least, and that a great majority of their turns were right turns, which may have meant they were in northern Israel, or maybe even in southern Lebanon.

The blindfold didn't come off until he was in a small, all-white room that he could tell was made to be moveable because its floor gave way a bit with each step he took. They stripped him naked, hand- and ankle-cuffed him to a chair that had been bolted to the floor, then left him all alone. He heard people talking outside— the walls were that thin—but couldn't make out what they were saying. It sounded more Hebrew than Arabic.

He tried to calm himself by taking inventory. In front of him was a clean white metal desk, but the chair behind it was the cheap plastic kind seen in all the cafés. Behind that chair there was a TV and a DVD player on a stand. Beside that was a door and a green metal filing cabinet. He couldn't read the labels on the drawers. They were in handwritten Hebrew. More even than the guns or the manhandling, the sight of those Hebrew letters sent a wave of weakening fear through him. He was in a Matilan mobile interrogation vehicle.

He'd forgotten about counting his heartbeats, but at least fifteen minutes passed in a state that could certainly have been seen as a period of serenity, if the surrounding circumstances could be ignored, for it was quiet, the temperature was fine, even for a naked man, and there was no one present to humiliate him. He tried to imagine he was in a medical clinic.

Without warning the TV on the opposite wall came on. A young woman was sitting on a double bed. The bedroom itself looked fine—nice wooden furniture, the bedstead matched the chest of drawers, which was all he could see. She sat on a pink duvet. She was wearing jeans and a sailor shirt with a straight neckline and wide blue and white stripes. She looked straight at the camera with a bright, round, expectant face that signaled an eagerness to please. She had an easy smile, wide, with white, perfectly spaced teeth. She was tanned, dark-eyed, with butterscotch blond hair, which she self-consciously shook back out of the way. She looked pure American.

For a long breath she just looked into the camera. Amin couldn't make out what this could possibly mean. Then a Lebanese Arabic voice behind the camera asked her: "Can you tell us a little bit about yourself?"

"*Yani* . . . I am eighteen years old. I am not married. Like that?"

"Yes, just like that."

"My hobbies are playing PS3, and I love reading fantasies such as Harry Potter."

"Where are you from?"

"That's my secret," she said, giggling.

Her Arabic was fluid and clear, Syrian more than Palestinian, maybe. It was hard to pinpoint. There was a touch of some foreign accent. Perhaps she had grown up in several different countries.

"Why is it a secret?"

"I don't know," she shrugged. "It just is."

"Are you still in school?"

"I study computing, online courses."

"Are you good with technology?"

134

"Yes, of course."

"You seem a little camera shy. Are you?"

"I'm only eighteen. I've never done this before."

"For a start, can you show us your titties?"

She smiled and without hesitation lifted her sailor shirt over her breasts. She looked down at them and squeezed each one. "How's that?"

"That's nice. Go ahead and take your shirt all the way off." She did that and tossed it on the floor. "Now your jeans."

She tried to remove them while remaining seated but they were getting in a jumble so she stood up on the bed and kicked them loose. Her pubic hair had been completely removed and replaced with a tattoo of a dolphin doing a tail stand on water. She tossed her jeans away, gave a little jump like a kid playing trampoline on the mattress, and landed on the bed with a big bounce. Her breasts rippled before settling into place. She smiled. "Sorry about that."

"You're doing fine. So tell me, are you a virgin?"

She giggled. "Are you kidding?"

"When was your first time?"

She counted on her fingers. "I was fourteen."

"Who was it with?"

"My mother's boyfriend. He was so hot."

"Who are you fucking these days?"

"Anybody I want. Maybe you?" Again she did that kid-giggle. "Or maybe you?" She pointed shyly to the camera lens.

Amin thought, This is exactly what I expected from these godless devils. They think they've got me bound up here hand and foot, but it is they who are prisoner. He closed his eyes.

"You like sex a lot?"

"Yes. Very much."

"And what do you do when you have no man in your bed?"

"I use my hand."

"Can you demonstrate for me?"

She began to rub her clitoris in swift, broad circles. Amin tried not to look when he heard her start to breathe hard. Her fingernails were long and pink, squared off rather than rounded. It seemed she took great care with her fingernails. She took breaths in

135

sharp gasps, then started to moan. There was a rising drama in the scene. The tension was in whether or not she could bring herself to an ecstasy, or whether it would elude her. The woman emitted louder and louder moans that became soft and then loud cries. Without the video, Amin might have thought it was a woman in deep distress. He looked down and was horrified to see that he was becoming erect. He watched helplessly as his penis ratcheted higher, redder, fuller veined. He tried to think of a verse from the Qur'an to distract his mind, but what appeared was ad-Dhukhan 44: 51-53. *Amid gardens and watersprings, dressed in silk, facing one another, we shall wed them unto fair ones, with wide, lovely eyes.* If he could have freed his hands and touched himself he would have exploded.

With agile fingertips topped by her carefully attended nails she strummed herself like a woman playing a lute. Amin tore his wrists against his restraints, jerked his legs against these monstrous betrayals, and shook his head like a man gone mad. When the woman seemed to be nearing orgasm she carelessly flung her head back out of camera range and convulsed as though in agony, in noisy epileptic spasms. She said, "Yes, yes. Oh my God."

With the drama resolved, she gradually relaxed. The spasms slowed, her breathing eased, her muscles allowed gravity to pull her deeper into the mattress. She slipped from the intense reality of sexual euphoria into a more composed state until , at last soothed and at profound and floating peace with the world, she released a quiet, whooping sound, more birdcall than laugh, and asked the cameraman, "Was that okay?"

A door opened behind him; he felt the floor give. He turned around as much as his restraints allowed and saw a man circling to face him. He saw a bulky, bearded, middle-aged man wearing a yarmulke. He was not dressed as an officer, just jeans and a loose, flowery shirt that was about ten years out of fashion. He was carrying a box the size of the packet Amin had been sent to deliver.

"Bastard," Amin said, determined not to hang his head.

"Hey, don't worry about it, kid. It's normal. Let me get a towel to cover you with. No need for further degradation."

He went through the narrow door beside the TV stand and

came out with a towel, which he laid across Amin's lap.

Amin saw that his penis had already gone soft, with a little streak of moisture oozing down his leg. He could feel the rolling drop turn cold, and wished he could free a hand to wipe it away with the towel.

"You didn't humiliate me. You humiliated yourself."

"Oh, stop complaining. You can call me Levi. What's your name?" He waited a few seconds. "What were you doing poking around so close to my border?" No response. "Maybe you don't even know why the hell you were poking around my border. In that case I can help you out, because we put the sniffer dogs onto your little packet." He placed the box on the table. "Know what's in it? I bet you don't, do you? I bet you're so marginal to your organization that you're not cleared to know."

Amin looked at the box, suddenly aware that he really did want to know what he had carried from Beirut to Israel.

"Care to guess? No?"

"You'd better be careful with me."

"Oh, is that the way you see it?" Levi pulled the 9mm Jericho from the desk drawer and laid it on the desk. "You're the one in handcuffs and I'm the one with the weapon, so to my mind you're the one who needs to be careful."

"My mom is best friends with a very powerful man in the U.S. He's running for president."

"Oh, really? This is most interesting. Tell me his name and I'll have him on the phone in a few seconds."

Amin did his best to remember, knowing all the while that it was futile, because Aziza had never even said the man's name, and anyway this Jew would only laugh at him.

"No? Not even a hint? I think it's sweet, though—you're a momma's boy. I get all these tough guys in here who say their daddy's going to blow my head off, because that's what you clan people do, why you've been slaughtering each other since prehistoric days. But, *My mommy's going to get you*, that's original."

Amin reminded himself of what he'd been taught: *They will try to take your dignity, though in the eyes of God they are but gnats.*

"By the way, we filmed you and your hard-on from beginning

137

to end. I loved that part near the end when your whole body went nuts and you gave that bad boy a shake. I bet your mommy would love to see that, too. We can post it online and send her the link."

Amin frantically pulled his wrists against his restraints. If only he could remove one hand, grab the pistol and shoot that bastard in the head. Even though he would be killed seconds later by the men outside, if he died with this *shaitan*'s blood on his hands, he would die a martyr.

"So guess, momma's boy! Guess what's in the box that has basically ended your miserable young life."

Amin didn't speak.

"These people you love and obey sent you on a fool's mission to deliver something so valuable that it outweighs your own life, so what was it? Semtex, Plastrite, C-4? What's your brand of plastic explosive? Or at least maybe a big stash of heroin that would at a stroke fund the *jihad* and destroy a few jewboy junkies?"

Amin refused to offer a guess, although he'd earlier convinced himself that it was C-4.

"Nothing? I'll move my pistol a little closer if you take a guess."

He moved it an inch or two as a tease. Amin could feel a friction burn developing as he struggled against his handcuffs. The guy seemed to really mean it about moving the gun. He remembered the Sheikh telling him he was destined for a job most *mujahidin* only dream about. "C-4, I think."

"Nope." Levi moved the Jericho to about the halfway point on the desk and removed the lid from the box. "Dates, kid! They sent you to your doom for a box of dates. *Medjhools*, nice ones too. Have one." He placed the box beside his gun. "Oh, your hands are bound. In this case, I'll have one."

Amin watched him pop a date into his filthy mouth. *Insha'allah it's poisoned!*, but the man seemed unconcerned.

"So you know what that means, right?"

"What what means?"

"You were sent on a mission to deliver dates to a fictitious address in Yaroun. What does that tell you?"

Amin tried to think of an explanation, but said nothing. No doubt the bastard was lying.

"It means you were a decoy. But a decoy for what, my dear

young friend? No doubt you'd like to know the answer to that as much as I would."

"You are lying about the dates. That's why you eat them without fear."

"Listen up for a second. 123Levi@hotmail.il. Levi, like the jeans. Memorize it. It's my private email."

"Why do you think . . . ?"

"You might need it. It may be that I'm not the most dangerous person in your life right now."

"I spit on you!" And he did.

"Look, somebody sent you on this death mission. It wasn't me. Go spit on them."

"I spit . . ."

"Did they give you that jacket?"

"Huh?"

"The people who sent you—did they give you that jacket?"

"What do you mean?"

"Was that your own jacket or did they give it to you as part of the mission?" Levi watched the boy's eyes carefully, saw something register. "You don't even know the game well enough to know what that was all about, do you? Do you?" He could see that the boy was dying to know, but wouldn't dare ask, not for love or money. "We found traces of heroin powder in the pocket. It's supposed to be your alibi, see? You're not some dangerous international terror menace; just a common drug peddler. That's what we're supposed to 'find out' in our investigation."

"I came to see my land," he said.

"Oh, I see! You're a landholder in this area, are you?"

"My father was, until you people drove him away."

"How old is your father? About a hundred and ten?"

"Okay, it was my grandfather. But the land would have been mine someday."

"Then why didn't your God protect it for you?"

Amin looked at the smirking Satan sitting across the desk. He thought, *That's why He's sent me here, asshole. I am Ibn Burak.*

"It's a funny thing, kid. You know what Napoleon said about God?"

"I don't care wh . . ."

139

"He said God was generally on the side with the best army. Isn't that an interesting twist on it?"

Amin said, "*Allahu akhbar.*"

"Yeah, sure. *Blah-blah-hoo-akhbar.* But isn't it interesting— both our sides agree on one thing: there's only one God and he's in total control of everything that happens. Yet isn't it funny that this land has been owned by the Canaanites, Jews, Babylonians, Persians, Greeks, Romans, Byzantine Christians, Sunni Muslims, Shia Muslims, Christian Crusaders, then back over to Sunnis, Turks, the fucking British, then Jews again. Can't God make up His mind? Why is He so fickle? Can you explain that to me?"

"I don't have to explain anything to you."

"No, absolutely right. But you have to explain it to yourself, or else you have to consciously choose to ignore one huge motherfucking gorilla of a disproof that's sitting right in the middle of the room."

"These are words of a fool."

"Is that so? Which one of us is going to be shot for importing a box of dates?"

Amin caught himself starting to smile at the irony of that, saw Levi smiling back, and so forced his face to remain blank. "You don't have to lecture me on history. My mom's a history professor and I've heard it all my life. I probably know more than you do."

"Then in place of a lecture we can have a fruitful discussion. Thanks to Professor Mom."

"She wrote a book about the Crusades. If you think I'm full of shit, look her up on Amazon.fr. Aziza Hatoum."

Levi scribbled the name on a notepad. "Then perhaps you know the really big event that happened here two thousand years ago? No, not the birth of Jesus Christ. I mean CE 70. Do you know what the year 70 means to Jews?"

Amin thought, The year Ibn Burak is martyred, CE 70 won't mean shit, but he said nothing. He realized that telling this guy his mother's name had been a huge mistake.

"When the Roman general Titus successfully conquered the city of Jerusalem in the year 70 CE, he entered the temple, the absolute center of Judaism, in fact the literal House of God, His abode. Where He hung up His hat and put on His slippers. Titus pounded his fist on the altar and challenged God to a duel. Titus is said to have laughed with great disdain at such a sniveling god who boasted that he would defend His chosen people but in fact could not even protect His own house. Then Titus had the temple laid to waste, laughing all the while at the emptiness he uncovered."

"So you're going to tell me that finally your god has returned to seek vengeance."

"Not at all!" Levi's head shot back at the absurdity of such a claim. "I am a hard-bench atheist. I think Titus was absolutely right. And Napoleon along with him. There is no God in this shithole patch of earth. It's military might that counts. When Hitler started rounding us up, we had God and he had guns. I mean, fuck, it was no contest. That's why now I prefer to be the one with the gun, which you keep looking at and slobbering over."

"So if you're a godless *mulhad*, why are you here? You're obviously an American—you didn't have to come here."

"I'm not a believer, but I'm a Jew. Is such a thing possible? Can people be a Muslim atheist, or a Christian atheist?"

"No."

"No. If you lose your God, you lose your religion. But Judaism isn't a religion any more. It was the Spanish who turned us from being a religion into being a race. After they took over from you guys—who by the way treated us better than the Christians did, so you get props for that—they forcibly converted thousands of Jews and Muslims into Christians. They were the "conversos." But that didn't satisfy the Spaniards. They said, Hey, wait a second! These Jews and Muslims we battered into becoming Christians aren't really sincere in their Christian beliefs! So it wasn't enough to be a Christian. You had to be born to Christian ancestors. Purity of blood became all the rage. *Limpieza de sangre*. So if your parents or grandparents were Jews, you were a Jew. It became hereditary. Same with Hitler. So I inherited Judaism, even though I don't believe in the Torah, or any of it."

"So why did you leave America?"

"If I'm going to be open and personal with you, I think you ought to do the same with me. Don't you think that would be fair?"

"Maybe. I'm not sure."

"Let's try this one. Don't you think 'Amin' is a nice name?"

Where did that come from? He hadn't googled Aziza Hatoum, didn't have anything beyond a pen and notepad, as far as Amin could see.

"Mentioning Hitler brought the name to mind. You may know about Amin al-Husayni. Would you consider him a great Palestinian leader?"

"I don't know the name."

"Oh, really? He's quite famous. Spent the war with Hitler—another brilliant Palestinian tactic. Advocated murder of all Jews everywhere, presumably even my parents playing hopscotch in Brooklyn. You sure the name doesn't ring a bell?"

"No."

"That's odd. He also had blue eyes. Like yours."

"A lot of Levantine Arabs have blue eyes."

"No need to be angry. I think you have nice eyes. I just wonder where you got them."

"Not from this guy, that's for sure!"

"Yes, that would be an odd coincidence. Hitler liked them, of course."

"Liked what?"

"Al-Husayni's blue eyes. He probably would have liked yours."

"What is this bullshit?"

"But make no mistake—you are no more Aryan than I am, and if Germany had taken over the world, you and I would be brothers, at least for our last moments. Maybe at last we would have found common ground, on the train ride to Auschwitz, and in the gas chamber, in the shower we had been promised after our exhausting journey."

Amin looked down at that pistol just sitting there, taunting him, beside those dates.

"That would have worked just as well, Auschwitz would have, to make you a martyr. *Kedoshim,* we call them. Victims of the *Shoah,* or even the Spanish Inquisition that we were just discussing. The Spanish got some of you guys too. Muslims are well-represented in the ranks of *kedoshim.* Do you see my point?"

142

Amin didn't see the need to answer that.

"I just grew tired of us supplying the raw material for the *kedoshim*. I say let you guys do it for a while. And since you're so eager to do it, well, then that works out nicely, doesn't it?

"You talk nonsense."

"I know from your facial expression that you are lying, even to yourself. Do you know any blind people?"

This took Amin totally by surprise. "No, just . . . you know . . . in the streets, like . . . sort of beggars."

"Man up, Amin! This is not bullshit! If I give the signal you will be dead within sixty seconds. Or I can pick up that gun, in which case you'll have two seconds. Only then I'd make a mess in my office."

"Such as it is."

"Ha! Too right!" Levi said. "It's an embarrassment. A fucking Winnebago! We should be camping in Yellowstone, or some such shit."

Levi paused, lifted his eyebrows, as if in invitation to . . . to what?, Amin wondered. To smile? To agree with him? He enforced his blank stare.

Levi didn't give up. "Wouldn't it be great if we lived in a totally different place and time, and we could hitch up this silly camper and drive way out into the wilds? Or even better, just walk right over there to that door and open it to find a quiet blue lake at our doorstep. Fishing rods, maybe a canoe. A campfire and a six pack."

"You do talk a load of rubbish."

"Hey, I not only talk it, I think it!" Amin actually chuckled at that. "So did you know that Hitler went blind?"

His blood ran cold again. This man was truly frightening, worse than a classic torturer. *They will try to separate you from your faith, but the God within you is indivisible.*

"It was right at the end of World War I. He had been wounded in a gas attack near the Lys River in Belgium. It was reported that when he heard of the German surrender he went blind, and had a vision in which he led a resurrected Germany to triumph. Do you think it's possible that blind people have special powers of revelations? A compensatory power, so to speak?"

"I have no idea."

"That Japanese wacko whose disciples tried to gas the Tokyo subway a few years ago—do you remember that incident?"

Amin nodded. It was true. He had seen pictures of that guy: fat, ugly, long hair, beard, eyes sunken into vacant holes. *Disciples*, he repeated in his head. This Levi guy was toying with him.

"I'm just wondering if you think there's anything to that?"

His wrists were sweating against the plastic of his handcuffs. He quietly pulled one against the other. He whispered, "*Bismillah*."

"Ah, yes. Back to our starting point. I thought maybe we had made some progress." He reached down into a lower drawer and pulled out a small notebook computer, raised its lid and watched the screen until a pop-up indicated that it was connected to the Internet. He looked back up at Amin and said, "I'll tell you what: I need to call it a day, so here's what we'll do. I know you can't keep your mind off that pistol lying there, any more than you could take your eyes off that pretty girl giving herself a bit of pleasure. So, let's make this fair. I'll put my faithful Jericho so near you that you can almost smell the powder. Here, just on your edge of the desk. Now, I'll take this box of dates and scoot my chair back. And I'll give you fifteen full minutes to somehow get your hand to that gun and blow my head off. It's you and your almighty God against me and a pair of cheap plastic cuffs. I think they cost about fifteen shekels a pair. Three or four bucks, U.S. You can pray and invoke and struggle, while I work online and enjoy a few of your dates. Fair enough? Time starts . . . now."

He knew it was a set-up, some sort of satanic temptation to cheapen the will of God, to cause him to call upon God and then lose his faith when God did nothing. But call upon God he did; he had to. He was a man without volition. He was driven by the notion of what a glorious world it would be when the divine entered his wrists and freed him to conquer this overbearing *mulhad*, then the soldiers outside, and to spread his destruction in a miraculous campaign of revenge and liberation until all of Palestine was free. He closed his eyes so hard that his vision sparkled into bright red shooting stars, and he prayed from the deepest part of his soul as he jerked first one arm, then the other, slapping his arms against the wall behind him, pressing and pulling even with muscles that could in no way be involved: his cheek muscles, his calves. Straining and praying in a wild, continuous effort that allowed no hint of doubt to creep through.

Soon he realized that the bastard Levi had again proven his genius by setting the time at fifteen minutes—far too long for a man to struggle and pray at full capacity, and not be overcome by the futility of it. For the last five minutes he just sat there, spent; occasionally twitching in a renewed spasm of hope, but really there was nothing left in him. Five minutes, at least. Five minutes, in a quiet room, ticking off the seconds as that fat bastard leaned back against the far wall, nonchalantly tapping laptop keys and chewing up one date after another. Five minutes is a very long time to wait for the aid of a God you know isn't going to show up. His wrists dripped salty sweat into fresh blisters, but it didn't matter. The weapon lay just in front of him, far, far beyond his grasp.

"So," Levi said, checking his watch, "I see I've let you go overtime. Those damn dates were just so sweet. Blame it on the dates! That's my excuse! And, oh! I see I didn't get shot. That's good news." He reached for his Jericho, put it back into the desk drawer. "Now—unfortunately—I have to release you to Central Authority, where things may get tough for you. You won't believe me, but right now I may be the best friend you have on this planet. I will try to get you a humane level of treatment and early release. If I succeed, we may need to pass messages between us. For that purpose I've just created a new email address for you and me and nobody else. Listen and remember: shakebadboy@hotmail. il. Password: *mommasboy*, no apostrophe. Got that? This is our little secret. shakebadboy@hotmail.il, password: *mommasboy*. No apostrophe. Only you and I will ever use this account, and it's only for private messages between you and me. If you've ever had any training, you'll know how to use it. If not, then you're a nothing flunkie or drug peddler, in which case I say get a life—you've got a spark of intelligence about you—but I don't need you and frankly I don't give a shit about you."

"Save draft," Amin said quickly.

Levi didn't respond to that, except inwardly, where he thought,

145

Ah! You want to impress me, do you? In spite of yourself, you want me to give a shit.

"To signal me that a message is waiting, find an Internet café far from your residence and write me in clear at 123Levi@hotmail.il. Say anything boring. The weather was great. The picnic was fun. The Dodgers should never have left Brooklyn. Anything I find there means I need to check shakebadboy@hotmail.il. Password: *mommasboy*."

"No apostrophe." Again the bastard had done it. Amin was sure he would remember it all, probably for the rest of his life.

To watch Amin flinch, Levi pulled out his Jericho again, put it on the table. "I have a few dates left. You want to give God another five minutes?"

Amin bowed his head. He just wanted this to end.

"Really, I don't mind. I'm not in any real hurry."

Amin didn't even look up.

"So, son, now that you know the whole God thing is a hoax, how do you feel? You okay?"

Amin was searching for an answer, not for the bastard Levi, but for himself, when a single rap struck the door and a man entered the room.

"You're to let him go. Right away."

"On whose authority?"

"The PM himself. And Washington's waiting on the office phone. Some congressman says we've made a mistake. Says this guy is his friend and he'll vouch for him."

Levi stood watching as a Ford Explorer drove away with Amin Hatoum, blindfolded again, but with one arm out the window giving him the finger. "*Motherfucker!*" he said, to no one in particular, as he slapped his hand against the side of his Winnebago. Three or four of his men looked around at him. "There goes a tremendous opportunity lost. An *unbelievable* opportunity! We need a kid like that on our side. What a huge fucking wasted chance!" This time he used his fist against the metal door. "Give me a few weeks with him, and I could turn that boy completely around."

146

14

WWW.FINDLOVE4LIFE.COM

ON FRIDAY BEFORE a committee vote on new interstate trucking regulations that Clark couldn't care less about, except that Wayne Redmon had phoned him personally to lobby for a thumbs down because it mattered a great deal to him and his coal hauling operation, a brochure sitting right on the top of the day's stack of mail caught his eye. Obviously Holly or Luke knew of his Beirut connection and had placed it there on purpose. It announced a four-day conference called *Unity in Diaspora,* and it set his mind to whirring. Aziza was his first thought, but she was off limits, obviously. Still capable of causing great pain and not much else. She might meet him for a lunch and a brief thank you for springing her son. Walter and Roxy had long since left Beirut for Dubai.

It took him a full minute to realize why he'd gone into a little tizzy over the idea of this conference, but then he knew: Tiberias. Even if from Beirut he had to get there through Cyprus, he could still be there in a day. This was his chance to sneak away from real life. He could find a hotel, Mara could take a day off, maybe a weekend, and he could be Danny Davies for a full day or two.

The following Sunday morning Clark didn't want to drive very far, so he took the nearly empty Key Bridge over to Arlington, past the Iwo Jima monument that he had rounded so often in his younger days that it was like an old friend to him now; a monument, as he had often said in public speeches, to the courage of young soldiers, and a monument—as he himself had never had the courage to say in public—to bad government. By now, as with so many monuments, to Clark and perhaps to Clark alone, it stood for his envy of all historians who could study, reflect, analyze and, eventually, no matter what reasoned conclusions they had come to—even if they concluded that the U.S. and European powers had penned the Japanese into such a corner that a Japanese leader might reasonably decide that death by fighting was better than

147

death by slow strangulation—these historians could say it right out loud, and write it in books, and still keep their jobs.

Historians could say that; politicians couldn't. Not and keep their jobs, anyway. So he thought about that for the billionth time in his life as he headed for the coffee shop in Piccadilly Center.

He'd read somewhere that white tea was supposed to be an aphrodisiac, so he ordered that, flavored with mango. He felt this was his way of getting into the right frame of mind; going tropical as he prepared to meet his young Filipina friend. He opened his chat box and typed:

—*Mara? r u there?*

He didn't even bother with other women anymore. This one supplied him with all he needed. While waiting for her, he opened his Danny Davies email and found a message from her, with a photo attached. He clicked on that and once again had to wait while the stodgy system took its sweet time.

A window popped up:

—*Of course! Where else would I be? LOL*

—*You could be anywhere.*

—*If I'm not there, I'm here, and if you're not here, then I must be there.*

—*I guess so.*

—*You don't get my joke?*

—*It's very early in the morning here.*

—*If we were married no way I'd let you leave our bed so early on a Sunday.*

—*What if I had to urinate? Us old guys do that pretty often, you know.*

—*Ha! I'd have a urinary bottle at my bedside. I'm a medical professional, you forget?*

—*LOL. No, let me go to the powder room (as you say). I promise I'll come right back to bed.*

—*Take a Viagra while you're in there. HAHAHAHA!!!!*

—*Hey, you sent me a pic. I was just opening it.*

It was still downloading in strips. A solid blue sky had appeared, and the fronds of some palm trees. Could this be the bikini scene he'd been hoping for? Her head and face came into

148

view. From the angle of her gaze it seemed she had adopted some stylized pose.

—*Is this a beach in the Phils?*

—*No, it's here. The Sea of Galilee.*

—*Sea of Galilee!!! Wow, that's cool.*

—*You know about it?*

—*Sure, from church.*

—*It's where Our Lord walked on the water.*

Her breasts were in profile view; they seemed to shimmer within the downloading photo. She thrust them forward as she looked over her shoulder at the camera. This was clearly meant to be a sexy pose. It became a kind of digital striptease. Her bare stomach was showing now; soon a small pair of bikini bottoms appeared, still wet from a swim and clinging to her rounded hips. He knew she was waiting for him to say something about the Lord walking on water, but he couldn't take his eyes from her rastering photograph.

Now came her thighs. She stood in profile to him, one thigh raised. He felt an unusual sensation in his groin—life stirring, enthusiasm within the moment, a memory of passion. Her bent knee seemed so perfectly round that he had the urge to trace its arc with his finger. A calf muscle was tensed . . . ah yes, it's because she's standing with one foot on tiptoe. It's a dare. It says, Come take me, if you think you're man enough.

—*My God!*

—*Everybody's God, silly.*

—*I mean your pic. You are so lovely.*

—*You like it?*

—*I love it!*

—*I think now that we are getting serious you deserve to see what you'll be getting.*

—*Really beautiful.*

—*Am I right?*

—*About what?*

—*You deserve to see all of me. ALMOST ALL! hehehe*

—*Yes, thank you.*

—*It's like marketing, you know? You get a little taste of the product.*

—*You're a tease, you know that?*

—*Only for you. No other man gets to see this.*

—*I'm sure there were a lot of men at the beach.*

—*I mean I don't send sexy pix to other guys. Only you.*

—*Yes. I see.*

—*Do you agree?*

—*Yes! Thank you so much!*

—*yw*

—*Many chats ago I asked you a question that you never did answer.*

—*What question?*

—*Are you still a virgin?*

—*Yes, but NOT FOREVER!!! LOL*

—*LOL Thanks for telling me.*

—*yw*

—*Me too, btw*

—*u 2 what?*

—*I don't plan on being a virgin forever.*

—*LOL Well don't delay too long, professor!*

—*LOL Good advice.*

—*I think we are getting serious, don't you?*

—*How do you know?*

—*I don't chat to any guy but you. Do you chat with others?*

—*No. You're the only one.*

—*♫♫ ONLY YOU ♫♫*

—*LOL*

—*You know that song?*

—*Sure. It's a classic.*

—*♫♫ Only you can make this world seem right. Only you can make the darkness bright. ♫♫*

—*Yes, that's it. It's a great song. The Platters.*

—*♫♫ Only you can make this change in me. For it's true, you are my destiny. ♫♫*

—*You're cheating.*

—*Why do you say that?*

—*You're not old enough to know that song. You googled it.*

—*Danny! I told you a thousand times. I like older men and older songs.*

—*Sorry.*

—*And I am a good singer, too.*

—*It seems like so many Filipinas sing very well.*

—*Yes, and I will sing for you alone. Would you like that?*

—♫♫ *Only me?* ♫♫

—*ROTFL*

—*Sure I would.*

—*So when are you coming over to see me?*

—*That's what I wanted to tell you. I have some big news.*

15

A TEAM SISLER PRODUCTION

AS SOON AS Aziza heard the voice coming through on its unsteady signal, she knew it was Roxy and that Roxy was back in Beirut. It meant something was up, that there was about to be an event in her life; a good one, probably; a bad one, maybe. But after all these years of slogging through by keeping her chin up, something, any damn thing, would be an improvement, thank you very much.

At the very least it included lunch, so to heighten the sense of occasion she drove out to the new Vero Moda in Achrafieh and bought herself a long, pleaty, gaia dress in a sort of purple stained-glass pattern, almost a tie-dyed look, that reminded her of that one grand, freewheeling year when she and Clark and the Sislers and her mom had formed a cobbled-together family. She topped her new dress with a white denim bolero jacket that didn't fit at all with the style but sure did look fine on her. She stopped by Lubna's to have her hair done, not, of course, in that lush tropical forest of a style that Clark had enjoyed getting tangled around his fingers thirty years earlier, but in a style not as short and practical as truly modern and mature Beiruti ladies are expected to wear. Her hair just touched her shoulders, draping her face closely as a foreshadowing of the way her dress cupped her breasts, and then her hips, in recapitulated arcs. She moved with unstudied composure these days, and why not? Her artistic mother used to joke that Aziza was her finest work.

She sat at her mirror and added a few more dabs of color, then a set of Indian gold ear chains. She looked at herself and thought, "There. That's about right." Roxy might well turn up in a sweat suit, but she'd be pleased that Aziza had dressed up.

She parked at her spot on the AUB campus, walked down Jeanne d'Arc and turned onto Hamra Street, past news kiosks, shawarma stands, and pizza joints, places where she—with her mind now on Roxy and whatever new development she had in mind, and on their heady days of thirty years earlier, and not at all on the intervening decades of disappointment and war—places where she could rewind the tape and see her young self with young Clark, buying newspapers right here on this square of sidewalk, and sharing them in that pizza shop right over there.

Roxy would meet her at the Alpha-Beta Club—too new for memories of Clark—where Aziza arrived first and decided to take an outdoor table. It was smoky, and breezy, but inside it was stuffy and packed. She told the waiter that her friend would be arriving in a wheelchair. He seemed not to mind, in fact seemed excited, for some reason, and scooted things around to make way.

An Indian man Aziza had never met came around the corner, apparently reconnoitering the territory, and approached her to ask, "Excuse me, madam, but are you Aziza *bint* Micheline?"

"Yes, I am," Aziza said, unable to suppress audible laughter at the man's innocent use of her jokey nickname from years ago.

The man nodded, glanced at the access path the waiter had made, pushed a couple of chairs a few inches further toward the curb, and disappeared around the corner, from where Aziza could not withdraw her attention until Roxy and her wheelchair came into view.

She wasn't wearing a sweat suit, but jeans, Velcro-strap sandals, and a colorful t-shirt that looked oddly familiar. The waiter hustled over and offered to take over from the Indian man, who reluctantly looked at Roxy and received her nodded agreement.

"It would be my honor to deliver you," said the waiter. "My mother is also confined, from a missile during the last Israeli attack. I tell her she should get out and live her life, but she only stays in her room. I will tell her of your visit and encourage her."

"You can give me your address and I'll come over and encourage her myself. Us old crippled biddies have to stick together, don't we sugar?" The *sugar* was addressed to Aziza, who had walked up to greet her. "And people I want you to just look here at this gorgeous thing! You're still every bit as pretty as one of your mother's pictures!"

"I am so thrilled to see you again." She bent to kiss her on both cheeks.

153

"Your mother taught me how to kiss like that. Can you believe that?" The waiter positioned her carefully, adeptly, at her table. To him she said, "I've known this young lady for over thirty years, and she hasn't aged a day."

He looked down and smiled at Aziza and then at Roxy. He recognized that he was in the presence of a real character.

Aziza corrected her. "Perhaps a day or two . . . or a few thousand."

"Not a one." She leaned forward in mock conspiracy, "And divorce looks good on you. Yes, buddy, it does." Then she indicated the waiter and said, "This gentleman's mother is another victim of our regional madness and she has to ride around in one of these. I'm going to have to light a firecracker under her."

When he left to bring their orders, Roxy told Aziza, "I was so sorry to hear about your mom. You know, she was my bestest, closest friend the whole time we lived in Beirut. I've missed her every single day since we left."

"She felt the same. She was so happy that you went to see her in France, during her last days. In spite of the danger."

"Oh, honey, I was in no danger. I used my Lebanese passport."

"You have a Lebanese passport?"

Roxy winked, clicked her tongue, rubbed her fingers over her thumb. "The reason I was hesitant about going to see her had nothing to do with border controls. I was afraid she didn't want to be seen looking so . . . so sick. She was just a stick woman when I saw her last."

"The cancer ate her up—years and years of Gauloise. Being an artist, she just had to smoke, preferably Gauloise. I joked with her that she had to die for her art."

"She never lost her sense of humor or her zest for life. Or for art."

"Hey—your t-shirt. I knew there was something about it. That's one of *maman*'s paintings, isn't it?" It was a landscape with trees, a little farmhouse beside a stream, a winding road, and cloud-covered mountains in the background. It was stylized and impressionistic, normal enough, only all the colors were wrong: the trees were blue, the sky green, the clouds lavender, the house black, the road silver.

"She gave the original to me during that trip to France, just before she died. I had it printed on this shirt. It came out really well, don't you think? Do you think she'd mind?"

"No, my god no. She'd be pleased it was running around the streets of Beirut."

"In a wheelchair."

"All the better. You're like a moving billboard for *maman*'s art."

"I'm glad you're not offended. Hey, listen, you and I have got some business to attend to." She took an envelope from her purse, bent toward Aziza and said, "Here's the letter I've written to Clark. Read it and tell me what you think."

Dear Darling Clark:

You've probably already received a brochure for our upcoming Unity in Diaspora conference to be held in Beirut about three months hence. It's a very moderate look at how the region can develop, nothing to get anybody's dander up. Some big names have expressed interest in attending. Both Sen. Laverty and V.P. Foreman have committed. Walter reckons the way things stand right now they'll be duking it out for the Democratic nomination. Some business heavyweights will be here, plus the usual assortment of sheikhs and emirs.

The reason I'm having this hand-couriered to you is because I want you to know what none of the others know: Walter is the guy behind the curtain working the machinery. Officially the sponsor is the Lebanese Alliance for Peace, Amity and Prosperity, or LAPAP in the logo, but between you and me and the gatepost, it's a Team Sisler production.

We'd love to see you. DO say you'll come. It's been so long. When was it you came to visit us in Dubai? Three years ago? Four, even?

??? I feel certain that Aziza would love to see you too. I just had lunch with her, and as you might suspect she hasn't changed one iota. She's divorced now—I don't know if you knew—and I'm sure that's a big burden off her shoulders.???

Sit down and write us your acceptance real quick, okay?

Much love,

Roxy (& Walter)

"The part there between those question marks is the part I'm not sure about. I wanted to ask your permission before I sent it."

"It's fine."

"The part about the divorce, too?"

"Sure, no problem."

"You know the reason why I put that in? Well, two reasons?"

"For one thing, I suppose you think I'm an enticement."

"Yes, exactly, and the other is I don't want him bringing Wanda along. Not that I have anything against her. When she and Clark lived here we were just as nice to her as we could be. You and Yousuf were too—if you don't mind me pronouncing his name!"

Aziza gave a short sarcastic laugh. "Yousuf who?"

"Atta girl! It's just for some reason I don't want Wanda here this time."

"You know something, Roxy? For some reason I don't want her here either."

"Perfect!"

"You know something else? I read an article not too long ago that indicated Clark might run for president. Do you know anything about that?"

"There were some supposedly quiet soundings taken in New Hampshire, just a basic name recognition and favorable/unfavorable poll. Then some reporter cottoned on and it came out in the papers. Clark told him that it must have been a private group of supporters, because he didn't know a thing about it—which was the truth right down to his shoe tops because it was a Team Sisler production."

"So how did he do? Is he willing to run? Could he actually win?"

"Sugar!" she said. "That's why me and you have got us some planning to do!"

When the driver dropped Clark off at the Sisler's residence in Beit Mery, Satish was outside the villa's formal walled gardens, in the wide lawn that led from the street to the front gate, directing a crew of groaning teenage boys as they transported large pots of hibiscus from a greenhouse some hundred feet down the mountain. He looked the real pro, with leather-wristed gardening gloves and a long pruner that he used to point out where each pair of boys should position their pot. The overall concept seemed to be that any guests at the villa would reach that first gate through a hibiscus-lined path. The instructions would have come from Walter, who had never liked the idea that the first thing his guests saw upon arrival was a security gate, so he'd had the wall moved back so that a few meters of his garden was on the outside. Clark stood there for a moment, unnoticed in the midst of this workmanlike bustle, and pieced this all together. He could almost hear Walter say, "I want my guests to feel welcome here, and if people outside steal a few flowers, that's their problem."

Finding Satish this way also meant that Clark could enter the villa grounds without ringing and could walk right in on Walter unannounced. He found him sitting alone on the great red-tiled terrace, at a table with a glass of something iced and fruity in it, gazing over the deepening blue of the bay toward the distant hills. He appeared a man at peace with himself.

"Who's this I see lounging in one of my favorite places on earth?"

"Hey, Clark!" Walter stood and walked briskly to greet him.

"You look so good, ol' dude! What do you do to keep fit?"

Walter patted his paunch. "I still manage to keep my weight up. But I have a gym downstairs, and I love roaming these hills."

"Are you back here permanently now? Or is Dubai still in the picture."

"It seems safe here now. But we keep our options open. That's one of the items on our agenda. Mine and yours, I mean."

"Options?"

"Well, I guess that's so, now that you put it that way. I was mainly thinking in terms of where we go next."

"You and Roxy?"

"Me, Roxy, you, and . . . everybody. But first you come over here and get an eye full of the view while I get you a drink. Satish!" he called into the house.

"I saw him outside dealing with flowers."

157

"We don't really have a staff here yet. I'll be right back."

"There's no need . . ."

"No trouble at all. I've got a little liquor cart I haul around with me. Roxy says it'll be my walker pretty soon."

It was like a little welcome gift, these moments alone on the terrace. Perhaps the two most significant moments of his life had occurred right here, leaning against this railing, with the sun glinting off the inlet far below, and the distant mountains in shade. Here he had met Aziza; here they had said their farewell. It turned out not to be the definitive *adieu* they supposed, because after graduation from Georgetown, after basketball and a PhD, he returned to Beirut and to AUB, this time as a professor, and as her colleague in the History Department. If he could add up all the hours he'd spent in her company during that second stint in Beirut, the papers they'd researched together, all the meetings, conferences, the complex discussions in the office, the quieter lunches on their secluded bench in the university park, they might actually have totaled more than all the hours they'd spent together during their one year as lovers, when they were nearly inseparable, but he couldn't compare them, for the latter were lacerated hours, an oozing rash that is scratched for a few ecstatic seconds, only to recoil into tortured hours, because when they closed their books or left their offices, he went home to Wanda, she to Yousuf. During those years they had played chicken with happiness, felt the prick of the needle against their arms, never courageous enough to pierce the skin.

But that first year they danced on this terrace. They were exempt for a while from reality. No, not so much that: they lived in a separate reality, one that made sense. So they danced.

Walter came back wheeling his liquor cart, poured Clark a scotch, a thirty year old Macallan.

"I see you're still doing well."

"Managing to stay out of the poor house, and then some."

"Well, cheers."

"Cheers to you. And welcome back to your second home. Do you still think of this as your second home?"

"Yes, I suppose I do. But I try not to think about it at all."

158

Walter replied, puzzlingly, "We'll see what we can do about that."

"Where's Roxy?"

"She's gone into the city to have lunch with Aziza." Walter watched Clark's face as that word stung him. He kept his gaze steady as he added, "They've been spending a lot of time together since we came back to Beirut. Did Aziza tell you she's divorced now?"

"No, but Roxy did. Can you believe I have heard from Aziza only one time since I left here? And that was to ask my assistance in some governmental red tape concerning her son. I think both of us felt it was safer simply to end all contact. We'd got ourselves into this 'you were the love of my life, the one that got away' mood. It wasn't healthy for our marriages or our careers. So we cut off all communication."

"Yeah, well . . . things evolve."

"We had to stop. She already had a daughter when Wanda and I moved here. Aliya? Have I got that right?"

"Sounds right to me."

"Then while we were here she had a son."

"Amin."

"Yes, Amin. He'd be a young man now."

"Nineteen, maybe twenty."

"Wanda never wanted children. She was afraid they'd ruin her figure."

"She had a good figure, I'll give her that. How is she, by the way?"

"You know Wanda."

"The ideal wife for a congressman, I imagine."

"Absolutely amazing at what she does."

"I've always thought she'd make a great First Lady, that wife of yours."

"She's got style, no denying that."

"Aziza's got style too, but she could never be First Lady."

"Couldn't keep her lip buttoned long enough! You think that was what made me love her so much? The way she could dish it out?"

159

"You two were quite a pair."

"Then she married lots of money. More power to her."

"Her father was nearly bankrupt. That was why. Did you know that?"

"Oh, yes. That part she told me. I married for politics and she married for money."

"What you mean to say is you both married for your fathers. Like I said, you two were quite a pair."

Clark stood, carried his drink over to the terrace railing, and looked straight down into the trees far below. He'd never really thought about suicide, but now knew that if he ever needed to try it, this would be the spot. He finished his drink, wished there had been an ice cube in it so he could dump it out and watch it fall, then on an impulse he let go of his glass. He watched it plummet all the way down, heard a whisper as it passed through the trees, then a barely discernable breaking sound as it hit rock. He thought of Aziza the Flying Nun's coronet, her windborne albatross that had lifted his heart on the wind and soared out to sea. He turned to Walter and said, "I owe you for a glass."

"You couldn't afford it."

"If you invite hillbillies into your home, you better allow for breakage."

"I take your point," Walter said, then the two of them sat in contented silence for a while. Walter recalled that one of the first things he'd learned about Clark was that he didn't need to talk all the time. Micheline was another one, just like that. She could set up her easel there in the corner and paint wordlessly for an entire afternoon, while Clark read a history book. Then Aziza would walk in with her book and the next thing you knew there'd be this almighty uproar over whether it was better to side with Herodotus and celebrate history, or Thucydides and analyze history. Or whether people were drawn to apocalyptic fantasies because history was so hard to understand that they just wanted to make it stop. Then here would come Roxy to tell them that all their blather didn't mean a damn thing if they didn't get up off their tails and act. Micheline would paint all this hubbub and it would come out as soft and congenial as a Renoir summer outing, so inviting and inspirational that you'd wish you had been there, even though you had been there. And you'd wish you were there again, seeing it through new eyes.

Walter let him think a long time, then said, "You know Aziza's mother died a couple of years ago."

"No, but I'm not surprised."

"I was surprised she lasted as long as she did, the way she abused herself."

"Did she ever stop smoking?"

"Ha! At the graveyard she sat up in her casket and asked for one last drag. She spent her last few years in France. Roxy went up to visit her before the end."

"God she was something. She was the quiet spot in the vortex that held the swirl together."

"I think it was Roxy's last visit with her that got us thinking about how we're going to end our days. We've got a whole shitload of money."

"I'd say between that and *not* having a whole shitload of money, you get the nod."

"But we can't go back home. We're still barred from entering the United States." Clark didn't say anything to that. "I reckon what we need is a presidential pardon."

"That should do it. Have you hinted to any president that you'd like to come home?"

"Yes, but no dice. Still, we've got a whole shitload of money." Clark looked at him, as though something had clicked. "Enough to fund an entire presidential campaign out of my foreign holdings alone."

"Personally I'm trying to work out a way I can get *out* of politics."

"To be honest, I never really thought you were cut out for it."

"Really?"

"You had all the skills, don't get me wrong. But you didn't have the drive. I saw you more as the pipe-smoking, corduroy-jacket professor type."

Clark thought of comfortable old Danny Davies, teaching away up there at Marquette, or wherever he was. Danny Davies

161

could wear corduroy and smoke a pipe, but Clark told Walter, "Wanda would set fire to any corduroy jacket I brought home— preferably with me in it."

"Yes, I can see her doing exactly that. Hey, do you remember all those big discussions we used to have on how to fix the mess in this part of the world? You always had ideas about that."

"I remember."

"You used to even teach a class about that, I believe."

"I lead some seminars."

"Aziza traces some of her ancestry back to Palestine."

"As does her husband. Her ex-husband. We did a joint paper on it. But Walter if you're hinting that I let down the side by dropping my grand ideas, you've got to realize that a congressman from Bumfuck, Kentucky, has approximately zero influence over affairs of state."

"Oh, sure. I understand that." Walter stretched way out to pull the liquor cart to him. "You need a fresh glass," he said, then thought to add, "And I do mean a fresh glass." Then on a whim he picked a glass off the cart and heaved it over the railing into the rocks below. "There!"

"I don't think we're nearly drunk enough to act such fools, do you?"

"Maybe not quite yet, but we'll get there." He poured two fresh glasses of the Macallan. "No, you're right. A congressman from Bumfuck is basically a non-entity."

"Well, I wouldn't put . . . "

"Rubber stamp, is more like it."

Clark decided it wasn't worth arguing over whether his mark on the world scene had been tiny, miniscule, or infinitesimal.

"*However,*" Walter continued, "a congressman with great, underused charisma, a fresh take on world affairs, a crack team of politicos, and a whole shitload of money . . . now there's a man who could make a difference."

Clark had actually for a moment forgotten the earlier hint of where this line of conversation was leading, and was as stunned as if it had never occurred to him. "Walter, you're fucking nuts."

"You have solid numbers in New Hampshire as it is."

162

"I knew you were behind that."

"Clark, face up to it: you've got what it takes. You've undersold yourself from the beginning."

"I'm just not interested in . . . "

"Think how Aziza will react. It was her dream too. You discussed it so many times right here where we sit now—a non-theocratic, one-state Palestine, people of all religions free to believe, or not believe. They're all dynamic people, Clark. If they only had peace, prosperity would follow right on its heels. And once the people there have a chance to make a decent living, all these extremists will dry up and blow away like yesterday's newspapers. It could be just as Hannah Arendt sketched it out way back then at our Conference to Change the World. Remember that?"

"Of course I remember that, Walter. That conference changed my life."

"But it didn't change the world. At least not yet. You could fix that. You—and only you—can still make the dream of that conference a reality."

"Walter . . . "

"I'll admit we've all been asleep at the switch, but we're awake now, we're alive to the possibilities."

"You're not listening to me. I don't have the stomach for it."

"You have the vision; you have the skill; you have the talent; you have the opportunity. You can develop the stomach."

"I told you, I don't want in deeper. I want out. I've been doing things that border on the insane, just because I'm so miserable."

"So here's your chance! Get out by being president! That's what they do: they serve their four or eight years, then they're out. Write your memoirs and make a mint."

"Walter . . . "

"And you could pardon us, Clark. A presidential pardon for Roxy and me. Let us back in on our own terms, not some unjust and humiliating admission of tax fraud. With our heads high, as proud Americans. Back home to lie together for eternity under good Texas soil."

"Have you actually thought about the logistics of this? You can't legally fund my campaign."

"Legally, schmegally. I've got a zillion ways. And when you start to be a real player other funding will roll in. And a few hundred million from me will just provide a few insurance runs. You know, a couple of runs in the seventh and eighth innings just to help out the bullpen."

"Both Laverty and Foreman will be at this conference?"

"You bet they will. You can take the measure of them up close before they have any idea you're in the race."

"What did the New Hampshire numbers say?"

"That's my boy! They were eye-popping. A whole state full of Celtics fans can't lead us wrong."

"This should have been my brother Jerry, you know. He would have made such a fine public servant."

"Well, it's you, old son. Let's deal with reality. But I'm sure he'd be your number one supporter. Along with Aziza—if you do this, think how proud she'll be."

"She always called the Palestinians 'my people'. Muslims, Christians, Jews; didn't matter. She said they were all trapped by hocus-pocus and violence."

"But remember—you can't utter a single word during the campaign about your intentions for the Middle East. Until Inauguration Day you're a straight down the middle backer of Israel. Got that? All the polls show that the slightest tilt away from that and your goose is cooked. I recall that you used to be very radical on that subject."

"I still am, inwardly. When I think about it."

"Of course you are. It's the moral choice. And if you have any trouble remembering your positions on the issue, Roxy and I can probably help you with that. We probably remember just what actions you had in mind."

"What do you mean by that?"

"It's just possible we have them written down somewhere. From years ago."

"You made notes on my Middle East position from thirty years ago?"

"More like twenty. From those seminars you led."

"Whose notes are you talking about?"

164

"Your own notes, of course. Hand-written. Israel as she stands now wouldn't exist, that sort of thing. I think we probably saved a copy. I'm sure I can find them for you. If need be."

16

THE MAN WHO WORE HIS DRESS TOO SHORT

A MAN OF my years! Clark had to laugh at himself, lying there watching the morning light begin to penetrate the curtains of his old room in Beit Mery. It was perhaps his favorite part of the day, this quarter-hour between waking and rising, for he always awoke just a little too early and for that had been rewarded all his life with a daily transformation of darkness to light. It was the perfect time for letting his mind run, and this morning, once it occurred to him what subject it had run to, he had to laugh at himself: a man of his years, lately given to dreams of retirement, and who, as of yesterday, should be dreaming of becoming president, was in fact lying there getting nervous about sitting on a park bench with his old college sweetheart.

He certainly wouldn't call it a date—he was such an old coot, he reminded himself, not to mention a married one. But by cracky, as his mom used to say, it sure felt like a date. Sometimes he still missed his mom. She would have approved of Aziza; probably would have adored her, and understood why he did. He let his mind keep slipping sideways—that was the bonus of his lifelong dawn-watch—and it occurred to him that those two women departing his life way too early had left him adrift, altering every subsequent event in his life.

Well, that wasn't quite fair. He couldn't blame it on that. Barbara had lived long into his adulthood, and he himself had been the one to leave Beirut, that first time, without Aziza. She had agreed, and had her own constraints to deal with, let's not forget that. And here you are with at least some long shot's chance to become President of the United States of America. It was Old Joe Hatling who made that possible. Not Aziza the Flying Nun.

All through the morning session of the conference his mind was mostly on that first meeting, and their lone year as lovers in

Beirut. He barely caught any of the presentations. During the first coffee break a conference steward found him, took him by the arm to inject him into a photo-op which had supposedly been arranged for the two major Democratic contenders, Senator Chris Laverty and former Vice President Stephen Foreman. They were clowning for the camera, poised to punch in classic pre-heavyweight-bout fashion. The steward inserted Clark right between them, introducing him as "one of your fellow legislators," as though the two announced candidates were eager to receive him.

Foreman clearly didn't recognize him at all. Laverty recovered quickly, stuck out a hand, and asked him how he thought the Wizards would fare next season. Clark said they might make the first round, probably not. The three of them had a courtesy photograph, and spoke no further. This was just fine with Clark, for Aziza was to meet him at noon on their old bench at AUB.

It was Clark's first visit to the AUB campus since the destruction of the Lebanese civil war. He signed in at the front gate and saw a new administration building where the old College Hall had been. The nearby arboretum, within whose paths and trails Aziza now waited in the same place where they'd shared so much time in years past, still formed its wild, graceful slope down to Green Field and the new basketball arena. Beyond these, the blue Mediterranean patiently scattered light across another perfect day in Beirut. He walked past the old observatory, over a century old and still standing as tribute to the long collective involvement with the heavens of both eastern and western scientists.

As he wound his way down paths lined by orange trees and myrtle, he met up with an old yellow cat that spotted him, stopped in its tracks, and decided to bound back to where it had come from, thus leading Clark straight to Aziza.

"Hello, beautiful," he said.

She turned and stood to embrace him. "The very first thing I want to say is to thank you again for coming to the rescue of my son."

"Hey, that's what heroes do, right? We ride to the rescue, say 'My pleasure, ma'am,' then ride away."

167

"He's been going through a rough patch lately. I think now he may be turning a corner. Anyway, don't ride away just yet." She held up a white bakery bag. "I have *manakeesh* with mutton and *zatar*. I hope you still like it that way."

"My god—I suppose I do. I haven't had one in years."

She tore off a hunk of the folded pita bread smeared with olive oil, thyme, and bits of chopped mutton. Her hands showed age, but she still cared for them, and her movements were adept. She had put on red nail polish. In handing over his share of the *manakeesh*, she put the calendar back by decades. He had the impression they had shared another snack on this same bench yesterday, last week, forever.

He told her, "You look great, by the way."

She laughed. "You mean I don't look like a woman who struggled through twenty-five years of loveless marriage?"

"Maybe I mean you look like a woman who's finally out of one. Where is Yousuf, anyway?"

"In Saudi Arabia, of course! Where do all Lebanese scoundrels go?"

"Really? Was he under any cloud of suspicion?"

"He came from a wealthy family and held important government posts all his life—so what do you think?"

"Is that why you sent him packing?"

"No. I knew he was out of favor here and was starting to worry, so I suggested Saudi. He liked that idea. Then I suggested he go to Saudi without me, and he liked that even better."

"His loss. But Saudi? Lebanese scoundrels can also go to Brazil or somewhere, can't they? Somewhere with beaches?"

"Don't they have beaches in Saudi Arabia?"

"Not with piña coladas. And bikinis."

"Ah, but you're thinking of the old Yousuf. When Saudi money started pouring into his bank accounts, he suddenly got all pious. Prayers, pilgrimage, the whole nine yards."

He nibbled on his piece of the *manakeesh*, tried to picture the young *bon vivant* as a middle aged mullah. "I can't quite imagine that."

She laughed. "It was pretty grotesque."

They let it rest there. After a moment Clark said, "Damn, this hits the spot. Can I have another bite?"

She tore off another piece for him. "Don't get too full—I'm taking you out for the best *kibbeh* in Beirut."

He ate silently for a while, just taking it all in. Below them he watched, in the stand of pines, two palm doves flying alternately between one tree and another. Above them the voices of students picked up volume, indicating the end of a class period. Beside him the yellow cat decided he was all right after all. It accepted a bit of bread from his hand.

Aziza asked him, "How long will you be in town?"

"Just two more days after this. Then I have to pop down to Israel for a commercial contact."

"You're a businessman too?"

"Not at all. I'm just a poor, honest congressman. It's for some workers in my district."

"Where will you stay?"

"At the Hotel Galilee in Tiberias. Just for a couple of nights. Then back to D.C."

"I don't suppose I can tag along." They both laughed at the idea of her visiting Israel, but the laughter ended when she added, "You're here for such a short time."

"How about this—I'll blow off the afternoon session and we can spend the rest of the day together."

"Won't that be difficult for you?"

"Not a bit. To be frank, I think my task here has already been accomplished. I hadn't been in the hall much more than an hour when somebody thrust me between the two leading presidential candidates and in front of a camera. And ten minutes after that a man with a laptop approached me asking for the email address of Luke Orniss, my communications director. So right about now Luke is waking up in Washington and soon every media outlet he can think of will have that photo. That's what this is all about: posing."

"It seems a lot of trouble and expense just for a photo-op."

"You still see the Sislers, right? You were out with Roxy yesterday."

169

"We shopped like maniacs."

"Did she tell you they want to make me president?"

"Mostly we were hatching plans to break up your marriage." She scooted close to him and laid her head on his shoulder.

He put his arm around her and said, "Done!"

"Excellent. Let's go house hunting."

"Here or in France? I've got my checkbook in my pocket."

She sat up and looked at him. "You remember that, do you?"

"Your dream of retiring in some little French farmhouse and growing carnations? Of course I remember."

"Not a dream. A plan. My mother's country. My mother country. Voltaire's country. The country that went from the center of holy war to the center of the Enlightenment in five hundred years."

"God I'm relieved to hear you say that. My biggest fear was that you'd gone native."

"You mean gone religious in my old age?"

"I certainly did not say that."

"Of course you didn't. Congressman. Though fair enough. It happens. But not to this sister, pal."

"As Roxy would say."

"Yes! I admire her so much. Her and *maman*."

"What a pair. Roxy the Lip and your quiet mother."

"Friends to the end."

He didn't answer what he was thinking. He looked down the hillside to check on those two palm doves, but they were nowhere to be seen. Perhaps they had settled their differences somehow.

Aziza gave him a moment before saying, "Go ahead and ask me the question that you're thinking."

"Not a question. Only that you and I will be friends to the end, too."

"You're wondering why I pretended to be a believer all these years. Why even my own children don't know me as well as you do."

"I wasn't wondering about that at all."

"But look, even you still go to church. I often go online to read your local newspaper. I see you coming from the church."

"I wasn't thinking anything! Do you want me to say we're both hypocrites?"

"Yes!"

"Okay! We're both hypocrites! So there."

Once again Aziza put her head against him, right on his chest, her ear nearly over his heart. She put an arm around his stomach and held him gently. "See there? Don't you feel better letting it all out?"

"You're completely nuts, you know that?"

"You know what Freud said."

"Stay away from Lebanese women with black hair and blue eyes?"

"He said that by rewriting human trauma as fantasy, we make it more bearable."

Clark had expected the place with the best *kibbeh* in Beirut to be a little swankier than this, but was pleasantly surprised by the noisy, congenial crowd, the scurrying waiters, the hubbub of serious cooking over flaring grills, where the cooks dripped sweat just as the meats dripped oil, all amid the smell of garlic, mint, frying onions and charcoal smoke.

They enjoyed an unhurried lunch, paying no attention at all to the scrum of patrons near the door waiting for any place to sit. She ordered both the deep-fried *kibbeh* and the baked version, along with one minty yogurt sauce, and one heavier on the garlic. They tried to nibble away slowly. Clark's biggest fear was that he would stuff himself before they'd said anywhere near as much as they needed to talk about.

She told him that Yousuf had been a distant father to both their children, but that Aliya, who had been a toddler when Clark taught at AUB, seemed to have made it through just fine. She was already a qualified pharmacist and was to be married in a few months. Amin, who had been born while Clark was there, seemed to have suffered more from the withdrawal of his father. He had gone through a playboy phase, then a pious one. Now, at last, it seemed he was changing again. She tried to be optimistic—the change from the scruffy Taliban look had to be an improvement, but if it meant he was now running drugs to the southern border, maybe not much of one.

Clark told her he was tired of politics, had never really taken it to heart. Almost every action he took seemed designed merely to get him elected once again in order to . . . well, in order to get re-elected for yet more terms. He told Aziza what he'd often told himself, that if his mom had outlived his father, or if his father hadn't been living with him and Wanda in Georgetown when dementia hit, he never would have considered running. He was perfectly content to teach history at Georgetown. It was mostly out of pity for Old Joe, who even while still serving in Congress could feel his grip on reality slipping away, and who, in the privacy of their P Street home, would weep bitterly and beg Clark, "Don't make me run again. Not like this. Please don't make me run." It seemed that one of life's aspects that Alzheimer's kept hidden from Joe was the concept of surrender, of resigning for reasons of health, or even simply announcing his retirement. The only end-game he could consider was passing his legacy on to Clark.

She asked him, "Once you took the step and were elected, why didn't you do more for the Palestinians? I kept waiting for a public statement or something when you would label what happened there ethnic cleansing. When the U.S. came to the defense of the Muslims in Kosovo against the Christian Serbs, I thought, Now! Now Clark will tell America that what they're defending in Kosovo is exactly what they should be defending in Palestine. Did you forget that my father was Palestinian? Did you forget about us?"

He tried to explain to her that it all went back to getting re-elected. He had started to lay out the numbers for her, just as Old Joe had done for him years ago, when her cell phone rang and, without explaining why, she said, "Let's get out of here. I need to take care of something." She tapped the table sharply—he couldn't remember her ever doing that—and as he was reaching for his wallet she pulled from her pocket some lira notes she'd kept ready there, and said, "This one's on me, toots."

The crowd had cleared out by now, so getting out the door and onto the street wasn't like trying to sack an NFL quarterback.

In spite of her sudden departure, though, once on the street she tarried, looking around as though she couldn't recall where she'd parked, then excused herself, saying, "You wait here a minute. I think I'd better go back in and use the restroom while we're here."

That left Clark standing alone on the street for a while. Not that that was an imposition. He was thrilled to pass the time watching Beirut happen all around him, waiting, for the first time in years, for the woman he'd loved more than any other.

The afternoon was warmer now that some clouds had moved in to trap the humidity, but still it merely supplied a softness to the air. A breeze was kicking up loose papers from the street. The owner of the news kiosk across the way was using clothespins to secure his newspapers in their racks. Near him a man reading a sports magazine while leaning against, or perhaps concealing himself behind, a corner of the kiosk, kept looking toward the restaurant, toward where Clark was standing. The man was wearing a solid black skullcap, the *taqiyeh*, and a white *dishdasha*, the robe-like garment style still common among Gulf Arabs, but by now rarely used as streetwear in Lebanon. His shortened *dishdasha* reached only to his ankles, indicating he was a very pious Muslim. He glanced back and forth between his magazine and the door of the restaurant. Clark pretended not to watch him as he pretended not to watch Clark.

Then a man approached him from up the street, in the direction he'd totally ignored while watching the kiosk.

"Well, hello again." It was Senator Laverty. He seemed to have just stepped out of a car, probably the black Mercedes that was just then drawing away.

"Twice in one day," Clark said. "What an honor."

"Are you here for lunch?"

"Just finished. Best *kibbeh* in Beirut, or so I was told."

"Who told you?"

It seemed an odd question, one he certainly couldn't answer honestly. In fact he suddenly realized that he needed to get the hell away from there before Aziza came out. "Oh, some website. It is delicious, too."

"What is a *kibbeh*, anyway?"

173

"Sort of a fried meatball, I guess. Well, I'd better be off. Enjoy."

He walked a good ten paces up the street, then turned around. If Laverty had still been standing there staring after him, Clark would have given him a hearty goodbye wave, and moved on. But Laverty had disappeared, presumably to sample the best *kibbeh* in Beirut. But what Clark did see as he turned to retrace his steps was the magazine reader in his old fashioned *taqiyeh* and *dishdasha*, crossing the sidewalk and entering the restaurant.

He waited a few more minutes for Aziza. He'd forgotten that she was the slowest restroom woman in the world. When she finally emerged, closing her purse, she was freshly combed, lipsticked and perfumed.

"I'm sorry for the delay. The place was full. And you know women and their toiletries."

"I've waited how long for you? Thirty years? What's another five minutes? Hey, you won't believe how close we came to blowing our cover. Guess who I just saw going into the restaurant."

"No idea."

"Chris Laverty! The guy I had my picture taken with this morning. The senator running for president."

"Was he following you?"

"No, just here for a meal. If you'd come out two minutes sooner he'd have caught us red-handed."

"Then it's just as well I needed to reapply my face."

"Your face is just fine."

"You're just saying that because I bought lunch."

She took his arm, just as in the old days. He loved that she did that. It seemed so European, so Old World. It implied a link, an interdependence. Why didn't American women do that more often? Maybe he could sponsor legislation requiring it during walks of over, say, five minutes' duration. If the Senate balked, he could offer a compromise of ten.

That's what he was thinking—the frivolity of the immediate. Aziza had deeper worries, and said, "You know, I think Amin would benefit from spending some time with you. Could you possibly invite him to the conference? Do you think you could get him in?"

17

NOW IT'S ISTANBUL, NOT CONSTANTINOPLE

AMIN HAD ONE last bit of preparation to finish before he reached the conference hall. He stopped at a café on Kennedy Street, unfolded a small Arabic note he'd been carrying in his pocket and began to translate it into English. *You are sinners against God and humanity. I claim as my right to strike at your heart as long as you hold my people in bondage. The crimes of America must be cleansed with blood.* He needed to memorize these words, the last words of a courageous warrior. He would quote them to his mother's powerful lover, watch the blood drain from his face.

Clark was watching from the lobby of the conference hall as Amin made it through the x-ray gates and past the security guards. He noticed that the young man's gaze swept the room, paused for an instant when it reached him, and moved on. Perhaps he didn't want to single out Clark for his height, or he wanted Clark to be the one to initiate the greeting. Maybe he wanted to leave Clark an opening to back out of this assignment, or simply hoped he would.

Clark put out his hand. "I'd recognize you anywhere. You look so much like your mother. You've got her eyes, precisely hers."

"A lot of Levantine Arabs have blue eyes."

"And none finer than yours. I've heard it descends from Tamerlane."

"What does?"

"This region's blue eyed gene." Clark hoped he had covered his misstep.

"I think that's a myth."

"Probably. But it's a good one."

Amin didn't smile, didn't meet his eyes. He surveyed the lobby and the long breakfast buffet set up there.

"Are you hungry? There are several kinds of juices and pastries here. All free for the taking."

"I've eaten already. What's the next speech about?"

"Not really a speech, I think. Three economists are going to talk about ways that Israeli-Palestinian cooperation could aid development."

"Development for who?"

Clark raised his eyebrows. "I don't know. Maybe everybody. I guess we'll find out."

During the hour-long session Amin hardly spoke. Clark wondered if he was always this quiet. Afterwards, as they approached the lobby, walking into the aroma of fresh coffee and a vanilla air freshener, Clark asked him, "So what did you think?"

"It all sounds just cozy, but you people forget—it was our land. They stole it from us."

"They took it from you by armed force. Not from you personally, of course."

"I was born here. You know that."

"Indeed I do. I held you in my arms when you were just a few days old." Amin looked away. Clark saw that he'd embarrassed him. "You were a damn fine looking kid, I'll have to say that. You had your father's wide jaw."

"You knew my father?"

"Oh yes. My wife and I often socialized with your parents. And with the Sislers. Remember them?"

"What was my dad like back then?"

"A lot of fun, really good story teller. Very athletic. We often shot hoops together. He was ambitious, of course—had to be in order to move up in the government. Had way more money than I ever did, and was very generous with it. He helped me buy a car—said it had been confiscated for road violations or something, but I'm sure he just bought it for me. Always saw to it that Wanda—that's my wife—got jewelry for her birthday or Christmas."

"My dad celebrated Christmas?"

"I don't know that he celebrated it. He gave gifts, though. Nice ones. This was in the days when I was giving hankies."

"He would never do that now."

176

"Do what?"

"Celebrate Christmas."

"Oh, I don't know why he shouldn't. It's a multi-cultural society."

"Not Saudi Arabia."

"There are thousands of Christians living there. Imported employees. Hindus, even, and Buddhists."

"No Jews, though."

"Don't be so sure. Maybe in *taqiyya*."

"You know *taqiyya?*"

"These days everybody knows everything about Islam. It just means denying your real religion in order to protect yourself."

"And Jews do that in Saudi?"

"I have no idea, but why not? Wouldn't you? Say you needed a job, got a good offer, but *oops*, it's in Saudi, and oops, you're a Jew. So, on the form where it asks your religion, your pen just has a little *taqiyya* moment and writes 'Christian.'"

Amin stopped, squared up, and looked up at him. Suddenly he realized that Clark reminded him of somebody—the bastard Levi! He wondered if the right thing to do was to walk away from him right now, or linger a while, learn more about the enemy in all his transmutations. "Can they do that?" he asked.

"I don't know. I'm just guessing somebody has. They can't send an agent out to track every applicant for every job, follow him to the synagogue. It's just a little white *taqiyya*. It's a human thing, not a Muslim thing. Don't be stingy with your *taqiyya*, my boy!"

It was the first time he'd seen Amin smile, and it was a good one. "I'll bet you knock the girls dead with that smile." It immediately disappeared.

"My mom says you're running for president."

"It's a distant possibility. Very distant. And still a secret. I'm in deep *taqiyya*."

Amin didn't laugh. "So why are you telling me?"

"Good! Do you realize what you've just done? You stepped outside the text of our conversation to look at the context."

Amin just looked at him as if to say, *Your point?*

"It's the first step to being a historian, that's all. Your mom said

177

you were bright."

"She did? I'm sure it was followed by a *but*. Bright but self-centered. Bright but misguided. Bright but bitter."

"Bright but searching, I think was the exact quote."

"So what's the answer?"

"I think I've forgotten the question."

"Why are you telling me this?"

"Oh. Yes. Very good question. Maybe it's because being back here brings out the teacher in me. Teachers prod students into asking questions. I think that's been our main job since at least Socrates. I loved being a teacher, and I think I was a good one. I am, at best, a mediocre congressman."

"So why did you switch?"

"Like most major shifts in history, or in life, it had a couple of causes. My wife thought her great calling was to be a Washington socialite. Certainly not to host teas in Kentucky or—god forbid—in Beirut. My mom had died, and my father was becoming overtaxed by his job. It turned out he had entered the first days of Alzheimer's, but at the time he decided to retire he just called it overwork. He always had this dream that I would take over his seat in Congress. My younger brother had the makings of a fine representative, but he was killed in Vietnam, so I guess I had greatness thrust upon me."

Amin nodded. Apparently he knew the quote.

"So if you're not a good congressman why do you want to be president?"

"For one thing, it'll get me out of Congress." Clark waited vainly for a chuckle, upped the ante with, "And it'll all be over in four years." Still no reaction. "Or maybe even less, if I get impeached." Goddamn, he thought. I guess a sense of humor isn't transmitted by the female chromosome. "See, that way I can go back to teaching and my ex-first lady wife can't grumble."

"Why do you think," Amin asked solemnly, "that you won't be reelected?"

"Oh, I was just making a joke."

"I know that, but there seemed to be something serious behind it."

178

Caught off guard, Clark wondered if he should level with this kid. While considering all the consequences, he breathed deeply through his nostrils, exhaled through rounded lips. It was how he'd been taught to prepare for a free throw. "Can I trust you to keep quiet about something?"

"Sure."

"Your mom said you were trustworthy."

"She did?"

"Yep." In truth, no, she hadn't, but Clark's teacher's instincts now told him to raise the bar on expectations. It might do the kid some good. Even if Amin went straight to the press with this, Luke Orniss would have it thoroughly denied and discredited within minutes. In any case, AIPAC knew his voting record.

"I can't believe she thinks that."

"Sometimes parents see things in their kids that the kids themselves don't even know."

"Did that happen with you?"

"I don't have any children?"

"I mean from your parents."

"Oh yeah, from my mom. All the time. Mind you, my father mistook me for Honest Abe Lincoln, but let's not talk about that."

"Okay, tell me your secret."

"Promise to keep it between us?"

"Sure. My mom was right, in this case. I keep all kinds of secrets."

"Fine. Then I'll level with you. I plan on being a pro-Palestinian president."

Amin looked at him like he was waiting for the big revelation. When nothing else came forth, he said, "That's it?"

"That's it. And dude—may I call you dude? That's plenty, dude. That's a political bombshell you just heard."

"Doesn't sound like so much to me. Every candidate should be pro-Palestinian. We were driven from our homes."

"Here's why every candidate isn't pro-Palestinian. It's a swing of at least thirty million votes. At least. Right now the polls show the Democrats and Republicans about dead even. The biggest loser in history was George McGovern in 1972. He lost by almost

179

twenty million. If I actually got the nomination, and word of what I'll try to do to Israel gets out, I'll be by far the biggest loser in history. Simple as that."

"And you tell me this because my mom says it's okay?"

"It sounds suicidal. Okay, forget I said it."

"No, seriously."

"Seriously, then. You won't say anything because we're on the same side. You want the Israelis out of their so-called settlements. So do I. You want the wall and those checkpoints to come down, and so do I. I'm going to bring as much pressure to bear as I can to make that happen."

"Maybe you can't do enough."

"Look, if I could roll the calendar back to 1945, and make myself Emperor of the World, I'd set up a Jewish homeland in Germany. Just like that. I'd say guys, you tried to kill them all, you lost the war, tough luck, you just lost Bavaria. But it's way too late for that, and even the U.S. President isn't Emperor of the World. But I'll do what I can."

"Have you talked this over with my mom?"

"We talked it over for years. And years. We go way back."

"And she's willing to share our land?"

"She knows you have to make compromises with history. Much of Palestine was taken by force of arms, but that's the usual case, and all the conquered peoples around the world can't be put back where they came from."

"It was ours. We should get it all back."

"Will you give back Istanbul?"

"What does that..."

"For more than a thousand years it was Constantinople, the greatest Christian city on earth, and the holiest site of the Orthodox Church, until the Turks finally took it in 1453. As recently as 1916 the Russian Czar listed the return of Constantinople to Christendom as a war aim. Let's say Christians today demand it back. If you were the Turkish president, would you hand it back?"

"Of course not. It's been Istanbul for centuries. And anyway, nobody cares any more."

"Now you're thinking like an Israeli. They figure if they hold out long enough, eventually the clamor will die away."

"Not as long as I'm alive. They stole my land."

"You don't mean your personal land."

"I do."

"No, Amin. Your ancestral land was sold to create a kibbutz."

Amin squared up at him again, this time with threatening eyes. "What are you saying?"

"Didn't your parents tell you?"

"It's a lie."

"Not at all. You didn't know?"

Amin held his fists down at his side, but clinched. His face was pinched and red. He was ready to fight over this. "I say it's a lie." He was nearly shouting. A security guard moved toward them.

Clark looked the guard away. "Let's take a walk. It's a lovely day. Let's walk along the Corniche and I'll tell you what I know."

As they entered the warm sunshine Clark removed his jacket and slung it over his shoulder, then felt the stiff wind through his shirt and put it back on. This was the Beirut he remembered, his Beirut, walking with Aziza next to the seawall, looking down onto the boulders below, and the churning surf smashing against them. "Listen bud, I'm sorry to just up and break this to you this way. I assumed your parents had told you your family history. I didn't mean to destroy any illusions, but the fact is your mom and I researched the whole issue of how much land was sold to the Zionists and how much they took by force. We did a big paper on it. You can read it for yourself if you want. I suppose it's still available in the AUB library. We went through the Turkish archives, deed by deed. The record is incomplete, but we did find the record of the title shift for your grandfather's land. Actually it would be your great-grandfather, early in the century. I can't remember the exact numbers, but it was a nice-sized farm, maybe a thousand dunams, and it brought him a small fortune, for that era."

"You say he sold out?"

"I'm sure it didn't mean that to him. It was a simple business transaction. A lot of well-to-do landholders were selling. The Rothschilds donated a lot of money to buy land for Jews fleeing Russia and Eastern Europe; even French Jews were leaving during the Dreyfus affair. I'm sure your great-grandfather just saw this huge offer for his property and it made good sense. It was all Ottoman territory, and he lived in Beirut anyway. His land in Palestine was just a holding, a farm that brought in revenue. I can't believe Aziza didn't tell you all this. This is important stuff."

Amin sat on a bench and squinted into the wind and the spray. The wind whipped the caps of waves. "Why would God let all this happen?"

"I wouldn't look at it that way. God's not a part of it. To me, it's just like my home in Kentucky. It sits there empty, except when Congress is in recess. I suppose I'll sell it when I retire from politics. If somebody offered me big bucks for it, I'd sell it right now."

"But they drove us out."

"Some they bought, some they drove. Your mom's grandfather never had any land. He was a serf. Before Jewish immigration started, serfs stayed with the land when it changed owners, but now they had to leave, because the new Jewish owners brought in Jewish laborers from the Eastern Europe. They were poor and homeless too. It was a nasty situation. When I was a boy, thousands of coal miners were driven out of Kentucky when the mine owners replaced them with machines. It was nothing personal. The machines worked cheaper."

"It's not the same at all."

"How is it different?"

"God brought the Prophet Mohammad, peace be upon him, to Jerusalem on a winged horse."

"A *buraq*."

"Again you know. Then you know that to Muslims, Jerusalem is a sacred place."

"Only since Saladin. He escalated it to holy status to build morale in the fight against the Crusaders."

"You lie. And no more *taqiyya* jokes."

"Hadn't even occurred to me. Ask your mom. I read it in her book."

"It was all the work of Satan."

"What was?"

"The seizure of my homeland."

"You need to be careful about crediting Satan. If you believe that Satan has power to do evil, then you believe in two gods."

"I don't see where you get . . . "

"Moreover, if Satan can do evil that God disapproves of, then Satan is more powerful than God. And if Satan can do only evil that God approves of, then you have a God that approves of evil."

I knew it, Amin thought. Another *mulhad*, just like the bastard Levi. To be a pious man in this age is to be confronted on every corner. "The *jihad* will sort out the truth from the lies."

"*Jihad* is the work of men, not gods. And I can prove it."

"How?" he asked, thinking, Go ahead and seal your stinking fate.

"Gods don't outlive their believers. Think of Zeus. He ruled this whole area for hundreds of years. Who's scared of him now? Then Jupiter took over. Seen any Jupiter Jihads lately?"

Amin laughed. Jupiter Jihads. This guy thinks history has all the answers. Let the *mulhad* Hatling discuss history with the *mulhad* Levi, in hell, while they watch their flesh liquefy.

"Okay, Professor History, let me test you on this one." He took the small piece of notepaper from his pocket and unfolded it. "I'll read you a quote, you tell me who said it. *You are sinners against God and humanity. I claim as my right to strike at your heart as long as you hold my people in bondage. The crimes of America must be cleansed with blood.*" He watched Clark's face, which glowed with relief.

"Oh, good one! A historian in the making, and you even did your homework for today's class. I love it! I'm proud to have lifted you from your bassinette. Maybe something rubbed off."

"Well?" Amin tried to keep his gaze steady as he accommodated two surprises: the *mulhad's* complete transformation of this obvious threat into some kind of game; the sensation of strong, warm arms around him.

"Is this a trick question?"

"Maybe."

"Where did you run across the quote?"

"Doesn't matter.

"Can we assume it's not the obvious?"

183

"Maybe."

"You're the cagey one. Can we specify that it's not a modern quote? Not a 9/11 message or the like?"

"Okay."

"Could it actually have been an American who said it?"

"This isn't Twenty Questions."

"No, it's more like Four-or-Five Questions. I'm going to guess . . . it sounds to me like John Brown's statement to the court as he was sentenced to hang for leading a group of slaves and abolitionists in a raid on a U.S. arsenal in Virginia. In 1859. How's that?"

"Correct. And how were America's sins cleansed?"

"With the blood of over half a million men."

"Exactly."

Clark didn't respond to that. He sat there thinking about how it must feel to actually be president and send young men to their death. Did he really have the stomach to apply for Lincoln's old job? And here he sat in a city cleansed in the blood of another civil war. A city he'd once loved, where he'd loved the spirited mother of this solemn young man.

"It's getting cold," Clark said. "How about we head back?"

So they walked alongside the windy sea, back to the hotel, through the x-ray screening gates and into the conference hall, where with some pride he introduced Amin to both Steve Foreman and Chris Laverty as, "a young man I've known since the day he was born."

18

USING HIS REAL name, Clark checked into the Hotel Galilee in the early afternoon, only to find the cameras already in place to record his big entrance. A small man wearing a sea-green silk suit, his hair in lovely wood-shavings of blond curls, came almost dancing out to meet him. He wouldn't have made a bad-looking woman, for proponents of a cocker-spaniel styled femininity, but as a man he looked more like a clown. In a thick Slavic accent he introduced himself as—Clark immediately forgot the name—a new Jewish immigrant from Russia, and the new owner of the Hotel Galilee. As the film rolled and the cameras flashed, he thanked Clark for being the first dignitary "to enjoy my hospitality" since his purchase of the hotel.

Clark fell back on, "Always happy to help," rather than, "Better thank my secretary."

The surprise formalities ended as abruptly as they'd begun, and he registered in good time for his meeting with the trade committee, leaving plenty of time to phone Mara and ask her to meet him for dinner somewhere. He hadn't quite worked out what to do about tonight. He might need a different hotel for her. He needed the Hotel Galilee as a shield and an office—the meeting with a small group from the Tverya Trade Commission might have accomplished some actual public good. One of the few non-coal industries in Kentucky Five was an old soap-making firm that had been near failure until someone had the idea of recreating it as a factory specializing in toiletries for the hotel industry. They sent it out in customized orders: shampoo, body gel, shower caps, any combination the customer wanted, all embossed with the hotel name and logo.

Actually it had been a pet project of Old Joe, who addressed the entire workforce at a picnic at the Floyd County Kiwanis club with the stirring words, "Every time I shampoo my hair in any hotel in the world, from Prestonsburg to Johannesburg, I don't care if it's apple scented or flower scented or what, the aroma I want is the sweet, sweet smell of success of each and every one of you." Old Joe could really lay it on thick, and Clark was diligent enough to carry on the crusade, at least by leaving company brochures with various hotel managers.

This time it was a brilliant idea, an Old Joe-worthy idea: tomorrow's Kentucky newspapers would report that Congressman Hatling was circling the globe in search of markets for Kentucky-made products. The feature photo would be of Israeli businessmen, smiling, lined up beside him, the magnificent Sea of Galilee in the background. Most of his constituents had never heard of Tiberias, certainly not of Tverya, had no idea that it was a bustling tourist town with dozens of hotels needing thousands of miniature bottles of shampoo each year. But every man, woman and toddler among them knew the Sea of Galilee. And come tomorrow morning they would be reminded that their gifted native son Clark Hatling, their modest champion who was always one step ahead of the competition, not only knew the Sea of Galilee as they did, and made pilgrimages there for them, but also knew about the insatiable demand for toiletries there, something nobody else knew—preachers didn't even know it!—and created jobs back home just by his knowledge and his gift.

When he handed his camera over to the Ethiopian waiter at the beach café and lined up those businessmen so that the sea dominated the background, it occurred to him that if he really did take up Walter's nutty campaign proposal, this photo might well resonate with voters outside Kentucky Five; all over the south; hell, all over a lot of places. It said it all: good old-time religion, union jobs, and capitalism in action. And Clark Hatling in the middle of it all, a head taller than anybody else.

The voters wouldn't know—didn't ever have to find out—that the tall man in the photo wasn't the good son Clark Hatling, but Danny Davies, the passionate spirit freed from earthly bonds to swoop down on Tiberias and ruin a young woman there. A Christian. A virgin. A caregiver; one who gave care.

Nor would they know—and Clark couldn't be the one to tell

186

them—that, fifty years earlier, half of the population of that same pretty seaside town had been Arab, both Muslims and Christians, and that in 1948 the Jewish militia Haganah had depopulated Tabariya, as the Arabs had called it, killing many, exiling the rest to squalid tent encampments hundreds of miles from the homes they, their fathers, or their grandfathers, had built with their own hands. Danny Davies could say that, in his classroom in Wisconsin, even show slides of the poor clods, backward, defeated and shamed, weighed down by the tied-up scraps of their old lives as they wept and trudged through miles of desolation to they knew not where. Danny Davies could do that. He didn't give a shit. But Clark Hatling had to smile, sell soap and pretend to walk on water.

After he'd emailed the photo to Luke, Clark phoned Mara and found himself suddenly agitated by two short, consecutive utterances, both of which he should have been prepared for. The first one was the oddness of his own voice as he said, "Hi. This is Danny Davies." It didn't feel as comfortable or liberating as it should have. In fact it sounded audibly fraudulent. He wouldn't have been surprised if Mara and the switchboard lady and anyone else within earshot had shouted, "Liar!" The second shock followed immediately, when Mara said, "Great to hear your voice at last. This is Mara." He had known, of course, that she would have an accent, and he distantly remembered what a Filipino accent sounded like, but during all their online chats he'd never heard it in his head. Suddenly he was this strange man speaking with this strange woman. Already, five seconds into this new phase of their relationship, a shift had occurred. At the time, the immediacy of the conversation was too great for him to understand why, but later he would know it went back to a bench in Beirut, one that had endured war, marriages, decades and distances. His alter ego was no longer Danny Davies, satyr and lying historian. It was young Clark Hatling, lover of Aziza *bint* Micheline, and honest student of history.

Mara said she could probably get away but he needed to come and get her, so he took a taxi up into the hills overlooking the sea, past vineyards and olive groves that might have been standing when Jesus walked these hills, and past bright, modern orchards of apple, peach, cherry, and pear. Potato fields, fields of tomatoes starting to ripen; lush, low vines of cucumber and melons. They drove past floral fields where Asian workers were cutting roses and lilies, with refrigerated transport trucks standing by. He wished he had a bouquet to give to Mara, but he hadn't thought of it in time.

They found the entrance to the villa, a blue gate in a solid white wall. He asked the driver to wait for him, and rang the bell. Mara wasn't the first to greet him. With some difficulty an old man in a wheelchair opened the gate and then wheeled himself back out of the way. He gave this tall man standing before him a good, long glare before saying, "Mr. Davies, I am Mordechaj Warski. Welcome to my home. Pay the man and send him away. You won't be needing a taxi for some time."

He complied, then entered a garden of citrus trees and flowering shrubs, all in full display, but Clark walked nervously past all that up to a wide porch where Mara had emerged from a chair partially hidden by bougainvillea. She looked up at him but quickly looked away, smiled warily at the old man and then at her feet. Clark hardly recognized her. Her hair was a little longer now than in her photos. She'd brushed it back, showing her small ears and hanging gold earrings. She wore no other jewelry, not even a watch. She'd chosen a carefree sundress for the occasion. Its cherry-blossom optimism was reinforced by her pale pink fingernails, and short-heeled suede sandals that showed off the stave of tendons running down her feet. Her skin had a beach-tanned shine, but there was no contour in its shading.

On a little patio table lay a box wrapped in white paper and tied with a green ribbon and bow. He felt naked, an empty-handed fraud. Tomorrow he would take her shopping. He would explain that he preferred it that way, so she could choose something according to her taste. Anyway he didn't know her size. That would work just fine to counter her feeling like a prostitute being paid after a night of sex.

She managed to step both gracefully and hesitantly from the veranda. She looked very young, criminally young. She'd told him she was twenty-five; probably it was true. He had no reason to doubt it. But she looked like a high school junior, a cheerleader,

188

circa 1965. It seemed beyond conscience that he would have her in his bed that night.

She walked to him and extended a hand. "I'm very glad to meet you at last." It seemed a line she had prepared for the occasion.

"It gives me a great deal of pleasure." He hadn't prepared anything, but this one of Old Joe's always fit the occasion.

"Mara, Mr. Davies will push my chair. Why don't you run in and pour us some of our fresh nectarine juice. With," he lowered his voice to a whisper, "just a little touch of vodka."

She didn't lift a hand to her mouth to giggle behind, as had the Vietnamese women he'd known, but smiled straight at the old man, gave a nearly silent chuckle, and suggested caution by pursing her lips in the general direction of an upstairs window.

"Who's the man of this house?" Morty demanded as he aimed a quick swat at her backside, but she was way ahead of him, giggling audibly now and slipping the blow by a good foot and a half. In answer to his question she pointed to the upstairs window, but kept moving toward the veranda. Her dress swayed pleasingly as she skipped up the stairs, slipped off her shoes in one motion and disappeared into the house.

Clark missed most of her adroit exit because his attention was on turning Morty without guiding the wheels into the flowers beside the path. He looked up just in time to catch the last sway of her hips and to notice her bare feet padding soundlessly across the tile floor. Morty turned his head as far as he could and said, "You're much too old for her."

While waiting for a response he kept his head cocked over his shoulder. Finally Clark said, "I am aware of that, sir."

The three of them sat at the kitchen table, drinking vodka nectarines and eating sesame cookies, with Morty holding court on Israeli agriculture, on the difficulty of making a profit when workers demanded so much for their labor, on the case for importing Thai workers in place of Palestinians, and on other fine points concerning the care of his orchards, from which this very nectarine juice was a product.

He seemed open to discussing the bus bomb, and the loss of his legs.

189

"Mara tells me you feel no bitterness about that. I really admire your generosity."

"Not at all. I consider it a great victory. Do you want to know why? Because that bomber blew himself up under the certain conviction that, one second after he hit the switch, I would be burning in hell, while he would be watching seventy-two belly-dancing virgins. Imagine his disappointment that I am drinking vodka nectarine in my sunlit kitchen, while he is a pile of ash. And best of all, he was dumped into a Jewish garbage truck."

"You lied to me, Mara. You said he was nice."

"He is also insane. A nice insane, maybe."

"No, *bubeleh*. I am perfectly sane."

"But how can he know he's a pile of ash?

"Maybe he doesn't. You have a point. But I know it. And I know about this." He held up his empty glass. "And I know there will be more of these before I'm a pile of ash."

"And you have your dancing girl upstairs."

"Shhh!" he said, and they both collapsed into the laughter of a private joke.

Morty suggested they tour the orchards. Mara filled a thermos with more vodka nectarine and once again Clark was called on to be the "chauffeur." Morty thought the quip hilarious. "One old guy pushing another down life's dusty road." In reaction Mara looked directly at Clark, their first sustained private understanding. Her unconcealed smile said to ignore Morty and his cheap shots; he's got it all wrong; he knows me well, but not as you do.

They traveled down hardened dirt paths between long, straight rows of trees bearing cherries, apples, apricots, nectarines, and even a few rows of quince.

"This is what I have to show for a lifetime of patient effort, Mr. Davies."

"The fruits of your labor, so to speak."

Morty laughed; Mara didn't. She walked a few paces ahead of them.

"Indeed."

"Not to mention government loans? Grants from the American Jewish Aid Organization? Did you have any help like that?"

"The world has been very generous with us. Especially your country, professor. You know the joke, 'How do you spell 'Zion'?"

"I'm afraid not."

"To do it right, you have to ask me that question."

"Oh. Okay. How do you spell 'Zion'?"

"HHH."

"Why HHH?"

"Hertzl, Hitler and Harry."

"Harry who?" He didn't know where to end his part of the joke.

"Harry Truman."

"Harry Truman?"

"Your State Department was opposed to the partitioning of Palestine. The UN vote was approaching. Truman's old friend and business partner, Eddie Jacobson, convinced Harry to meet our very persuasive Zionist leader, Chaim Weizmann. And since Harry believed that Deuteronomy 1:8 was the law of God, he instructed his UN ambassador to support partition, then muscled dependent countries like Haiti, Liberia, and *bubeleh*'s Philippines to do the same. Did you know all this, professor?"

Mara turned to look back at them. She seemed to disapprove of this 'professor' tactic. It was just Morty being snide.

"Well, yes, some of it. I teach history."

"Another H."

"Ah, yes. Indeed so."

"You know in this part of the world when two men dispute 'Mine is longer than yours,' they mean history. Professor."

From the last row of trees they emerged onto a short ramp leading to a wooden deck, more of a viewing platform, overlooking neighboring farms further down the hillside and the cluster of houses along the shore and beyond, to the deepening blue of the sea. Clark parked Morty, fixed his handbrake, and sat down on a wooden bench nailed to the floor. Mara sat down beside him, her leg nearly but not quite touching his. The sun was low behind them. Soon they would be in shadow watching the late evening sun glint off the smooth surface of the water.

There were a few boats out even now. The fishermen had

191

put in for the day, but some wooden tourist boats glided along, throttled down to a slow drift. On one such boat a Christian group was singing a hymn. The breeze carried their song across the calm waters, and up the sloping hill to the platform. He could make out the tune, could almost put the words to it. Mara, beside him, started to sing along, but not in English. He didn't know whether it was Tagalog or Visayan, but he didn't interrupt to ask. It was none of his business, anyway.

He could remember his mother in church, sitting just like this, next to him but not quite touching, singing this same hymn. Something about throwing a lifeline across dark waves, there is a brother whom someone must save. Something something dare, his peril to share. Somebody's brother, sinking, sinking. He was sure his mother would know the whole thing. Suddenly he wished he had thought to bundle her onto one of those Holy Land tours, watched her reactions as she walked where Jesus had, and brought her to this very spot. He wished that together they had crossed the Israeli barricades into the destitute Palestinian areas, through the massive prison walls into Bethlehem, where surely she would have sided with the dispossessed and poor, those to whom Jesus had given the kingdom of heaven, and damn little else.

She would have been at home on that boat out there, singing her heart out, only at the same time she would have dropped a fishing line into the water and all the while kept a sharp eye on the bobber, hoping for tilapia, or for that delicious catfish she loved so much, grilled in a cornmeal and pecan coating, served with cole slaw, baked beans and hush puppies. That's how she would have seen that boat ride: half hymn, half catfish. Would he have told her that the bad fish—the ones that in Matthew Chapter 13 were separated from the good, right here on these shores, just as in the coming End of Days the wicked would be cast into hell fire, wailing and gnashing their teeth—that those fish were the non-kosher catfish; all that tasty protein, a symbol of the coming fire?

She had believed every word of it, the sinking soul on a storm-tossed sea and the safe harbor that awaited. In her fervor to believe she had dared not analyze any of it, for fear that picking at a single thread would cause the whole fabric to unravel. Would he tell her

192

that her two fine boys had studied it all point by point and didn't believe a word of it?

Mara finished her song and looked up at him for recognition. He could tell she wanted him to take her hand, to somehow be together blessed by it all. But he couldn't. His mother would have been disappointed in him.

As the shade deepened, the temperature dropped. They rolled Morty back into the kitchen where they switched to a lager called Maccabee because Morty had a sudden craving for pizza, and that meant beer. Soon after Mara had put a couple of pizzas in the oven, a shrieking voice from somewhere upstairs seemed to crack the plaster. "What is that stinking up my room!"

Morty sighed and said, "A great number of possible answers come to mind," but he shouted, "It's pizza, Yetta dear."

"Maricel!" Soon there was a clomping of stairs and the echo of approaching footfalls. The kitchen doorway filled with a large silhouette of a woman in a housedress and cotton nightcap. "My stomach will become bloated by the stench of this Italian garbage! Maricel, bring chicken livers and *ratzelech* to my room. Did you prepare the guest room for this man? When you come to bed do so quietly . . . *please!* . . . for with this stomach of mine if I am awakened in the night, I will never get back to sleep and my system will be out of balance for days."

And that was it. She went back to her room and Clark never saw her again.

"Man, oh man," Clark said.

"I met her in Poland during the war. She was a *Waffen-SS* officer disguised as a lovely young Jewish woman. Or was it the reverse?"

They left Mara to get on with her work in the kitchen. Morty directed Clark to a large dining area with a wide view of the sea, now a vast dark space discernable only from the ring of city lights outlining it. Clark eased Morty's chair into its obvious place, the vacant space at the head of the table, then sat at the side where he could enjoy the view. Mara soon followed with a tray of sliced pizza and two fresh Maccabees. She had put a gray apron over her sundress. She placed their food down gently, wordlessly, and went

193

back to prepare the old lady's order.

"She really was my beautiful Yetta, Mr. Davies. It's only the infirmities of age that have made her so . . . *Waffen*. And she loves Mara, in her way. Make no mistake."

He fixed his eyes on Clark. He seemed to want him to declare himself, right here and now, but Clark wasn't biting.

"So it must have been one hell of a journey—your life, I'm referring to."

"Perhaps life is not easy for any thirteen year old boy, Mr. Old-Enough-To-Be-Her-Grandfather, but imagine that same boy's life when the Nazis invade his town, seize his neighborhood, and send him and all his family to a friendly little Polish town called Oświęcim. Do you know of it? You should. It's quite famous."

"Auschwitz. I've been there. Mr. Treats-Her-Like-a-Servant."

"Oh, really? Funny I didn't bump into you. Mara! Bring two beer glasses."

"Sheez, I'll get them." But she met him with the glasses before he reached the kitchen. She smiled at him, and shrugged.

Morty poured their beers and proposed a toast. "Here's to bringing the truth out into the open."

Clark clinked glasses with him; he more or less had to.

"Imagine this scene: It is a frozen winter morning in Poland. All the inhabitants of one vast section of a city, the Jewish section, have been rounded up and driven away from their homes. While they are being processed into either death camps or slave labor camps, their old neighborhood lies nearly deserted. In the lobby of the municipality building there is a long row of desks, each desk manned by an official of the new German city government. In front of the desks are long, and more or less orderly, rows of Christians waiting their turn. Behind the desks are large boards with thousands of nails sticking out. What is the purpose of these nails? To commemorate the crucified Messiah? No. They are for holding sets of keys that will unlock the houses and flats of the expelled Jews now being welcomed into the friendly Polish town of Oświęcim. At the front of the lines of waiting Christians are German-speaking Polish Christians left over from pre-independence days some twenty years earlier. Following them are lower class Polish Christians, hopeful of finding better living quarters than they now had. Not many of the Jews had lived all that well, but perhaps it would be a step up, or perhaps now a son and his wife and child could finally get a place of their own.

"When they reach the desk they present their papers, are assigned an address and given a set of keys. They hurry with great anticipation to their new home, eagerly survey the layout to decide which room will be Papa and Mama's, which little Felka's, which little Boleslaw's. Then they with equal excitement scurry throughout their new neighborhood to greet their new Christian neighbors, who are just as eager to greet them."

"I see where you are going with this."

"Because you are a historian. This is the middle H of Zionism. Hitler and his ilk kill millions of Jews, but some survive. Some strong young men and women were not sent directly to the gas chambers, but were chosen to be slaves in the nearby factories. That was me. I manned a furnace for Krupps. The lovely young Jewish woman whom you just met was a fitter-trimmer for IG Farben's rubber factory. And we survived. Freed by the Red Army in the bitter January of 1945, we were shuffled from one refugee camp to another until eventually we received JDC money to come to Israel."

"Where you turned the tables, though unfortunately not against the Germans. Against an unsophisticated, poorly educated and innocent Arab population."

"Do you think we don't know that? Do you think that when Yetta and I lined up to receive the keys to the small house that used to stand right here on this patch of ground, do you imagine that we didn't remember our mothers and fathers, who had handed over their keys to the German occupiers? Do you think that when we Jews excitedly surveyed our new house and then eagerly met our new Jewish neighbors that we didn't think of the Arabs who had been driven out?"

"Yes, that's exactly what I think."

"Yes, well. Maybe for a while. And maybe some never think. But I do. I think of them each time I tour the little olive grove just out back. They planted that grove. They planted those trees

195

decades ago, perhaps some father and his little boy, teaching, This is how we plant an olive tree. Now we will water it and care for it, and if we are patient we can watch it grow and by the time you are in school we will eat from it. Yes, I think of that. There may even be slices of olives from it on your pizza right now."

Nobody talked for a while, as they finished off their pizza and emptied their glasses. Clark figured that under the circumstances he could help himself to the refrigerator, so he got them each another Maccabee. Mara was washing up a few dishes. Her look, at first pleading, expectant, grew pouty and resigned as she saw him go for the fridge. When he returned he saw that Morty had a pencil in his hand and a little notebook in front of him.

"I want to list ways Palestinians and Jews can cooperate."

By now they were both pretty drunk, save-the-world drunk.

"You know," Clark said, popping Morty's beer and pouring it for him, "the early Christian leaders wanted the Roman Empire to separate religion from government. As far as I can learn, it was the first ever proposal to separate church and state. Of course it was bloody unlikely to happen, since the Romans believed the gods had built their empire. And these early Christian leaders quickly dropped the idea when the Emperor Constantine became a Christian. But still . . . "

"But still what?"

"The idea hung around."

"It didn't hang around here."

Mara came in. She started towards the table where they were sitting, but saw they were talking an animated bullshit, even taking notes on it, so she veered toward an armchair and curled up in it. The day that was to have changed her life had come to nothing. She cried silent tears that neither man noticed, and fell asleep.

"Music," Morty wrote. He was looking for areas outside religion where both camps could operate together. "Art. Films."

"Sports."

"Business."

"Video games. Shit like that. Oh, let's not forget: history."

"Stupid idea, professor. They'll fight like dogs over history."

"But take the gods out of it. If the gods are in it, it ain't history."

196

"If the gods ain't in it, people around here will not be interested."

"History is the study of surprises. Maybe they will surprise us."

Morty hesitated, wrote it down.

Clark heard a soft, rhythmic snore from across the room. He looked up at her, his fantasy made flesh, curled tightly inside the soft chair, waiting, still willing, no doubt, to accompany him upstairs, if he wanted her.

"I need to get back to my hotel, Morty."

"No. Stay here. I'm too drunk to phone a taxi, and you'd just get robbed by some Russian taxi driver. She's already made up your room."

She had told him, *Take me away from here and I'll love you like you've never been loved before.* But that was no longer possible. For thirty years his love had sat waiting, on a park bench in Beirut.

"Since we're saving the world, before we call it a night let's make a plan to save that precious child over there."

After their long discussion had reached a sense of resolution, Morty said, "You go on up to bed—second room on the left. I'll wake her so she can help me to bed. That's her real job anyway."

Clark had brought along a toothbrush and some toothpaste. No pajamas, but he was too drunk to care. He stripped off all his clothes into a big pile on the floor and climbed into bed naked. As he eased his way between the cool sheets he unexpectedly found himself transported back to his little flat in Beirut, during his one year with Aziza. They had both slept in the nude—her idea. She couldn't see any sense putting on a nightgown, just to take it right back off again. This might have been the first night in thirty years he'd gone to bed with nothing on. The memory, and the soft, cool, sliding sheets, seemed to caress him. Deep in his groin an erection announced its intentions, then slowly started its creeping accession. He touched himself, wished he could phone Aziza and say, Look what you've done, and not for the first time.

He heard a little rap on his door, heard the doorknob rattle. A click against the door frame meant she was putting some effort against the door, but he had thought to lock it as he closed it. He knew not to trust himself to ask her to leave once she got in, so he'd locked it. He could hardly trust himself not to get out of bed

197

just like this, let her in and rid her of her hymen before she'd so much as said a word.

She gave up easily; the door was abandoned. What if instead of Mara it had been old Yetta, checking if he needed towels or a pillow, and in his dark room he'd pounced on her? Wouldn't that have been a trip? That gave him a good laugh. He wondered if in the morning she would have swooned over him, called him *bubeleh*, and made him breakfast. A chocolate babka or something. Did Polish Jews eat chocolate babkas? He wondered about that, let his mind drift. His erection had disappeared, but he didn't notice that. He didn't imagine Mara removing her sundress for him anymore, either. He thought of those two old drunks, Danny Davies and crippled-up Morty Warski, prescribing peace in the Holy Land on a notepad.

As he was falling asleep he might have heard Mara at the door for one farewell try. There was a single thud, muffled and obscure, like an explosion far, far away. The trailing wail of sirens, he didn't hear at all.

The next morning she was at his door again, but this time only to say, "Danny? If you'd like anything special for breakfast, tell me, okay?"

He already had his shirt and trousers on. He had brushed his teeth, swished around some amazing mouthwash layered like a *pousse-café*, and slapped some sort of lavender powder under his arms. He had no hangover to speak of. He hadn't despoiled a comely, wide-eyed maiden, but had hatched a plan to transform her life. Another hour of being Danny Davies and he could drop that whole bit forever. In general he felt fucking wonderful. He bet if he'd had a pair of running shoes he'd sprint right out and do a lap around the lake.

He opened the door for her. "Hi. I'm just putting my shoes on."

"How did you sleep?"

"Fine. Just fine. How about you?"

"Not so great, maybe."

He had only one shoe on at this point but left it that way and

198

walked to her. For the first time he took her in his arms. "You know, Mara, I am truly sorry about yesterday, and about . . . everything. Let's hold off breakfast for a little while, okay? Let me get my other shoe on then I'll meet you on the veranda. You and I need to talk alone for a while."

She was waiting on a long, wrought iron bench. Her look showed none of yesterday's expectant readiness. She was wearing a plain pink t-shirt, striped Capri pants and simple tennis shoes. She smiled up at him, but it was an enigmatic Asian smile that might have meant, I know you're going to punch my lights out and there's nothing I can do about it.

"Morty and I talked a long time about you while you were sawing logs last night." She probably didn't know what sawing logs meant, and he didn't bother to explain. "What I see now that I didn't before is that I'm a real shit, and don't deserve any place in your life. I also see that you have undershot your potential. I know it happens all the time—gifted, deserving people end up doing menial jobs just because they were unlucky in their place of birth, or the family they were born into. People who miss their calling are heading for trouble, so we've got to fix that. And anyway, I'm much too old for you . . . "

She started to go through the usual denial, but he stopped her.

"Many beautiful young women want to accompany their husbands into a happy retirement, but not right after the honeymoon. After about forty years or so, is more like it. If you had lots of money or opportunities, would you be on the Internet looking for some old fart?"

She smiled at the thought of herself with lots of money, and at his honest presentation of her station.

"You're a caregiver who's used as a servant. You're not even matched with your qualifications, much less your potential. What work would you do if you had a choice?"

"Probably be a real nurse. You know, hospital, ER, ICU. Something like that."

"Or a doctor?"

She laughed.

"Because what Morty and I are going to do is set you up with a bank account in your name. I'll send the funds and he will help with the setting up. You'll have enough to attend a fully certified nurse's course at a college in the States. I can help you get in, help you with a student visa, that kind of stuff. You start checking out schools online, and we'll get started. Or, of course if you want to do something different, even stay here and chop chicken livers . . . "

"You're crazy," she said, but kissed him.

"At times I have been, but I don't think this is one of them."

"It's still so hard," she said. "I loved you. It seemed I loved you so much."

"It's easy to love a fantasy. But reality . . . "

"I can really become a doctor?"

"I don't know about that, but here's your chance to try." Walter didn't even know about the nursing program yet, so why would he mind upping the ante to med school? The old boy could pay for it out of his hip pocket.

"Try the University of Kentucky. I have some clout there. Let's go find the URL."

"After breakfast, professor. I want to cook you one decent meal before we say goodbye."

The wrapped gift from yesterday was still sitting there on the patio table. She picked it up but didn't hand it to him straightaway. "Yesterday things got crazy and I forgot to give this to you. It will seem very silly and small now after what you've given me, but I bought it for you."

"You're such a sweetheart, Mara. If I were thirty years younger . . . Can I open it now?"

"Sure."

She handed it over. He ripped it open and held up a bright red t-shirt with a big basketball logo and the words *Hapoel Jerusalem* on it. "Wow! What a great souvenir."

"I picked it because I know you like basketball. It means Team Jerusalem—it's the IBA team me and Morty like. I hope it fits. It was the biggest size they had." They both stood up and she held it up to him. "I think it will be perfect."

"Perfect is exactly right. I'll never part with it. The University of Kentucky has a great basketball team, too. I played for them a little while." At once he knew to shut off that line of conversation. He wondered if it was possible to google every UK player ever, even freshmen. She smiled and said, "Maybe that's why I like you so much."

She'd no doubt mean it as a quip, but, as she watched his face, waiting for a smile, he looked down at the floor. Finally, before the awkwardness tinged an otherwise luminous morning, she said, "Breakfast," and he followed her into the house.

In the kitchen Clark finally got a glimpse of what life might have been like as Danny and Maricel Davies. She prepared a breakfast of the sort that American soldiers must have transplanted to the Philippines: scrambled eggs, real ham—this bought from a Russian butcher—fried potatoes, ketchup. The two outliers were sweetened bread rolls and quince jam; easily explained, as the quince had come from Morty's orchard, and the bread, Mara said, was the true Filipino style *pan de sal* that she had learned from her grandmother.

It was a quiet time. He wondered, but didn't ask, if she'd somehow convinced Morty and Yetta to leave them alone for the morning. Mara didn't say much. He thought she might yammer on excitedly about med school, but she didn't. She hummed while she cooked. Maybe doing a servant's chores, but as a housewife, was work of a completely different category. Maybe it was the status that mattered. He didn't ask her about that, either, or about much of anything. He asked light questions about the food, about the morning sun, and the day's weather.

She hadn't yet heard a forecast. She switched on a small TV.

They saw the smoking rubble of a large collapsed building. "Oh my God!" she said.

"What is it?"

"This is a local newscast."

It was in Hebrew, so she quickly switched on CNN. With the same video feed as before, a voice announced that a truck-bomb had destroyed the Hotel Galilee in Tiberias, Israel. An unknown number of people, many of them Christian pilgrims to the area, had been killed. After the explosion, a previously unknown group calling itself the Jihad for Islamic Revenge had phoned the

Jerusalem Post to claim responsibility for the attack. Nobody knew exactly why they had chosen Tiberias or the Hotel Galilee, but speculation ran to . . . and then they flashed up a photograph.

It showed five men standing by the sea, under the palms, one man a head taller than the rest. This was a United States congressman who had been registered at the hotel. His name was Clark Hatling, of Kentucky. In the rubble his body had not yet been positively identified. Police, emergency crews, and sniffer dogs were combing through the rubble, searching for any trace of Congressman Hatling, or any survivors.

Clark and Mara were looking at each other. The potatoes kept frying but she just looked at him.

"Jesus," he said, taking his cell phone from his pocket as he moved toward the back patio. "Do these things work out here? I need to make a phone call right away."

As she watched him close the kitchen door behind him, Mara said, "Good-bye, Danny. Goodbye Maricel Obrador Davies."

19

THE WILL OF GOD

AMIN WOKE UP late and walked into the kitchen at about nine o'clock, hungry as hell, only to find his mother and sister sobbing over a pile of crumpled tissues. On TV, Zionist rescue workers were picking their way through what was left of the Hotel Galilee. Occasionally all work would stop while men with headphones connected to sound-sensitive meters listened for the faintest hint of life underneath. They even had dogs running over the debris, sniffing for the not yet dead.

Aziza seemed unable to speak, so Aliya said, "They can't find Clark! That was his hotel but they can't find him anywhere!"

"It is the will of God. Thanks be to God."

Aziza shot him a look. "What complete nonsense!"

Amin didn't say anything back to her. Aliya said, "You've always been an insensitive little monster. I can't even believe I'm your sister."

"I'm sorry! It just happens that what I said is what religious people say at times like this."

Aziza told him, "You don't even seem shocked."

He shrugged, lowered the level of dispute, saying, "I had it on in my room." He hadn't slept well, turned on the TV at about 2 a.m., said his *fajr* prayer at 5 a.m., and finally went back to sleep.

Aliya said, "Your face just looks dead and blank."

"I didn't sleep very well."

"Probably Amin is showing his grief in his own way, Aliya. Of course he's sad. During Clark's last week on earth he probably spent more hours with Amin than with anybody. I wish there could have been hundreds of hours more. A million more."

"He was a well-read man. We had some good talks. Did I tell you that on the basketball court one guy ran me over, and Clark was right in his face, waving his finger under this dude's nose, like, no more of this stuff. Let's play fair."

203

"That's exactly what he would have done to the Israelis," Aziza said. "He was our salvation. If he had made it to president . . . there's nobody else out there, *nobody*, who sees the solution the way he did. Years ago we talked this through, over and over. He was the Palestinians' last, best hope. And now he's gone. Our hope is gone. And my dear friend."

Aliya moved to put her arms around her mother. "Maybe not gone, Mom. They're still searching. They've found a few survivors."

"Yes, but look . . ." She waved a hand at the TV, a scene of broken cement slabs connected by bent steel rods, with smoke still rising from the corner that had housed the power plant. She had said "Look," but looking is exactly what she wanted to avoid at the moment, so she took her phone and a wad of tissues out to the back garden, where instead of sirens and a dozen breathless interviews with experts who knew nothing, she could weep in peace, surrounded by birds singing. Aliya brought her a cup of tea, then left her alone. She sat there under a lemon tree for over an hour, paralyzed as by a state of deep dreaming, with a shattered desire to wake up being the closest thing to a thought in her mind. Then her phone started flashing its commanding red screen and she heard, "Hi. It's me, Clark."

She came running through the house, waving her phone and shouting, "He's alive! He's alive!"

"Oh, Mom—thank God!" Aliya ran to hug her.

"Thank a Ukrainian hooker, more likely! But yes, thank somebody!" Amin hadn't said anything, but when he, too, moved to embrace her, she told him, "There's your will of God."

With Aziza back in the house with Aliya, both of them watching the news and crying, Amin felt the urge to point out to them that's exactly what they were doing when they thought Clark was dead, but then he realized that now his stomach felt hollow, his legs felt drained, so he could hardly claim that since Palestine was still captive nothing had changed. Something inside him had changed.

He took his mom's vacated chair in the back garden, stayed there just long enough to formulate a message in his head. When he thought he had it just right, he rode his Vespa to an Internet café near AUB, logged on to shakebadboy@hotmail.il and wrote, *Were my dates sweet in Tiberias? Or are you the biggest fuck-up in the history of Zionist security? Or both? Asshole.* He saved it as a draft. Then he used his own anonymous email to write to 123Levi@hotmail.il. *Sounds like the party was a blast. Were you there?*

20

THE FIRST CALL he made was to Aziza. "Hi, it's me, Clark."

Nothing.

"I know what you've probably seen on TV, but I wasn't in the hotel when the bomb went off. I'm just fine."

Finally she made sense of it. He heard her catch her breath. "*Ya Allah!*" She spoke a string of rapid-fire Arabic, then asked, "What happened? How did you get out?"

So he repeated for her, "I wasn't there when the bomb hit. I wasn't in the hotel at the time of the explosion."

"You mean you left the hotel before two in the morning? What was it—some sort of angelic warning?"

"No, silly. I spent the night elsewhere." He knew he was going to have to explain this about a million times, so he might as well start now. "I know some people in Tiberias so I spent the night at their house."

"Wow! Clark Hatling, it was a hooker! You picked up a hooker and . . . no wait. She'd have come to your room. I can't believe this! My darling! I've been crying all morning."

"I just woke up and turned on the TV."

"You just found out?"

"You're the first person I called."

"God bless that lovely hooker! Was she Ukrainian? They usually are, right? God I love her. Did she take you to her place so her boyfriend could steal your wallet? I'll replace it! And send flowers to her and her boyfriend!"

"No need. I kicked the shit out of him. Actually there were three of them."

"My darling!"

"*Habibti*," he said, using the word for the first time in years. "*Habibti*." My love. It felt natural on his tongue. "Listen—I've got to go. I've got lots of calls to make."

206

"And tell the emergency crews—they've been searching for you all night. And for the others. God, those poor, poor people. Do you think you were the target?"

"I don't know. I'll call you again soon, okay? Don't worry about me."

Next he phoned Wanda at home, left a voice message. What time was it in Washington, anyway? Four in the morning or something? He tried her cell, couldn't connect. He sent a text: *I am ok. Where r u?*

He phoned Luke, his communications chief. He could tell he'd been sleeping.

"Hey, wake up! You should be pacing the floor and praying for my safety."

"Who is this?"

"It's your boss, you bonehead."

"Oh my God! How the hell did you survive?"

And here it went again. "I spent the night with some people I know." It was good to get in some extra practice before he reached Wanda.

Luke said he would prepare a statement for the Washington media, and advised Clark to inform immediately the Israeli media. "This thing broke in prime time on the East Coast, was breaking news on the West Coast nightly news. It's been going hot for eight hours. Your photos have been all over the channels, and getting big online play. Yahoo had one of you in your Celtics uniform, in those little short shorts. Maybe we can play it to our advantage, but . . . how? I'll need to think on it. The first word that comes to my mind, though, is Chappaquiddick."

Fuck! It hadn't come to Clark's mind, but it sure stuck there now. Senator Edward Kennedy's long lapse in reporting that he had driven a car and its young woman passenger into the sea off Chappaquiddick Island had cost Kennedy a shot at the presidency, and now, decades later, everybody still remembered what Chappaquiddick stood for: the arrogance of the powerful, weakness in a crisis, a married man and a young woman. A young woman ruined—and with what punishment exacted of the man who had destroyed her?

Forget about being president. You can't treat a young woman like that and ever become President of the United States.

Did that matter, though? The rumors about him contesting New Hampshire were about as low-level as presidential rumors could be. Nobody besides Walter and Roxy knew anything about this new phase of the plan, and he wasn't even sure he liked it himself. Aziza was divorced now; she clearly retained some of her old feelings for him. Maybe he should drive Wanda off a bridge and take Aziza to France. Or maybe he could move back to Beirut, marry Aziza, reapply for his old AUB job, hang around some with Amin, mentor him along a bit. Either way sounded fine.

He mulled over all this on the ride back to Ben Gurion airport. And he thought about the dozens of sleeping believers killed by the Galilee bomb, all those peaceful dreams of hymns sung on wooden boats, of drifting along where Jesus had fished for souls, and sorted them into two piles. He thought of the hotel workers on the night shift, the guys on the loading dock unloading shipments of Haifa oranges, Kentucky shampoo, or C-4 plastic explosive. He thought of the insomniacs lying awake at the moment of the blast, back in bed after a trip to the bathroom, but unable to lay aside intensely private worries about a child's failing math scores, about that endoscope that shows some kind of discoloration in the esophagus, the payment that hasn't arrived yet and the bank that doesn't care, about the spouse who occasionally comes home late with no explanation, or sometimes seems to have been crying, and goes to bed early. Some must have lain awake wondering how to make peace, or war, in this sacred land. Did it matter? Did it make any difference at all whether you were awake or asleep, if you died a millisecond later?

In a crowded conference room at the airport in Tel Aviv, he made a statement to that effect, although much more anodyne, embroidered with prayer and sympathy for the surviving families of the victims, full of praise for the emergency crews who had labored so long to save so many lives. He condemned the cowards who had planned the attack, and their stooges who carried it out. Indicating his t-shirt, he apologized for looking so casual in the aftermath of the tragedy, but reminded the reporters present that all his clean clothes had been destroyed. Privately he thought that the sudden dislocation implied by his appearance in a bright red *Hapoel Jerusalem* basketball shirt would say volumes about the kind of guy he was and would remind everybody what a near-miss victim he had been.

Then he accepted questions.

"Congressman Hatling, can you tell the world where you were last night?"

"I can say that I was visiting a private residence, not for any sort of government business, just a purely personal visit with an acquaintance of mine. With good conversation and good food, the time flew by. I was graciously offered the guest room, so I accepted the offer. Nothing more complicated than that." He shrugged his shoulders as if to add, We've all done it, right? A couple of Maccabees and you stay the night. But he knew it sounded scandalous. If poor Mara was dragged into this, her new vision of a bright future would be crushed within hours.

He called on the next reporter, who said, "First of all, nice shirt."

"Thanks. I needed a change of shirts so I just grabbed this one from a shop here at the airport. I hope I don't offend any Maccabi supporters."

"Don't try to run for office in Tel Aviv wearing that shirt."

"I'll bear that in mind. I have to admit I don't possess great political instincts. It's just that it was my size and had a picture of a basketball on it, so I bought it." He stood there, tall, commanding, still an athlete under that t-shirt; triumphant, and knee-deep in irony. He knew it, and knew that they all knew it too. They were all inside the guild, the actors' studio of political theater. And he knew that outside the guild, the good voters back home were thinking, Look at this guy! He's one of us, only in concentrated form, the distillate of us. He is us in a more rarified and perfect state. He is what we are made of, in efflorescence.

"So, you had a question?"

"Yes, Congressman. We've heard that the search through the destruction uncovered the wall safe from your room, completely intact, but none of your personal effects were inside, and that was

209

because you had taken your passport and everything else with you as you left for the evening. Can you confirm that?"

"I don't know that they found a safe—I simply have no information about that. But I assume it would have been empty. I didn't put anything in it."

"Why?"

"I'm sorry?"

"Why did you take your valuables as you left for the night?"

"Who did you say you write for? *Paranormal Monthly*?"

A lot of people laughed. But he could tell they thought it was a great question. He wondered if many people here knew what Chappaquiddick meant.

"Actually I'm with the *Jerusalem Post*."

"I keep my valuables in an old leather passport case my father gave me years ago. I always take it with me. Sometimes you might need your passport for identification, if there's an emergency, say. Or to cash a traveler's check. I also keep some photos in there of my loved ones." Take that you little shit. It always amazed him how he could think on the fly. "Maybe it comes from years ago when I couldn't afford nice hotels. I don't know—it's just an old travel habit of mine." But really, why *had* he taken his passport case with him? He never did that. "I assure you that even in this land of celebrated revelations, I received no such revelation. Otherwise I would have informed hotel security and many innocent lives would have been saved from this heinous attack." Oh, right—it seemed so long ago now that when he recalled the real reason, he almost lost concentration: he'd thought he might need those things at another hotel. With Mara. Thank God these guys didn't know about the toothbrush.

He tried phoning Wanda again several times throughout the afternoon, most recently from aboard the plane before the take-off from Ben Gurion. By then it was 4:00 p.m. Israel time, which was well up in the morning for Wanda, assuming she was on the East Coast. Even if she'd flown to California for some reason, wasn't it time to get out of bed? But even so how could she have missed all the hubbub of the previous fourteen hours? At every failure to pick-up, he texted, *Where r u?* Later it became *Where the hell r u?*

He thought, Let's be honest about this—do I really care where she is? Let's say she's run off with her yoga instructor. That solves everything, right? I can quit politics, move to France. Or Beirut. Doesn't much matter. Or maybe I can win the presidency as a wronged husband; get the men's empathy vote and the women's sympathy vote, then let Wanda wither with envy as other women parade royalty through the White House. Or marry Aziza in a White House wedding! The country can like it or lump it. They couldn't impeach a man for marrying his college sweetheart, could they?

He laid his head back and welcomed the embrace of these simple daydreams. His press conference had gone rather well, in his opinion, and it was over. His depositions with the Israeli investigators had been entirely congenial. The only thing he'd been forced to lie about was the list of people he'd told about the Galilee. Wanda, Holly—that was it. Aziza's name never came up. There was no way around mentioning his night at the home of Morty and Yetta Warski, but the police would sit on that. Probably Mara would be invisible to them—the hired help of a crippled Israeli hero. So, everything was under control. He had asked Luke to inform Wanda when she surfaced. In a moment the plane would rise from the ground and his spirits with it. Soon cell phone communication would cease, and he would have twelve blessed hours of repose between here and JFK.

The cabin crew was still checking seat belts when his phone rang. First class wasn't packed, but still he took the call in the toilet.

"Hi, Wanda."

"I've got a dozen messages from you. Why are you keeping tabs on me? This isn't like you."

"Whoa! How long have you been out . . . "

"See there! I don't appreciate this *scrutiny*." She emphasized the word as though she'd substituted it for *fucking shit*.

"You must have been way out of touch."

"Stop it! You go running off anywhere and everywhere, so I guess I can enjoy myself sometimes too."

"Absolutely!" He laughed out loud in the small toilet. "I'm all for that. Just where have you been enjoying yourself?"

"I'm in Key West, if you must know. We just got back from a lovely sea voyage."

"You just got back?"

"My phone started beeping before we even pulled into port."

"Well, that's fine. I hope you had calm seas." Her stomach could be a source of controversy.

"It was for *you*, if you're interested."

"For me? How thoughtful."

"I've been pouring champagne for some of your biggest supporters. Chuck Abshire and his wife; the Kiethleys; and Wayne Redmon. You remember him."

"Oh, I think I do. Good-looking guy, nice eyes."

"Yes. It was his boat."

"Old sailor Redmon. Popeye Wayne, people call him."

"You're not nearly as funny as you think you are."

"Don't be cross with me. I've had a rough day."

"Ha! I've been playing hostess for that bunch of hillbillies."

"I know you did a great job and loosened up their wallets real good."

"I'm sure I did, and I don't appreciate your insinuations, either."

"Totally uncalled for. I couldn't be sorrier."

"I don't think you realize how important I am to your success."

"No doubt you're right. For now though, listen . . . "

"Without my influence you'd be a nothing history professor in the armpit of the earth."

"I couldn't agree with you more, but I feel the plane starting to move . . . "

"The plane? You're on a plane?"

"Don't panic, I'm not on my way to Key West. I'm on my way to Washington."

"So soon?"

"Little change of plans. I'll tell you what, you go flip on CNN, and then spend the rest of the day asking yourself whether being First Lady would make you any less of a bitch."

212

21

TAKE NOTE OF SILENCE

MARA HEARD THE bell for the door in the thick garden wall and opened it to find a bulky man in a bright sunset-scene Hawaiian shirt standing there. She noticed that his baggy jeans were held up by a belt that had a gun and holster attached to it. Before he could say a word she slammed the door and was up the veranda steps, almost to the door of the house, when she heard, "Sorry, miss! Israeli security. Please don't be alarmed."

By this time Yetta was at the door and in control. She motioned that Mara should return to open the door, and made sure that whoever was there could see that she was giving her hyacinths a leisurely inspection when the door opened. When the man started inside, Yetta, still examining a flower, pointed to the ground at his feet and said, "Stop right there. You'll show me some ID first and you'll also be kind enough to stop frightening my maid."

"Of course. Chief Inspector Levi Hershko of Internal Security, North District. My police ID." He showed her his card. "And my apology to the little lady. I'm one of the good guys. It must have been my sidearm that frightened her, not me personally." He looked at Mara, who stared right back. "Little lady" made her want to throw up.

Yetta asked, "And what brings you here, chief inspector?"

"I just want to check out the statement of the American congressman Clark Hatling, who conveniently didn't die in his hotel room. He says he was here all night. Can you confirm that?"

"I can indeed."

"Maybe I could speak with your husband."

Yetta Warski nodded to Mara, but didn't invite the good guy in. Morty appeared at the door to the house. Mara eased his wheelchair out the door and onto the veranda.

"Please have a seat up here, if you don't mind."

Levi accepted, and, as his bulk cleared the garden door, three

213

other security agents, these in uniform, followed him and strode directly into the house. Yetta barked, "What do you think you're doing?" and followed them in.

Levi settled himself comfortably in a cushioned porch chair, sighed as though he could finally take a break after a long day.

"Would you care for a drink, Mr. . . . "

"Hershko. Chief Inspector Levi Hershko." Once again he produced his ID. "No, thanks. I'm just fine like this. Lovely setting, this."

"It's fine for us. We all love flowers."

"Does it hurt?"

"I beg your pardon?"

"Where your legs used to be. Phantom limb pains."

"Isn't that why God made vodka?" Morty asked with a straight face.

"Maybe. Yes, maybe so. The answer to our prayers. Two blown legs and you get a nice stiff drink."

"I'm glad you're not offended by my tone."

"It's just that I might have prayed for two legs *and* a bottle of vodka."

"I've survived Auschwitz and a Palestinian bus bomb." He didn't add, *you fat-assed nudnik.*

"So he was here all night?"

"Indeed he was."

"Why?"

"Why not?"

"Why?"

"This could go on a long time."

"I think *why* is more to the point. And I don't mean to offend. This is routine procedure, but for a very non-routine matter. If Congressman Hatling had anything at all to do with planting that bomb, I need to uncover it. If he was the target, I need to know who's targeting him. And why."

"There could be a million other reasons. Maybe the target was American tourists. Or some ruthless business dealing. Or Chechen fanatics! There's where to start your search. Not with us."

"We know about Chechens. And we've heard the rumors that

214

the new owner had ties with the Russian mafia. We're on all that, and more leads that you'll ever know about. We've got teams on all those. But the Hatling connection is my assignment, and I will get to the bottom of it."

"*Why not* will get us there. The congressman knew my history and paid me a visit. Cynics such as yourself may see a motive in it. You perhaps think he was trying to pick up votes by parading me in front of a camera. But I tell you we made not so much as one photograph together. I showed him around my orchards, we watched the lake as the sun set behind us, we had dinner, had a lively conversation on how to rescue this land from the very kind of destruction you are investigating now. The hour grew late. I offered him our guest room. Now, tell me: *why not?*"

"Indeed, as you say . . . why not?"

One of Levi's officers came onto the veranda holding a pink notebook with some rag-dolly cartoons on the cover. The officer opened it, pointed to a name, and handed it over to Levi. Mara blushed and looked away, far down the slope of the hill and onto the blue waters of the Galilee.

"And who is Danny Davies?"

"I have no idea what you're . . . "

"It's mine," Mara said. "That's my notebook."

"Why do you have the name Danny Davies written over and over in it?"

"He's a friend of mine."

"A boyfriend?"

"Well, sort of an online boyfriend."

"Where is he now?"

"In the States, I guess. We don't chat anymore."

"And what's this Maricel Obrador Davies written all down one page."

Mara was too humiliated to answer. She sat down and buried her face in her hands.

Yetta stepped from the house and toward Levi. "It's what young girls in love do, chief inspector. They practice writing their married name. And they dream. Haven't you ever been in love?"

Mara started to cry into the palms of her hands. She caught

her breath to say, "It's probably not even his real name." She tried to wipe her nose on her sleeve. Levi reached for his handkerchief but Yetta put a hand on his arm, and handed her a tissue from her pocket. "He's disappeared. They all just disappear. They get your hopes built up and then . . . half of them are just old married guys looking for . . . " She decided not to complete the thought. Let them figure it out. Yetta sat beside her and put an arm around her. "Oi! The man is a *momzer*! All men are *momzers*! Forget him! Forget them all!"

"So, Chief Inspector Hershko," Morty said, "as one *momzer* to another, I'd say you've done your job here, and a bit more, wouldn't you?"

"I would, for now."

"Are you sure you won't accept a drink? You seem to have some phantom pains of your own. Vodka in fresh nectarine juice might help."

He doubted it, and walked down the steps and through the garden.

"You've noticed?" Morty's voice stopped Levi at the gate. "You've noticed the silence?"

"What silence?"

"Nobody's rioting. Following the bombing you might have expected Jews to be slaughtering Arabs in the streets. But it's not happening."

"That's because most of the dead were Christian tourists. American Christians."

"What difference . . . "

"Haven't you seen the polls? Hatred of Arabs in the U.S. hasn't been this high since 9/11. We feel secure with American support. We don't need to riot."

"Or perhaps we are sick of blood."

Levi started to let it pass. What did it matter to anyone that one old stump of a Jew and his old bitch wife were soft in the head? But Levi had three officers with him, and in any case it wasn't in his nature to let things pass. So at the gate he turned to them: "If we're sick of blood, we can kiss our country goodbye."

22

IT HAD BEEN dark and light and dark again by the time Clark exited the plane at Washington National. When he switched on his phone he found a message from Wanda: "Call me. I'll pick you up." When he did he got Holly, using Wanda's phone, and driving, he soon saw, Wanda's big Navigator.

"One heck of a trip, right, boss?" she said as she walked around to open the rear door, forgetting that he had no bags. She gave him a big hug right there at the curb, but she was from Pinsonfork, Kentucky, so it was okay.

"No kidding."

"Surprised to see me instead of your wife?"

"Look, if you've murdered Wanda and stolen her car, that's fine, but if you bought this on your salary, then I'm paying you way too much."

"She asked me to come and get you."

"Is she still in Florida?"

"Um . . . okay. Let's say she's still in Florida."

"What does that mean?"

"I'm sorry. I've been instructed to be mysterious."

"The Mystery Woman of Pinsonfork. Why the hell not?"

She turned to smile at him. "I like this car," she said, and gunned Wanda's monster.

He was happy to sit back and watch the world whiz past. The worst of the rush hour was over. The onrush of all these big American cars made him feel a foreigner. *Jesus*, he'd only been gone a few days, and what a few days they had been, yet back here life just went on. The Potomac looked black along its banks, under the lights of a few tourist boats, and the Key Bridge always seemed welcoming, wide and unpretentious, with its view of Georgetown and the spires of the Riggs in the background. As they crossed the bridge he looked down along the river toward the view of the great national landmarks, the Lincoln Memorial, the Washington Monument, the Capitol. The White House. Was he home now? Was this his true home? Was this what he really wanted? No denying he was looking forward to reaching his genteel townhouse on primly ordered P Street, but wasn't that just because he was exhausted?

As they turned onto P he relaxed into the congenial attraction of the proudly methodical minds that had created these streets. It said, There there now, take comfort in what the hand of man has constructed. Here is the architecture of reason; here is a Haydn string quartet in brick and wrought iron.

The doorways and fence posts and trees went past in a spellbinding rhythm. He would have allowed himself to doze off, only he was minutes from his own bed.

Up ahead there was an interruption in P Street's regularity. There was a crowd of people gathered on the sidewalk, even spilling onto the street. Holly slowed and announced, "Ta-da!"

"What the hell is all that?" He saw a banner stretched out across his front stoop.

"It's a reception! A welcome home reception!"

They saw him too. The lights of TV crews came up and pointed at him. As he got out of the car he was blinded for a moment. He smelled meat on the grill and then heard "Darling! Thank God you're back home, safe and sound." Wanda was running toward him, out of the pitch black and through the bright lights. She rushed into his arms and kissed him. Luckily he had glimpsed her in time to brace himself, or she would have knocked him flat. But within that glimpse he did brace himself, and he noticed that she looked great, dressed in something red and silky that showed off her shoulders and her legs. She took his face in her hands, looking as sincere as a woman could look. Even later, on replay, he couldn't discern any duplicity in her reaction. Was it the shock of almost losing him? Or the prospect of choosing a new china pattern for the White House?

He made a nice statement for the press. He was getting good at it: Stayed at a private residence. Didn't want to allow their hospitality toward him to create an intrusion into their lives. We

Kentuckians, and—just in time he remembered to broaden his market—we Americans, are a hospitable people, so we can easily understand the circumstances. You kindly offer the guest room to a visitor, you don't expect to find reporters tromping through your flower bed because of it.

It seemed his whole staff was there, along with a crowd of neighbors, their kids, and some people he didn't even recognize. Clusters of balloons floated from the handrails of his front stoop. Somebody—he would kill whoever it was with his bare hands—had tied yellow ribbons onto the tree in front of his house. Luke, in a silly apron and baseball cap, supervised a catering crew as they made sure everybody had a hot dog and something to drink.

As he was finishing up his statement, his panning vision paused on a tall, thin, elderly man with white hair, a white rimming beard, and prepossessing blue eyes. He stared at Clark as though any second he expected Clark to recognize him and return the rapturous smile. He looked like an old man from his childhood called Stringbean Maynard, the odd-job man who helped clean up the back yard after snowstorms, and the like. But that was ridiculous. Whoever it was, it wasn't Stringbean Maynard. Other than the face, this guy looked normal, as far as Clark could make out. He was wearing a sport shirt and a golfing visor, but his face gave off the worshipful brightness of a pet dog, or—perhaps this made more sense—a person sliding into dementia. Clark forced himself to pan on past the man. Good speakers don't fixate on one listener. But on his return sweep of the crowd, that puppy dog stare hadn't changed.

After answering a few questions from the print journalists, Clark excused himself to go looking for the Stringbean Maynard look-alike, but he had disappeared.

Aside from that it all seemed to go pretty smoothly, until, after Wanda had thanked everybody and asked for their forbearance, as the Congressman was naturally exhausted in the extreme, and they had all started drifting away, with the kids untying the balloons and the caterers starting to bag up trash, a reporter from the *Post* walked up to Clark, leaned in menacingly, and said, "We're giving you a bye this time, Congressman. But eventually we'll find out where you spent the night. We're all dying to break that story."

Once inside, Clark closed the heavy front door, leaned his back against it as though keeping something at bay, and stayed that way a moment, reflecting on the success of the evening. He wasn't going to let that one asshole reporter spoil it for him. It had been a great evening. The banner, so many friends outside, hot dogs, both beer and soft drinks. Wanda beaming for the camera, first with one big smacker of a kiss, then little snuggly ones. Very convincing. Her performance even had him wondering if perhaps the shock of almost losing him . . . no, certainly it was the prospect of a run for the White House. Even so, she'd cuddled right up to his side, cameras rolling or no. Then again, you never knew when or how far away a photographer might be shooting stills with a zoom.

His impromptu speech had struck the right chord. He was pretty sure of that. He was eager to hear it again to be certain.

The back of the house was locked down solid, and all the downstairs lights were off. Wanda must have seen to that. He could hear her making little sounds upstairs: unpacking, he supposed. He grabbed two glasses and a bottle of their best scotch, punched the alarm code, and as he was climbing the stairs he heard her call out, "Hurry, honey! It's coming on!" They sat together on the end of the bed, not saying a word, just sipping their drinks as NewsNight's opening graphics unfolded in their accustomed sequence. The co-anchors made a show of straightening papers and checking monitors. Then one said: "*Tonight: a congressman's safe return to a relieved welcome home.*"

"Lead story, baby!" Wanda turned to her husband and they clinked glasses at last.

The story opened with Wanda's flying embrace and big smooch. It all showed up surprisingly well: her sexy but still appropriate red dress blending cozily into his red t-shirt, the casual man's man and his glam wife; the banner, the balloons, the kids holding hot dogs and hopping around. A tall, white-haired old guy wearing a golfing visor. Clark had kept his statement to under two minutes, and sure enough they ran the whole thing. In the beginning they showed him on his front stoop, in his *Hapoel*

Jerusalem shirt, but when his voice grew grave and he spoke of the need to combat terror, they ran a sequence of the destruction of the Hotel Galilee itself, with forlorn emergency crews pawing through the rubble. There were close-ups of victims, and of their mourners. "Ironically," the anchor allowed his voice to fall solemn as he concluded, "Congressman Hatling was in the Middle East to attend a conference—a conference to bring peace to that troubled land." Their closing shot was the photo taken in Beirut, with him standing tall and stately between Laverty and Foreman, presidential timber for the whole wide world to see.

"Wow. It's been one hell of a week."

"You can say that again!" She drained her glass and kissed him again. "And don't I love those whisky kisses!" She took his glass and poured them each another drink.

She still looked good, years younger than her age, which in any case was six years less than his. He'd often accused her of using fitness club memberships as an excuse for socializing. No doubt there was some truth in that, but she'd kept herself fit in the process. Her skin tone glowed from her trip to the Keys. She still had on the cocktail dress and the face she'd made perfect for the cameras, but now she was barefoot, with her calf muscles stretched agreeably long. She gave him the look of a woman who had returned home from a long hike: flushed, famished, and delighted at the prospect of gratifying her hunger. It was a look he remembered from long ago. She took something powder blue from the bag that presumably she had just brought back with her from Florida, went into the bathroom, and came out wearing a powder blue babydoll nightie.

"I'm still your wife, remember? You can screw me if you want. At least that's my understanding of the way it works."

He was still sitting on the edge of the bed. She lifted his left foot, popped off the shoe without untying it, removed his sock, then did the same for his right foot. All the while she stared at him. He watched the tops of her breasts as she started to breathe harder.

"Since we're starting to have so much fun, let me make one little observation. It didn't escape my notice that on the passenger

221

manifest for the Good Ship Lollipop, everybody there was a couple, except you and Wayne. I take it Connie was busy, so Wayne asked you aboard to make up a pair—for bridge, maybe? Or was it shuffleboard?"

"Don't be ridiculous. I told you, I was there for you, silly. I'm your fundraiser extraordinaire. We're going to need lots more money now that we're running for president. Hurry, finish your drink."

"If we're running . . . "

"Yes, Clarkie, of course *if*." She took his glass and he raised his arms like a child as she removed his t-shirt, then she shoved him onto his back and started undoing his trousers.

"Let me put it another way: Where was Connie while you and Wayne were playing shuffleboard?"

"Oh, didn't I tell you? Connie and Wayne are getting a divorce."

"A divorce? Those two? I never dreamed . . . "

"Ho! Listen to this one! Connie found out he was on one of those websites men use to pick up Asian tarts."

He sat back up. "Connie found what?"

"Yep. He was listed under a phony name. Said he was single."

"Holy Shit! This is unbelievable."

"Sure is. As hillbilly scandals go, this is a juicy one. His caddy caught him. Isn't that just too perfect?"

"His caddy? This is insane!"

"One of the caddies at his country club was a Vietnamese girl named U Bum Suk."

"You're making this whole thing up."

"Okay. Maybe U Bum Suk is Secretary General of the United Nations. I don't know the girl's actual name, but she caught him on this website and told him she'd keep quiet about it for five thousand dollars."

"She blackmailed him?"

Wanda pushed him back down again, pulled down his trousers and underwear. "Five thousand dollars. Isn't that too funny? As much as he hated Connie? He might have paid five thousand to kill her, but not to keep her."

"I didn't even know he hated her. I thought she was nice."

"Well, she isn't, and he does. So when he reported the blackmail to the staff manager at the club, they fired Little Miss Bum Suk, who in turn went straight to Connie. And the rest is history." She knelt down on the floor, spread his knees apart and began kissing his inner thigh, working her way up.

"Shit! Listen, Wanda . . . stop it. I need Wayne's address in Florida. I need to see him."

"Tomorrow. I have his email address in my list. His cell too. But right now you just relax and enjoy yourself. You were getting hard, and now . . ."

"And now I need the name of the marina where he docks his boat. I have to see him personally."

"Shut up, silly. You're about to get the sweetest little blow job ever and all you can think about is poor old Wayne Redmon."

23 COLE GIBSON WAKES UP

IN TALLAHASSEE, POLITICAL consultant Cole Gibson was also watching the late news that night, and he thought he noticed something. He wasn't quite sure he'd heard it right. It seemed too bizarre to be true. He even thought he might have dozed off and dreamed it, so he turned toward the sofa, intending to ask Danielle what she'd heard, but she wasn't there. He looked around for her and saw her coming down the stairs.

"Just checking on the boys," she said. "I thought I heard Jack crying."

Cole started flipping through the news channels. "There's something you need to see. I just saw—or I think I just saw—the most astonishing thing." He clicked through them all, gave up and put it on CNN. "They're bound to run it again. In fact, let me set the recorder."

"What has got you so buzzed all of a sudden?"

"You know the congressman they thought had been killed in Israel?"

"Hatling? The one connected somehow with your trip to Dubai?"

"Yes! Something really strange is going on here."

"What was the connection? I forget the details."

"Those Texas oil bazillionaires wanted us to recommend to them some pro-Palestinian politicians who might become president. Well, guess how many of those there are."

"None."

"Precisely. So we handed in this bogus list, and then they asked us to spend a whole day assessing the chances of this guy, Clark Hatling. Had you ever heard of him, until this week?"

"Just when you came back from Dubai. After that I started watching for his name when I updated the regional news links on our website."

224

"Really? Did you find anything?"

"Only very local stuff. He looks good in pix. That's about it."

"All I knew was that he was from some little hillbilly dynasty and played basketball. So why did they ask about him? He's voted straight down the middle on Israel. AIPAC rates him at 97%. I couldn't find any trace of a reference to Palestine."

"He was about as obscure as any politician out there," Danielle said. "There was that blip about a poll in New Hampshire. That died a quick death."

"All three of the consultants I was with in Dubai have called me about him lately. Why? I don't know why. He has no chance."

"Maybe they see something we don't."

"I seriously doubt that. In Dubai we all ridiculed the suggestion. And now suddenly he's all over the news."

"He was in the wrong place at the wrong time."

"Or he *wasn't* in the wrong place at the *right* time. And just now . . . I didn't catch the whole thing . . . I was half-asleep until I heard what I think I heard . . . but he was on there again."

"On where?"

"On the 11:00 news. He was lead story again, just for coming back home."

"He got lucky. It's a slow news day."

"This guy seems to get lucky a lot. And there was something about that speech tonight." Cole looked at his watch. "I wish they'd hurry up and run his fucking statement!"

Danielle pointed to her ears and then upstairs. Cole lowered his voice.

"After Dubai I got interested enough to look deeper into Hatling's past. Did you know that while he was in college he studied for a year in Beirut? He gave up one full year of basketball eligibility at Georgetown University to study in Beirut. And then, after a knee injury ended his pro career, he got his PhD in London, and went *back* to Beirut for three years. Does any of that strike you as weird?"

She yawned and pushed back her hair. "Only for politicians. Normal people jump all over the map."

"But he is a politician. Born and bred."

225

"Maybe that's the problem."

"You mean he just rode his father's coattails?"

"I mean maybe his heart wasn't really in it."

"Then what's he doing running for president?"

"Maybe he's not. It's just his people pushing him."

"Simon Angelo isn't 'his people'. Albert Tollson and Jeremy Allenberg aren't 'his people'. No doubt all of them have received feelers from both Laverty and Foreman. I know I have. So what's up with this no-hoper?" He tried spinning through the channels again. WTXL was showing Hatling's photo, and a voice was introducing the film clip. "Here it is!" Cole said. "Pay close attention to this."

There was Clark, wearing his red t-shirt, Wanda diving at him and planting a big whopper on him.

"Wow! Don't expect that from me when you're his age."

"Quiet. Listen."

Clark was explaining, "We Kentuckians—and we Americans—are a hospitable people."

"Hear that? See what he did?"

"He wants people to quit bugging him about where he was."

"No! That's not my point. He's so used to addressing his district that he did it from habit, but then it occurred to him: Hey! I'm not running for Congress now. This guy's running for president. I'd bet anything he is."

Danielle thought about it. "It's possible. But answer me this: Nine hours unaccounted for? Where was he all that time, anyway? Why all the secrecy?"

"Very good question."

"So tell me—obviously you don't buy his story—what's your theory?"

"I don't have one. Not yet. But one thing I do know—there's intrigue oozing out of every gap. Some grand scheme, a hidden hand. I'm not coming to bed until I figure it out." He swiveled his chair around toward his laptop.

Danielle yawned again. "Great idea. You investigate; I'll sleep. Then in the morning we'll call in the good Congressman and put him through the wringer."

24 A POP TART BREAKFAST

BLACKMAIL.

It was Clark's first thought of the morning. By now the idea must have occurred to Mara as well. She'd probably lain awake all night calculating exactly now much she could extract from him, her mind toying with staggering numbers. He recalled how promptly she'd bumped his nursing school offer up to med school. Clearly gold-digging was second nature to her. He recalled too how readily he'd acceded. That tactical error alone would have told her that he had access to very deep pockets. If a man offered that amount of money just to ease a guilty conscience, how much more would he pay to continue his presidential run?

How would she contact him, anyway? She couldn't go straight to the press. That would destroy the blackmail scheme. He tried thinking from her perspective and it hit him: she would email her demands to Danny Davies. That's where she would notify him of the dollar amount of her opening gambit. He opened his laptop with the idea of checking there, but soon realized he'd rather not know. It didn't matter now anyway. She would learn soon enough, probably on CNN, right there in the kitchen where she'd learned his true identity, that her plan would come to nothing. His confession and apology to Wayne and Connie Redmon would put that little daydream to rest, and the resulting scandal was bound to make the news.

He couldn't expect Wayne to say, "Oh, that was *you* using my picture to find Asian tarts? Well then, never mind." No, the recriminations would be bitter and long-lasting. Especially if Connie knew what Wayne and Wanda had been up to on his yacht. The press would spin weeks of fun out of this one. Screw the presidency—he might even lose Kentucky Five.

Poor Mara. He really did feel sorry for her, now that her second plan to transform her life via Danny Davies was about to blow up in her face. Or maybe Walter would just dig deeper. Was this presidential run important enough to him and Roxy that they would throw mounds of cash at Mara *and* Wayne *and* Connie?

The one course he would not consider was to let Connie divorce Wayne over Danny Davies, even if they did hate each other. His mother used to say, "Every tub sits on its own bottom." Well, Mr. and Mrs. Redmon, this is my tub, and it sits on my own bottom. Expose me if you want. Blackmail me if you must.

Blackmail. He tried to isolate the word in one corner of his mind, like a computer virus that can't be deleted. There really wasn't much else he could do.

He could try to direct his mind to other topics. That was the cunning scheme of a man fresh out of cunning schemes. As usual, he lay awake in the last dark of the morning, listening to the song of the cardinal in the beautyberry bush under the bedroom window, the bush his mother had planted years ago. With the week he'd survived, not to mention all the airplanes and jet lag, his hope had been to sleep in, to try to ignore the fact that today he had to fly to Florida to confess everything. Instead he would sleep late and allow his internal machinery to perform whatever healing was necessary. And yet, that cardinal's pretty call, for all the world the whistle of a paperboy calling his dog to their dawn labor, and the memory of Barbara and her trowel making her contribution to the colors of P Street and to everyone close to her, made him cherish even this wakeful, miserable dawn.

He knew what he had to do that day; understood it to be the climax of a madcap week, the abrupt end of a half-hearted presidential run that had lasted . . . he tried to count back to his conversation on the terrace with Walter, the day he'd dropped a crystal glass down the side of a cliff just to hear it crash through the cedars and smash to bits on the rocks below. Six days? Could that be right? Only six days? And here he was, resting on the seventh. He had to laugh at that. Genesis could have said, And on the seventh day, God slept in. Or even better, On the seventh day God woke early and couldn't fall back to sleep because of the racket from that damn cardinal He'd created a couple of days earlier.

He missed Aziza. If she'd been asleep beside him he could have awakened her and recited his redacted Genesis. She would have laughed; he was certain of that. Then they would have made love. He missed her with an ache deep in his stomach. One day together after twenty years apart, and the emptiness nearly doubled him over.

He could try it with Wanda: Hey! On the fifth day God created the birds of the air and on the sixth day said, It's five o'clock in the morning *so shut the fuck up*! She wouldn't think it was hilarious, but she'd make love to him. Again. And probably for the last time, since later today he would confess himself before the killer gaze of Wayne Redmon, and that would be that. Bye-bye White House dreaming. Bye-bye Kentucky Five. His name would be added to that long list of comic losers whose genitalia had tainted their political careers. Argentine strippers in the Tidal Basin, teenage boys in a bathhouse, an intern in the Oval Office. And now, an online affair. Wanda would feel the humiliation more than he himself would. At least his downfall was groundbreaking—the first-ever Internet love scandal in American political history.

Then again—his silver lining for the day's clouds—maybe Mara wouldn't blackmail at all. You can't blackmail an honest man. He released *blackmail* from its virus vault, let it roam around at will, but replaced it with *president*.

He finally gave up on sleep and was downstairs making coffee when Wanda, apparently awakened by his kitchen fumblings, walked in, looking pleasantly sleepy and still wearing only her babydoll outfit.

"You should have waked me up. I was planning to fix your breakfast today."

"Where's Juanita?"

"I gave her the week off, since you were gone."

"And you were gone."

"Stop it."

"I was just teasing."

"It hurts. False accusations always hurt worse."

"Sorry. That's the last time."

She started rummaging through the fridge. "Unfortunately there's not much here for breakfast. I haven't had a chance to order groceries."

He didn't say anything; just let the silence hang there.

229

"There's cereal." She opened a bottle of milk and gave it a sniff. "Oops. Maybe not."

"Coffee's enough. I have an incredibly busy day. I wonder if it's too early to pester Holly."

"Oh, here are some Pop Tarts."

"That's fine. I'm really not very hungry."

"Well, shoot! I had planned to make sausage gravy and biscuits, some fried apples. A real big mountain man's breakfast for my real big mountain man."

"Don't worry. It's the thought that counts."

"Oh, shoot, anyway." She stomped a foot in mock pique, a little girl thwarted in an attempt to play grown up.

"I'll fix your coffee if you'll run back upstairs and get me Wayne's contact details."

"You said you'd knock off the . . . "

"No, really. This has nothing to do with anything. I'm concerned about his divorce, that's all."

"I can *not* for the life of me understand why. You and Wayne were never close friends, and now you're going to fly all the way to Key West just to give him a big hug?"

"He's been my supporter for years. Let's just leave it at that, okay? For now. Run and get your address book for me."

She adjusted the toaster, pressed down the Pop Tarts, and did as he asked. She looked away from him, but he had already noticed the redness in her eyes.

He phoned Holly's cell. She answered quickly, with her usual expectant lilt, the phone equivalent of a big smile. "Oh good, you weren't asleep."

"When do I ever sleep?"

"I'm happy to say I don't know the answer to that question."

"And why does that make you so happy?"

"Because I'm in enough trouble already."

"Fair enough. I thought the party went well, didn't you?"

"Did you see the late news?"

"Oh, yes. And the early morning news."

"Listen, I need to get to Florida *asap*. Can you make the arrangements?"

230

"To Tallahassee?"

"No, Key West. Why Tallahassee?"

"I just got a fax."

"You're at the office already? Jesus."

"I'm too amped to sleep, boss. You're the media darling of the moment, and I knew there'd be a *shitload* of invitations to deal with. And I was right. The one from Tallahassee is from Cole Gibson! Even I've heard of him. He's so famous that even Senator Laverty wants him to run his southern strategy."

"Who told you that?"

"Luke. He beat me here this morning."

"Sheeze. You guys are going to be so disappointed."

"For now, we're on a roll."

"I'm sorry Holly, but no. Just get me to Key West, and forget about Cole Gibson. All of that is pointless now."

"C'mon boss! This is the thrill of a lifetime. Let's ride it out."

He hesitated a bit, moved the phone away from his mouth so that Holly couldn't hear him take a deep breath. If it hurt this much just to disappoint his secretary, how could he bear his approaching ordeal? How could he explain to Walter and Roxy that they must die on foreign soil because of his Internet deceit? And Aziza. How could he ever look into her sad blue eyes again, when all he would find there was the recognition that the man she'd once seen as the savior of her people was in fact an impostor; a cheap, emasculated fraud. But he couldn't break up a marriage, even a bad one. Not for love, friendship, or the greater good. The truth trumped all those, and it had to be told.

"Sorry, Holly. Just give it up, and book me through to Key West."

25

FRIDAY *FAJR*: **04.56.**

That's all the message said, but Amin knew what it meant, so as the day was breaking he rode his Vespa into the city center to the al Omari mosque, made his ablutions along with a scant few other worshippers, prayed, and was sitting on a bench outside the mosque, lacing up his shoes, when at last someone sat down beside him.

Amin didn't much like the way this thing was playing out. Abu Ali hadn't even been one of the worshippers. He plopped himself down, no *salaam* or anything, did nothing at all with his shoes; simply sat there flipping a set of worry beads as though he were alone on a park bench.

His shoes tied, Amin sat up and in the dawn light noticed three men standing at what amounted to the three points of the parking lot. He recalled from his training that in any situation designed to menace you, the thing to do is relax, act as if you're way too thick to take note of the intimidation. Good advice, surely, but advice not normally thought necessary within your own group. It took him a while to convince himself that it wasn't his imagination. It wasn't normal anxiety juiced on the sight of a hotel in ruins, and of a man whom you know with complete certainty to be an agent of Satan, walking out of his grave to give TV interviews. But he tried to collect himself, tried to be cool.

Abu Ali finally spoke. "A couple of things I just don't get. Get up and walk to that white van over there. Open the side door and get in the back."

Amin did that. It was empty inside, and would be quite dark with the door closed. In spite of his dread of this darkness, he had started to pull the door shut when a hand caught it. Two of the perimeter guards followed him inside, while the third took the wheel. Abu Ali hadn't joined them, and when the van started moving Amin wondered what that meant to his situation, but the van simply pulled the fifty feet to the bench, and Abu Ali got in. Amin laughed to himself, *Lazy bastard*, even though he knew it was really a status move. The high and mighty don't walk.

Here we go again, he thought, as the blindfold went on. Mercifully he wasn't handcuffed this time. One of the guys even said, "This is just for everybody's security," and it was removed as soon as they'd parked the van, climbed some crumbling cement stairs, and entered a room that smelled of mint and of old oil in a deep fryer.

They all sat down at a long, metal table, four of them on one side, facing him, but then one guy seemed to pick up a signal of some kind, because he stood up and walked around and behind to where Amin couldn't see him at all. He could sense him only as a shadow thrown by the lamp in the ceiling. Across from him, Abu Ali sat between the other two. Clearly this was his court to hold.

"In the name of God, the Compassionate and the Merciful," he began. "Clear up one little thing for me. Ibn Burak. So-called Ibn Burak."

"I'll help any way I can."

"I'm sure you will, whether you want to or not. First, fill us in on this powerful American you've been spending so much time with."

"He's not very powerful. He represents one small district, one of about four hundred, I think, in America. His vote is valid in only one-half of one of three branches of the U.S. government. Maybe you've studied the structure of the American government."

"I wonder what type of person would know about this. But never mind . . . continue."

"All I mean is that he's a tiny part in the American power machine."

"He's been on TV a lot, for a nobody."

"Only because he happened to be in that hotel. Before that nobody ever heard of him."

"Two points here: *You* had heard of him. And he wasn't in that hotel."

He couldn't very well say, *My mom's theory is that he was with a*

233

Ukrainian prostitute, so he said, "He was an old family friend. But I don't know where he was at the time of the blast, any more than anybody else does."

"And what else don't you understand any more than anybody else does?"

"Uh, not much, I guess." For the first time he looked at Abu Ali not as a better, an adept worthy of some awe and respect—not like the Sheikh, of course, but up the ladder a ways from himself. Now he saw him as an ordinary human, not a very handsome one at that, with blood and muscles and bone, with only one life to live, that one probably already more than half completed, a man with ordinary skills and intelligence, if that, trying his best to make his mark as high up on the doorpost as he can jump; a man not past cheating a little in the process, if it'll gain him an inch or two.

"And what does that mean?"

"I think mainly it means I didn't understand the question."

"Then let me make it simple for you: This nobody American you describe—so nobody that his face was all over the news all week—you had this American dog on a leash for two full days and he's still alive. How can you call yourself a *jihadi* if you can't execute a man like that? Why didn't you even report this to us? Can you imagine the impact his beheading would have made? We could have milked it for weeks, then sawed his *kafir* head off, posted the video on *mawsuat.com* for all the world to see. We could have every *kafir* in the world trembling at the sound of the name Abu Ali. But because you let him go, now he's a *kafir* hero."

"Hey, he's an old family friend. He's known my parents for years. He held me in his arms when I was a baby. Or so I hear. I can't quite remember." He gave a quick smile to the two men flanking Abu Ali. It seemed that they wanted to share it, but dared not. "It's a sin to kidnap a man like that and murder him."

Abu Ali leaned forward across the table and slapped him. It caught him completely by surprise. He wanted to stand and challenge, but he saw the shadow lift an arm, and sat quietly.

"We decide what's a sin and what's not."

"You, or the Qur'an?"

"Me *and* the Qur'an." He lifted an eye toward the man behind

Amin. This time the arm came down. Delivered from behind, a fist to the side of the face does instant damage to the ear, the eye socket, to the delicate capillaries of the temple, as well as to the psyche. He'd once crashed his Vespa into the seawall along the corniche, and it had felt like that, only this time he had no helmet. He used a sleeve to wipe a trickle of blood from his ear.

"And another thing, Clark Hatling is on our side."

"What does that mean?"

"He believes in the Palestinian cause. He knows we got kicked out of our homes and he wants to help."

"Does he want to drive all the Jews into the sea?"

"Well, no. He wants a non-religious state where we can all be free to follow whatever religion . . ."

"And you call that our side? You know what I think? I think it's *your* side."

"Meaning?"

"Meaning I think this guy who held you in his arms was holding his own baby! His own blue-eyed little *kafir* baby."

"That's ridiculous!"

"Who got you out of Israeli custody? Nobody's in and out of Israel the same day."

"A Lebanese policeman saw them kidnap me. He ran the number plates on my Mom's car, and notified her. She called her old friend in Washington. Simple as that."

"She called her old *lover* in Washington. Your blue-eyed mother and her blue-eyed lover."

He addressed the other three: "He's just making shit up as he goes."

"Is that so? Then think about this: Does your mother's true husband have blue eyes? Answer: No. And we all know that the father's power determines eye color."

"This is unbelievable!" he told his guards. "Your boss doesn't even know about genetics."

"Unbelievable? Why do you think that the Prophet, peace be upon him, ordered that a Muslim man could take a Christian wife, but a Muslim woman must marry a Muslim?"

"So the children would be Muslim, of course."

"Yes! It's the father's power that carries it. Just like your blue eyes, you son of a *kafir*."

He started to stand but the one behind pushed him down. "A lot of us have blue eyes. You'd better think before you talk like that."

"Look who's threatening who." He stood and pointed down at Amin. "I know you destroyed the whole operation. You warned your father not to stay in that hotel that night."

"Pure nonsense. You're hallucinating. Maybe you're on some of those drugs you've been selling in Israel." He remembered something that galvanized his courage, this time something Clark had said. Most of history boils down to petty factions competing over petty prizes.

"How else did that man know to leave the hotel?"

"Was it your operation? Did you even know about it in advance? Hell, after it was over, a dozen groups claimed responsibility, but before? Not a word from anybody. If you knew about it why didn't you call CNN two minutes before the blast? That's how you get credibility."

"You're in no position to instruct me . . . "

"Look, I'm just following orders! I don't know what else to do."

"Whose orders?"

"The Sheikh's."

"He ordered you to spare the *kafir*?"

"No, he only said to live my normal life as before, until I got new instructions. In my normal life before I never killed any old family friend. So if you don't like my action, take it up with the Sheikh."

"I agree that the Sheikh was a great leader."

"We all agree on that." But he thought, *Was?* "So let me get this right. You're saying I aborted the Sheikh's operation in order to save my father's life?"

"That's what I'm saying."

"That's easily proved."

"How? Can we ask your mother who she was fucking?"

He could have slapped him right then, but he had him where he wanted.

"No. I mean let's go ask the Sheikh. Let's get in the van and go right now."

Abu Ali hesitated. He had overplayed his hand. Even his three henchmen seemed to know it. The two men Amin could see turned to look at Abu Ali. The shadow seemed to draw in on itself.

"This is just a final warning, Ibn Burak. So-called Ibn Burak, rich kid son of a *kafir*. I'm warning you that we've got our eye on you. One more misstep and you're history."

26

THE BLACK BEAUTY was anchored at the Westin, so Holly went ahead and booked Clark there for the night. He sent his bags to his room and headed straight for the marina, where he soon spotted it—a fifty-foot yacht with a white hull and white sails. There was nothing black about it, except the name of the coal company Wayne Redmon owned. This grown man's toy had probably set him back a decade's salary for the average coal miner he employed. Clark stepped behind a paradise tree, took out his phone and dialed the number Wanda had given him.

"Yellow."

"Wayne, it's Clark Hatling. How are you doing?"

"Clark! I've been watching you on the news."

"How does it look?"

"Looks damn good. Where are you and what do you need? You know I'm always here to help."

"Actually I'm here to help you."

"Here? Where's here?"

"Key West."

"You're in Key West right now? No kidding?"

"I just flew in. Can we meet up?"

"Sure, Clark. But I'm out at sea now."

Clark watched as Wayne, dressed in an orange Speedo and nothing else, hustled himself into the cockpit. "So your phone works out at sea, does it?"

"To some extent, yes. I'm probably at the limit about now."

As he had expected, Wayne fired up the engine. Clark climbed up the rear ladder, made his way down into the salon and by the time Wayne had backed out of the slip and maneuvered his way out of the marina into the ocean, he had poured himself a neat whisky and was sitting comfortably at the table.

"You still there, Wayne?"

"Just barely."

"Why don't you cut your engine and go fix yourself a drink?"

Wayne figured it out but couldn't believe it until he walked down into the salon. Clark watched his hairy legs scurry down the steps.

"Well, fuck me with a hoe handle! You're not armed, are you?"

"Of course not."

"You can see I'm not. Are we going to be adult about this?"

"I don't see we have much choice."

"Wanda phoned to warn me. She said you were coming tomorrow."

"Because that's what I told her."

"You're a sneaky bastard."

"You should know."

Wayne just stood there for a moment. He had a thick cover of gray hair right down over his paunch. Clark wondered what Wanda found attractive about him. But Wayne had never suffered for women, so he must have had something. Great eyes and a yacht, for starters.

"Maybe I will have that drink. Yours needs refreshing?"

"Sure. And an ice cube. I didn't know where . . . ah, there they are. Next time I'll help myself, since what's mine is yours."

"And what's yours is mine?"

"I suppose there's no great harm in sharing ice cubes. But I'm not here to talk about my ice cube. I'm here to talk about yours. I hear you're getting a divorce."

"Yep. You want Connie? She's going for a discount."

"I hear you got caught online."

"Never trust a caddy, that's what I learned. Next time that little bitch says use a 3-wood, I'm going with my 9-iron."

"Ha! You're taking this pretty well."

"It's costing me a lot of money, but I'll be honest with you, Clark. I never could stand Connie. I got control over her daddy's mines at his death. I knew I would, and that explains the whole thing. Including years of torment. Not to mention this cruiser."

"It's one hell of a canoe."

"Thanks. Welcome aboard. I forgot to say that."

239

"You were too busy looking me over for weapons." They both smiled, quietly sipped their drinks. The sea was so calm they might have been alone in a bar. "So, the caddy who spotted you . . . I think I might know her."

"God, let's hope not. The bitch."

"Do you think if I spoke to Connie and I explained the truth to her . . . "

"Shit buddy, she *knows* the truth. She caught me red-handed. That gook bitch laid in ambush and the next time I came online she called Connie, who swept into my study at about 2 a.m. and caught me pumping my little sawed-off to beat the band."

"Connie *caught* you?"

"Mount Fucking Vesuvius. Haven't you ever used those sites? They're the greatest innovation since augers in a coal mine."

"What are you talking about?"

"These women from all over the world have these webcams, you know, and for a few dollars they'll take their clothes off for you, squeeze their titties—anything you want them to. Finger themselves. Pet the bunny. While you whack off."

"Sheeze! I've heard about them, but never actually saw one."

"They're great, man. Cost effective; no cops; no STD's. You feel so powerful, like a god, man! You type "Suck your finger," and in seconds, from halfway around the world, a woman obeys. You should log on, give it a try. Log on and log off, if you catch my drift."

"No need to now, Wayne. Something's turned Wanda into a real firecracker."

27

THE NEW WHEELCHAIR van was a lipstick red one, because, as Walter admitted, he chose it while in the throes of a mid-life crisis. Roxy said that it was more of a crisis for her, since that meant he would live to be about a hundred and fifty, but she liked the color anyhow. It got some stares from Alpha-Beta Club customers as it pulled over to the curb on Hamra Street and began to unload its passengers. Mushtaq, the Indian driver imported from Dubai, stepped out of the van and operated the lift. First he wheeled Roxy out, then a paraplegic Lebanese lady who looked older than Roxy, although in fact she was younger than Aziza. Walter followed with Roxy, as Aziza rose from her café table to greet them all. Roxy introduced the Lebanese woman as Umm Sami, or Mother of Sami. This Sami, the Alpha-Beta's waiter she'd met while lunching there with Roxy, wheeled his mom to a table on the patio.

Sami asked Aziza what she wanted, hurried inside and came back wearing his Alpha-Beta t-shirt and carrying a tray of evidently pre-ordered drinks. He hammed the officious waiter routine, as they all laughed at him. His mom scolded him at some volume, insisting she had ordered something completely different, but she would drink this anyway, but only because she was a kind and generous woman. Other customers overheard the complaint, looked around, and joined the following laughter. Sami said, "You are most gracious, my dear mother," and Walter said, "Here, you can have mine," because he had ordered a beer, and everybody laughed some more. They told Aziza about their tour of the malls, showed her the pretty pashmina shawls they'd bought. Using the small screen of Walter's camera, they showed her a video of their wheelchair race along the Corniche. Clearly they had enjoyed a rollicking outing.

She wished her mother had been painting them with some detachment, from behind her easel across the street. She wished she didn't have to tell Walter and Roxy what she had figured out about her ex-husband.

As the little group broke up, Sami stayed to work his shift, and Aziza asked if it would be all right for Walter and Roxy to stop off at her office at the university while Mushtaq delivered Umm Sami to her home. It was an unusual request. Of the few times the Sislers had been to her office, it was only as a convenient place to meet, usually for some university function: a concert, or a lecture. This invitation, however, involved inconvenience, so both Walter and Roxy knew something had gone wrong, mostly likely something to do with Clark.

Once the three of them had settled into her cramped, private space, she forced herself to do what she'd so far managed to avoid: weave together the strands of an unfolding tragedy.

"So . . . I don't know how to begin this. This is totally hush-hush, okay? If I'm out of my bloody mind, just forgive me from the start. It may be that my divorce has unleashed an overactive imagination. Maybe I watch too many newscasts of political-religious violence after all those years researching the political-religious violence of a thousand years ago. Or maybe I'm just a new single parent finally wakening to my duty to be a father as well as a mother."

"Sugar," Roxy said, "if you're asking us to not leave this room thinking you've lost your ever-lovin' mind, it's way too late for that."

Aziza smiled at her. "Good. Well . . . here's how I . . . " She paused to look down at her hands and folded them across her knees to force them still. "Here's one important point. When Clark left here after our one year together, married Wanda, became a basketball star, all that, and my father so nearly went bankrupt that he asked me to marry into money, I thought, what do I care? What difference did it make to me at that point who I married? And Yousuf wasn't a bad guy. You remember him from then, right? He was totally secular, good-looking, suave, had the patter. Generous with his money, if not his affection. He knew I'd been in love with Clark, but didn't seem to take it personally. A non-jealous Lebanese? What a find! He would even read the

242

sports page and say, 'Boston won again. Clark scored twenty.' Years later when Clark got on at AUB, almost the first thing Yousuf asked him was to see his championship ring."

Walter said, "That's odd—I remember him as being so jealous he stopped coming to our place if he knew Clark and Wanda would be there."

Aziza laughed. "Oh, he didn't mind Wanda one bit, I can tell you, and for a long time he seemed friendly with Clark. But little by little he started to hate Clark. He thought I would soon come around and see rich-and-important Yousuf as a towering figure over lowly Professor Hatling, but what he in fact saw was that Clark and I were so perfect together, researching, writing papers, attending conferences, that Yousuf's money meant nothing. Clark even had a sexier wife!"

"Yes, but you had his children," Roxy said. "That must mean something. And Wanda soon enough hauled Clark back home, the civil war came, we left for Dubai. Surely all that would have damped down any intensity of his jealousy. And anyway you're divorced."

"Divorced, yes. With Clark back in my life. And now in Amin's life too. I've no doubt that Amin wrote him about that."

"Oh sugar, that old tom cat is probably up to his neck in wives and mistresses in Saudi Arabia."

"Saudi Arabia," Aziza repeated with a little laugh. She imagined a swarm of raven-robed women pecking him away bit by bit. "Let me ask you, Walter, do you still have contacts there?"

"In Saudi? Sure. Lots. Why?"

She hesitated to extend this line of thought. "I'm worried about Amin. For whatever reason, I've never really known him well, and now it seems he's more of a stranger than he ever was. At times he's his old happy-go-lucky self, but there's a strain on him now that I don't recognize. He went through a religious stage, then seemed to grow out of it. But see, that's one thing that tipped me off. He didn't grow out of it into anything. He simply reverted to being a teenager."

"But he is a teenager, dear."

"He's twenty now."

243

"But a switch doesn't turn on the lights the day you turn twenty."

"Yes, I told myself that. But did you know he was arrested for possession of narcotics?"

"I never heard a word."

"In Israel."

"In Israel! Good Lord. Then how is he out now?"

"Clark. I phoned him and he used his influence. I hadn't talked to him in years. He got in touch with Prime Minister Ben-Nun somehow, and they let Amin go free."

"Clark said you'd contacted him over some government red tape, but I had no idea. This is red tape on steroids."

"And Yousuf should be grateful to Clark. Not want him dead."

"No, he would see it another way, that Clark now was the one with the clout. His own son, saved by his old rival."

"Does Amin look like a drug user? Does he give off any signs?"

"None. And I supply him with plenty of money, so he wasn't peddling drugs out of financial need. I couldn't imagine what he was up to."

"Oh, baby. I'm so sorry."

"It gets worse—I think. Sometimes he slips out of the house before dawn. One time I followed him. He went to a mosque."

"That doesn't sound so bad. It's not like he was off to an opium den."

"Crack house, Waldo. What century are you living in?" She thought it would lighten Aziza's mood, but she seemed not to hear.

"And he seems so dead at heart. When we thought Clark had died, he was absolutely frozen about it. He'd just spent two full days in his company, yet he was completely unmoved."

Now Walter made the connection—what Aziza was trying desperately not to say, or even think. The Israeli connection; the Saudi connection. Two days with Clark, and then the blast— maybe the time frame was not a coincidence. He had to force it out of her, so he asked, "And why did you ask me about my contacts in Saudi Arabia?"

"I'm not really sure. Maybe it's just me being silly."

"Lay it out straight for us, Aziza. I know it's not about how many wives Yousuf has."

She shrugged in resignation. "He was never very religious until all the Saudi money started pouring in. It was only when Yousuf got religion that Amin started acting so pious. He always craved his father's approval. Not that he ever got much of it. It's only that . . . okay . . . just answer me this: Do you think that some kind of family link with radical jihadists could open up . . . I don't know how to put it . . . revenue streams?"

"Let me say it for you honey, so you don't have to say it yourself. You think maybe Clark told Amin where he was staying in Tiberias, Amin told Yousuf, and Yousuf tipped off some of his less savory customers?"

"Yousuf phones him sometimes—more than he used to, that's for sure, and I know they're in email contact. He probably pumped Amin for information about Clark. Amin just innocently divulged everything he knew."

"I'll put it even plainer than Walter did. Can Yousuf enrich his nasty self by offering his son up to the *jihad*?"

"Yes, something like that. Maybe exactly like that."

"I don't know the answer myself," Walter said, "but I know some people who would love to find out for us."

Later, at home in Beit Mery, he told Roxy, "That last part was true. I know just who to contact. But the first part was a little fib. I do know the answer: there's a fortune in it. And the more the blood flows, the more the money flows."

The following week Walter phoned Aziza to tell her that Amin was probably out of danger now. Yousuf was under arrest in Saudi Arabia.

28

CAMPAIGN NOTE TO *self:* Never again start the afternoon with Wayne Redmon and a bottle of bourbon.

Clark clasped his head and attempted to triage which body part needed the toilet bowl most. The words "six hundred dollars" also came up, as that's how much he could have saved by skipping the Westin altogether and heading straight for the boat. He and Wayne had spent the night far out at sea, in an area that Wayne and his GPS deemed suitable for an incredibly unpresidential trio of activities: drinking, deep sea fishing, and planning how to murder their wives. What rescued the night from being just one more span of half-remembered, alcohol-abetted nonsense—in addition to not drowning forty miles offshore—was hooking his first deep-water fish, a massive swordfish that was seduced by a squid and a six-inch blue glow stick, and which struggled mightily for hours in bitter repentance of that single moment of weakness.

They released it. In the process it nearly pulled them both over the side of the Black Beauty and into the black water. Back at the Westin the next day, as he stood motionless in the shower and let the pulsing water batter him back to sensibility, he tried to imagine what tales the world's press would have weaved around his death at sea following so closely on the near-miss at the Galilee. How would it all have fit together? Hamas, Hezbollah, the Islamic Revenge, al Qaeda, *jihad*, Team Sisler, the United Arab Emirates, big oil, big coal, the Southern Baptist Church, a transgressing wife and her coal-baron lover, a beautiful Filipina in Israel. An empty Black Beauty adrift on the high seas. A lone Muslim woman weeping silently on a bench in Beirut.

The asshole from the *Washington Post* might have parlayed it all into a lucrative tour of the conspiracy-theory circuit. Who would buy: he got drunk and a swordfish pulled him overboard? Nobody's that naïve anymore, not since Oswald.

He recalled his reaction, months earlier, the day he first encountered Mara online—that instant of irrational fear that flooded every cell of his body when his eye fell on the word *Israel* in her profile. It was a primal fear, as when a dog scents a snake. He'd wanted to click off and flee that coffee shop as fast as his feet would carry him. But he had talked himself down, unwilling to believe how minutely incorrect the irrational could be at predicting the future. He remembered the hymn the church group sang: *Throw out the lifeline. Your brother is sinking, sinking.*

The shower was a good one, though not worth six hundred dollars, surely. The nap that followed seemed to bring the price down, and a lunch of sesame mahi-mahi made him feel so much better that he decided to think of his total bill of $645.35 as a very reasonable charge for a hospital stay. The scent of ginger mingled with the salt-sea smell that somehow remained in his head, and the pain in the muscles of his back and arms, right around his shoulders and up both sides of his neck, reminded him that the swordfish was still within him, still fighting. He put *blackmail* back in the virus vault, and gave *president* free rein. He called Holly for Cole Gibson's phone number.

"Congressman Hatling! This is quite a coincidence. My wife and I spent most of the night discussing you." He hesitated to say, *researching*.

"Most of the night? I trust you're not losing sleep over me."

"We're dealing with a sick little boy here, so let's just say we were going to be awake in any case."

"Nothing too serious, I hope."

"Strep throat. Woke up with it about midnight. He gets it a lot."

"Poor little guy. How old is he?"

"He's five."

"At that age they tend to get sick suddenly and just as suddenly get well again."

"We hope he'll soon grow out of it. But it did give us a chance to run some numbers on you and sketch out a strategy."

"*Pro bono*, at that."

"Yes. For the time being."

They both laughed.

"It seems I'm suddenly a matter of public interest."

"Amazing how these things happen, isn't it?"

"You see it happen to other people but you don't expect to be at the center of it."

"It took you by surprise, did it?"

"Sure did," he said affably, but wondering, *A bomb in a hotel? How could it be otherwise?* "In fact my thoughts were running more to retirement as an adjunct professor of history somewhere."

"And now?"

"Now I'm entertaining options."

"I'll take that as politico-speak for *I'm on fire with ambition.*"

Clark paused for a few seconds. Why bother to contradict that? It was a mere quip. But he decided on, "No, let's start out with total honesty. I have always been a lukewarm politician. You should know that from the start."

"And you should know that you'll never become president with that attitude."

"I totally agree. My most basic decision is whether I want to stoke that fire or not."

"I gather from your basketball career that you can be a tremendous competitor."

"I have that capacity, yes. Do I want to loose it onto an unsuspecting world?"

Again Cole laughed. Humor in a politician was worth more than a whole series of attack ads.

"When can we get together, Congressman?"

"Call me Clark. At the moment I'm in Key West. I'd previously cleared my agenda right through the weekend."

"You mean for your visit to Israel?"

"Exactly."

"Don't worry. I'm sure you sold more than soap this way."

"You have been reading up."

"My wife. We collaborate these days. She'd love to meet you too. Would it be possible for you to stop in Tallahassee on your way north? You're welcome to stay with us. We're a bit trapped here at the moment."

"You've got a five-year-old with strep."

"Exactly. You remembered. I'm impressed."

Impressed is one thing, Cole thought as he watched Clark enter the arrivals area at the Tallahassee airport, but taking you to the presidency is another. Still, he looked the part—tall, slope-shouldered, rolling his modest black suitcase along, walking with a grace that, even at his age, spoke of an athletic past. Onlookers noticed him and hung back, discreetly pointing to him and whispering. Was it just because he cut a figure, or did they recognize him from the news?

Cole smiled and stuck his hand out a good ten yards away, giving him plenty of lead time. He knew that politicians didn't like to be pounced on, especially one who'd nearly been assassinated just a couple of days earlier.

"Congressman! I'm Cole Gibson. It's a pleasure."

"*Igualmente!*" Cole didn't know how to react to that until Clark showed him the Spanish phrase book he was carrying. "My airplane reading. Bought it in Key West. I figure, when in Florida . . ."

"I'm not sure that will win Hispanic votes these days, but we can discuss that later. For the moment the only Spanish you need to know is margarita."

"That's a relief. And how's the kid?"

"Much better. He was reading *Harry Potter* when I left."

"I'm glad he's on the bounce-back. And a budding genius at that."

"Gets it from his mom, I assure you."

"In that case I look forward to being intimidated by her."

It didn't take long. He was sipping his margarita on the back deck, where Cole had the grill going and Jack was putting together some castle sort of thing with Lego blocks. Danielle walked out the back door carrying a stuffed trout wrapped in foil. She stopped, cocked an ear as though listening for something both faint and important. "Hear that?" she asked. Clark listened carefully to the light breeze from the lake. Cole looked at him and rolled his eyes. "Do you hear a bird, Congressman?"

249

"You can call me Clark, if you don't mind."

"Okay, Clark. What kind of bird do you hear?"

"None at all."

"Exactly. And now Nature Boy will tell us what that non-bird sound means."

Jack looked up at them. Through a screen door Clark could see that Joe was watching them.

"Yes, dear," Cole said. "I'd be happy to interpret for these unfortunate human beings who can't speak with animals."

"Like Dr. Dolittle!"

"Yes, Jack. Dr. Dolittle and Mommy. And now Daddy knows that what the silence means is that when Mommy says something we should all stand awestruck just to be in her presence."

"Yes," she said, "and . . . "

"And it means our friend the horny grebe is now flying somewhere south of Omaha, where he will meet his girlfriend and have a bunch of little horny grebes."

"Horned."

"Whatever."

Clark said, "I hope you boys will pay attention and try to remember the conversations that your parents have while you're little, because you will certainly treasure them all your life."

Jack looked up toward Joe, behind the screen door. Danielle and Cole looked at each other.

"This fish needs a few minutes on each side." Cole set something on his watch. "Shall we use the time to run through what Dani and I see as your best strategy?"

"You bet."

"Another margarita while we talk?"

"Get me tipsy and make me president? I smell something fishy." He winked at Joe behind his screen door.

"First of all," Cole opened, "if this *Where was Hatling* media fever doesn't die down . . . let's just say we have to make it go away. If it sticks, then this is just a meaningless chat before dinner."

"Not my first, nor my last, I assure you."

"Fine. The way we see it is that right now the nomination is Laverty's to lose. Foreman can charm children and old ladies, but he's completely gaffe-prone. He'll shoot himself in the foot, probably with a bazooka. He only gets a mention now because the press wants a horse race. Even if Iowa should make him a real threat, Laverty can splice together enough of Foreman's previous bumbles that he becomes his own attack ad. Donors know that. He'll run out of cash before Super Tuesday. Maybe before New Hampshire is truly decided."

"Elise Torsvik is also contesting Iowa," Clark mentioned. "She's an excellent congresswoman. I know her from the Agriculture Committee. I vote yes on ethanol for her, she votes yes on tobacco for me. Two incredibly stupid products continue to churn out lots of money, and we both get reelected. Democracy in action."

Dani said, "I think she'll get her fair share of votes. Old Senator Torsvik is almost a beloved figure in Iowa."

"In my estimation," Cole said, "she's not really running for president. She wants Daddy Rolf's old Senate seat, and this is a tactic to raise her profile statewide. She's reluctant to leave her cozy Iowa Two with its Democratic +7 partisan voting index. Statewide the Iowa PVI is a dead heat."

"Wow. You guys really have been doing your homework. What's my PVI? Would you believe I haven't even checked it since before the last election?"

Dani said, "Don't ask. It's way Republican, maybe +14 or so."

"That's great for you, though. You're a proven winner in Republican territory."

"I'm not the winner. Look at my voting record. They're the winner. They've turned me into a Republican."

Dani laughed, looked around at her sons. "You boys disregard that statement. What the congressman means is that he's a moderate Democrat."

"Hey, it got you elected."

"Only because I was a local sports star back when being a Democrat was still cool. And my dad laid the groundwork."

"Just as Senator Torsvik did for his daughter in Iowa. Still, Laverty will take the caucus. I've been in touch with Simon Angelo, who's totally up on the mid-west, and he says Laverty will win handily. As much as fifty percent. With Foreman and Torsvik basically splitting the rest. That's why you need to skip Iowa. The best you could hope for would be to pick up the scraps. You'll do no more than show your face in Iowa, just enough to say you're not starting your real campaign until New Hampshire."

"Meaning you'll blanket the state with a thousand speeches to tell everybody again and again that you're not in the race."

"Oh! I've got it!" Cole said. "You'll remind Iowans over and over that you would never contest Iowa against your good friend Congresswoman Torsvik, daughter of the great Rolf Torsvik, whom you have respected for years."

"As did my father. At least that has a kernel of truth behind it."

"Close enough for politics, right?" Cole looked toward the door for Joe, to see if he got the joke, but Joe wasn't there.

"How vulnerable is Laverty nationally? In my opinion, by the way, he's quality. I could endorse him with no problems."

"How about being his V-P?"

Clark couldn't say, I've only got two issues—freeing Palestine and pardoning Walter Sisler—so the vice presidency would be useless. He couldn't say, Actually I'd rather retire with my college sweetheart to a small town in France. He probably couldn't even say, I'd rather run a horse farm or teach history at AUB. So he said, "Uh . . . no. That wouldn't interest me at all."

"Good. Then we'll have to beat him, and the way I see it, the best way to do that is to skip the primaries altogether and run against the Republicans."

"What he means," Danielle said, "is that while Laverty is clearly the most popular candidate among Democrats, he will look a lot weaker against Republicans. We need to remind the Democratic voters, right from day one, that come next November we've got to beat a Republican."

"And as we lay out the numbers, the way to do that is to put forward a more centrist Democrat than Laverty. In fact, if I were a Republican politico, I'd be watering at the mouth for a run at Laverty. Dani put together a spreadsheet."

"Basically we think that against any Republican they can throw out there, Laverty could only take: Oregon, Washington. In California he's extremely vulnerable. That's it for the West. In the East he'll take New York, Massachusetts, New Jersey, Connecticut,

Rhode Island, Delaware. Maybe Maryland. D.C., of course. In the South, nothing. In the Midwest, maybe Minnesota. Possibly Wisconsin, but we doubt it. That's it. Plus Pennsylvania, his home state."

"Illinois, very unlikely. But even giving him all the toss-up states, we're looking at a total in the range of 220–230."

"Way short of the 270 he needs. The other heavyweights: Texas, Florida, Ohio—he'll never take them. Michigan—probably not even Michigan. The union jobs have all gone somewhere else."

"To Asia, by way of Walmart," Clark said. "Not that I'm a protectionist. But just between us, that's where they've gone."

"Exactly. So now let's look at you. Dare I say it, but you, or someone like you, who's less liberal than Laverty, more in tune with grass roots . . ."

"What my husband is trying to say without saying it, is that you're a white male of Scots-Irish heritage. You're a Southerner. You're a Baptist. You could possibly take back the South for the Democrats, and still hold most of those liberal western or northern states. If we could win back the South, we wouldn't even need those dead-red states. Texas? They can keep Texas. Let them have their Nebraskas and Montanas. A moderate, Southern Democrat could beat a Republican. Chris Laverty can not."

"There's layer after layer within this analysis, groups we can target any number of ways, but as an overall sketch that's how we see it."

"But in order to get that far we'd have to defeat Laverty on his own court. So to speak."

"That's good. Use sports metaphors. Nothing wrong with that."

"But you're right in what you imply. A few months ago I would have put your chances at 99-1. With all this new publicity, the odds are much better."

"We have to say, though, that we've never seen you on the stump, or in debate."

"But we can work on all that. We can do wonders with image packaging. Far more than what you've needed to win Kentucky Five."

"And," Danielle added, swaying with a gentle flounce, "I'm

253

becoming a whiz at Internet campaigning."

"We calculate that if you can sneak a few delegates in Iowa and make a strong showing in New Hampshire, then Super Tuesday will make you or break you. The trouble is, we're a little bit unlucky with the dates, because the only southern states voting on Super Tuesday are Georgia, Alabama and Tennessee. And Laverty is lucky, because his backyard—New York, New Jersey, Delaware, Massachusetts—not to mention the big cahuna of California, they're all that day. You may take a few western states, but they'll be Republican anyway in November, which won't really demonstrate that our southern strategy can swing the general election our way."

"So if I understand you, you're saying we could reverse the southern strategy of Richard Nixon, which was basically the Republican Party's way of saying "Racists Welcome Here."

"And of course it worked for him, but we think things are different now. We're in with a gamble on general cultural affinity, rather that race."

"You know that straight out of high school I went to a college that had an all-white basketball team."

Danielle said, "Yes, but you did that because it was your state university and your father wanted you to. That's what my research shows. Is that about right?"

"Yes, it's exactly right."

"And you left UK very soon after you got there. To join the military. And when you started playing again it was always on predominately African-American teams. Right?"

"I didn't count. Probably fifty-fifty.'

"Then we can use that to good advantage."

"She's right. We get three spins from that one: loyal to your father and your state; stood up for civil rights; left to fight for your country. Three big winners there. We can have a field day with this."

"So that's our Southern Strategy. And that what makes South Carolina so crucial."

"South Carolina?"

"South Carolina is the first southern state to vote, and they do so before Super Tuesday. Plus, they allow crossover voting, so with a big win there we will be able to demonstrate that you have a wider general appeal than Laverty."

"Then, only a week later, for Super Tuesday, with California, New York, Illinois, and half of everybody else up for grabs, we can plaster the nation with one thought: A vote for Laverty is a vote for a Republican next November. Keep it simple for the average voter. Laverty Can't Win; Hatling Can."

Cole's watch beeped. He walked over to the grill and turned the fish. The soft breeze from the lake carried charcoal smoke and a distantly Mediterranean aroma across the deck. Once again Clark thought of Aziza. Wouldn't she love to be here right now, in this discussion, sniffing this breeze? He decided he would phone her later.

"And Congressman, do you think Gov. Kastner has a lock on the Republican nomination, as most pundits have it?"

"I would think so, yes. He cut Michigan taxes by some huge margin. That's all anybody thinks makes good governance these days. Slash taxes. Is this a trick question?"

"No, not at all. That's the way we see it. All the polling trends point that way. And he's bankrolled to the gunwales."

"Slash taxes *and* one more thing," Danielle added. "Family values. Code word for the religious right wing."

Unaccountably, Clark said, "As if Jesus preached family values." Cole and Danielle shot looks at each other, then at Clark, who added, "Come on. Did thirteen Jewish celibates support family values? Did Paul? Paul said it was preferable for a man *not* to marry." He noticed the eyes flaring at him. "But don't worry—that's just between us. I hate hypocrisy, but a hypocrite I must remain. In public anyway. My daddy taught me well."

"Lucky damn thing," Cole said. "Otherwise the only reason you're here is for a fish dinner."

"Because the religious right wing may well hold the balance of power in the next election. But guess what?" When Danielle saw that neither Clark nor Cole would finish her thought, she finished it herself. "Guess who's the practicing Baptist?"

Clark looked at Jack to signal that he was about to do something silly, then raised his hand, in overeager schoolboy fashion, fingers snapping. "Um . . . that would be me?"

Suddenly Joe was back at the screen door. "Mr. Hatling, sir? Can you come inside?"

"Sure. What's up?"

"They announced you're going to be on TV."

The trout needed another good ten minutes anyway, so they all went inside, even Jack. By this time there was a commercial on, but they all waited, standing there with nothing to say. Clark thought he knew what the others were thinking: that all the campaign strategy they'd been discussing would turn out to be just more hot air before dinner; that as he waited through these endless commercials, his heart must be in his throat; that this newscast would be, at a minimum, yet another piranha assault in the *Where was Hatling* feeding frenzy, or perhaps even the ultimate revelation of the events preceding the Galilee bomb; the end of all his presidential hopes. At worst the beginning of a criminal prosecution.

In fact he was thinking that it mattered little to him which way it broke. If it was a rerun of his P-Street statement, fine. If it was Mara revealing the truth, fine. Aziza would forgive him for that, in effect had already done so. Now he wished he'd cleansed himself by confessing his Danny Davies episode to her. But he could still do that. They could be together in France by tomorrow night. Maybe the bookstore at the Tallahassee airport had a French phrasebook and a copy of *How to Grow Carnations*.

Finally the newsman came back on to announce:

The mystery of how Kentucky Congressman Clark Hatling escaped death in the bombing of the Hotel Galilee has been solved. This from Israeli Channel 7 News:

Mara's face filled the screen. It remained there long enough for even the most detached viewer to absorb her penetrating beauty. The camera pulled back to reveal a necklace and crucifix, the bright gold made dazzling by her sandalwood complexion. The scalloped collar of her white blouse nearly hid the tops of her breasts. She was looking down, as though concentrating on something. As the camera withdrew further the viewer learned that her eyes were

256

fixed on the path of a wheelchair as she navigated the ramp to a platform overlooking the sea. Morty looked irritated, but resigned to the process. Mara turned, apparently at the direction of someone, so that the sea formed the background to the scene. Clark recognized this as the deck where they had sat together, not quite touching; where she had sung a hymn in a language he didn't understand. An unseen interviewer spoke:

"I believe you have information on the whereabouts of U.S. Congressman Hatling at the time his hotel exploded."

Morty answered, "He was with me."

"And could you tell us how he came to be with you?"

"He had apparently heard about my injuries, so he contacted me, asked if he could pay me a courtesy call when he came to Tiberias. So, sure, fine with me. I figured half an hour. But we started having such a fascinating conversation about ways to bring peace to this land, that I invited him to extend his stay through dinner. He's a man overflowing with ideas, and they coincide with my own. In the end we talked well into the night. My wife suggested that instead of going back to the hotel he should stay in our guest room. And he graciously accepted. End of story."

"What sort of ideas did you discuss?"

"We both feel that Israelis and Palestinians need more opportunities to see each other as people, as normal human beings, rather than as the enemy. I had been thinking along the lines of a Mordechaj Warski Foundation, to try to set up such opportunities. The congressman believes that sport can break down barriers. He told me of the segregation of black and white children when he was a schoolboy, and how integrated sports teams brought strangers together as teammates and friends. He said that America as a whole grew accustomed to cheering for sporting heroes of any color. He contends that this process aided the movement toward a tolerant society. Things like that. That's what we spoke about."

"Until what time?"

"Until well after midnight. Maybe even between one and two a.m. My nurse thinks it was as late as that. At my age, what do I care what time I go to bed?"

"Is that how you remember it, miss?"

"Yes. It's part of my job to help Morty . . . Mr Warski, to bed. I was asleep through their conversation, but was awakened to help, sometime after one o'clock."

"And is it true that you were alone with the congressman when he learned of the tragedy?"

"Yes. It was sort of mid-morning. Everybody except me was sleeping late. I was preparing breakfast when the congressman came into the kitchen and asked if I'd heard the day's weather forecast. I had not, so I turned on the television. We have a little TV on the counter there. That's when we learned about it."

"And how did he react?"

"He went straight to telephone the police, and his wife."

Clark watched Mara's downcast eyes as she said "his wife." Perhaps no one else saw it; perhaps he imagined it. But the brave girl had stood up for him. There was no blackmail in her. She would make a fine nurse, or doctor. A fine wife, no doubt. Through thick and thin. She would make a fine anything.

While he was thinking that, he saw a sudden movement to his right. Startled, he turned, almost ducked, in fact, and saw Cole Gibson's right arm held high in the air.

"High fives, Congressman!"

"Yes. Indeed." He slapped hands with all of them.

"Wow!" Joe said. "I never high-fived a Boston Celtic before."

"You may have just high-fived the next president of the United States."

Danielle went to her spreadsheet and announced, "I'm putting the New York and California primaries back in play. Maybe even Florida."

29

WHAT MADE THE MORNING SO UNUSUAL . . .

WHAT MADE THE morning so unusual was that even before Senator Laverty and his wife had said good morning or anything, when Lucinda Laverty looked up from her newspaper and said across the breakfast table to the senator, "Oh my word, this is a hoot!" and when at almost the same split second he looked up from his newspaper and said, "Goddamn son-of-a-bitch!" they were talking about the same thing.

Throughout Chris Laverty's political career, he and Lucinda had always done their best to start each day together at breakfast. They didn't have to say much—quietly reading the newspaper was perfectly acceptable—but this one last vestige of family life was very nearly a sacred ritual. It couldn't happen every single morning, of course. Lucinda acknowledged that. He had to be away a lot, and occasionally she was the one to break ranks for some out-of-town engagement, but it was always seen as the norm they needed to return to at the earliest opportunity.

A subset of this rite was that whoever carried the *Post* to the table (usually Rosa, these days, but everybody knew the drill) would put the sports section by his plate and keep the rest for Lucinda. Even though he was always itching to get his hands on the political news, the couple adhered to a belief established years earlier, soon after he had become District Attorney for Allentown, that, for a man like Chris Laverty, starting the day with the engrossing yet non-partisan and essentially inconsequential world of sports was beneficial to his long-term sanity. Not to mention hers. This system often meant she would offer him juicy *amuse-bouches* of political news while he rejoiced at a Penn State blowout or suffered through another Redskins loss. But this morning they were, like many long-married couples, harnessed together, even if not on the same page. For while she read "Kentucky Dem to

259

Challenge Frontrunner Laverty in New Hampshire," he read, "Former Celtics' Star in NH Primary Race."

He later got quiet chuckles from the journalists outside his home by telling them: "The Democratic Party encourages diversity. We welcome basketball players, football players, cheerleaders, majorettes, you name it. It's what makes us America's party." But later that day, when he heard that Frank Baker and other Celtics from their championship team would be stumping New Hampshire with Hatling, he privately reverted to his original summation: *Goddamn son-of-a-bitch!*

30   FASHIONABLE NECKWEAR

"THE LAST TIME I wore a necktie was at my wedding," Levi Hershko liked to tell his junior officers, "and the next time will be at my funeral." But the latter prediction would turn out to be wrong, unless his meeting with the Prime Minister went far worse than he hoped. He'd met Aviram Ben-Nun once before, but that was at a fund-raiser at beach resort in Tiberias, where his Hawaiian shirts were countenanced, perhaps even envied, by the poolside Likud types in their custom-made suits. And anyway at that time Ben-Nun wasn't yet even the Likud party boss. Today's meeting, though, was with Aviram Ben-Nun, Prime Minister of Israel, at his office in Beit Rosh Hamemshala itself, so a necktie, and a conservative one at that, was in order.

Simply being granted this meeting had been an accomplishment. Even if the PM had some dim memory of the headstrong security agent he'd met up north, by now he would know Levi Hershko as hardly more than a name in a dossier. Given the current state of the region, Levi supposed he'd succeeded only by grounding his request in language that must surely have sounded paranoid. He knew that in the Middle East these days, only maniacs could expect to be taken seriously. So, okay—Levi could do paranoia, because, as he liked to teach his apprentices, being paranoid and wrong is better than not being paranoid, and dead wrong. The subject line of his memo sounded insane enough: *U.S. President a Palestinian Operative.* Perhaps it also explained why he'd been x-rayed and patted down at four different security points along the way, and why three bodyguards remained in Ben-Nun's office after the door closed.

Ben-Nun offered him coffee, nothing more, then got down to business. "So tell me what you've got on Hatling."

"Well, Prime Minister, we know that he spent a year in Beirut as a university student, that he has studied both Arabic and Hebrew, and has a PhD in Near Eastern History from the London School of Economics. We know he returned to Beirut as a professor, and stayed for three years."

"Get on with it."

"We know he had a lover there, a Miss Aziza Aruri. She later married a government official named Yousuf Hatoum, whose highest post was Deputy Minister of Industry. It's reported that he skimmed a lot of cream off big international contracts and is now self-exiled in Saudi Arabia. Maybe in prison. He's gone very quiet—at least the bank account we know about has gone quiet."

"And this somehow impacts on Hatling?"

"The only direct link we can trace is to the son of this Yousuf and Aziza Hatoum. We know that last year, while Hatling ostensibly went to Beirut for an economics conference, he in fact spent almost all his time there with his old lover Aziza, or with her son, Amin."

"That's the prisoner I ordered released from your custody following Hatling's request."

"That's right. We picked him up just north of the Lebanese border. Apparently he was either doing reconnaissance, checking our intelligence into his group and what our response to his probe would be, or he had been sent on a fool's mission. I suspect the latter. A factional dispute; somebody's trying to get rid of him, and disgrace his side in the process."

"Tell me more about this group."

"They call themselves *as-Saif-ul-Muntaqim*—the Sword of the Avenger. The 'Avenger' refers to Allah. *Muntaqim* is one of the ninety-nine names of God. They're a splinter group based in Syria, funded from Saudi Arabia, and headed by the blind imam Issa Abu Fakhr, the one his followers call simply the Sheikh."

"So you contend that Hatling intervened on this boy's behalf because he's sympathetic to their cause?"

"We've got more than that. This boy's mother is Hatling's former lover. And guess when he was born? Exactly during the three-year period when Hatling was teaching at the American University of Beirut. And, the boy has blue eyes."

"Lots of people have blue eyes, Levi. You're saying Congressman

Hatling's own son is a member of a Syrian terrorist squad? Don't you know how preposterous that sounds?" He glanced around the room at his protection, as though to ready them for the flick of his finger that would put this madman under observation in Sha'ar Menashe Hospital.

"Not at all, Prime Minister. We must never forget that although these people make incredibly stupid short-term mistakes, their real strength is that they think long term. They think they can drive us out by continuing a birth rate twice our own. And they are capable of putting moles in place to lie in wait for years and years."

"So tell me your theory in a nutshell."

"I think Hatling fathered this child and the boy was brought up to hate Israel. Meanwhile, I believe Hatling took up his father's position in the U.S. Congress to bide his time until he could make a run for the presidency."

"And who tried to kill him in Tiberias?"

"He did, sir. By that I mean he planted the bomb himself. Someone is trying to seize control of *as-Saif-ul-Muntaqim* from Sheikh Abu Fakhr. Hatling and his son are aligned with the Sheikh. It's a nasty little war they've got going."

"Have you got any evidence at all for this, or is it pure fantasy?"

"Only Hatling had the means—as a U.S. congressman he knew he would bypass strict security. And Hatling had the most to gain. Recall that this was the event that made him famous in America and set up his presidential campaign. Or some ally inside Syria could have smuggled in C-4 explosive—paid off a fishing trawler, tourist cruiser, anybody with a boat. An Ethiopian in a skiff could have done it. It's not impossible. Then someone inside Israel loaded a van with it and handed it over to Hatling. He parked it in the underground lot at the hotel, caught a taxi, paid a nice long visit to his old friend Mordechaj Warski—who, by the way, he'd never met in his life. Never even heard of, from what we can determine."

"We have Warski's statement to the contrary."

"He's lying. He could produce absolutely no documentation of any correspondence between them."

"It might have been by email. Deleted and gone."

"He's lying, sir. That's all I can say. Both him and his wife. I interviewed them both and I know they're lying. And the girl, their Filipina maid. Why did she suddenly turn up a student in Kentucky, Hatling's home state? More to the point, where did she get the money?"

"From Dubai, it says here. From the United Bank of the Gulf."

"And where did UBG come from? It's a reincarnation of the old CCB—Commerce and Credit Bank. Or 'Crooks and Criminals Bank', as regulators called it. Registered in Luxemburg, but largely run from Syria, formerly with complex connections to the Abu Nidal terror group."

"So? Formerly is right. Saddam Hussein had Abu Nidal killed, and the Emiratis turned a cleaned up CCB into UBG. It's a totally legitimate establishment now."

"And a huge depositor there is Ammenstar Oil. Owned by an old friend of Clark Hatling, who just happens to have been running with Gulf oil sheikhs for the past forty years."

"Do you know for sure he bankrolled that Filipina?"

"No, it's not an absolute certainty, but in my business we don't have to convince a jury before we take action."

"No. But you have to convince me."

Levi looked around at the bodyguards. He wished he could ask them, *What the fuck's he think I'm doing here?* He was sure they were following this better than Ben-Nun was. He took a deep breath and started all over. "So why exactly did that Filipina maid turn up in a college classroom in Kentucky?"

"You tell me."

"It was hush money. Hatling gave it to her—it had to come from him. She had something on him, and he wanted her where he could keep an eye on her."

"He's a devout Christian. Didn't you have any of our Christian allies in the U.S. check him out?"

"If you don't mind my saying so, those people are crackpots. They think they can convert us all and then the Messiah will come roaring back to Jerusalem. Sir."

"I know they're out of their minds, Chief Inspector. But they have their uses, and one of them is keeping tabs on supporters of

Palestine. Let me repeat my question, this time for a yes-or-no response. Did you check him out with the Christians?"

"Yes, sir, I did."

"So did I. And what did you find out?"

"They said he was a devout Baptist."

"Exactly. A good Christian Baptist. So let's assume he's educating that Filipina out of Christian kindness. Maybe she's a charity case."

"Prime Minister, with all due respect, you and I are both functioning males of the human species. As is Hatling, I presume. When an aging alpha male pays a bunch of money to a pretty young girl, how often is that charity?"

Ben-Nun didn't say anything. Levi Hershko wondered if he might not have made a huge blunder. Maybe the PM was paying off tarts by the boatload.

"Sir, think about it. Right now this guy may look like a no-hoper, but he's got guts and he's got guile. He has everybody fooled—or, maybe not quite everybody. If you'll seriously consider the scenario I'm laying out here, then that makes two of us he can't fool."

Ben-Nun put down his pen, removed his half-moon glasses and pushed his chair back. His protection tensed. "One more question, then you can go. AIPAC certifies him as our man all the way, right through every vote he's ever cast. And his father too, for that matter. Neither father nor son has ever cast a single House vote against Israel. How do you explain that?"

"Sir, how else would you vote, if you were a Palestinian mole? And if I'm right, by this time next year the principal agent of our deadliest enemy will be sitting in the Oval Office."

31

CLARK WOULD HAVE attended the *History in the Present* colloquium in Brussels no matter what, because he'd done so for the past twenty years, meaning nobody would take much notice when he left the campaign trail—such as it was at the moment, with Iowa and New Hampshire still two months away, and Super Tuesday a month after that. The press wouldn't bother with this; he had had his fifteen minutes and was once again a nobody. And Wanda never wanted to tag along to these thrilling lectures on the most up-to-the-minute gossip in palimpsests, so that was a plus. But even if this was his twentieth straight "the Brussels," as attendees referred to it, as in, "Will you be at the Brussels this year?" this one was special, because Clark had texted that very question to a phone number in Beirut, and had received the reply, "Such cheek!"

Aziza wasn't there, though, not *as such*, as she liked to say, so he fought back the disappointment and tried to distract himself in the mock debates, such as the lively one where one Muslim historian played the part of Averroes defending Aristotle and another was al-Ghazali condemning Aristotle as anti-Islamic. He managed to lose himself for a while in the hammy costumes and wisecracks, in the serious undercurrent of the arguments, but these moments of absorption were short-lived, for now that Aziza was back in his life he would soon turn almost reflexively to his right, where years ago he would have found her, his confederate at so many such gatherings, already looking up at him, her importuning blue eyes waiting for the connection, willing him to make it.

But back at the hotel he found a message from her. It instructed him where to go, and at what time. The time was tomorrow afternoon; the place wasn't in Brussels, nor even in Belgium, but in some little town in France he'd never heard of: Vézelay.

He supposed she had chosen this tiny speck of a French town for some good reason—secrecy, presumably, or a nearby aunt, or cousin—but really he had no clue. He took the early morning *TGV* to Paris, then a regular train to Auxerre. From there a *TER* filled mostly with giggling, shrieking schoolgirls finally dumped him out at a station in Avallon. An older man who spoke clear English directed him to a bus marked Vézelay that was quickly filling with more schoolgirls, so Clark walked in the dead opposite direction and waved down a taxi. Whatever it cost, he would have paid double just to get far away from that bus.

Finally, as an early winter's dusk began to settle on the late afternoon, he stepped from the taxi into a brick-laid square, tightened the scarf around his neck and found himself facing an enormous basilica. It was so off-scale in the tiny town, so dominant, grave, imposing, that for a moment Clark couldn't approach it. It took him by surprise, loomed above him, seemed poised to threaten and demand. He felt a splinter of fear run through him. As the taxi pulled away into the darkening silence, he had an urge to call out after it.

One of the weighty red doors to the narthex was slightly open. He had to put his weight into pushing it. The groan of the hinges signaled intruder. He didn't notice that above him the tympanum, which normally in Romanesque churches held scenes of the Last Judgment, with Jesus separating the exalted from the damned, here in the Basilique Ste-Madeleine featured Christ on His throne as the rays emanated from His fingers to direct His missionaries to go out and conquer the world. Clark didn't notice the unbelievers portrayed as misshapen monstrosities trapped in cells surrounding the commanding Christ. These were the ungodly, to be converted or exterminated: the dog-faced Moor, the Siamese twins, deformed Jews in their caps, midgets, men with ears of elephants, with snouts of pigs. Non-Christians, non-humans; vermin so much easier to revile and slaughter.

Clark walked under all that, ignorant of it for now, his mind fixed on a single thought: Within these walls perhaps there waits a solitary woman who loves me. A woman whom I also love, as I have for thirty damaged years. She may be here in this vast space—yet limited, enclosed, not the whole wide world to hide and to deny in. And if she is here, so what? What does it signify? A

267

brief meeting? A week of pretended reality? A pledge unto death, as the setting encourages? Is that why she asked me here? To make vows before a God neither of us believes in? All this formed one single thought so imposing as to choke off all others, leaving his mind obstructed and spent.

In the half-light filtering down from the clerestory he could make out only one person in the church, an old woman in a peaked scarf, sitting with her head bowed, apparently in prayer. Her breath fogged around her head. Clark started to check the side chapels and then realized: *of course.* She who would never be cowed into wearing a hejab in real life, would willingly wear a scarf in church, in disguise. He walked up to her and as she turned to him she smiled her old smile, her young smile, and he said, "You're as beautiful as ever."

"And you look like hell. What took you so long? If I'd sat here much longer they would have made me a saint."

"I rather doubt that. Not if you did confession first." He sat beside her.

"But you really did come! I knew you would. I want to kiss you. Is it allowed to kiss in an abbey?"

"No," he said, and kissed her. "Absolutely forbidden." He kissed her again. "Violates every rule in the book."

They embraced awkwardly. It should have been outdoors, this moment of renewal, in a park, under a big sycamore whose leaves hovered in an autumn breeze, then landed on their shoulders and stuck there, but here they were in a cold, dark, empty basilica, sitting in folding chairs and making the best of it.

"I've always loved you," Aziza confessed abruptly. "I'm sure I must love you even now." Clark's reaction surprised him but not her. He pressed his face into the wool of her headscarf and without making a sound wept free-flowing tears, wept for all the intervening years of continued love, uncelebrated devotion; silent toasts offered but never acknowledged, no champagne uncorked, no special vacation spots, no tucked-away bistros. Nothing but an empty park bench that civil war couldn't blow away. Aziza stroked the back of his head, giving him as much time as he needed. An early congregant of this church would have seen demons fleeing his body and flying away with bitter rebukes, as had done the seven demons Jesus cast out from Ste-Madeleine herself.

Clark began to feel buoyant from the evacuated weight of those demons. The windows of the church seemed to capture a late ray of sunshine and refract it in colors just where they sat. *I know, I know*, Aziza said to him, smoothing the hair at his temples.

He soon felt giddy, immaterial, a child after a cry. "So," he finally caught his breath. "Where do we go from here?"

She released her hold on him so they could collect themselves. "First off, tell me about the campaign."

"You mean how I'm doing?"

"Yes. Can you win?"

Here Clark finally allowed his gaze to ease upwards, towards the arresting dark-ribbed ceiling arches, illuminated way up there by the narrow clerestory windows, and then onwards, toward, if the psychology of religious architecture had it right, heaven itself. He knew he had been granted a moment of grand action, such a moment as will determine the rest of your life. He could simply say, *It's not going so well*, and that would be that.

Aziza let him work his way through all this. She knew that he was thinking what she was, that what was to stop them? Screw the campaign: they could walk out of that church right now, find a real estate agent, buy some broken down farmhouse outside some little French village, work on that cantankerous farmhouse by day, and in the evening drive to the village *brasserie* for a wholesome dish of white bean stew or *choucroute* and a nice bottle of wine. Grow carnations for the farmers' market, where she could also sell her famous *manakeesh* with *zatar* and minced lamb. Clark could meet the locals for *boules* or even basketball, while she and her neighbors laughed at them, and talked of flowers, herbs, and rainfall.

What was to stop them? He could call it a day with Wanda and let her party on. Inside the beltway it would cause a lively scandal for a press cycle or two, but who paid any attention to that stuff? Certainly not their neighbors in Provence, or the Auvergne, or wherever they ended up. What's more those neighbors could care less who ate pork or drank wine, who wore a scarf or who didn't. They only cared that you ate and drank with gusto, improved your

269

French daily, and learned their names.

Whose lives were we talking about, anyway?

Well, the Palestinians, for starters. Then the Israelis and all the Middle East, and Muslims all the way from Morocco to the Philippines. Not to mention all the restive Islamic groups in America and Europe. Millions upon millions of people who, if Clark was right, would be helped into the Enlightenment by enlightened U.S. policies.

Was that enough? He imagined himself bicycling to the village in the early morning mist for a *baguette* and some *pains au chocolat*. Returning home he would inhale the aroma, the joy, of fresh pastry rising from the basket at his handlebars. Arriving invigorated, blood up, roaring with life. Scenting dark coffee from the back patio. Peering through the kitchen window as Aziza laid out rounds of cheese, cups of yogurt, jars of honey and of cherry jam. Did millions upon millions of strangers counterbalance the joy of the single instant when Aziza looked toward the window and saw him watching her?

"Do you want me to win?"

She just looked at him. She was giving nothing away.

"First of all, congressmen almost never win. People tend to see the office of senator or governor as the stepping stone to the presidency."

"But it is allowed."

"Oh sure, it's possible. Gerald Ford had been a congressman. But then he didn't get to be president by popular vote, so he's sort of the exception that proves my point."

"But still . . . "

"How much do you remember about the primary process?"

"Very little, I'm afraid."

"Well, it's complicated. It starts in Iowa, where people don't exactly vote in the normal way. They meet up in caucuses and vote that way. I'm not even contesting Iowa."

"Is that a tactical retreat?"

"Not exactly. The way it'll happen is that my campaign manager tells the press that I'm just not bothering with Iowa, not spending any money there, will hardly even show up in the state.

He puts out the word that I'm concentrating on New Hampshire, which by the way has a proper voting method and used to be the traditional opening state anyway. Their primaries are a week later than Iowa. So press speculation on Iowa hardly mentions me. I've only got one ad there, a sentimental one of people walking through corn fields to find me playing basketball with a bunch of kids. It comes from a baseball movie. It's low-keyed and sweet, a little bit humorous, very Iowa. Also the press won't really notice the hundreds of young people canvassing the state. The Ammenstar Foundation has quietly told its student interns that I will be the candidate to promote their views, whatever they are. Basically that means ethanol from corn, I'm told. A couple of weeks before the election I'll quietly meet with some groups there and tell them that my old granddaddy was so pro-ethanol that he drank it by the jug. That sound bite is expected to get blanket press coverage, and alone to be worth eight-to-fourteen percent of the vote.

"So let's say I'm a surprise third-place finisher there. Suddenly the buzz in New Hampshire is that I'm the dark horse. I already have good name recognition there—people remember me from my basketball days. One of the all-time Celtic greats also happens to be my best friend right from high school. He'll be campaigning actively for me. Some of the other Celts will do media spots. If I do well in New Hampshire, then I'm in a reasonable position for South Carolina, a southern state that I must win. It's that simple. If I lose South Carolina, it's all over." February 7—mark that date.

"I'll watch the morning news on February 8. If you lose, I'll put out an extra plate for dinner."

"Better still, get all dressed up. We're going out for dinner."

"But if you win?"

"If I win, I'm in reasonable shape for Super Tuesday, the following week. In with a chance; no better than that. A senator from Pennsylvania named Chris Laverty is way out in front. You very nearly met him in Beirut, remember?"

"Where? At Walter's?"

"No, at that restaurant you took me to. You had just stepped into the restroom when he walked in. If he had seen us together ..." He didn't bother to finish the sentence.

271

"We wouldn't have such a difficult decision to make right now."

"That's about the size of it."

"So Laverty is your main rival."

"I wouldn't put it that way. I'm not even his main rival. Remember Steve Foreman, used to be vice president? He's a real force—nice guy, too. Sort of an airhead, but people like him. A local congresswoman is contesting Iowa. There are others. I'm still a decided underdog, you realize that. In fact, I'm way down the list, but somehow I've landed some heavyweight consultants who think I have a shot."

"And if you should beat the odds and get elected, what will you do for my people?"

"You mean the French?"

"Ha-ha. I mean the Palestinians."

"One thing I will definitely do is shout from the rooftops that no revealed word, no matter how sacred people think it is, I don't care if it's the Bible, the Torah, the Qur'an or the bloody Bhagavad Gita, has the authority to grant anybody legal title to a piece of land. It's not a deed. God can't take somebody's house and give it to somebody else. If He could I'd suddenly have it revealed to me that He meant for me to own one of those lovely Bluegrass horse farms. It would all be right there in my gospel. GPS numbers and all."

"I was thinking more of our little French farmhouse."

"You got it, babe! I'll add a verse to that effect. Make it a big one if you want. My God is a mighty big God. How about a beachfront villa on the Mediterranean?"

"Can I see the kitchen? I want granite counter tops."

"Done!" he said, and sang, "*God gave this kitchen to me. This brave and ancient kitchen to me! And when the morning sun, reveals her granite counter tops . . .*"

"Shhh, idiot," she laughed. "An imam or somebody will come and kick us out."

"Right. Serious business. What will President Hatling do for your people? In an epoch-making address to the UN General Assembly he will state categorically that the creation of the state of Israel was the last gasp of a colonial era in which a few top dogs could order land takeovers and population transfers, an era underpinned by the erroneous presumption of European superiority, an ideology as dead as Disraeli except in the conflicts it spawned, a legacy that lives on and on. How's that so far?"

She took his hand, lifted it to her lips and kissed it. Such a routine gesture, in abeyance for thirty years, stymied him, until she said, "Go on."

"I do love you still, too. I don't know if I said that."

"Yes, you did, in your way. Go on."

"I will withhold every nickel of U.S. aid I can, and encourage every other civilized country to do the same, until Israel has pulled those disgraceful settlements out. Unsettlements, they should be called. Listen—maybe you can't get into the West Bank, but I've been there, and do you know what I saw with my own eyes? Here's a big piece of fertile farmland with a wall running through it. On one side of the wall it's lush and green; on the other it's a pale scrubland of withering plants. Who do you think owns which side?"

"Uh, scrubland to the Arabs?"

"And do you know why?"

"Just a guess: because God favors the Jews and can't stand Arabs?"

"Because Israel controls the water distribution and takes eighty percent for Jewish farmers, that's why. That figure is from the World Bank, not me making it up."

"Do you remember how we used to sit and discuss what needed to be done in Palestine?"

He looked away. "I'm afraid I got sidetracked along the way."

"No! I didn't mean that as criticism. Most of us got sidetracked. I mean now you have the chance to actually do something—when you win."

"If I win."

"When you win."

"The main thing is that U.S. policy will turn toward a one-state solution. One secular state, nobody's religion calling the shots. That's what we talked about, remember? In my little flat

273

when we should have been . . . "

"Or after we had been . . . "

"Wow, that was so much fun. That was easily the best time of my life. Sad it came so early, and was over so fast."

"Not over yet. Look at me, *habibi*." She took his face in her hands and pulled his gaze to her eyes. "Now listen to me very carefully. Take these next words as your real Bible: *I will wait for you*. You win the presidency, do your best to save my people. I will stay far, far away. No trysts, no phone calls, no emails, no chats, nothing. Nothing that could get us caught and ruin everything. You stay married and let Wanda host her teas—I remember how well she does that. She will help smooth out your presidency. But when you get out, so to speak; when your eight years are done, come for me and I will be here, waiting."

"Four years. When my Middle East policies become known I'll never get reelected."

"All the better. Kick ass for four years, then we will make a home for ourselves."

"Four years . . . it doesn't seem so long, but god it is. I've been so miserable. You wouldn't believe some of the things I've done to escape my own life. Four years is a big ask."

"I'll be with you all the way. Well, maybe not *as such*," she said, to make him laugh.

"I'm afraid if I miss this chance there will never be another."

"Don't worry about me, big guy. My concern is that you'll be in danger."

"You mean assassination?"

She hadn't wanted to say the word, or even to hear it spoken, but she answered, "Yes, exactly. I was beside myself when the Galilee blew up. I had phoned that evening and left you a phone message. You probably didn't even get it."

This was the first he'd heard of it. "What was the message—do you remember?"

"Just that seeing you again had been really special. In a husky, sexy voice. You would have laughed. That's all."

"Oh, yeah! I did get it. I thought it was from one of the hookers down in the bar."

"So you said, Sure, come on up!"

"Nope. I was broke. A presidential candidate can't have a thing like that on his credit card. *One Ukrainian Pro: Priceless.*"

"It's easy to laugh now, but the next morning when you didn't return my call I was certain you'd been killed and I just wanted my life to end right then, with yours. Honestly, if you had been in it I would have died."

"Don't be silly. Of course I'll have plenty of lethal enemies, but I'll also have the best security force in the world protecting me. That's as much assurance as I can offer."

"It's bound to be better than those Israeli morons who still don't have a suspect. They still have nothing, right?"

"Not a thing. Just the ruins of the van that held the explosive. Presumably the bomber was blown to giblets."

"But they have no theory about who was behind it?"

"If they have they're not telling me."

"Or even who knew in advance that you would be staying at the Galilee?"

"I can only think of a couple of people. I emailed it to Holly, my secretary. She says she just looked up their phone number, wrote it on a notepad and put it in a drawer, which was locked that night. I emailed it to Wanda, of course, but she was away from home and didn't even check her mail until after I'd phoned her to tell her I was ok."

"Ah-ha!"

"Maybe she's had fantasies, but she would pick a more subtle method. She's more the poisoning type. And you. That's the list. You didn't tell anyone, did you?"

"Of course not. I take it you didn't give my name to the investigators. I wasn't even contacted about it."

"No, I kept your name out of it. But I thought somebody might question Amin, in any case."

"If they did, it didn't last long, and he didn't tell me. Not that he tells me everything, but he still lives at my house and I know when he's gone for any length of time." This was her chance to ask her most relevant question, although she dreaded the answer so much she almost preferred ignorance. But she couldn't let

275

suspicion poison her reason, so she asked him, "Did Amin know where you were staying?"

"No, I'm almost sure I told only Holly, Wanda and you. After my arrival in Tiberias—a lot of people knew then. But did that give anybody time to organize the attack?"

"In Lebanon a lot of people say Syria did it, that they managed to slip across the Golan Heights and ferry the van across the water."

"Or from Jordan. I've heard that one too. I think that's just gossip."

"In Lebanon some people blame Syria if the wind knocks their knickers from the clothesline."

"The border's too tightly controlled; they couldn't sneak anything across the Golan. The consensus theory is that someone was hacking into my emails. Before I left Beirut I used the business suite at the conference center. Or they could have hacked into the computers at the Galilee. One of those two sources—that's the general opinion. Or of course there's always the possibility it had nothing at all to do with me."

"You mean a mafia or drug lord reprisal, something like that?"

"Maybe. Russians or Chechens. Or just a terrorist bomb already planned for where I happened to turn up."

"Whatever it was, you can still see my point. You're only here by the thinnest thread of a coincidence."

He put his arm around her and drew her to him. She rested her head against his shoulder. "But I am here. And as I say, the Secret Service is the best there is."

They both sat quietly for a minute, allowing the silence within the basilica and the serenity on the face of a crucified Christ to assay whether the best was good enough.

"Okay, enough of that!" She sat up.

"Fine by me. Why are we here, anyway? Why did you pick a place so remote?"

"Do you know who Philip Augustus was?"

"Maybe an old boyfriend? That's probably who'll assassinate me—one of your jealous suitors."

"What a sweet thought. No, Congressman, he became King of France at the end of the twelfth century. He was at war with

276

England, but then Saladin captured Jerusalem from the Christians, so he and Richard the Lionheart made peace and vowed to crusade together."

"Yes, I read your excellent book."

"Oh! You didn't mention it in Beirut, but I knew you had. I just felt it." She clapped lightly, one time only, but the sound echoed throughout the great hall and then the side chapels.

"I should have heaped praise on you then. It's just that my mind was whirring all around. But honestly, it was brilliant. I was so proud of you."

She leaned in, pulled his face toward her, and kissed him again. "You really liked it?"

"I devoured it."

"I'm completely thrilled." This time she gave herself a full round of applause that sounded from the walls like firecrackers. "I think it's a shame we can't make out in an abbey."

"So what's your point?"

"My point?"

"Philip Augustus and Richard?"

"Oh, they put their differences behind them, knelt side by side, and vowed to conquer Jerusalem. Right there." She pointed to the altar, not twenty feet away.

Clark looked up at the altar as though it had just materialized from the ether. "Right there? Richard the Lionheart and Philip Augustus?"

"Kneeling. Making a sacred vow for the Third Crusade."

"Was that the one that went way wrong and ended up destroying Constantinople, the greatest Christian city on earth?"

"No, that was the Fourth."

"But the Third was a failure too, right?"

"Not for my side! And do you remember Bernard de Clairvaux? He preached the Second Crusade from here. It was supposed to be in this church, but so many knights turned up that he had to preach in a field outside the walls of Vézelay."

"The Second was a failure, too, if I recall."

"A total disaster. For your side. We pretty much kicked your butts all over the court."

277

He was preparing to make a basketball joke when suddenly he realized what she had done. He actually stood up from his chair, turned and looked down at her. "A *crusade*? That's why we're here? You brought me here to launch a crusade? And here I was thinking it was to pledge some kind of lifelong devotion!"

"*Habibi*." She gave him a second, then took his hand, arrested in mid-air after its accusing gesture. "Sit. No." She stood instead, put her arms around him. "I'm here to do both of those things. Together we launch a crusade. Together we pledge our devotion. Put your heart and soul into both vows, but the crusade comes first. If we don't try, if we don't go all out to recreate Palestine, then our lives have been wasted. You sacrificed us for . . . what? A political career, right? Yet what have you done with it? Cleaned up a few strip mines? Limited the tax on bourbon whisky? Let's face it, these things don't stack up against our missing thirty years. And I married into money and power to save my dear old feckless dad the embarrassment of bankruptcy? My mom advised me against it, by the way. She said they could live off her painting and that I would forever regret marrying against my heart. But, my heart had already disappeared. Then it returned—with Wanda in tow."

"I've made some huge mistakes."

"We've both made huge mistakes, but we can turn them into one grand triumph if you put all your tremendous, underused talent into winning that goddamn election and saving my people. That's why we parted thirty years ago—so we could reunite four years from now in a better world; a world you created."

"And you."

"And me, if this pep talk works."

"You do remind me of Red."

"Who?"

"An old basketball coach of mine. He'd hold out an old beat up leather ball and make you think it was the holy grail."

"This time it's the whole round world he's holding out to you, and believe me, *habibi*, for peace in that world, this *is* the holy grail."

She had said her piece and now rested the side of her face against his chest. He wasn't surprised that he remembered just where she fit against him, right where he could rest his chin on the top of her head, her ear just at his heart. She was right, of course. How could they lie together in happy old age if they had tossed away their one slim chance of righting the wrong done in Palestine? The original Crusades, misguided as they were, had at least been right in their basic intentions: righting wrongs, and, ultimately, attaining salvation.

A cleaning lady came in and switched on some lights in a side chapel. She was young, attractive, friendly, and black; the emblem of the modern Catholic Church. She smiled apologetically at their embrace, an accomplice, but one who had to call a halt to it all. It was time to close up.

As they left the abbey, Clark dropped a two-euro coin into the collection box and took a pamphlet with a verse on the cover, translated into a half a dozen languages, including Hebrew. It was Mark 8:36, *For what shall it profit a man, if he shall gain the whole world, and lose his own soul?* He hadn't bothered with Hebrew for so long that he wondered if he could still read it, so he stopped in the light of the doorway under the tympanum. It turned out to be an amateurish attempt at translation which, as he translated it back into English, froze him as stiff as any of the sculptures adorning the wall. Aziza was pointing to the rays from Jesus' fingers as He in turn pointed to a world awaiting conquest. She said, "See the dog faces on those humpbacked human forms? Those are Muslims—vile beasts, as Pope Innocent the Second called us. That's me up there."

Clark heard her, in a way, and later wished he had said, "Don't be silly! You're much prettier than that. More of a collie, maybe," but he hadn't spoken a word. He was paralyzed by the juvenile Hebrew: *Do you want the world or your soul? Please choose.*

Aziza pointed across the rows of houses and down the hill towards a farmed field. "There's where Bernard preached the Second Crusade in 1146. At the time he was probably the most revered man in Europe. He laid his enormous reputation on the line and when the crusade proved a disaster he never recovered. How could God's team be so humiliated? He couldn't say God had switched allegiance to the other side, so he tried to blame

279

Christian defeat on Christian wickedness. It was all a scourge for errant belief. While attacking Peter Abelard he said 'Faith doesn't dispute; it believes.' I've often wondered whether he later wished he had disputed, rather than believed, the Second Crusade. You do know who Peter Abelard was, don't you?"

"Well yes, of course I do. How could you think . . . "

"Who was he then?"

"Why, he was a bitter enemy of Bernard de Hoozit. Everybody knows that."

"You didn't even read my book—tell me the truth."

"I *did*. I told you I did. I didn't memorize the damn thing though."

"Tell me again what you thought of it."

"I thought it was a superb work by a first-rate historian, a magnificent achievement."

"Don't hold back—this is no time for understatement."

"Magisterial. One for the ages."

"Yes! Perfect! Now tell me one more thing."

"Shoot."

"And this time I want the real truth. Got that?"

"Got it."

"The absolute truth."

"Absolutely, for chrissake."

She came up close to him, touched the lapels of his overcoat, lightly at first, as though she were examining the material, then grabbed them in her fists and pulled him toward her.

"Then answer me this one, Congressman. You're Danny Davies, aren't you?"

32

AN HOUR OUTSIDE Beirut and two hours before dawn, passenger cars became rare. Normal people were home in bed, yet traffic didn't let up. It coalesced into a convoy of transport trucks filing toward the city. They moved either too fast or too slowly for road safety, each one jockeying for any possible advantage. Amin rode his scooter mainly on the paved shoulder, when there was one, and did his best to stay on asphalt when there wasn't. The one thing that every trucker seemed to agree on, and which they signaled persuasively with their blaring horns and flashing lights, was that at 3 a.m. a Vespa was no more a vehicle than was a dog or a chicken.

An hour later, on the long, straight stretch of road that cuts through the vast agricultural estates of the Bekaa Valley, even the line of trucks thinned out. The weak headlight of the Vespa poked a jittery tunnel into the darkness, providing Amin with an almost contemplative atmosphere inside the purr of his little engine. At times now, in place of diesel fumes, he picked up the scent of turned earth, or, where the nomads camped, the smell of their hobbled animals, or even the fires of the women who rose early to heat a griddle for making flatbread and to boil chunks of goat meat in buttermilk.

Amin began to wonder if he shouldn't envy them. Not that their lives were easy, or even simple, but because their lives were defined. It was an odd way to see the Bedouin, as living within boundaries, but as he thought on the subject that's exactly how he was different from them. Everything that they would ever be asked to do, from birth to death, no matter how long they lived, was a simple repetition of what their ancestors had done for generations, while he, an urban man of fixed abode, found himself riding into the night, into the unknown and unknowable world of revolutionaries at war. What if his job for the day was to move goats from one field to another? It didn't sound so bad. Goats don't even get excited. They might lose concentration and drift a little, but they willingly rejoin the flock when you wave a stick and cluck at them. Wouldn't that be a better way to spend the day than informing on a treacherous comrade, divulging the plot of an internal coup to its intended target?

Instead of spilling his guts and possibly his blood, why didn't he marry one of these young goat-smelling girls, and beat her occasionally, just because he could? These donkey-riding illiterates could get into paradise just as well as he could. Why didn't he take up the riding stick and become one of them?

He had to amuse himself with such nonsense. That such a life was a reality for someone didn't make it any less ridiculous. Maybe he seemed silly to them. He was sure he would seem silly to Clark, if he knew, him with his history lectures and his philosophy. No good could come from thinking of that guy now, but the face kept sneaking its way back into Amin's consciousness, just as his own face had lain in hiding behind his full *jihadi* beard, only to jump out later and reclaim him.

Approaching Baalbek, he passed the Palestinian refugee camp at Wavel. At the spot where he passed the entrance to the camp he always thought, "Sisters and brothers! You and I are one! I am a warrior in our common cause!"

He did so this time as well. He tried to think it with as much sincerity as ever, but...but something. There was a little blade of a notion that found a crevice in his solidarity, where it introduced a new, unwelcome consideration: I was the landowner; you were my peasants. I called you *fellaheen*; you called me *ya sidi*. I now live in a great house in Beirut while you live in a shack and beg for scraps from the U.N. This is because my great-grandfather had the good sense to sell out for a vast profit. Baron Rothschild was offering a bag of gold, so he took it. It wasn't treachery; just good business sense. Our prophet, peace be upon him, was a businessman, too.

He couldn't go on thinking like this. It was a Satanic intrusion, delivered by a Satanic envoy.

If you believe that Satan has power to do evil, then you believe in two gods.

How could he let this *mulhad* fill his head this way? Or was

282

that the other one, that Levi prick? Damn it! Which one had said that? Those two were getting mixed up in his head! They both needed to be dead, yet they both lived. Let them get mixed up in hell; God would see to that. Or was that Satan's domain?

He stopped the bike, removed his helmet and shook his head violently. He took a drink from his water bottle and squirted the rest down his head and face. The sleeve he used to dry his face came away black with diesel film.

In Baalbek he passed the tourist cafés, dark now, their rusting metal shutters pulled down and padlocked onto the cement floor, and the outdoor tables that later in the day would appear so cheerful to European visitors, now chained together like prisoners. He passed the ruins of the great Roman temple to Jupiter, a god now dead to all but tourist buses. He recalled Clark's wisecrack about how many Jupiter jihads had made the news lately. He also recalled how he had shared Clark's absurd laughter about it, but this time, passing the dark and silent temple grounds, passing Jupiter's looming pillars, barely visible gray projections against the black sky, tombstones for the eternal deity, it wasn't so funny anymore.

In fact the whole Clark connection made him squirm.

As he rode into the city, he tried to make sense of it all.

Somehow Abu Ali moves in and tries to use Clark to undermine the Sheikh's position. What a disaster it has all become. And what a pity that Yousuf, my real father, has gone silent in the holy city. When will he reappear and clear up the whole mess? This much is clear—it all goes back to Aziza and her French *kafir* mother. They no doubt saw marriage to my father as a path lined with gold, so they took it. Why did he open his soul to that nest of impiety in the first place? No doubt they tricked him somehow. Was it with some gypsy spell? Everybody knows that Catholics have easy access to their sorcery. Or did they just lie? My father wouldn't have married an uncovered woman, not of his own volition. No doubt those conniving women assured him that marriage would bring piety to the feisty little whore, and, long since betrayed, he finally got fed up and left them all for Mecca. There, amid the holiest sites in Islam, he will regain our family

283

honor and rebuild the family fortune that his fast-dealing ex-wife had cost him. Thank God my father notified the Sheikh that my misguided soul needed guidance. God must receive praise in these matters of destiny.

Inside the cramped back streets of Baalbek he located the one he needed, saw that there was still no light on in the bakery where the owner, an old woman he knew only as Khadija, could arrange the most important contact of his life. He parked the Vespa down a tiny back alley and tried to wedge himself between some stinking garbage bins and the back stairs. It was about the best balance he could achieve between concealment and physical comfort. The sour stench of old dough overpowered him at first, but soon enough its strength seemed to die away, as did the tension in his muscles and the muddle of his thoughts. He really needed to get some sleep.

When he woke up he noticed that a light was on inside the bakery, but as he had not been disturbed, Khadija must have entered through the front door. He pulled himself upright and knocked at the flaking blue back door. A weak light bulb went on over his head and a face was peeking at him from behind a curtain.

She smiled at him from behind the window, and he read her lips as she said, "Ibn Burak." Just that much—not even hearing the sound, but only seeing it on her lips—put away all the unrighteousness he had been wrestling with. It was as though a soothing natural balm had been applied to a burning rash. Internally he said, *In the name of God, the Compassionate and the Merciful.*

He greeted her and she returned it, adding that he looked exhausted and hungry. "I haven't started the ovens yet, so let me take you home. You need food and a place to rest."

He followed her down the back lanes. Lacking streetlights and pavement, these poor sections of town made nighttime walking a drama, but his spirit soared. This was exactly his place in the universe at this moment. He knew that just as surely as he could follow the glimmer of moonlight off Khadija's kaftan, he could also follow the *sunnah*, the path of rightousness.

Inside her house, Khadija motioned for him to have a seat on a sofa and then called out for Samira. Her daughter, he supposed. A woman he'd never met. He heard her coming down a narrow flight of wooden steps, her brocaded slippers tapping each stair. When she came around the stairway door he got his first glimpse of her, hardly more than that, for she slid quickly around a partition and through another door. He had seen that she was also wearing a kaftan, hers a quiet pastel more yellow than green, and had her head covered. He heard metallic sounds, soon a kettle whistling, and the aroma of fresh coffee reached him.

Samira came in with a tray of pastries and his coffee. She said, *as-salamu alaykum*, and looked around for a place to put the tray. She balanced it precariously on a sofa cushion, smiled at him to indicate, without speaking, that she knew it was a risky base for his breakfast, so he'd better be real still while she found a better spot. Her teeth were perfect and her smile pressed her cheeks into bright knots. Her face was clean and fresh, with no need for cosmetics, and none applied. She pulled a folding gate-leg table from behind a door, placed his breakfast on it, and said, "Ah, much better. If you need anything else, just call out. Feel free to get some sleep while my mother arranges for your contact." Then she was gone.

He saw her only one more time that day, when she came in to remove the tray. He was already stretched out along the sofa. She left the room and returned with a blanket, which she spread over him. He pretended to be asleep, but in fact as he heard her walk away he opened his eyes to catch one more glimpse, this one of the delicate curve her hips formed, just where her kaftan rubbed against her.

He kept her pure face in his mind as he tried to drift towards sleep. And the arc of her kaftan as it touched her. He found himself wanting to be the one to touch her there where her kaftan rubbed. He thought how sexy she was in her modesty, how this was the kind of woman who could provide her husband with the true Islamic life. Why weren't all women like this? Didn't they see how superior this way was? He found himself wishing he owned this overcrowded little house with it cheap furnishings. He imagined himself married to Samira, coming home to her in the evening, being greeted with a cup of tea and some dates. He imagined the composure he would feel when at night Samira came into their

285

bedroom, took off her scarf and shook loose her lovely hair for him, for him alone. He imagined that she swayed in an easy dance as she began to remove her clothing; imagined the excitement of their lovemaking, yet at the very heart of the excitement he could feel the center core of deep peace that came from knowing beyond any doubt that no other man had ever touched her soft skin. No other man had even seen the curves of her hips and breasts, the lines of her thighs or the bend of her knees. No man outside her inner family had even seen her hair. No man, period, had ever seen her toss it back, her arched neck tensing as she accepted his penetration. She would be his for life, all his, never to share with anyone. He would be her lone focal point. When she thought of sex, she would think only of him. The two would be one in her mind. There would be no one to compare him with. He would never have to worry that another man had loved her better.

These European whores had it all wrong. He knew plenty about them. They approached him on the beach or in an *arghile* waterpipe café. They would ask the time, or directions to somewhere. Maybe ask if he had change for a 50,000 lira note. Didn't matter. There was really only one question: Would you care to come to my hotel room and fuck me? He knew them all so well. He would flatter them with a few simple phrases. They would scream and moan. Sometimes he wanted to say, Just shut the fuck up. I don't even recall your name.

How did such whores ever find a husband? He wondered how European men could stand to be even near one of these. They weren't men, that's how. They were dogs that smell the swollen organs of a bitch, mount her for two minutes and then let another dog at her. That's how much they knew of honor and virtue. Otherwise how could such a husband come to his wife knowing that an untold number of strangers had been inside her? How could they even kiss them, if they knew, as he knew, where those mouths had been? It made him sick to think of it.

That's what made Samira so sexy. One look at her and you knew who she was. She wasn't dressed or made up to plant ideas of lust in men's minds. Of course he was having lustful thoughts about her—he had to smile at that—but he was imagining himself married to her. In a sanctioned, holy marriage, not some hotel room on the Corniche, where a quick screw was followed by room-service fish and chips, followed by a longer screw, and a taxi to wherever he'd parked the Vespa. It would be the fire for those sluts, and worse for the gelded cuckolds who married them.

He had no idea how long he'd been asleep when Samira shook him awake. Waiting for him outside was a big black Nissan Patrol with its rear windows blacked out. He hadn't realized that by becoming a revolutionary jihadist he had entered a life of blacked-out road trips, but he had to make peace with that now. At least this one was a lot less threatening than the others: no blindfold, no security guards on the muscle. This secrecy was simply a precaution against the possibility of an in-house traitor, and since this trip was all about an in-house traitor, there was no denying the wisdom of precaution.

Soon he felt the bump and vibration of tires over a cattle guard, and he knew they'd crossed into Syria. They picked up speed along the hardened tracks through the cotton fields, slowed to a crawl as they crossed a ramshackle bridge over an ancient irrigation canal, jostled along donkey cart trails until the fertile valley declined into rocky *hamada* desert, where they picked up speed and kicked up a dust cloud thick enough to obscure the horizon for a mile behind them.

Amin knew this road well. He didn't really need a window to know that when gravel starting slapping against the Patrol's skid plate they were within minutes of the camp.

He still hadn't detected trouble even while walking between two men, not in the direction of the Sheikh's receiving room, but toward a cement block building he'd never been in before. He was put into a small room with cobweb tags hanging from corners and the dank odor of debilitated air. The two office chairs were normal enough, with cushioned seats and backs, but one, the one he was directed to, was bolted to the floor.

He had been in this room before, or a mobile version of it, and this time, as before, he whispered a prayer.

A man came in wearing a Syrian police uniform. Amin said, "If I could speak with the Sheikh for just a minute—this is really important."

"First of all, just a few questions. We understand you bring

287

important information about someone you know. Your American?"

"No, not him. He's not 'my' American in any case."

"Then if you want a confrontation, we can oblige."

"What does that mean?"

"I didn't want to say 'your mother's American'."

"No, wait a minute! This is starting out all wrong. This isn't about him at all."

"We have rumors that you spent three days with a candidate for the U.S. presidency, yet you didn't inform us."

"I'm not here about him."

"Are the rumors true?"

"Yes—but . . . "

"Then you are either a fool or a traitor."

"No! It's not like that at all. If I could speak with the Sheikh . . . "

"The Sheikh's attention is occupied at this time."

"But this is really important. It's about his Beirut cell leader, Hafid al-Ghanim. You may know him as Abu Ali."

"We are aware of your personal dispute with Abu Ali. And your close ties with the American Hatling."

"Not close ties! That's what I want to say! No, that's not my main reason. What I mean is . . . "

"You are a scared child. You are either a coward or a spy." He nodded toward the guards by the door, who grabbed Amin's arms from behind and secured his wrists with three quick bindings of rope.

"No, wait! This is all unnecessary!"

"What is necessary, Mr. University boy . . . " he said, adding, with menacing irony, 'ya sidi,' is for you to explain yourself."

"I'm here to explain to the Sheikh that someone is out to undermine him."

"Do you think I don't know what happened to you in Israel?"

"Look, forget Israel. I got out only because my mom used to work with Hatling. I'd never even met him." He hoped they didn't know about, or wouldn't count, his infancy, but even as he thought it he knew his eyes had fluttered an instant, and that this policeman had caught it.

288

"Forget Israel? This is a *muhajid* talking?"

"I just mean forget that incident. It's not relevant to this discussion."

"*Not relevant!*" he mocked, looking up toward the guards. Only one laughed. Maybe the other one didn't know the word.

"I was only with Hatling because the Sheikh ordered me to live a normal life until I received further instructions."

"Why did you go straight to Israel?"

"Abu Ali sent me."

"He sent you?"

"Yes! That's what I'm saying. Maybe 'set me up' would be more accurate."

"You seem determined to betray him."

"It's the other way around. He's betraying us all. I have proof. If I could just speak to the Sheikh, I could clear this up in one minute."

One of the guards left the room. Amin hadn't seen any signal to that effect. Furthermore his interrogator looked up in apparent surprise as the door opened, and was quietly pulled shut. Then he finally started to understand. He actually felt himself grow in the wisdom of revolutionary politics. This guy was in uniform because the Syrian government had, for whatever reason, decided to take control of the movement. Maybe they were afraid the group's capability to do harm would be turned against them. Maybe it had to do with the large sums of funding involved; money flowing like oil into a land deprived of both. Abu Ali had allied himself with the Syrians, and Amin was seen as the Sheikh's man. Why all this, he couldn't say, but he had been right back at Abu Ali's place to recall Clark's dictum: petty factions and petty prizes.

Then the second guard left as well. Not a word from him, only the sound of the door closing and an astonished look on the face of the Syrian.

"You won't leave too, will you?" It felt good to taunt this arrogant usurper. What right did he have to inject a secular government into God's arena? "If you leave too, I'll be strapped in here all alone."

The Syrian stood up, maybe to slap him, maybe to flee. Amin

289

would never know, because the Sheikh walked in, holding the arm of a guard.

"Ibn Burak, my son." He held out his hand, which Amin took, kissed, and placed against his forehead. Again, just as happened the last time they were together, the fingers absorbed the light like eyes, and emitted the certainty of God's truth. Amin felt peace settle throughout his body, as though he'd been burning with fever and had stepped into a cool, flowing stream.

"*Ya Sheikh*, I have some information that might possibly save our movement."

"Tell me."

"It appears that Hafid al-Ghanim, the man also known as Abu Ali, has been accusing me of associating with a powerful American in order to cover his own treachery. I can assure you that he was seen with the American presidential candidate Christopher Laverty during his visit to Beirut."

"This is a lie!" said the Syrian. "You're lying to cover your tracks!"

"I know this sounds odd, *ya Sheikh*, considering your blindness. But would you like to see a photograph? I have it here on a disk."

The old man threw back his head and laughed. "Yes, *walidi!* I would love to see that photograph. I'm sure we all would. Especially our Syrian brothers."

33   THE PROMISE

"LET ME THINK a minute how to explain Danny Davies," Clark said. He and Aziza were walking toward a little Peugeot rental car parked at the edge of the Vézelay church square.

She took his hand, soon felt how cold it was, and put her hand, still holding his, into her coat pocket. "You don't need to think about it. Just tell me whether or not you wrote that review."

"What are you . . . ?"

"On Amazon, *idiot*," which, just as way back then, she pronounced *ee-dee-o*. "You're way too slow to be president. Maybe we should give your poor country a break and start looking for that rustic cottage right away."

"Oh, that! Yes, of course. For a second there . . . yes, that was me. I have a junk mail account. I used that when I wrote your review."

"I *knew* it! I read it and thought, My book isn't *that* good. This reviewer is somebody who . . . then it hit me. Who else would send me a love letter hidden behind a book review and a *nom de plume*?"

"Was it obvious?"

"No, darling. Not too obvious. 'One for the ages' was a strong hint, though. 'Enduring impact' was another."

They got into the car. He knew he was completely in the clear now. Danny Davies would never come up with her again, yet he felt something much like regret. Was that possible? He'd nearly convinced himself that he needed to confess, to nobody else in the world, surely, but to this one, to Aziza, yes. Didn't he need to explain to her his escape in Tiberias? Shouldn't she know what contortions had resulted from thirty years of living someone else's life? But perhaps now wasn't the time, and anyway she was whistling! Women usually didn't whistle, and Arab women never whistled, but she started the car with her own tuneful accompaniment, ad-libbed a few sour notes as the engine burped against the cold, and finished with some kind of Vivaldian finale. No, this was not the time to flesh out Danny Davies.

"So Congressman, how many days are you cleared for?"

"I fly back next Sunday. Until then no one cares where I am. I'll phone in daily, but other than that, I'm all yours"

"Don't you want to know what's up?"

"Okay. What's up?"

"Cathar Country. That's what's up. You and me and five free days in the Languedoc, in little towns even I'd never heard of until I started researching my book."

"The Albigensian Crusade. The Catholic Church wiped out some Christian sect in southern France, hundreds of years before Martin Luther. See, I did read your magisterial tome."

"Are you game?"

"For Cathar Country? You bet! Wait. Leave the brake on and look at me for a moment."

She turned to him, perfectly willing to humor him, knowing that the tenderness in his voice came from emotions needing to be shared as well as felt. A sorrow around his lips told her she was right about that, but she hadn't expected eyes about to puddle over. No one else had ever looked at her that way. Thirty years between loving gazes, that's what he wanted to say, that there's nothing more indescribably painful than great spans of lost time. Moreover, that a moment such as this should be commonplace: Hey, let's drive over and check out this village I've been reading about. It's supposed to be really interesting.

"Okay," he finally said. "Let's go."

She noticed he wasn't concerned to question her. That much hadn't changed. If she led him somewhere, he was an avid follower. If she'd waited for him to ask for that first dance, they never would have met. And now, if she hadn't said, "I've booked us a room in Bourges," what would he have done? Had he even considered that? But once she had said it, he would run with it. There would be no need to add, "Where we will make love for the first time in thirty years." He would take the key from the front desk clerk, ignore the *porteur*, take the stairs two at a time, and shut the door behind them with a *whack*. He would take her wrists in his hands and pin her to the door. The first kiss might be gentle, but it would leave no question about where it led. He would undress her without her assistance and carry her to bed. But it was hers to say, "I have booked us a room in Bourges." If she had said, "two rooms," that would have been the end of it.

She supposed it was the same for becoming president. Her impetus would transform inertia into fervor. Wanda's love of center stage would help, too. It was funny to think it, but Wanda would be her ally in this effort.

Thinking of tonight, and of Wanda, she asked, "Have you ever cheated on your wife before?"

"Never," he said.

"I don't believe you."

"Then why ask?" He smiled at her.

"Because I want to hear your answer, of course. And because I want you to ask *me*. Have you forgotten everything I taught you?"

"About making love?"

"About women."

"Did you ever cheat on Yousuf?"

"Not once."

"Oh. Okay."

"And . . ."

"And what?"

"Follow up question."

"Umm . . . the choice is huge. Why didn't you? Or . . . Wait! I've got it! Were you ever tempted?"

"You know I was tempted, *ee-dee-o*."

"Oh yeah, I forgot about that. Okay—last try: Don't they have male prostitutes in Beirut?"

She reached out and slapped the back of his head. "Ask me if I ever cheated on you."

"Ah! I almost had it! Did you ever cheat on me?"

There was no traffic on the road. She slowed to look at him. He perceived that she'd turned toward him, met her eyes. She answered him, "Every single time."

It had started as jest, but her mind had tricked her, and all at once she knew she had to pull the car over and cry. To Clark it seemed it was simply her turn, so he held her until it passed. He knew the tears were not from sorrow, or even from happiness. They were tears of redemption, not in a religious way, but in the original sense, the sense where the religious metaphor had come from: a slave was redeemed, as in a pawn shop. The owner had been paid off. She was free.

They got out of the car. Clark leaned back against the warm grille and Aziza leaned into him. He felt the warmth of the engine against the backs of his legs. In the dead silence the sound of a fish jumping told them they had parked by a river, probably the Yèvre. He pulled her toward him and folded her inside his big winter coat. In her coat pocket his hand found the scarf she'd been wearing in the church, so he took it out and tied it around her head, mostly so she would smile at their unspoken understanding of what the scarf stood for, but also because he knew its warmth would be welcome.

The road followed the river, which along this section was straight, but it rose and fell over low, rolling hills. From far back they heard a car approaching, its lights visible, then gone, as it rode the mounds. Illuminating them once again, the car pulled alongside and stopped. Two young men were inside. A window dropped and the passenger said something. Aziza answered something that made them laugh, and they moved on, perhaps shocked at finding an elderly couple in such a teenage setting: embracing by a parked car on a dark country road.

"Good Samaritans?" Clark asked.

"They asked if we were all right. I said I haven't been in this man's arms in thirty years, how could anything be wrong?"

"I bet they're laughing their asses off right now."

"When they're our age they'll remember this moment, and they won't be laughing then."

"Shall I drive for a while?"

"I'm fine, and I know where we're going."

But they didn't move for a long time, until a wedge of swans in silhouette against the last patch of light in the western sky flew right over their heads and landed on the Yèvre, those great wings canted up like airfoils to slow the decent. They couldn't see the landing, but heard it, the skiing along of rubbery feet, then of breasts plowing deep into the river, the onrush of water as though passing a ship's prow.

That small drama signaled that it was time to move on. Clark looked her in the eyes and kissed her again before relaxing his grip on her. She smiled, removed her scarf, and got back into the car.

A light fog had moved in. She drove into the night, the Peugeot's headlights disturbing wisps of it, like tufts of kapok on the wind. Clark rode silently now, except for a few hopeful stabs at pronouncing something from road signs. *Dégustation gratuit*, he tried. "Gratuitous disgust. That's worth knowing about." And, "Blank wine. You wouldn't think they'd advertise that."

"Clark, darling. Never, ever make a state visit to France, okay?"

"Why not? Look over there! Petite Pricks! They're so honest about it. I admire that."

"It's pronounced *puh-tee pree*; low prices. Do yourself a favor and do not try to speak a word of French during this trip, or the whole time you're president. Five years from now we'll buy a cottage, and I'll teach you French."

"Deal! Strong, silent type, that's me in a nutshell."

"For the time being I'll settle for silence."

It's true he didn't have much to say during the entire trip. He grew tired of planning his campaign, tired of political topics altogether. Even Aziza, at first so eager to put some specifics into their policy on Palestine, suspended the subject in favor of the small, brief world they shared—which restaurant looked inviting, what kind of flowers those were, how did they get them to bloom in this weather.

They talked of the massacred Cathars, and of what it must have been like to hold to a worldview that said all solid matter, even the fetus you carried, was evil, a receptacle where Satan entrapped the divine spirit, yet as you watched the material horizon with your material eyes and saw the material evil of soldiers and horses and swords coming to release your divine spirit from your evil body, how you feared and fought them, how amid the chaos of battle you clung to your material children as their evil blood spilled, how

295

what you embraced and wept over was not the freed spirit of your husband, but his evil corpse.

They sat on the cold steel seats in Beziers cathedral and felt the Crusader flames that burned the thousands who had taken shelter there. Aziza quoted the words of Abbot Arnaud Amaury from 1209, identical to t-shirt slogans Clark had seen on American streets: *Kill them all. Let God sort them out.* Just who were *they*, he wondered. Catholics and Cathars? Muslims and Christians? Warriors and peacemakers? Tilapia and catfish?

They climbed the slippery stone steps of the fortress of Peyrepertuse, and explored the banks of the Verdouble near the fortress of Padern. They made Carcassonne their home base and watched helplessly as their own immaterial treasure—one hundred and thirty-two hours of precious time—hardened and fell away in the form of baguettes with black currant jam, of onion and nutmeg gratin, braised lamb, white beans, and Cotes-du-Rhone; of deep mattresses and cold sheets. The spirit of their diminishing hours was made the flesh of mountain walks in the foothills of the Pyrenees and boat rides on the Midi canal; into English movies with French subtitles, into the *Herald-Tribune* and coffee. At night they watched a half-hour newscast from the BBC, which never once mentioned Clark Hatling.

One night, though, Clark shushed Aziza mid-sentence as a bloodied face came on the screen. It was a heavily-bearded man wearing a black skullcap and a white, collarless *dishdasha*.

"In other news from the Middle East, the Muslim extremist Hafid al-Ghanim, widely known as Abu Ali, was found dead of gunshot wounds in his Beirut apartment. It is not yet known who his assassins were, but there has been speculation that he was a victim of the factional fighting within his radical arm of the Syrian-backed group that calls itself the Sword of the Avenger. Police in Lebanon say al-Ghanim received at least a dozen bullets to the head and chest."

"Jesus!" Clark said, "I've seen this guy!" He took a good, long look, to be certain. "I'm pretty sure he's the man I saw lurking outside our *kibbeh* restaurant in Beirut. I watched him as he pretended to read a magazine at a kiosk across the street. I thought he might have been security. Under cover, obviously."

"For you?"

"No, not for me. God no. Nobody even knew I was there. I thought it was for Laverty."

"I wouldn't worry about it if I were you."

"What do you mean by that?"

"Just it's no big deal if some terrorist gets what he deserves."

"But I've *seen* this one. He passed right by me. You had stopped off at the restroom, remember? He went in right after Laverty."

"I remember now. You said we almost got caught."

"Laverty even stopped for a brief chat. How's the food, that sort of thing. Then this Ghanim guy followed him into the restaurant."

"To *meet* with Laverty?"

"I have no idea. Obviously not to kill him."

"Don't dwell on it. Maybe he was just hungry for the best *kibbeh* in Beirut."

"Looks like he bit off more than he could chew."

Reminded now of the near-exposure they'd had in Beirut, Clark wondered why they were taking the risk again, this time on a tryst that could not possibly be explained away. They would have to stop. If he became president there would be no chance of any future meeting. Phone calls, emails—all had to be shut down. Once the campaign got going, reporters would sniff out every move. Until the election he would chance his weekly calls with the phone he used exclusively for her, the number nobody knew he had. After that, it would be four years of silence.

At the bistro, their last night together, Clark left Aziza at their table and walked over to the pianist, who then looked toward the singer. Aziza saw this, and knew that this time it would be Clark who led her onto the dance floor, and knew as well that her heart would fill, and soon burst, with the pressure of its contents. He raised her arm as the piano began, pulled her to him as the woman sang, "*If you wait for me, then I'll find my way back to you, wherever you are, where all my journeys end.*"

Her hair was warm against his throat, her tears cool on his neck. He felt the slight motion of a nod against his chest, so he lifted her chin, forced her to look at him. "You promise? Say it out loud. Otherwise I quit politics right now and stay with you."

The musical promise was in the sorrowful air, but she had to say, "*Habibi*, we need you. My people need you. It's bigger than our love; even our great love."

"Promise me."

"Of course I promise. Right here in Carcassonne. Five more years."

"Or one."

"You? A loser?" She smiled at him. The crinkling of her eyes stirred the film of tears there, fresh facets sparkling up at him. "Clark Hatling has never lost at anything."

"I lost you."

She placed her ear back over his heart. "We misplaced ourselves."

"For a reason, it seems."

"For a big reason." She circled her arms around him and drew him tighter. "To put muscle behind our ideas to repair this insane world. That's why you have to stay in the fight, and win it."

"And you'll be here waiting?"

"I promise."

He stopped dancing; she looked back up at his face. Motionless there among the other dancers, he resolved to go all out; he resolved to win. That's who Clark Hatling was. He was the championship son. "The day my successor is inaugurated, I'll welcome him to the White House, board a helicopter for Dulles, fly to France."

"And that same day I'll book our room upstairs, watch the inauguration there, and count down the hours. I'll be waiting here. Right here on this dance floor. I promise."

"And I'll say, 'I'm the former president of the United States, and you're going to dance with me.'"

34

Iowa

January 10
Total Votes Cast: 138,475

CANDIDATE	TOTAL VOTES	PERCENTAGE	DELEGATE TOTAL
Uncommitted	47,569	37	20
Laverty	34,688	27	15
Foreman	21,841	17	10
Hatling	17,987	14	8
Torsvik	16,424	5	3

New Hampshire

January 15
Total Votes Cast: 220,831

CANDIDATE	TOTAL VOTES	PERCENTAGE	DELEGATE TOTAL
Laverty	97,166	44	12
Hatling	97,025	44	12
Foreman	19,875	9	2
Torsvik	6,619	3	1

Cole stood up at the head of a table of Hatling workers at the Thoroughbred Club in Charleston, clinked a glass for attention, and said, "There are two ways and only two ways to look at the results from New Hampshire, and both of them explain why I'm drinking this." He held up a bottle of Bud Light by the neck. Everybody around the table applauded and cheered. Other Thoroughbred guests looked around at the commotion, but nobody said anything. They didn't even seem all that cross, because they'd all been following the election results from New Hampshire. They knew from the goofy hats that these were Hatling people, and they

299

knew the impact of the day's primary.

"Tell us, Brother Gibson!" Toody Baker called out, in a mild parody of himself at a Sunday service. "Tell us what they mean!"

"One, the actual delegate total is tiny, but the impact is huge. For one thing, Foreman spent himself dry, and fell to single digits in the process. He'll withdraw now for sure. Meanwhile Laverty, by concentrating his fire on Foreman, has made a lot of enemies, so I estimate we'll pick up seventy to eighty percent of Foreman's base. But even leaving that out of the calculation, it's impossible to overstate what a monster victory we've had in New Hampshire. I know that by the numbers it's a virtual tie, but remember that in 1968 Eugene McCarthy came within seven points of Lyndon Johnson, and before the month was out Johnson *quit the race!* Seven points away and it knocked him cold! A sitting president, gone! Yet here's our congressman neck and neck with the guy who only a few weeks ago was selecting a tuxedo for his inaugural ball. This isn't a tie, good people. We *WON!* That's why I'm having this." He held up his Bud Light bottle again as they clapped and cheered.

"The other thing is that while these results may seem momentous, in fact the delegate total is tiny, so we've got a tremendous amount of work ahead of us." The applause this time was slow and determined, accompanied with some pumping of fists and a low growl of dedication. "So that's why I'm drinking this stuff—which tastes like water, only with less alcohol."

A burst of laughter and cheers seemed to affirm that at least a few people at the table had managed to consume a little alcohol. There seemed to be the general sense that no matter what the future held, they had played their small part in a great drama, they had lived through this night, it was theirs; nobody could ever take it away.

He took a small notebook from his jacket. "Let me run through this schedule once again, briefly. The congressman will spend the night in Concord and fly down here tomorrow morning. He has a speech at the university in Columbia tomorrow evening—and I warn you, no Gamecock jokes, none at all, got that?"

A lot of people laughed, even at the other tables, when one of the Hatling supporters reached into her bag and came out with

300

a cap that said, "I'm a 'Cock fan." She stood up, doffed it for the room. There was hooting from all corners. The Hatling victory celebration was contagious. It seemed to Cole that it was sweeping the nation, and suddenly, if belatedly, even as he was saying, "Okay, Maureen, you've had your moment, now hide that cap until after the polls close next Tuesday," he had the idea to create a theme around that. The guy was a winner. It was as simple as that. People rallied around a proven winner, just to bathe in the aura. No matter how far down the ladder you were, you felt more like a winner just by getting emotionally involved with real winners as they made their triumphant journey through life. He flipped to a fresh page in his notebook and wrote, *Sports franchise theme. Caps, jerseys, pennants, mufflers, etc. Job for Luke.*

"Sunday morning: church service here in Charleston. It's currently penciled in at some place called the Jubilee Faith Tabernacle but it turns out that's one of those mega-mall behemoths and I know for a fact that the congressman would prefer a smaller scale venue, so how about you, Slater? You know these woods. Fix that, okay? By tomorrow noon and I'll notify the Secret Service."

Slater nodded his head, gave him the thumbs up. Toody spoke. "I'll find him one for Sunday evening service. How about that?"

"Great idea. Ditto—details tomorrow noon. So, except for church, the rest of Sunday and all of Monday will be devoted to prepping him for his biggest moment so far. That's the Monday night debate here in Charleston. I can't tell you how much is riding on that. Laverty's reeling, but he's a fighter, and if we lose South Carolina, Super Tuesday will be his for the taking, and then for us it'll be all over but the tears."

One way the fighter in Chris Laverty showed was in the blunting tactic he adopted toward Hatling's Southern Strategy. He and his team divined right away that Cole Gibson had chosen to "fight November in January," as one aide put it. Everybody knew that in November Laverty would take not one single electoral vote from the entire South. After the primaries they would spend hardly any money there, and even less time. But, as Laverty reminded his staff, this was January, and he'd be damned if he'd let some broken down hillbilly jock jump in at the last minute and steal the prize that he'd been paying his dues for all these years.

Certain voices in his campaign advised him to skip South Carolina; in fact, just skip the South altogether, even the Super Tuesday south. Concentrate on the Democratic strongholds and on the battleground states. Come November, California alone was worth fifty-five electoral votes, almost a fifth of the total needed to hand him victory. New York had thirty-one, Illinois and Pennsylvania twenty-one each, Ohio twenty. South Carolina's eight electoral votes were meaningless. In fact, a Democrat could lose the entire South and all the prairie states, and still become president. Why are we wasting this week in South Carolina when we should be flying all over the north and west?

"Because," Laverty told them, "if they beat us here they can say, 'See? If a centrist Democrat that nobody ever heard of can beat the mainstream Democratic frontrunner in a conservative state, in November Hatling will keep all the liberals—they're not going Republican—and he will siphon off centrists votes as well.' This isn't about South Carolina, people. This is about Ohio, Florida, Michigan. This is for the November toss-ups. And if we lose here, all we'll hear through Super Tuesday is, 'Laverty can't win the Big One.' But to my mind the idea that a pseudo-Republican can beat a real Republican in November is nonsense. That's Alice-in-Wonderland politics. So here we stay, and here we fight."

It seemed these days that Clark couldn't face any public gathering without first surveying the crowd for the puppy dog leer of the old man he called Stringbean Maynard. After the eerie moment of precognition in Georgetown, he'd spotted him at least twice in Iowa, at a speech on the campus in Ames, and in a town meeting in Des Moines. The one in Des Moines spooked him to the point that, under the pretext that he thought the old man had been a friend of his father's, he asked a state trooper to station himself at the door and delay him as he left. But the old guy had slipped through the crowd, or perhaps out a side door.

He'd seen him nearly everywhere in New Hampshire,

302

sometimes in deep disguise. In the bitter outdoors wearing a knit Patriots hat and a Mackintosh meant for a much heavier man. It made him look sickly, a wasting stick of the man he'd once been when that coat was new. At a panel discussion for NHPTV in Durham, he was far back in the crowd. This time he was clean-shaven, and had dark hair. He wore those big fish-eye glasses graded for clear vision at any distance. Clark couldn't even be sure it was him. He was seated, so the matter of his height was not in evidence. But, however he was dressed, he always looked straight at Clark with wide-eyed worship. There was never a trace of menace there.

Clark stopped being spooked at the sight of him. In fact until he could locate him in the crowd, or—he was still sane enough to know he might have invented him, like a child's imaginary friend—until he'd chosen a man to identify as the day's Stringbean Maynard, he couldn't really relax into his speech. By the middle of the New Hampshire campaign Clark had learned to scope the crowd during his introduction and pick out old Stringbean. He felt much safer that way.

"There he is," he would tell himself, "watching over you. Your guardian angel. Now go out there and give the speech of your life."

He knew it was silly, this guardian angel nonsense, but as Aziza had said, the trauma of reality is made easier by rewriting it as fantasy.

At Duncan Park in Spartanburg, Clark spotted him immediately, at the far back rim of the crowd. Once again he was a white-bearded old guy, but more stooped this time, and wearing no glasses at all. He was done up hick-farmer style, bib-overalls and a straw hat. His white hair ran down from his hat, over his collar, and looked as though it could use a good shampooing. Even burdened with his new stoop, his face peered at Clark from above the crowd. Clark felt confidence course through his body. It was a rush of near impudence that had once been as familiar to him as the smell of a locker room or the squeak of rubber soles on hardcourt. He recalled the feeling from his basketball days, from when he had the ball and saw Toody looking at him. Not really looking, but thinking at him. Great athletes think with their bodies, and when Toody's body told him, *I have an idea*, Clark got this same sensation, this certainty that he could make the future happen.

He gave his usual stump speech. Very moderate and genial. He said we need to be aware that we are all one big family and we need to pull together, but we can't bankrupt ourselves in the process. The best welfare is a job. And so on. It was all as soothing as a warm water spa, and its entire message was, I'm one of you, and that big-spending northerner Chris Laverty may be a nice man, but he's something of a misguided flake.

At the end of the speech he fielded questions. A reporter said, "Congressman, as you may know, there's a controversy raging here in South Carolina over whether to include the Confederate Stars and Bars on our state flag. What are your thoughts on this?"

He had been prepped on this one, had his answer ready, but paused to indicate that he was just now considering the question for the first time. "Well, I will tell you exactly my feelings on the matter, sir. What is your name, please, if I might ask?" Every inch the southern gentleman.

"Jason Farley, sir."

"Mr. Farley, we all can appreciate the pull of the past, the attraction of an identity with our forefathers. But I have to be honest with you. When my brother came back from Vietnam, it was not the Confederate flag that draped his casket. The flag those soldiers at Arlington folded into that pitiless triangle and presented to my mother was the American flag. The same one I have here on my lapel, and the same one that flies proudly over this lovely amphitheater here."

He could hear the crowd's collective pain, like a cry stuck in the throat, and then the burst of applause. He had them in the palm of his hand. This was the sound bite for the evening news, maybe the crowning sound bite of the South Carolina campaign. He knew he should stop right there. But he felt more coming, and it seemed he had no choice in the matter.

"You know, there's a high school right in my home district in Kentucky that has the Confederate flag flying in the school lunch room. And of course this high school includes several African-

304

American students. Now I ask you ... don't they feel that same pull of the past that we do? Don't they share the same attraction of an identity with their forefathers? And what if instead of being soldiers of that flag, your forefathers were held captive under it? What if the soldiers of that flag were fighting and killing American soldiers in order to make you work for no wages, to separate you from your wife or husband, to sell your children? How would you like to be told you had to go to school and eat your lunch every day under that flag? Does that sound right to you?"

He just kept winding it tighter and tighter. He couldn't stop it. It was him and Toody hugging at center court at the state final. It was Aziza looking at herself above the cathedral door, depicted as a dog-human before all the believers of Christendom. He had to let it roll. Fuck being president if it meant stopping short of the truth.

"What if Jewish children today went to a high school in Germany and had to eat their lunch under a swastika? Back to your question, Mr. Farley, what if Germans wanted to put the swastika back on their flag? Can you imagine how evil a debate like that would look to you and me and the rest of the world?"

He pulled himself up, took a drink of water. Had he really just done what he'd done? Had he really insulted the white voters of the most important electorate he would ever run in? The crowd fell into a shocked silence. They all seemed to be waiting for someone else to react first. Clark couldn't think of another word to say. He might have added, So go screw yourselves and your forefathers too, but instead he just stared right back at them.

Then the old guy at the back of the crowd took off his hat, slapped his thigh with it, let fly with a squeally version of a rebel yell, and said, "Hoo-WEE! I like 'im! He's a straight shooter!" He cheered and clapped, dancing his own adaptation of a geriatric two-step. Other people took his lead and applauded. He repeated, "A straight shooter, that's what he is! I'll vote for the man you can trust to speak his mind!"

By the next day there were "Straight Shooter" bumper stickers and billboards all over the state. On the *Hatling for President* website there was a logo of a cartoon-cowboy Clark, cocking his

305

thumb and pointing his finger, with smoke coming out. If Clark's cerebral, university professor past had been a liability among white voters, it was gone now. Here was the straight talking he-man who wasn't afraid to speak his mind, no matter whose feathers got scorched. And thousands upon thousands of black voters dropped their tepid affection for Chris Laverty and moved into the Hatling camp. They made up nearly a third of South Carolina's electorate. The next day's tracking polls showed Clark up by eleven percent.

Then that evening a Secret Service agent approached Clark in his hotel room. There was an old man in the lobby asking for a private meeting. The agent added, "He resembles that Straight Shooter gentleman from Spartanburg, sir."

"Pat him down thoroughly and let him in. But not for a private meeting. Have somebody stand just inside the door."

Clark was at his desk when the old man was allowed in. He approached in a loping stride, his hand far out in front of him. Clark stood to greet him.

"I owe you a big thank you," Clark said.

"Not at all. It's been my pleasure to serve you."

"You've been following me around the country."

"Not any more. They've spotted me now."

"Who's spotted you?"

"The media. I've come to say goodbye."

Judging only from the words he spoke, it was still entirely possible that the old boy was a schizo off his meds, but his manner didn't bear out this theory.

"Is it possible that I knew you a time long ago?"

"How kind of you to remember. It's been over forty years. It was at The Conference To Change the World. I met you and your late brother and father there. My name's James Lahnert, but everybody calls me Jimbo. I've worked for Walter and Roxanne all my life. I recall very clearly how you immediately offered Walter legal help. And you just a kid still wet behind the ears. It was a very kind thought."

"So they paid you to watch over me?"

Jimbo Lahnert laughed. "They said sure's this world you'd say something troublesome, and when you did I was supposed to turn it around."

306

"So who was it that thought up this Straight Shooter thing?"
"Roxanne, I'd bet. It sounds like her."

And so it did. Clark saw Jimbo Lahnert only one more time, at a great distance, on the night following his televised debate with Laverty, the night that ended any serious threat Laverty might have been to his campaign. The debate had ended—whether it was a draw or not would soon be of no consequence—and Clark was exiting the auditorium through the back tunnel. As he was being led through the final set of security doors and into the parking lot, Laverty rushed up to him. His face was so red, and his gestures so threatening, that if Clark's guards hadn't recognized him right away they might have pinned him against a car. Laverty was brandishing a wad of paper in his fist, shaking it in Clark's face. He shoved the paper straight into his face like a shaving cream pie and, in a sort of whispered shout, said, "I was working for *peace*, you son of a bitch!" He turned away, almost breaking into a run.

Clark and his guards watched him disappear into the dim lights of the parking lot, then a guard retrieved the paper and unfolded it. "Any idea what this means, sir?"

It was a digital photograph, printed out in color on slick paper. It showed Laverty sitting in a restaurant, sharing a plate of *kibbeh* with a man in a black skull cap and a white *dishdasha*. The caption said, "Sen. Chris Laverty in a secret meeting with the terrorist Hafid al-Ghanim, a.k.a Abu Ali."

Clark looked up from the photo and noticed that the wind was whipping up identical copies underneath every windshield wiper blade in the parking lot. "What it means, I think, is that I'm the next Democratic nominee for president."

He looked up and saw a man, barely visible at the far edge of the parking lot. He was a tall, thin man, with a stack of papers in his hand, and he was waving goodbye.

35 APOCALYPSE SOON

IT WAS TYPICAL of the morons in Magav Central to send a bloody Third Sergeant all the way to the Tiberias office to hand deliver an order for Levi to be at Megiddo Prison the next morning at seven. Even the pretty Third Sergeant, in her garrison cap and a tight skirt that was almost certainly shorter than regulation, didn't quite make up for the insult. Although Defense Force women in garrison caps—and nothing else—did constitute the most enduring bit of kink that he'd yet to check off his list, this one was so unsmiling and sour-pussy that he couldn't even treat himself to a fantasy of her. And why this wasted trip? Why didn't they just send her in the morning to pick him up? Phone him up today, tell him to be ready at six tomorrow, our driver will bring you. You can look at her legs as she changes gears. Why the big secrecy with the seals and signatures? Hell, they were summoning him to a fucking maximum security prison. They could broadcast it on Hamas Radio and it wouldn't matter. But nobody ever said that brains rose out of Task Force into Central. Common sense would actually disqualify you for Central.

The bottom line is: you don't summon Levi Hershko. Levi Hershko summons you. And if you do pull rank, especially for some bullshit time like 7:00 a.m., Levi Hershko just might be a couple of minutes late. He might have something pressing to do on his way in. Like he might have to stop at a bakery and pick up a bag of *burekas* for his breakfast, the buttery gold triangle kind he likes so much, the goat cheese ones where the phyllo wrapping puts up just enough resistance that if you're not real careful the warm cheese will dribble right down your chin and onto your aloha shirt, thus ruining your whole day.

The traffic was thin, his *burekas* were still warm, and anyway no traffic cop would mess with a Matilan badge, so he tore along Highway 66 at almost twice the new speed limit. He pulled over

308

at a coffee kiosk outside the park at Megiddo Hill and enjoyed a leisurely breakfast at one of the picnic tables. He was the only customer, but up the hill he could see teams of workers at the Armageddon archeological dig. They had the look of American volunteers, with their sand khaki shorts, and their bright red windbreakers tied around their waists. Baptists from Oklahoma or some such, he figured. American do-gooders trying to prepare the landing strip for the Lord's return. A group of them were kneeling; praying, Levi supposed, exactly what the warden of Megiddo Prison was thinking: *Hurry up, man! You're late!* On the other side of the rise was another group of worshippers, this a scragglier and livelier bunch, wearing funny costumes and doing some silly ritualistic dance. They had a sign that said, "*Say NO to the end of the world!*" Some of them knelt to pray as well, maybe to cancel out the other group, maybe just to piss them off. Levi chuckled and, although he was already full to bursting, ate his last *bureka* in one go. He sipped the last of the liquid coffee from its bed of coffee powder, and looked at his watch. It was 7:15. That would do just fine for the warden of Megiddo Prison.

What he didn't know was that the man drumming his fingers on the warden's desk was Aviram Ben-Nun, Prime Minister of Israel.

"You're late, Hershko!" Levi stifled a burp and started to make up something, but Ben-Nun cut him off. "Do you know that the Warski Foundation is conducting a memorial service on the anniversary of the Tiberias bombing?"

"Yes, sir."

"And do you know who the main speaker will be?"

"No sir."

"Good. Because so far it's a secret. And you don't need to know."

"But sir, that's my patch."

"No Commander, not for this event."

"May I ask . . ."

"Because the Secret Service will be in charge, that's why. They need someone to liaise with, and that will be our man from Jerusalem, Asher Yaari."

"The Secret Service? You mean the U.S. Secret Service?"

"I mean exactly that."

"But sir, I was born there. I'm perfect for the job. I know a hit-and-run from a Texas leaguer."

"You may have your strengths, Hershko, but liaising isn't one of them. Come the memorial event, you're on leave for two weeks."

"It's Hatling, isn't it?

"Two weeks. Full salary of course. Take a vacation. Go climb the Eiffel Tower. Go climb Mt. Everest. Go climb some damn place."

"But sir . . . "

The prime minister stood up and put out his hand.

Levi rose with him, shook his hand, and moved toward the office door.

"Hershko. Don't think for a minute that this means I've discounted your theory. But this is very delicate. We need kid gloves on this one."

"I understand, Prime Minister. I appreciate your telling me in person."

He drove away, but not far. Once again he bought coffee at the park and sat at his old picnic table, watching the diggers, the worshippers and the pranksters on Megiddo Hill. And why not? He had plans to make. The PM had told him to climb some damn place. Maybe he would climb Megiddo Hill, help these good Christians find Armageddon. Maybe he would attend the memorial service in Tiberias and meet Herr Hatling in the flesh.

36

"BANG."

BACK AT HIS hotel suite Clark couldn't make himself relax after the shock of seeing that Chris Laverty/Abu Ali photo distributed all over the parking lot—by now, no doubt, all over the country—and of watching Jimbo Lahnert's retreating farewell. At midnight he sealed a hand-written message and asked an aide to deliver it to Chris Laverty's suite at the Francis Marion. The message read, *I swear to you that I knew nothing of that. It came as a complete shock to me.*

He waited up for the return message, but none came, except for his aide's embarrassed, whispered repetition of Laverty's response: *Tell that hillbilly to eat shit.*

He tried to get some sleep, but his restlessness provoked a groan and a nasty look from Wanda, then finally a sharp jerk on her edge of the blanket, so he located an extra blanket and took it to the day-bed, with the intention of stretching out there as best he could, but ended up only sitting there, thinking.

He wondered if Chris Laverty, too, wasn't sitting upright in his hotel room, wide awake, thinking. Thinking what? Most likely thinking what he could do to totally destroy Clark Hatling. For one thing, he could go straight to the press and cry, Dirty trick! But that route was risky, because it makes you look like a dupe, a weakling who can't control events. Nobody likes a crybaby.

His best strategy might be to simply say, "I think it's valuable to talk to all sides in any conflict. For me it was a fact-finding mission. By the way, just before I went into my meeting I saw Hatling there too, standing at the door of the restaurant. I wonder what that was about?" Then let the press start digging. Somebody would interview the waiters. Was it likely that somebody there knew Aziza? Was she a regular? He couldn't remember her saying anything about that. But then she knew about the *kibbeh*. Was that only by reputation, or from personal experience? If so, would their

311

waiter remember the tall, foreign man who had accompanied her on the very same day that an oddly dressed cleric sat down with the now-famous American Senator? Who would believe *that* was a coincidence?

Clark squirmed, sitting there under the spare blanket. He could hear Wanda snoring now, and, outside, the metallic clip-clop of horses' hooves, and the rattle of wagon wheels over cobblestone. A carriage driver heading home for the night, or perhaps taking a tourist for one last run. A couple, more likely; honeymooners lost in the fantasy of new love in the Old South.

When that soothing sound left him even more awake, he knew he was in for a sleepless night. He got dressed, asked the agent at the door to summon a car and driver, and rode over to the Francis Marion. His plan was to ask Laverty's security detail to find out whether the senator, too, was awake. If so, he would request a few minute's chat. If not, then all he could do was write another note protesting his ignorance of the whole thing, and return to his hotel.

Chris Laverty was still awake, still seething. If he'd been anywhere near six-foot-four, he might well have thrown a punch.

Clark tried to defuse his anger. "Again, Chris, I swear to you as one honorable man to another, I was as ignorant of this as you were."

"Do you know how empty that sounds? How can you expect anyone to believe that?"

"Maybe because if it weren't true, it would be too lame for anyone to invent."

"I don't buy it, Hatling. Not for one nanosecond. I saw you right there."

"I'd just finished my lunch. It was as simple as that. I did see al-Ghanim standing across the street, reading a magazine at a kiosk, but I didn't know who he was."

"Oh, come on! Do you think I'm a fool? You followed me in and took that photograph. Then you had it distributed on the biggest night of your life."

"Again, all I can say is that I was as stunned as you were."

"Then how did you just happen to choose that restaurant, in

all of Beirut?"

"Somebody recommended it, that's all."

"Somebody at the conference?"

Clark paused. He thought, Oh no. Please, don't let it be that way. "No, as a matter of fact. Not somebody from the conference."

"Who, then?"

"A website."

"That's twice you've said 'somebody', then changed it to a website."

"Well hell, Senator, somebody writes those reviews."

"If you'd read it in the *Post*, you'd say, 'I read about it in the newspaper. Not, 'somebody told me.'"

"It's just a shortcut. I read it or heard it and wrote it down. What difference does that make?"

"It makes your highly improbable denial even more suspect."

"Still, it's the truth."

"I think I'll let the press determine the truth or otherwise."

"Actually, I don't think you want to do that."

"Actually I don't think *you* want me to do that."

Clark laughed quietly. "I suppose you're right about that. If I couldn't smear you real dirty with a refutation, it would certainly kill my campaign. But it would kill yours too. Probably automatically elect a Republican in November."

"So basically I get to sit right here and choose the next President of the United States. One man, one vote, you might say. Kastner or Hatling? Who gets my vote? The man who'll cut my taxes? Or the one who stabbed me in the back?"

"Let's reframe the question. Do you vote for the man who'll launch an investigation, cost you your Senate seat and quite possibly stick your ass in prison, or the man who won't?"

"What are you talking about?"

"Look, a man was murdered soon after he met with you. A man you met, either ill-advisedly or maliciously—we don't know which—but those are the only two possibilities. Either you were duped, or you were a cat's paw for some CIA operation. Either way you don't get to play senator anymore. Even in these cynical times there's probably some dusty law on the books about senators

313

becoming accessories to murder."

"I'll take you down with me."

"Me? I can go home and run a horse farm. An investigator will drop by to ask me what I know about the incident. I can say—honestly—that I was as stunned by that photograph as everybody else. Then he'll head out on your case again while I hop up on Old Seaweed for a gallop around the track. That's as low as you can pull me down, Chris. And frankly, it doesn't sound all that bad to me."

Laverty didn't say anything for a while. He checked his wrist for the time, realized he wasn't wearing a watch, and abruptly seemed to lose interest in any of it. Clark sat back to let him think it through. Chris Laverty was no fool; he just needed time. Finally he smiled and said, "Old Seaweed?"

Clark smiled back at him. "Out to pasture. Just like me."

"Do you absolutely swear on your brother's grave that you were not involved in any way?"

It sideswiped him. He felt prickles around the rim of his eyes. "I do, Chris. On Jerry's grave."

"That comeback about the flag on his coffin—that was one hell of a sound bite. You would have taken South Carolina in any case, after that."

"You know, I still miss him. Thirty years gone, and I can still hear him laughing."

"My apologies. Maybe I chose the wrong expression."

"No, you chose just right. I do swear on Jerry's grave. He's the one who should have been president."

"Maybe not. Some people are too good to be president."

"No, Jerry would have changed that. He was like Lincoln, but without the melancholy. Or the height."

They smiled at each other.

"You know I'm still going to fight you all the way."

"I wouldn't have it any other way. But tell me, how did you get set up with Hafid al-Ghanim?"

"One of the organizers at the conference approached me saying that a Hamas leader was in town. Supposedly he was sick of the cancer eating through the whole region, and was seeking a legitimate peace. I just thought, well, he's right. There is a cancer

314

affecting not just the region, but much of the world. Iran is getting nuttier and nuttier. Egypt is ready to collapse into chaos. I figured if he was willing to tell me his ideas, I was willing to listen."

"Then listen to this idea of mine. If you rally and take Super Tuesday and go on to win the nomination, I'll support you fully, no question."

"I thank you for that, but we both know . . . "

"We both know that nobody knows the future. But if it turns out that I am the nominee, will you help me out?"

"What did you have in mind?"

"I was thinking, Secretary of State."

Sitting in the back of the car on the ride back to his hotel, it finally occurred to Clark to check the news penetration of the Laverty-al Ghanim story. Old Joe would have been appalled that he'd waited that long. He might have rethought his whole electable-son position. Nearly seven hours had passed since Laverty had first thrust the photo in his face, and he hadn't even checked CNN. He'd merely recounted the incident to Cole, left instructions that he needed to be alone, and sequestered himself in his room with his sleeping wife. She hadn't even gone to the debate. She pleaded a migraine. He had no clue and no desire to know what that was all about.

He asked his driver to find an all-news radio station, where, as he might have known, it was the lead story. All they seemed to know about al Ghanim was that he had been a member of some terror gang, killed by a rival. An Israeli government spokesman was saying they would wait until all the facts were in before they responded officially and specifically, but that as a policy they never approved contacts with terrorists, not even by representatives of their allies. A columnist from The *Jewish Daily Forward* urged AIPAC to call an emergency conference to discuss their neutral position on Laverty's candidacy. Even better for the Hatling southern strategy, the Christians for Israel leader in Columbia, Rev. Cletis Scalfe, said that "Strictly speaking in my own opinion," the meeting was Satan's attempt to postpone the Second Coming.

They listened to this for a while. The driver didn't say a

315

word, but did laugh when Clark repeated, "Strictly speaking in my own opinion." He asked the driver to cruise the peninsula down to the historic edge of Charleston. As he stared into the passing landscape on this serene, lovely, pivotal night, Clark found it curiously simple to run the film back to the beginning, to the chained and bewildered Africans who had found themselves ensnared, imprisoned, penned into a ship's hold, and now somehow the centerpiece in an outdoor market seething with white men and bags of gold. He passed gray-clad regiments of marching men who knew that as low as they might be against other white men, they were nonetheless men of honor, unlike the brutes who worked the fields. And they all agreed that you died for that honor; you had nothing else. Passing the now-idyllic Hampton Park he saw corpses wearing no more than blue rags, lined up in the prison camp of the old racetrack, being covered with an inch of dirt by their captors. As Charleston fell and the white citizens fled, he saw congregations of freed slaves rebury, in proper coffins, with prayers and crosses, these rotting corpses, these fallen soldiers of the United States of America, these liberators. He watched the great procession of May 1, 1865, as the freed slaves held services and placed flowers on this hallowed ground. He imagined Jerry's grave, with Toody's mother praying there, spreading rose petals over her own little white boy angel. He watched as, eleven years later, the former slaveholder Wade Hampton III and his terrorist group of Red Shirts murdered and intimidated their way to power, and set back by almost a century the dream of freedom.

He wondered whether in this military-loving state anybody remembered that the first U.S. Memorial Day had been held right here, in a field of death, hard by today's Citadel. Where freed slaves wept and sang hymns. Right here, in this pretty park, a place for picnics, lovers; for jogging and softball. Hampton Park. Named for the man who put the chains back on.

He wished he could address a crowd with this. He wished he could say, I know I'll lose your vote tomorrow, but here's what really happened. Like some colossal Stalin, your gallant forefathers air-brushed it from your collective memory, but you can't censor me, and you can't change history.

316

But they could. They had.

Clark broke his silence and told the driver, "I apologize for the way this sounds, but can you pull over and get out of the car for a couple of minutes? I need to make a phone call."

Once she'd figured out how to add custom ring tones to her phone, Aziza downloaded a U.S. Army Band version of *Hail to the Chief* for Clark. It was great for a laugh, but he only phoned once a week, usually very early in the morning, so no one other than her ever got to enjoy it. She couldn't let anybody in on the joke anyhow. That's why it was such a kick when it rang while she was having her late-morning coffee on a Starbuck's patio on Hamra Street. It was a lovely, sunny, January day, and the tables were all occupied. She saw several people look up and smile as *Hail to the Chief* roared forth. People didn't even need to know that the next president of the United States was on the other end. It was just a funny tune for a cell phone.

Aziza stopped *Hail to the Chief* and her fanciful red flashing screen and said, "Darling."

"Darling me later," she heard. "First I want to know if you've heard the news."

"About the cute little photo that will make you president?"

"So it was you."

"With a little help from our friends. But yes, I pulled the trigger, so to speak."

"That's not the least bit funny. You killed that man, you realize that."

"I did no such thing. Nobody even knew about that photo until we distributed it last night."

"Then why did Abu Ali get killed right after Laverty met him?"

"I have no idea. Because he was a very bad man, I suppose. And ran in a very bad crowd."

"What puzzles me is, how in hell did you even get him to agree to such a meeting? Did Walter hand him a wad of cash?"

"It wasn't the *real* Abu Ali, silly. It was an imposter, an actor Walter hired. With a little work he was a clean double for Abu

Ali. And Laverty was a pushover. He was too credulous to be president, anyway."

"I just spent two hours with him protesting my innocence, then right in the middle of it I realized I was connected after all."

"Did you convince him?"

"Here I am trying to be the honorable candidate, and it turns out I'm Mr. Dirty Trickster."

"I love your righteous anger. You'll knock 'em dead at the U.N."

"Why did you do that? It's a low, sneaking deal."

"We had to dethrone him, somehow, before next Tuesday. He was way ahead in all the big states, except Texas. I think you could have gunned him down in Texas. My big straight-shooting cowboy."

"Bang."

"You didn't answer my question."

"What question?"

"Did you convince him?"

Clark took a deep breath, as he'd always done at the free throw line, and let it out slowly. In place of a dribble he patted the seat beside him, three times. "I think so. For the general election, we're going to need him. I offered him State."

"What do you mean?"

"If I win in November, I'll nominate him for Secretary of State."

"Wonderful idea! I knew you would rise to the occasion. Wait till I tell Roxy and Walter. They'll say it's a brilliant tactic, I just know they will."

"It's more than that. He'll be a good one."

She secured a five thousand lira banknote under her coffee mug and carried her phone out to the street. She watched the crowds of careworn pedestrians, felt that she could read their thoughts as they struggled to create and hold a place above third world poverty, to fight down the demonic impulse to divide up into tribes and start killing one another. To recover the lost dignity of a once proud race. "Oh *habibi*, it's really going to happen, isn't it? This is the first time I've actually felt it in my soul."

"I don't think they'll give me the remote control to the White

House TV just yet—not unless you have some dirty linen on Michigan Governor Arthur R. Kastner."

"Let me take a look through all my closets, see what I've got."

37

THE HATLING TEAM decided on Elise Torsvik as their vice presidential candidate. Her gender almost worked against her, with both Simon Angelo and Albert Tollson arguing that the whole unknown-female-as-running-mate gambit had been done to death, but Jeremy Allenberg persuaded them that the real benefit here was to put old Senator Rolf Torsvik on the campaign trail in a big way. He would gather his waning energy for the big finale. His daughter's victory would be the crowning glory to his great career. That basically clinched Iowa for the Democrats—not that their seven electors meant much—but far more than that, Allenberg argued, old gray-maned Rolf was such an iconic presence in the entire Midwest that Minnesota, Illinois, Wisconsin, maybe even Michigan, would be in play. Those states, plus Iowa, totaled sixty-five votes, almost a quarter of the two hundred seventy needed to win. Any extra women's votes she could pull in were just gravy.

Clark asked how anybody could think that he had any kind of chance in Michigan, since it was their own Governor Kastner who had a lock on next month's Republican nomination. Allenberg contended that at the moment Kastner's tax cutting agenda played far better with voters outside Michigan, but was starting to backfire at home, where voters were finally connecting the deterioration in their own neighborhoods with the lack of funding from Lansing.

"Our job," Allenberg said, "is to help them make that connection. And who can do that better than the attractive Elise Torsvik and her senator daddy, with his thirty-year history of moderate fiscal policies?"

Cole added, "Our job is to help the whole country make this connection."

"I'll grant you she looks the part," said Angelo. "Young and pretty, but not too young or too pretty. More wife than mistress."

"But a married woman you could have thoughts about," said

Tollson. "Not that I would, of course."

"Don't look at me," Angelo said, because they all had.

Clark liked this whole rationale, but more than that he liked Elise. She had always been a worthy colleague, and something of a friend, a co-production of a father's vision. In a funny way, his offer to her of a place on the ticket reminded him of a marriage proposal. He left Wanda to entertain Ed Torsvik with witty and flirtatious conversation in the hotel lounge while he and Elise went into his suite, alone. He joked that he had to stop himself from falling onto one knee, with a big bouquet of petunias in his outstretched hand.

"Petunias! You gotta do better than that."

"In fact, I think I can. Here's what you'll soon have to deal with." And he told her: "Tiberias, three weeks. I'm coming out of the closet."

"Well, I must say, it never showed. In that case I guess I'm perfectly safe in your hotel room."

"I wouldn't go that far, but I will warn you—in all seriousness this time. I'm a closet supporter of the Palestinians. I identify with them." She squinted one eye at him; he'd lost her. "Like our mountain people a century ago, who were uneducated, unsophisticated, had no one in power to look after their best interests; who in fact found that their own government was working for the interests of the very people who wanted to grab their land, the Palestinians got slickered and then they got shellacked."

"Your people weren't driven off by force of arms."

"No. Lack of jobs. The blood didn't start to spill until coal dust hit their lungs. But the root cause was the same: asymmetric information; asymmetric power. Big Money versus peasant nobodies."

Clark saw that she wasn't trying to withdraw from the pairing. She was a clear-eyed child of the prairie.

"And this affects me . . . how?"

"Okay, now I have to reveal something that, so far, nobody in this world knows."

"Oh! And I'm a devil with secrets. Do tell."

"In Tiberias I'm speaking at a memorial ceremony marking

321

one year from the blast. In that speech I intend to announce that I advocate movement toward a single, secular state for all of Israel/Palestine."

She laughed. "You're joking!"

"I wish."

"And this is because . . . "

"Because it's the fairest way. The injustice committed fifty years ago created an instability that is eating away at our national interest. Plus those unfortunate people got a raw deal. Muslims and Christians alike."

"Clark, I've always admired your intellect."

He noticed she didn't say courage, and liked her all the more for it. "I know we can't fix it. And I know we'll lose when I come out, but at least this way we get the conversation on the table. And let's not forget, we're underdogs anyway."

"Great slogan: *Probably lose either way. Might as well be honest.*"

"So what's it going to be?"

"I'm the daughter of a senator. Senator is all I ever wanted to be anyway. Let's go for it."

They left the convention together for the now-traditional tag team bus tour across the country. They met with big crowds along the way. It was clear from people's faces that they looked good together. This was a star couple, but not some Hollywood schlock pair. This couple carried moral weight. They were the offspring of two good-citizen fathers who had instilled in them the importance of public service. These were bedrock Americans you could trust.

Clark wasn't often asked about his policies toward the Middle East, and he didn't offer much in return. He told people to check his record, that it spoke for itself. AIPAC said, Yes, he's a friend of Israel. His record speaks for itself. The American Muslim Council said, Just look at his record. He's no friend of the Arabs.

Unfortunately for Clark, it wasn't so. His record, in fact, was a lie. Unfortunately for his campaign, he had recently turned into an honest man.

The stateside campaign was left to Elise, while Clark went off to look presidential on "the world stage," as reporters liked to call it. He wondered if they were secretly echoing Shakespeare,

322

whose men and women were merely players, with their entrances and exits. It didn't bother him to recall that he had but a bit part in the whole drama. His churchgoing mom had always cautioned him not to stick his nose up above his eyes, because if it rained he'd drown. These days he thought of her every time he thought of Tiberias and the Sea of Galilee. He should have taken her there. It was where he had made his big entrance onto the world stage; it would do just fine for his exit.

AUB invited him to speak there, saying that "obviously" he was "welcome home anytime." The trouble was, Wanda had to accompany him on this trip, and, even though Aziza wanted his marriage to last out his presidency, he couldn't face her with Wanda by his side. He agreed instead to speak at the American University of Dubai, so Walter and Roxy decided to return to host him there. Not officially, of course. That would be too risky, but they could all meet in private at the Hotel Marrakesh.

The final stop on the Middle East tour would be Israel. Morty and his foundation were setting up an anniversary memorial for the victims of the Tiberias bombing. This would be the place, Clark decided, and this would be the time. He could campaign no longer on a premeditated lie. He would come clean, as he defined it to himself. He would announce his true policies on Israel and the Palestinians. In fact, he wouldn't even define the areas as two entities. He would label it an Abrahamic civil war. Let 'em puzzle over that one for a while.

All this sounded fine as he dozed back and forth on the plane, thinking it through, sipping, from time to time, on some tepid scotch with lots of melted ice in it, but after he'd reached the Marrakesh and been led through the droning laundry room with its overripe lavender air, through the steamy oppression of the cinnamon and onion kitchen, and into a private room where Walter and Roxy were waiting with hugs and kisses and delighted faces, it started to feel more like a betrayal of friendship. He dared not think of Aziza as he planned the best way to destroy the hope of her people for the sake of an honest election.

Wanda was headachy and queasy again, and why not after the

long flight? Her abrupt exit from the reunited group puzzled them all very little. Roxy said they had a nurse on the staff, she would send her up. Wanda said no, she only needed sleep.

That was fine. It was simpler, if not easier, to approach the subject without Wanda sticking in her two cents. He nibbled on olives, cheese bits and, to hear Walter tell it, the only decent Moroccan bread in Dubai. It reminded Clark of his mother's cornbread. He found he could hardly swallow it. He had to break the news.

"I need to tell you both something that you may not like." They both stopped chewing and looked at him. "I'm going public with my Mid-east policy. I know you think I'll blow the election, but I have to do it anyhow."

The Sislers looked at each other, as though they may have misheard. Walter said, "You can't be serious."

"I'm afraid I am, Walter. I can't lie my way to the White House and then be an honest president."

With an audible effort to control her voice, Roxy said, "Just what do you have in mind?"

"I'm speaking in Tiberias next week. It's a memorial for the victims of the Galilee terror. I plan to lay out my true policies."

"You don't mean '*If the world had known in 1948 what we know today, Israel would not exist.*' Surely not that."

"Israel *as now constituted.* That's a crucial part."

"Crucial to you maybe." Roxy was losing the will to control herself. "But not a bucket of warm spit to the American voter."

"Look, I know what you guys have riding on this."

"How the hell would you know? Tell me that. You're no spring chicken, but Clark, we're *old*. We could go snuff in the blink of an eye."

Clark instructed himself not to say, *Then calm down right now.*

Walter led the exchange into a quieter tone. "Son, without you, we're going to die right here in this foreign land. Do you realize what that feels like? You can head home tonight, if you want. We're stuck here waving bye-bye."

"I understand your position, and I sympathize with it, but Walter ..."

324

"Then never mind us. If you lose this election, nobody will do squat to square things for the Palestinians for the next fifty years. At least fifty. The blood spilled so far will look like a trickle compared to what's to come. The whole Muslim world is going to blow, and any calm Muslim voice gets blown away by a thousand others screaming *They stole Palestine!* You could fix that, son." Walter held up a thumb and forefinger about an inch apart. "You're that close."

"Next you're going to say that makes me a mass murderer."

Walter looked at him and saw that all the time Clark had been watching Roxy. "I couldn't say that to you. I know you have your conscience."

Roxy met his stare. "I'll say it then. You can't make peace in the Middle East while you're sitting on your ass in Kentucky, reminiscing about all the great jump shots you made."

"You're almost there, Clark. One more victory and you can move mountains. You're almost even in the polls; Kastner's got weaknesses. Can't you smell victory? Can't you just taste it? Six months from now you could be signing your name to executive orders that will set this place on its ears. Then with some elbow grease you can recreate the whole area, or at least give them a decent chance to remake it themselves. Think of it: political cover for moderate Arabs! Never in history has it happened. Imagine what they could do with it! Imagine them and moderate Jews pulling in tandem! How can you throw that away for some namby pamby guilt game?"

Clark stood up to pace the room. It was closing in on him. The curtains were wide open onto a view of the Gulf, roiling like molten lead to the horizon, yet the room squeezed him in. He straightened his posture and jerked his shoulders back violently. He felt like one of Michelangelo's unfinished slaves who strain endlessly to throw off the marble yoke. He wanted to slam his way through the big window, cross the beach at a full run and plunge into the sea. But he loved this old couple; a love that went back forty years. He needed them to understand. He turned, walked toward them, sat back down. By now their faces registered the pain of trust and hope betrayed.

325

"I'm truly sorry. I can't even tell you how sorry I am, but think about this: remember Richard Nixon? Remember how he campaigned on some secret plan to end the Vietnam war, but it turned out all he had was a secret plan to win the election? That would be me, only in reverse. I really do have a secret plan, but I tell the country I don't. Do you want me to be another Richard Nixon?"

"Nixon beat the living crap out of George McGovern. Would you rather be Richard Nixon or George McGovern?"

"George McGovern. Hands down. He ran an honorable campaign and was beaten by a man who lied to the nation; a man who resigned in disgrace three years later."

"Well, I'm sorry old buddy, but I can't let you do it."

"I don't see how you can stop me."

"We can pull all our funding out from under you, let you scratch for pennies like everybody else."

"Walter, you got me off and running, and I'll always be grateful for that, but to be honest with you I haven't needed your money since New Hampshire. After that, it started rolling in faster than I can spend it."

"That'll dry up fast if you make this announcement."

"In which case I'll cut spending."

Roxy said, "I'll go straight to the press. I personally know the senior editor of CNN right here in Dubai. I'll tell him you got your start with some very suspicious funding from the Gulf. And brother I don't mean the Gulf of Mexico, either."

"I doubt you'll do that. Once you calm down you'll see that by destroying the Hatling campaign you destroy any chance you have of a presidential pardon. With me in the race, you've still got a chance."

"Fat fucking chance."

"A theoretical chance, anyway."

Roxy leveled her eyes at his. "Does Aziza know about this?"

Clark looked down at the floor. He didn't whisper a sound. To a stranger, he might have been a man inspecting the carpet, but both Walter and Roxy knew they'd found their best weapon. Walter looked around at his wife. She had Aziza's number in her

326

phone, and her phone in her purse. He expected her to reach for her purse, and, if she did, wondered whether he would keep silent, or say "No, not that." He tried to imagine what was going on in her mind. Probably that Walter was older than her; that the wife usually outlives her husband; that she would be the one to bury him, probably in Beirut, and then every evening she would sit on the terrace and watch the still water go dark, and the mountains behind go dark, until her own life, too, went dark. But her hands, her lovely, twisted hands, remained unmoved in her lap, until one lifted to her face to wipe away a tear.

"Listen," Clark said. "You know I love you, don't you? I dearly love both of you. But it would be a crime against democracy."

Roxy looked at Walter. She shrugged, tried to force a smile. "A lifetime of bad presidents, and wouldn't you know we'd draw Honest Abe."

Clark thought of Amin's riddle: *The crimes of America must be cleansed in blood,* and of how Honest Abe had opened the floodgates to let it flow. He said, "I'm going to need you there with me, in Israel, for my speech. Without your support, I don't think I'll have the courage."

38

WANDA DIDN'T FEEL up to the sweetie-pie hugs-and-kisses ceremony with the Sislers, not immediately after the flight, but she accompanied Clark to their private office and went through with it anyway before announcing that she needed to lie down for a while. Once back upstairs in her hotel room, she brushed her teeth, freshened her face, and had reception put her through to Cole Gibson's room. He answered on the first ring, always a good sign.

"Hey you made it. Is Clark there?"

"Would I be phoning for a toy-boy if he was?"

He decided that the best response was a polite chuckle. "Do you know what your husband is doing right this minute?"

"Do you?"

"What I think he's doing is downstairs with Walter and Roxy basically withdrawing from the race."

"What do you mean by that?"

"Can I come over?"

"You're always welcome in my *boudoir*." She purred more than articulated the word.

But two minutes later she greeted him with a simple handshake and led him to the sofa set in front of the wide French windows that led to a balcony. She took the big red bow from a cellophane-covered fruit basket, stripped the peel from a mandarin and popped a segment into his mouth. But for one tiny tic of surprise, he didn't flinch from eating straight from her fingers.

"So Wanda! What the hell are we going to do with that husband of yours?"

She had no idea what he was talking about. He had to explain it to her, right to the end, which was, as he saw it, a record defeat in November. They might not even carry Kentucky. He asked her

328

if she thought she could sway him away from such a foolhardy course.

She'd always half-expected her husband to self-destruct. It was just like him to go soft as soon as he'd pulled even in the polls. The stuff it took to make something of himself—grit, guts, gall, whatever you wanted to call it—Clark Hatling was way short on it.

"Ha! I can't even get in his pants."

Cole's face registered something. Interest? Yes, that, surely, but interest in what? She sensed that her increasingly blunt attempts to seduce him were finally getting through.

"But you are indeed a very sexy woman. I've been thinking about that."

"And I must admit that the sight of you at poolside has forced me to take the plunge a time or two."

He smiled at her. Did *taking the plunge* mean diving into cool water? "Well then," Cole told her, "maybe we'd better do something about that."

"If my poor, measly excuse for a husband can't dig me out of this rut, I'll just have to dig for myself." She pulled a bright red grape from the basket and held it up to the light from the window. Its thin, translucent skin glowed like some magical eastern crystal ready to explode with liquid light. "I don't see any pips. I do hate grapes with pips, don't you, Cole?" She moved it slowly toward his mouth, noticed that his eyes narrowed as he watched it close in. As the cool grape just touched his lips, he parted them, and didn't back away from contact as she slowly rolled the grape left and right, moistening it for him with his own lips, and popped it in.

"You should close your eyes before you bite down. Close, squish, then feel the flesh and the juice. That's how you should eat grapes."

"Yes, well, I should learn some lessons on sensuality from you. In a funny way I think that's what brought me into your room."

"Oh, goodie." She closed her eyes and ate a grape. "We must take care not to let Clark catch us."

"Exactly. We need a plan. Let's get started."

"Honey, I'm as ready as a woman will ever be." She rose to lock

329

the inside bolt on the door, and when she turned back saw that he had moved places. Not to the bed, however.

He was lowering himself into a desk chair. He found a pen and note pad, then picked up the phone.

"Hi, sweetheart. How you feelin'? Excellent. Could you drop over? No, wait—better we move to our room. We'll be there in a second."

The door of the Gibson's hotel room was standing wide open when Cole and Wanda got there. Danielle was over in the corner, bent over a laptop. She looked up, waved at Wanda, and bent back to her task, saying only, "I've already found the still. I'm just checking YouTube for the video."

Cole motioned Wanda to a soft armchair under a brass reading lamp. It was the kind of corner set-up that would seem to beg for a rainy evening and a good book, yet here, on a day that seemed overcast only because of the dingy dust, the pollution and the summer haze that coated the sky, and by a window moist only with condensed humidity, it seemed an inadequate place to rescue a presidential campaign so close to dying by its own hand.

Cole sat opposite her and said, "It seems that your husband is determined to deliver a speech that will almost certainly wreck his campaign. That's beyond the control of any of us. However, Dani and I faced a situation something like this before—though on a much smaller scale—and we lucked out. What we're thinking about right now is how to duplicate that luck, only this time it won't be luck. It'll be strategy, and we'll need you and your sex appeal to make it work. Dani, tell Wanda what happened before."

"We were running a Democratic challenger for governor of Georgia. Martin Breciant, you may have heard of him. He won. Great guy. But while still a candidate Martin decided, after studying the state's energy and transport situation, that he simply *had* to add a nickel to the state's gas tax. It was a *must*, he said, for a whole bunch of very good reasons. He had to announce it immediately. We said, fine. Announce this brilliant plan immediately—immediately after your inauguration. But he didn't want to be tricky, and he argued, wisely, as it turned out, that

330

without electoral backing he couldn't get it through the legislature. He was inflexible on every point, except the precise timing. We advised him to unveil this plan at a meeting with urban planners, a sympathetic audience, in late October, late on a Sunday evening, too late for the evening news. We hoped that by the time the late news came on, everybody would either be in bed or watching the Atlanta Braves in the World Series.

"So that's what we did. The trouble, of course, is that Monday's going to roll around all too soon, and you know how everybody goes bazooka over a gas tax. I never have figured this one out. The price of a gallon of milk can go up a dollar, and nobody peeps, but if gas goes up a nickel, there's revolution. But let me show you how we got lucky."

Danielle started the YouTube segment. It showed a distinguished-looking middle aged woman in a flowered party dress, getting ready to enter a taxi. Not a limo, just a normal taxi, which emphasized the woman's inclusive attitude. Here she was, wearing a wide paper braid sun hat with a scarlet satin band tied into a rosette bow, and carrying a pair of white lace gloves, clearly on her way to a garden party, probably some country club affair, yet she was taking a standard yellow cab with an African-American driver.

The photographers had been positioned for this moment. Her driver was opening the door for her, and just as she turned to wave, she dropped a glove, which the obliging driver stooped over to retrieve for her. Unfortunately for everybody, except the photographers, as the driver stood back up, his head caught underneath the edge of her skirt, providing, for one moment's click of the shutter, a terrific shot of her exposed legs, and that driver with one of the great political crotch shots of all time. As he pulled out from under all that expensive cloth, and after they stood there frozen for a moment, she slapped his face with her one remaining glove.

"Most stations cut the tape there. The next day this "gauntlet affair" dominated the news. Later, after a lot of bitter debate over whether her act was the reaffirmation of proud southern womanhood or petulant abuse of an unlucky underling, over

331

whether race was an issue or not, and after her own protest that it was all blown out of proportion, that her "gauntlet" was in fact a playful slap at the bad luck of the incident, they got around to finishing off the scene, which really did show both driver and passenger laughing at how embarrassing it was for both of them."

"By this time," Cole said to Wanda, "I'd bet a hundred bucks that you've forgotten that the point of this little story is . . . what?" He gave her a couple of seconds. "The Breciant gas tax, of course. See, the voters missed it, too, just like you did."

Wanda laughed. "You set me up, you jerk. So now you want me to show my crotch to some Arab cab driver?"

"Or the moral equivalent," Danielle said. "What do you think?"

"I have to say, I do like the sound of that hat."

On the afternoon before Wanda's press conference and Clark's speech, Danielle downloaded a copy of the first *Hatling For President* advertisement in the series that Jeremy Allenberg came up with after mulling over Cole's strategy of announcing to the nation what Michigan voters were just starting to figure out— those deep tax cuts and Michigan's steep economic decline were more than a coincidence. It was the kind of message that people would reject if you preached it at them. They, like the Michiganders, needed to see it developing around them. All Allenberg's crew did was put a camera out the window of a car as it drove along almost any Michigan road they chose, and let the deteriorating pavement jostle the video while a voice-over praised Governor Kastner for cutting state taxes. While the camera lens, and presumably the viewers' eyes, bounced over ruts, broken lane dividers, separating bridge joints, and potholes; across pothole patches that were worse than the potholes; as the car swerved around chasms and danger cones and once-orange sawbucks whose paint had peeled away and whose warning flashers had gone dead, a cheery, teenaged, feminine voice tallied how much revenue had been forgone thanks to our own Governor Arthur R. Kastner. A graphic appeared on the screen with each item on her list. When she said, "He cut state taxes by twenty-seven percent," the screen showed "Minus 27%," but the words bobbed up and down the screen and finished

332

in a blur. It made you dizzy just to watch it. Wanda had to close her eyes. "State Revenue Down: $1.2 Billion," bounced all over the place. "Unemployment: 15.7%" "Workers lost to other states: 327,000." "Homes for Sale: 537,021." "Homes Sold: 120,483." "Home Sold For A Loss: 120,483."

As it went on, the young woman's voice betrayed a growing fear as the car went more and more out of control. Then Allenberg's real breakthrough: "Note To Michiganders: You too can make a film like this." This one bounced a while then flipped off the screen, and was soon replaced with: "Pick a street. Any street." It ended with an out of control "KASTNER FOR PRESIDENT" careening around the screen with bumper-car-like ferocity, and the teenaged narrator saying, "Oh. Ouch. OW!!! Hey dude, slow down, will ya?"

39

SO WANDA HAD her special bit part in the political drama, and the anticipation perked her up for a while, gave her self-deceiving mind enough space to avoid confronting the truth of her failed seduction scene with Cole. When she recalled that the man she'd targeted as her next conquest had actually been thinking—and at the very moment she was ready to strip him down in her own locked hotel room—of his wife, then at that point her head would shout, Whoa! Stop right there! Soon you will hold your own press conference and stand before the world, the temptress with the will of iron.

The look she provided for the cameras was about as hot as a mainstream Protestant woman can look and not lose votes, and—here's the expertise she brought to the table—that's pretty damn hot. She'd been playing the church game right along with Clark, so she knew where the line was. What the modern church voter cared about was their standing in the community, and being a frump was no longer a status symbol. Copping a Christian attitude though, that brought big points, and the hotter you were when you copped, the bigger the payoff. So when the planted journalist asked her the planted question—a question Cole had practiced with him word for word—and Wanda sent his ass packing, now that was pure Moral Majority adrenaline in its most potent dosage.

The "journalist" was in fact a French-Arab engineer who'd lived in Dubai for years, a friend of the Sislers. He didn't want payment; he just wanted to help. He easily got into Israel with his French passport, grew a week's worth of whiskers, and delivered his line with as much indecency as he could muster.

"Mrs. First Lady," he started, already showing his ignorance, "You look so much sexy all the time, to all the men. Maybe since Jackie Kennedy no woman so sexy. How you feel to know young American boys see you and think bad things? Feel happy, maybe?"

Wanda stared at him. They had determined that five seconds was the optimum length of surprise at such a question, proceeding in a slow burn to a brisk response. She let her eyes grow bigger, took in a sharp, shocked breath, and told him, "I assure you, sir, whoever you are and wherever you come from, that is not a question you should ask any woman on the planet. I don't care if my husband is running for president or not, I will ask you to leave this room at once."

The French-Arab-Engineer-Journalist had been practicing a sideways look that meant to convey, Are you sure you're not just playing hard-to-get?

Wanda said, "I am serious as a heart attack, sir. You will leave this room immediately, or this press conference is over."

At that point the action depended on how the other journalists reacted. If the crowd stayed silent, Wanda would wait thirty seconds and walk out. But since, as Cole predicted, the real journalists joined Wanda in hissing this fool out of the room, she continued to field softballs about her ideas on fashion, child welfare, and all the rest.

She carried it off brilliantly, and she knew it. She knew it within herself, and when she walked away from the microphones and through a set of curtains into the privacy of backstage, both Dani and Cole greeted her with high fives. She felt it right to the nerves in her fingers. She'd done exactly what needed to be done, perhaps even with a touch of class that couldn't be rehearsed, and no one would ever have guessed she'd worried over it for days.

Clark didn't even know about it. He was off rewriting his Tiberias speech for the fiftieth time. He knew she had a press conference scheduled for that afternoon, but he didn't know it would plant a little Tiberias bomb of its own.

As successful as it was, though, with the high-fives and a quick toast, by the time of Clark's speech, retaining her glow required effort. As she sat in the great auditorium of the Tiberia Convention Center, beside Cole in the first row of seats, behind Roxy and her wheelchair brigade, she hardly listened to her husband's words, or to the audience reaction to them. Her mind was too busy replaying her own star turn. But—it was funny—

somehow the melancholy of the hall seeped inside and filled the empty crevices. All those wounded people, or the bereaved loved ones of the bombing victims. Maybe it was because Clark kept talking about Lincoln. She knew that Mary Todd Lincoln had succumbed to clinical depression in the White House. Could that happen to her, too? Or maybe it was the hopelessness of the cause that her husband had espoused. She was supposed to sit there giving him adoring looks, in case the cameras focused on her, and she did that. Faithfully. At least she thought she did. She tried not to let it slip. She certainly hoped it concealed the one thought that started to crowd out all the others: why are you throwing away our future on this? Don't you know these people are never going to get along? A dozen presidents will come and go and these clowns will still be scratching each others' eyes out. She wanted to take the microphone from him and say, Fuck you people! Why can't you just let us be president? What hold do you have over him that I can't release him from?

Tears started dribbling down her cheeks. She didn't sob or make a big show of it; just let them go where they wanted. It had all become too much. The stakes were too high, and losing was a certainty. Cole handed her a handkerchief. He smiled sadly, perhaps telling her that tears look great on the six o'clock news.

She joined her husband on the podium as he received his ovation. The crowd rose and called his name. The wounded rocked their chairs back and forth or drummed their crutches on the floor in time to the call of *Hat-LING! Hat-LING!* She looked up at his face and realized she'd never seen him so happy. This was the moment of his supreme victory. This was his mountaintop. He'd assured this mixed audience that they'd already suffered all the pain they had to. They'd suffered enough for the entire nation; that part was over, and now they could all be friends. Individual members of the crowd paused in mid-chant to embrace a neighbor, a stranger an hour ago, now a friend, a human being of like mind, freed of a forced allegiance to a false doctrine, emancipated from their bondage to history. The waves of cheers set sympathetic vibrations running across her skin, and deeper down inside her, until her own heartbeat seemed to ride the onrush of adoration.

336

For Wanda, though, that was it. She didn't go backstage after the speech. Much later Clark found her in their room, sitting on the sofa, in the dark, with the balcony doors wide open. Even on this upper floor he could hear waves breaking on the beach as the heavy night air rolled in, smelling of dead fish and seaweed.

He turned on the overhead light, but quickly turned it back off when she winced and threw her hand up to shield her eyes. He closed the balcony doors and switched on the desk lamp. Her smeared eye make-up, and the caved-in way she slumped against the arm of the sofa, gave him the impression she'd been attacked.

"Wanda, what happened?"

"Nothing," she slurred. "Not one single thing."

"Are you okay?" He moved to sit beside her, carefully, as on a hospital bed.

"Oh, sure."

"Have you taken anything?"

"Maybe a couple of sleeping pills."

"You have sleeping pills?" When he reached across her for the phone on the end table, he noticed a collection of empty mini-bar liquor bottles stuffed down beside the sofa cushion. "Prescription pills?"

She didn't respond. He called reception and asked them to send the nurse up right away.

"Come on, let's walk around. Just put your arm around my waist, right there. That's it. Now let's take a nice stroll around the room." She put the side of her face to his shoulder and closed her eyes. He was carrying most of her weight. "Isn't this like dancing? How long has it been since we danced? Stay awake now. I need a dance partner." Her legs just trailed along. He gave her face a little slap.

She muttered, "So you wanna play rough, do you?"

"Ha! Yes, that's my Wanda. Let's play a little rough."

She took more of her own weight, moved around to face him, and said, "We need music."

The easiest thing to do was grab his iPod from the dresser, so he waltzed her in that direction, got it going for himself, and fitted one of the little speakers into Wanda's ear. The first song that came

337

up was *Harvest Moon*.

She looked up at him and smiled before cozying her cheek once again against his chest.

"No, none of that. We need to liven this thing up a little. He sang, "*Da-da—dada-ta. There's a full moon rising...da-da-dada-ta...I wanna see you dance again.* Wanda, you're not sleeping are you?"

"Nope. I'm too sexy to sleep."

"Yes, you absolutely are! Way too sexy too sleep!"

"Maybe you'll make love to me tonight."

"Yes, excellent suggestion."

In a mumbly British accent she mocked, "Excellent suggestion. Excellent suggestion, my dear Wanda."

"You're not very nice," he said, and gave her a sharp slap on the butt.

"Hey!"

"See there? See what happens to naughty girls?"

"So you wanna play rough."

"Are you awake yet?"

She nodded groggily that she was, then suddenly broke free of their dance, left her earphone hanging against him as she rushed for the balcony. Her head banged into the door frame, but she got it open before Clark could grab her. She reached the balcony railing and leaned way out over it into the heavy air, far above the narrow beach. Clark got his hand under the collar of her dress as her whole torso constricted. She vomited repeatedly into the distant sand.

When he got her back inside, a nurse was at the door. All Clark could do now was to assure her it had been a big misunderstanding and send her away. With Wanda out of danger he didn't need to risk a witness who might be tempted to go to the media. He carried her to bed, wiped her face with the dampened end of a towel, and told her it was perfectly okay to sleep now. Perversely, now she fought it. Like a child, she struggled to stay awake as though the darkness of sleep held unimaginable evils.

"I saw your face tonight."

"I know you did, love. You were right there."

"I never saw you look so happy."

"Really?" By now it seemed years ago.

"Not even with the Celtics' championship."

"Well, yes. This is much bigger, I guess."

"You know the sad thing?"

"Don't you think you should try to sleep?"

"It was my happiest moment."

"Tonight?"

"The Celtic days. They were the best. Weren't they the best, Clark?"

"They were damn good."

"I loved being a Celtic wife."

"You were great."

"I never cheated on you."

"I never doubted that."

She lifted her hand to his face. "Aren't you going to make love to me?"

"Sure, if you still want to. I think maybe sleep would do you more good right now."

"That's what Cole said."

"Cole was here?"

"For a little while. Not very long."

"Don't think about it. Tomorrow night then."

She turned her face to the side, cuddled against the pillow. "Why do we get old, Clark? It's a perfectly ridiculous system, isn't it?"

"You're right about that, love. It is pretty silly."

"It's a pretty silly idea, isn't it?"

He didn't say anything; just brushed the dry end of the towel across her exposed cheek. He thought, What are we going to do with you, my temperamental wife? He'd never really thought through what he would do about her when it was time for him to be with Aziza. Probably she would just run off with somebody, and be happy. That was the easy way out, and, he'd always assumed, the most likely. She was so full of surprises that her exit would be just one more, her last.

She turned to look up at him again. "Even Yousuf quit writing.

I sent him my photo and he stopped."

"You've been in touch with Yousuf?"

"Of course. He loves me, did you know that?"

"Well, no. I guess I didn't."

"He said we were mismatched. It should have been you and Aziza, me and him."

"Honey, you're getting things out of whack. All that was years ago. Close your eyes and sleep some."

She lifted her head from the pillow. "It was not years ago. I guess I know. It was recently. Roxy sent me his email, so you see, I don't need you." She relaxed once again into her pillow. "But then he stopped writing."

"I'm sure he still wants to write you, but he's in jail. He's under arrest in Saudi Arabia."

"Really? He still loves me, but he's in jail?"

"Otherwise I'm sure he would write you."

"My poor, dear Yousuf. Get him out tomorrow for me, okay?"

40

IN THE OLD DAYS HE WOULD HAVE KILLED HIM.

AMIN WATCHED AS his mother flipped obsessively from CNN to BBC to the Hezbollah station Al Manar—as though Al Manar would get access to Israeli signal. If all that wasn't enough to drive him batty, she was jabbering maniacally into her cell phone, all the way to Brazil, where Aliya and her new husband were combining a honeymoon with a visit with the in-laws family in diaspora. Amin could hear Aliya's voice pip-pipping away, just like his mom's. They couldn't possibly be listening to each other. This was the anticipation of Clark's big speech coming out as delirium. From the way they carried on, you'd think that Manchester United was playing Flamengo. Clark had told Aziza, privately, that the speech would be momentous, so of course Aziza had tipped off everyone she knew. She said she'd read about it on some website. The story gave no details, just that the speech would be aimed over the heads of the governments of the region, including the Israelis. Hatling would address the people of the region, let the governments be damned.

If this was true, Amin was as anxious in his own way as were his mother and sister. Clark had told him—and Amin in fact *could* keep a secret—that such a change of course against the Israelis would lose him millions of votes. He'd be the biggest loser in American history. A fitting place for the presumptuous, godless *mulhad* who dared parley a bit of affection during Amin's infancy into the lifelong right to an emotional tie. It was certainly this interference into their lives that had caused Yousuf to distance himself. How could a proud Arab father suffer such indignity? In the old days he would have murdered him, simple as that. The modern era, run on European rules . . . rampant promiscuity . . . women openly asking for it . . . this would have to be exterminated, and wouldn't

341

a wonderful marker in that process be a world record defeat for his father's old enemy?

"Found it!" Aziza said. "It's on BBC World. Try it there. Oh good! Hang up now—I'll call you when it's over. Love you, baby. Bye-bye."

41   IT WAS A PRETTY LONG SPEECH, BUT ONLY ONE MAN LEFT BEFORE THE END

A MUSCULAR YOUNG Arab pushed Morty's chair up the ramp that the Tiberias Convention Centre had recently installed for the occasion. Clark watched through a gap between the heavy stage curtains as Morty took the microphone and the nearly three thousand guests cheered. Clark noticed that the entire area in front of the center section of seats was lined with people in wheelchairs. They were Muslim, Christian and Jew, young and old, Israeli and not, all of them injured in political violence of one form or another. The Sisler's friend from Beirut was there, seated beside Roxy. Roxy herself was the exception, an American crippled by muscular dystrophy, but still a deserving member of this collection, just one of the gang, bound to that chair through no fault of her own.

He spotted Wanda behind her, in the first row of seats, beside Cole and Danielle. He recognized some of the other faces along that row—his assistants for the course of the visit, mostly Warski Foundation volunteers. He saw members of his Secret Service detail and their Israeli counterparts standing in all four corners of the hall, and at all the exits, facing the crowd. He always had to remind himself that they should reassure, rather than unnerve, him.

As a sort of inside joke that was so inside only he knew about it, he surveyed the crowd for a tall, thin, elderly man to nominate as this event's Stringbean Maynard, but then he realized the honor belonged jointly to Walter and to Roxy, the real guardian angels of the whole endeavor.

Levi Hershko sat in the far back of the hall, as near to the rear door as he could get. He saw one of his own corporals, a true lummox, lovesick half the time, posted at the door near him. He

343

made a stupid mouth at Levi—not that he meant it to be stupid, it was just the only kind of mouth he had. It probably meant, What are you doing spending your vacation here? It might even have meant, I'm getting paid overtime for doing the same thing you're wasting your leave on.

Whatever. Levi just looked him over. He had a Glock 20 sidearm, and probably a concealed Cobra somewhere. Nice new jacket for the occasion, must have twenty pockets.

Morty introduced Clark as "the future President of the United States, who will arm this region not with weapons, but with ideas." Clark walked out to generous applause. He bent well over to hug Morty and waited for him to be transported to his space in front of Yetta. Once settled into position at the lectern, he pointed down to Wanda and his little delegation, smiled, and lifted his hands for the crowd's attention.

"Thank you all for this overwhelming welcome. First I'd like to thank Morty and Yetta Warski who made it possible for me to be here, and I mean this in the least ceremonial, most literal way possible. One year ago, on a night much like tonight, they offered their guest room to a weary traveler. Otherwise I would not be standing here before you now. It has often been observed that a close brush with death puts everything else in stark perspective. I can confide with you that this run for the presidency, this request for the power to effect improvements in a dysfunctional world, this whole improbable saga that I am on, and that I think it fair to say all of us are on; this attempt to create a region that rejects violence and enmity in favor of human charity; all of this was born at the moment an explosion of light lit the night sky over Galilee.

"Tonight my happy task is to deliver the bad news to those who hoped to trigger a bloodbath in this wounded land: you indeed triggered a movement, but not the one you were hoping for. You lit the fire of human compassion. You exploded the myth of your own moral foundation. You exposed yourselves as no better than any of the other deluded, power-crazed, self-righteous and petty criminals who have attempted to push decent people around throughout history. I say to those who planted the bomb, You

344

started this movement. The night that these good people here in their wheelchairs were sleeping peacefully in their beds, you started it. The night when the absent loved ones of the people filling this room checked into a hotel to conduct their daily commerce, or to walk where Jesus walked, or merely to spend a couple of days at the seaside, you started it. Perhaps they returned to their hotel from a visit to the tomb of Moses Maimonides, the great Jewish philosopher of al-Andalus who found himself linked, during a period of Islamic intellectual fervor, with the great Muslim philosopher Averroes in admiration for Aristotle's powerful legacy of reason. Perhaps these pilgrims lay awake for some time, hearing the echoes of Maimonides' voice across eight hundred years as he still guides the perplexed through the underbrush of wizardry, witchcraft and fanaticism. And then the bomb. You started it. We shall finish it.

"Maybe our missing loved ones came to see the site of the Battle of Hattin, where Saladin turned back the Crusaders before retaking Jerusalem. These history buffs fell asleep thinking what a better world it would be if warriors and politicians didn't disguise their ambition in religious robes, so that we all could spot them easily, and unmask them.

"I look at my dear friends here in their wheelchairs. One of my advisors suggested I deliver this speech from a wheelchair, to show solidarity, but I said no. I thought it might look like a political stunt. But now I kind of wish I had taken her advice. I wish we'd all come here in wheelchairs. I wish everybody in the whole Middle East would take to the wheelchair and be family with our brothers and sisters here.

"Isn't it funny that no matter whose side you're on, no matter which God you pray to, or even if you don't pray at all, when the bombs explode and your spine shatters, your legs don't work anymore. Doesn't it seem that if your God is the right one and the other guy's God is the wrong one, your spine wouldn't shatter like his? Or even if it did, you could still walk just as well as before, while the person with the wrong God would never walk again? It sure seems that way to me, and perhaps to the wounded and heartbroken in this hall, and around this world, now that we have

345

begun to ponder these grand questions.

"Who caused us to seek the truth behind religious warfare? You, the unknown bomber. You made it clear for us all that your only weapons are the bomb and the gun. You offer no philosophy, no argument, no book, no moral purpose. But for your belt with the bombs attached, you stand naked before us, while we stand as one against you, fully dressed in rational thought, spun from the material of free minds. Our dear friends here in their wheelchairs—they stand taller than anyone.

"I plan to structure my speech tonight around two great American presidents, one Democrat and one Republican—I must be fair about this. Both of these men were wartime presidents, both left America a better place than they found it, but both had serious flaws that can shed light on what this meeting is all about.

"You may or may not know this, but one of the great American presidents, too, was in a wheelchair. Some of you may even remember him. He died not long before I was born. His name was Franklin Delano Roosevelt. He caught polio when he was thirty-nine years old, and he never walked again. As president, his main early task was to pull America out of the worst economic crisis she had ever known. He attempted to do this through measures he called the New Deal. Nowadays most people think of a "deal" as a business transaction, but that wasn't what Roosevelt meant by the term. He used it as in a game of cards. In a country built on the belief that even people of humble birth could, through their own efforts, improve their station in life, Roosevelt saw a flaw in the nation's system of commerce that had undermined that principle and those efforts. Poor people were dealt a hand of cards that would inevitably end in loss. It didn't matter how skillfully you played your hand, you were defeated from the start. He called for a new deal. Shuffle the cards and start over. Give people half a chance.

"How well he succeeded is a matter economists still debate, but he lifted people's spirits, and while it might be a stretch to say he saved democracy in America, there's no doubt that under his care democracy survived in the face of its greatest challenge in U.S. history. However, he was no great friend of the Jews.

"What many people nowadays forget—or perhaps they never knew—is that even after Hitler came to power in 1933, most average Germans were not clamoring for anti-Jewish actions. The decrees to boycott Jewish merchants were largely ignored. People just tended to keep shopping where they'd always shopped. German police or paramilitaries had to be posted outside Jewish shops to prevent business as usual. The many acts of violence carried out against Jews by Nazi party members, and tolerated by the police, provoked some of Hitler's advisors to complain that the unrest was damaging the economy. On August 8, 1935, Hitler reluctantly ordered a halt to these acts of quasi-official terrorism—an order that prompted a backlash by the Nazi hardcore *Alte Kämpfer*, the Old Guard.

"Hitler's economic advisors may have preferred a more settled commercial environment, but his own inclination was with the Old Guard. He wanted a legal framework to support his policy of persecution, so in September of that year he opened a session of the Reichstag in Nuremberg. The site was symbolic. Until 1543, Nuremberg had always hosted the first diet of the Holy Roman Empire. In 1935 the city saw the inauguration of the infamous Nuremberg Laws which rescinded German citizenship from all German Jews.

"So now a half a million Jews were suddenly stateless. The annexation of Austria and the Sudetenland in 1938 brought the total to nearly a million. Hitler had long dreamed of a Germany that he described with that hideous word: *Judenrein*. "Cleansed of Jews." But where were they to go? This was the Depression; most countries had firmly closed their doors to Jewish immigration. Chaim Weizmann observed that the world was now divided into two parts: places where Jews couldn't live, and places where Jews couldn't enter. So Roosevelt called for a conference to decide what to do about the stateless Jews.

"It was held in France, at Evian-les-Bains. From the start it was clear that the conference was a sham. The U.S. didn't even send a government official, but a businessman. The other major countries said from the start that they were full up. Great Britain and the U.S. had already made a secret agreement that the U.S. wouldn't press the British into offering Jews more places in Palestine, and the British wouldn't ask the U.S. to increase its immigration quotas. The nine-day conference was filled with ringing calls for humanitarian action, but by the end only the Dominican Republic had agreed to accept any of the refugees—they took seven hundred.

"The result delighted Hitler, who claimed that the world community had vindicated his policies by demonstrating that Jews were not only unwelcome in Germany, they were unwelcome everywhere.

"On February 14, 1945, King Ibn Saud of Saudi Arabia came aboard the USS *Quincy*, anchored on Great Bitter Lake in the Suez Canal, to meet the president, and they seemed to get on. The king had bad feet, so Roosevelt presented him with his spare wheelchair.

"On the subject of Palestine, Ibn Saud said the proper place for the Jews to find refuge was in the lands they had been driven from. Roosevelt agreed that Poland should have space for many of the homeless, as three million from that country had been slaughtered. Ibn Saud warned that the Arabs and Jews could never cooperate, not in Palestine, not anywhere. Arabs would choose death over the loss of their lands, and he asked FDR why the Jews coming into Palestine weren't in Europe fighting Germans instead of Arabs.

"It was a sobering meeting for FDR. He told a press conference that he'd learned more about the Middle East in five minutes with the king than in all his previous years. He left the meeting more pro-Arab, promised to do nothing to assist the Jews against the Arabs, and to make no hostile move against the Arab people. In November, 1944, FDR was elected for another four-year term, but he died only five months later, in April of 1945.

"It's impossible to say in what ways this region would be different today, had Roosevelt lived out his final term of office. Historians love to speculate on these things, but of course it's a futile, if interesting, pursuit. The obvious point is that he would have been president right through the fateful year of 1948, which Zionists celebrate as the year of their independence, and the Palestinians mourn as the *Nakba*, the year of cataclysm.

"The other president on my mind for this occasion is a man

348

born in my home state during the days of slavery, Abraham Lincoln. Lincoln had always been opposed to slavery. His greatest hope was that in time it would fade away, a process he believed to be inevitable as long as it couldn't spread. His greatest fear was that it would escape the southern states and find new markets, either in the north, or, more likely, in the vast new lands bought from France in the Louisiana Purchase, or wrested from Mexico in the 1846-1848 war, a war Lincoln, a congressman at the time, opposed for several reasons, one being that the geographical location of that territory would place it in the American south, therefore allowing it to be seen as prime territory for slavery.

"Lincoln was a man of high moral standards, but he was also a man of his time and place. He abhorred slavery, but he could not imagine an America where whites and blacks were co-equals. In this sense—and in this sense only—he had a common problem with Hitler. Or indeed with the modern Israeli government: he had a minority population that he wanted to get rid of. He saw the best solution as "colonization," as it was known. It didn't mean taking overseas colonies for the U.S. That was still seen as old-world European oppression, and would continue to be scorned for another thirty years. The colonization that Lincoln had in mind was to purchase a huge parcel of land somewhere, creating a homeland for freed American blacks.

"By the way, we cannot use the contemporary term 'African-American' when referring to slaves. The term wasn't yet coined, and in fact could not have been coined, because slaves were not American citizens. Like the Jews of Germany after Nuremberg, they were stateless. By the mid-1800's, they numbered four million.

"They tried colonization in Liberia, where a few thousand Amerigo-Liberians, in one of those episodes that make us despair for mankind, quickly set themselves up as an aristocracy modeled on the plantation owners of the American South, complete with hoop skirts, top hats, and fine homes with big, shady verandas. But yellow fever killed many. The survivors had trouble with the natives. And not many American black people wanted to go there.

"Lincoln invited a group of free black ministers to the White House in 1862. He explained that it was his view and the majority

349

white view that the two races could not share the same country. He wanted them to be free, but he wanted them to leave the U.S. He said he'd located a great deal of land with excellent coal deposits in Central America, and he wanted these ministers to recruit people to go there and work it. They could sell the coal to the U.S. Navy and use the money to improve their situation and bring in more blacks.

"Not many people wanted to take Lincoln up on the idea, and then—in a prefiguring of Roosevelt's Evian Conference—a delegation for Nicaragua, Costa Rica and Honduras said they didn't want them either."

Levi Hershko wanted to laugh out loud. Surely nobody was buying this rambling drivel. He felt like standing up and shouting, Yeah, yeah, we get it already! We were niggers in fair old Deutschland, the Araboush are our niggers. *Judenrein. Araboushrein. Niggerrein.* Herr Hatling has all the answers. You're way ahead of the rest of us. Lincoln and Roosevelt can't hold a candle to you. You fucking Houdini. Come back to my country and rub my nose in it. Try *Hatlingrein.* Now go crawl off and die a while, because you know *nothing* about our situation.

What he enjoyed most about the presentation was watching Hatling's face on the big screen, because there was a scratch or smear or something on it that with a little imagination could look just like the crosshairs on a scope. When Hatling moved his head just so, it locked on for a second, plenty of time for Levi to think, *Pull.* He had long ago stopped listening to the words. He stood up and left.

Clark paused as he saw one man in the back row rise from his seat, but a local security officer opened the door for him, the man departed quietly, and Clark continued. "We teach our young to be polite to their elders, that the elders are wise, that they deserve our respect. As a man of some few years myself, I'm not going to stand here and campaign for the young to be rude to the old, but if one of the wise ones tells you, 'Take this gun and go kill those people. I know this to be moral because God is on my side,' then

350

what you need to ask him one little question. It's a question that a polite young person might be reluctant to ask, especially a young person who is seeking the side of God and hopes he, or she, has found it. But always be aware of something: the wicked also claim to be godly. This guy might not be who he says he is. He might be a power-hungry fraud. Statistically, he probably *is* a power-hungry fraud. He might be such a power-hungry fraud that he's even convinced himself that God is on his side.

So if he gives you a gun and asks you to kill the others, because that's who God wants dead, this should be a red flag to you. Before you sell him your soul, you need to make sure he's really one of God's elect, because, let's face it—if you do his bidding and he turns out to be a fraud, and on the Day of Judgment God asks why you killed for a power-hungry fraud when God Himself had told you *Thou Shalt Not Kill*, and all you can say is that you were kinda caught up in the moment and didn't want to ask the one, perhaps impolite, question that would have saved you your immortal soul—that will sound pretty lame. God will be displeased. God will say that you and this power-hungry fraud will spend plenty of time together in hell, so you can ask him there.

And what is this big, telling question? You merely ask, as politely as possible, 'May I first use this gun to shoot you in the head?' Because if God doesn't want this man dead, surely the bullets will be repelled and fall harmlessly to the floor.

If the answer is, 'Sure. No problem,' you go ahead and shoot. If the bullets do indeed fall harmlessly to the floor, then you've found your guy. If he thunders, '*Have ye no faith?*,' then you know you have exposed a fraud. If he says, 'Let me show you here in this book where it says...' then you have exposed a fraud. If he tells his aides, 'Behead this boy,' then you have exposed a fraud.

"As for the question facing the nation—What can we do about this group of people we don't like?—neither Lincoln nor Roosevelt can help you there. Neither of those two great and powerful men knew what to do, nor does the state of Israel or Hamas or the Palestinian Authority. But the thing is, we in this room, we *do*. We know that the solution can't come from the government. They can't set you free, because they have to get elected by a majority of the people. The most effective way to do that is to control what Lincoln called 'the public mind' and the most effective way to control the public mind is with fear and hate, with a stirring of the bitterest enzymes of the human soul.

"They can't set you free. You have to free yourselves. We know it can be done. Any time one Jew and one Arab form a friendship, our side has won. Any time a black man and a white man share a laugh, our side has won. Whenever any two people on this planet embrace upon meeting, or shed a tear as they part, our side has won. In this way we rise up from our wheelchairs, lift our stricken spirits from their year of mourning, honor our dead, and the Hotel Galilee rises from the rubble like a film of demolition shown in reverse. This is how we finish the great movement that was started here by a simple-minded dupe with a brick of plastic explosive. Neither ruler nor superstition can chain the human mind. Free yourselves, and stay forever free."

42 DO BULLETS BOUNCE OFF HIM?

FROM A CHAIR recessed into the dark corner of the room, Amin watched his mother. It was a disgusting sight. She was at it again, back on the phone with Aliya, wiping tears, blowing her nose, repeating this line of the speech and that line. She sounded both exhilarated and worried at the same time. She had recorded the speech and was now replaying it as she talked. "It was a courageous speech. I can't contain my elation. *Your governments can't do it for you. They divide by fear. Free yourselves.* But it was foolish. The Jewish lobby will turn on him now. It was a magnificent moment, but the election is lost. . . . You don't think so? How could they possibly let this . . . No, sweetie, that's you thinking with your heart. Just like Clark . . . Yes, I agree, but . . . "

He left them to cry themselves out, walked into his room. He had an email to write. *Shoot him in the head*, he thought. *See if bullets bounce off.*

Levi Hershko heard the cheers all the way out in the lobby. He thought, Let the sentimental little darlings stand and applaud and slobber over this fool all they want, but his day is coming. Levi couldn't stand all the blubbering and the snot. It was more like one of those evangelical crusades he used to see on American TV, where they passed around enrollment cards and everybody got saved. It was one of the reasons he had left that sickening country behind. And now here it was in his own back yard.

But never mind. After this speech there need be no extraordinary action to keep Hatling out of the Oval Office. The coward had just blown his election chances, and in the process proved Levi's point. As he walked to his car he remembered PM Ben-Nun, who hadn't even been invited to this travesty. No doubt he'd watched it on television, and by now he must be on the phone with AIPAC, all the while thinking, Damn! That Levi Hershko

353

guy really knows his stuff! He's heading for the top!

On the drive home he felt it, and it got stronger as he parked. He hurried into his building and down the corridor. Would there be a message waiting? He punched the elevator button over and over. If he'd been in just a little bit better shape he would have charged up the stairs. Even in the elevator it seemed he was going nowhere. He felt like a lover, expecting a call. When Mrs. Herrnstein looked at him weird for jogging down the corridor, he just said, "Toilet." Luckily he'd left his laptop on, so he went straight for his *shakebadboy* address, clicked on Saved Drafts, and found a new one waiting. "*I knew it!*" he said to the empty apartment, and read:

I think he just shot himself in the head, don't you? Do bullets bounce off him, like Superman?

"HERE's HOW I say we spin it," Cole told Clark. "Bold and conservative in the same way our own Constitution was bold and conservative. Never mind that our Constitution was bold and radical."

"Not to mention," Clark piped up, "that it was drawn up by a bunch of atheists." Cole's head shot up at him. "Or deists," Clark amended, "if you're fond of euphemisms."

"Don't even say that in private," Cole said. "Don't even think it very loudly."

"Go look it up. Lincoln too. Believed in nothing. Never joined a church."

"Respectfully request the honorable candidate for president to put a sock in it."

"Don't blame me. Blame Abe. After he'd written a speech he had his aides stick in the *God*'s and *Almighty*'s and so on. Go look it up."

"You're on a real high aren't you? Or are you stoned?"

"High on life, my good fellow."

"Did you get laid last night, or what?"

"And how could that have happened, with Wanda in Washington and us in Chicago?"

Cole remembered. Clark had been in session with Elise Torsvik. "Ah. Oops. Sorry, boss."

"Not at all. Think nothing of it."

Cole couldn't let it go at that. "Surely you're not balling the vice-presidential candidate."

"You are absolutely spot on correct, Squire Gibson, although I must confess that when she told me she shares my vision of a one-secular-nation for the combined Palestine and Israel, and that at the conclusion of my Tiberias oratory, the word 'wow' formed her concise analysis, I felt a sensation in my groin that could send

Viagra sales into a . . . let's call it a tailspin. If you catch my . . . "

"I get it, I get it. And that's the only . . . er . . . congress, with her that has you so cranked?"

"Most assuredly so. A congress of the mind. Always the best sort."

"You're very weird today."

"The same sort of congress you had with my wife."

"Hey, whoa . . . "

"Which makes you either very gay . . . "

Cole smiled at last. "Or what?"

"Or a very good friend."

"You're baked. I swear to God you are."

"High on life, my dear fellow. I speak with the eased conscience of an increasingly honest politician, and human being. How do you like, as they say, them apples?"

"I somehow doubt I like them as much as you do. Now shu'up and listen. Here's how we spin it."

The polling numbers held firm, but the contributions started to dry up, and nobody in the Hatling camp could quite make sense of that. The consensus view was that eventually the two streams would have to coincide, but there were opposing opinions on why it wasn't happening now. One side had it that this was bad news, because it meant the average voter hadn't really focused on the implications of the Tiberias speech, and the numbers wouldn't react until those hostile to it got the word thoroughly spread throughout the electorate, but any potential contributor would have been paying much closer attention and therefore wouldn't want to throw money at a doomed candidate.

The opposing view—meaning, in the beginning at least, mainly Clark's—was that while it wasn't great news, it certainly wasn't disastrous. All it meant was that the calendar had reached the period when summer vacation credit card bills started showing up, and back-to-school expenses reared up, so small contributors suddenly found they didn't have the extra fifty or hundred bucks to spare. He told them not to worry, that this always happened at the same time of year in Kentucky Five. They said the trend didn't reflect the historic national pattern. Maybe it was because of the recession. Clark said it reflected Kentucky Five's historic pattern, because Kentucky Five was always in recession.

Danielle had her theory. It was Wanda's handling of that jerk. The poll numbers rose because every woman in the world was proud of her. Contributions were down because men didn't like it one bit, and it was the men with most of the money.

Albert Tollson said no, they'd all missed the point. It was simply that any major speech that mentions Roosevelt and Lincoln and sounds like a preacher, no matter what is said beyond that, people see as pure Americana, and it makes them feel safe.

Whatever the reason, by the second week after they'd returned from the trip abroad, it was clear he hadn't killed his campaign. Moreover, the bouncy Kastner ads shot on the streets of Michigan were having the best possible spin-offs: they had gone viral. Danielle linked the Hatling website with YouTube, and every day there was something new for her to add. People just stuck their video cameras out their cars and made their own jiggly ads.

Allenberg's even more fertile idea was the *What did you buy with your Michigan tax cut?* Every Michigander with a camera seemed to get in on it. One guy wearing an Altima cap said, "With my Michigan tax cut I bought a bus ticket to Tennessee and got a job with Nissan." A young woman standing in front of a football field said, "I bought season tickets to the Lions' games," and the camera pulled back to show little kids in a Pop Warner game. An elderly lady said, "I bought the factory where my husband used to work." The camera panned across a vast and dilapidated pile of rust and broken window panes. Another jiggly one said, "I bought four new tires and whole new set of shock absorbers."

The campaign rolled out two separate initiatives. One, an image campaign, added *May I shoot you in the head?* to his old Straight Shooter persona. This got huge play in the gun-rack states of the south and west. The west was always seen as a write-off, and they could possibly even squeak a victory without the south, if they ran the table in the north and on the west coast. That scenario was anything but assured, though, and Cole wanted to build on the southern strategy that he had devised to defeat Chris Laverty.

357

Their most important initiative was the ReTool America campaign. This was the Hatling New Deal, where the north would be won or lost. He told the voters that a Hatling administration would build an America that built things again. They would put the man back in manufacture—and the woman, too. They would restore railroads as the great arteries for moving cargo. They would make cities more livable and cleaner by installing world-class mass transit systems. They would concentrate on creating jobs that couldn't be sold off overseas down an Internet cable. People who were by now accustomed to getting up and heading off to the Food Stamp or unemployment office would become breadwinners setting off to a job that meant something. When children were asked, "What does your daddy do?" they would no longer look away in humiliation. They would say, "He builds America."

Everything was right on track until the morning the news broke that Saudi intelligence had uncovered and destroyed a terror network run by the Lebanese exile Yousuf Hatoum. This development, taken alone, meant nothing to the campaign. Kastner couldn't out-hawk him on the issue of terrorism. Clark was by now Mr. Shoot 'em in the head, and could anyone forget that he'd nearly lost his own life to a terrorist's bomb?

Even when somebody dug up a connection between Clark and Yousuf, his brain trust seemed to think that a social connection from the distant past, broken off nearly twenty years ago, could be explained away with little aftermath. Hatoum wasn't a terrorist back then. He was a highly respected governmental official, and the husband of a colleague. Anyway, who didn't have an old buddy who'd taken a wrong turn?

The carryover seemed minimal until Clark got home late that night and found Wanda on the floor, with a stream of vomit leading from her mouth.

All of Israel rejoiced at the news of the extermination of the Yousuf Hatoum network. Matilan, Magav, and all the units assigned to stop terror wherever they could find it, were especially elated, and within Matilan no one had more reason to cheer than Levi Hershko, who opened his email to find a new draft on *shakebadboy*.

358

Asshole didn't shoot himself in the head after all. The man needs our help, so get this through your thick Jew skull:

The whole world knows where Hatling is, all the time. But only I can get you his own personal mobile phone number, and when he's using it, IN REAL TIME. No Secret Service. Then it's over to you, assuming you can IMSI-grab and triangulate better than the average dickhead.

Levi Hershko found himself wanting to please that boy. He didn't want to let him down, wanted to erase *dickhead* from the boy's memory of him. He wondered who was turning who. He typed and saved:

Standing by . . .

44 IN THE NAME OF THE FATHER . . .

MOMENTS MATTER. ALL these years later and Clark still tried to follow at least that portion of the Buddhist path that his brother had just begun to explore for himself when the tanks rolled into Loc Ninh. Moments matter for themselves within the instant they occupy. This moment matters: the headlights of a rental car opening a cave of light in the rolling black mountain of midnight darkness that covered this backcountry Bluegrass road. Horses stood sleeping, breathing two streams of fog into the chill of the October night, their heads stuck out over fences, over greener grass and nearly out over the narrow road where Clark was driving. He noticed how their breath came out round as pipes, then diffused into clouds. From memory he could almost physically feel the velvet tips of their noses in his hand, their careful, dainty lips nuzzling his palm for a few oats.

This was home. This was Kentucky. As he drove he wondered whether Aziza might not forego France and move here with him. Would she love it as much as he did? Maybe it didn't have France's history of the Enlightenment's triumph over religious persecution, but in its short history it had won its own grand victories. A century and a half ago those horses would have been groomed by slaves. He would mention this to her tonight when he phoned. Just plant the seed there in her mind. If the polls were right it could lay dormant for four years.

Before his phone call he had to decide what to tell her about Wanda. Should he tell her that her ex-husband and Wanda had been having a sort of Internet affair, an exchange of passionate email fantasies? Should he tell her that Wanda had attempted suicide when she learned that Yousuf was dead? Should he tell her that her husband and Wanda had had a real-life affair in Beirut, right under their noses? Should he tell her that private nurses would stay with Wanda, in Pikeville, out of easy public view, until after the election?

Yes, he decided, if she asks about Wanda, I will tell her the whole story. I will not be the one to bring it up—we have four years to work this thing out. But if she asks, she gets all the facts.

He checked his phone and saw that he had a signal. The timing was fine—just after six in the morning in Beirut. By now she was used to taking his call even before she'd had coffee. Sometimes he could even hear her clinking around the kitchen making her first cup. That moment, too, mattered: her in a bathrobe and slippers, her hair every which a way, the phone scrunched between shoulder and ear. Then, with a coffee cup in one hand and her phone in the other, opening the back door with her elbow, and finally relaxing with him under the lemon tree in her back garden as dawn broke over Mount Lebanon and sunlight tipped the waves of the Mediterranean.

"Darling," he heard her say.

"Hi, love. Listen, I heard about Yousuf. Are you okay?"

"I'm fine. At least now Amin can escape his clutches, once and for all."

"Do you know the story behind his death?"

"Just what they're saying on the news. I knew that he'd been arrested. He was mixed up with some al Qaeda-type cell and the Saudis found out. Selling arms, is my guess. He wouldn't let a little innocent bloodshed stand between him and a pot of gold."

"Actually there was more to it than that. Hard line Saudi oil money was funding that training camp inside Syria, the same one that shot Abu Ali. The U.S. learned about the Saudi connection, told both the Saudi government and Syria to shut it down, or U.S. missiles would do it for them."

"Who told Washington about this?"

"Don't know. Probably Mossad. Maybe Saudi intelligence."

"Oh my God, Clark!"

"What is it?"

"I think I know! If it came through the Saudis, I may know who tipped off the U.S."

"Don't say anything else."

361

"No. But if the Saudi investigators started with Yousuf, I know how."

"They did start with Yousuf, worked their way backward and forward along the funding trail, and wiped out everyone they could find. Once he was exposed, he had no chance. I'm sorry."

"To me he's just another casualty of the war you need to stop. I can only hope he died without suffering."

Clark didn't answer that. Secret police don't uncover money trails by being merciful.

"The Syrians, for their part, want to act quietly. They're scared shitless the jihadists will win the loyalty of the average Syrian citizen—a fear the U.S. shares—so they don't know whether to try to co-opt them or snuff them out. They're trying to fracture them and contain them that way. At this point the U.S. is willing to give them time."

"How did you learn about all this?"

"I get briefed now. If the election goes as the polls predict, I'll be president in about three months."

"Then we'll have to shut down these phone calls."

He drove on silently for a few moments, wondering how he could get through the silence of four years. "I just thought you should know what had killed your ex-husband. You can't mention this to anyone, even the Sislers. Not even to Amin."

"Years ago Yousuf had the chance to be a decent man, but he couldn't resist the ambition to reach that pinnacle of power where the rules don't apply to you anymore. His end was inevitable. I was more concerned about Amin than anyone."

"How's he taking it so far?"

"I think he's going to be all right. He's back here with me now, back in his old room. Spends most of his time alone in there. He's trying to work his way through it."

"I wish you both could be with me right now. It would be therapeutic. It's so lovely here. I wish you could live this moment with me."

"Where is here, anyway?"

"I'm driving down some rural roads in Kentucky, outside Lexington. I have the roads all to myself." As he was saying that,

362

he glanced in his mirror and saw headlights closing the distance. In an instant a four-door pick-up slid past him and an instant later was disappearing red taillights. College students, he guessed, probably high on something. He wondered whether Jerry hadn't once traveled this same road, so much closer to the end of his life than anyone could have imagined.

"Are you having a brief rest before the final push?"

"I wish! There's a rally at the university tomorrow morning, lunch with somebody important—I forget who. Great photo ops at the Keeneland racetrack in the afternoon, and then off to Atlanta. But at least for this moment I am home. And I wish you were here at home with me."

"I am there with you. Not *as such*, perhaps."

"Here's a little secret for you: it's *as such* that I want you here. I hope that doesn't shock you."

"You shock easier than I do, *habibi*. I love that about you. How did you slip away?"

"I paid a kid in my campaign to rent a car for me. It was a great idea, too. As long as our signal holds up. This must be one of the ten happiest moments of my life. You and Kentucky and me, all together. Maybe you'd like to retire here? There's an idea."

"You just don't want to study French."

"You may be onto something there. But wouldn't you like to be here on such a night as this? We could put on wool hats and down jackets and walk down a country lane, checking out the clear skies for meteors. It's the Orionid shower, I think."

"Isn't it too early for wool hats?"

"That's what I was thinking, too. It's too bloody cold for October. Hey! I've just this second made a big policy decision. During my presidency I will give priority to speeding up the process of global warming. Down with catalytic converters! Up with . . . hang on . . . there's a couple of hunters standing in the road up ahead. Somebody must have been wounded. Don't go away."

She heard his brakes whine, heard his window coming down, and heard him say, "Can I help you boys?"

Then she heard, "In the name of the Father, the Son, and the

363

Holy Ghost." Then she heard gunfire.

It felt so familiar, sitting there in her bathrobe with CNN on, mourning his death, yet the very familiarity of it broke her grief with waves of rage. It was a betrayal. She'd already been through this once. She'd been through it and had come out the other side, in triumph. Nobody should have to do this twice in one lifetime. Nor should her people have to endure another catastrophe, another *nakhba*.

She sat and watched. Nobody knew about it yet. CNN was running a documentary on the Sahara eating up grain fields in Africa. Clark was dead and now here were a million more dead, with another million leather-bound skeletons waiting to die. The reporter said they were praying for rain. He didn't add, And a fat lot of good that will do them, but the final helicopter shot of the rolling dunes said it for him: graceful flowing sand lines with the odd minaret piercing through, and the odd church spire.

It took a long time for the news to break. At times Aziza could withdraw from the dramatic event. She knew he was dead. There was no tension about that. It seemed she'd been granted this short respite between hearing his death and hearing about it. There was this little vacation before the festivities started. BBC World was showing us around a museum in London. It was the Wallace Collection. There was a racy Eighteenth Century painting of a man lying on the ground to get a sneak peek up the billowing skirts of a pretty girl in a swing. They had a nice collection of medieval armor. Aziza caught herself thinking, That's a destination for Clark and me, when we retire.

Back on CNN it was the sports news. Apparently there had been a big badminton tournament somewhere. It never ceased to amaze her what people could take seriously. She realized that of the millions around the world who had turned on the news to find out whatever it was they were interested in, only she right now knew what would soon send a tremor through them all. She drank her coffee and for the moment hoped that if she kept quiet about it, it wouldn't really be true.

It took so long that when the big yellow letters of BREAKING

364

NEWS appeared, to Aziza it seemed more of a documentary. She managed to keep a historical distance until her phone rang, its flashing red screen mocking her detachment. It was Roxy, saying, "Darling, we'll be there in fifteen minutes."

45

THE FIRST OF the riots broke out in Gaza. Hamas had filled the streets with its foot soldiers, its old ladies and hangers-on, for some wild ululation and chest pounding. The crowd waved placards showing Clark's picture, with a fur hat and long sidelocks photoshopped onto it to conform to the Arab's stereotypical Jew, the comic Jew, the dirty, smelly, ignorant Jew, the dog-Jew. Surrounding all this was the big red circle-slash symbol of prohibition. The marchers carried signs saying *No Union With Jews* and *Drive Them into the Sea*. They shook their fists in rhythm to lots of *Death to America*'s, sprinkled liberally with *allahu-akhbar*'s.

Not one of the marchers seemed to know what was going on when people lining the streets also starting shaking their fists—not at America, but at the marchers themselves. The Hamas security men weren't prepared for anything more than a few onlookers. In fact their main brief was to spot those among the hand-picked demonstrators who didn't ululate shrilly enough or spit out *America* with sufficient venom. They didn't know how to react when people started to catcall the Hamas crowd, calling them government stooges and slaves to ignorance.

University students led the challenge into the streets. They dispersed the marchers at Islamic University and occupied the open quarter of Tel al-Hawa, still rebuilding from Israeli attacks. In the Olive District in eastern Gaza they blocked the narrow streets leading onto the square facing the Greek Orthodox church, and crowded toward the closed border crossings of Erez and Nahal Oz. In Jabaliya, students were joined and soon outnumbered by workers and housewives holding photos of the children killed when Israel bombed their United Nations school, alongside Clark's photo, his real photo this time, and his slogan, *Free Yourselves*.

In Jerusalem the ultra-orthodox poured into the streets with doctored placards of their own: Clark's face, draped in a black-

366

and-white *keffiyeh*, sporting an unkempt beard but no mustache. Fights broke out when onlookers plunged into the streets to seize and rip up the offending placards. The nasal cry of Israeli sirens cut through the afternoon air with wave after wave of drama as police filled their cells with the unwilling.

The next day Morty Warski's wheelchair led a Hatling commemoration march in Tiberias. By now Tiberias had adopted Clark as its own, and there was open weeping on the streets. Later that night a hundred thousand people carried candles down Dizengoff Street in Tel Aviv. By the third day marches had been held in Amman, Cairo, Dubai, Haifa. They were everywhere. In the U.S., every city of any size saw a massive turn-out of Hatling sympathizers. Arabs outnumbered Jews in the Detroit demonstration; Jews outnumbered Arabs in New York. Everywhere the police were out in strength and in armor, but incidents were rare. It was the time for the mourning that lays the foundation for renewal. The signs said, *You Can't Assassinate the Desire for Peace* and *Kill the Dreamer, the Dream Lives On.*

However, on the fourth day, from somewhere in hiding, the assassins released a video that changed everything. Three men in hunters' camouflage, their faces hidden by balaclavas, were shown standing in front of a plain plank building, apparently a barn or outbuilding. Only one of the men spoke. His accent was more central Kentucky than eastern. He said they were affiliated with a local Christian group called the Rapture Tabernacle. The group was committed to preserving Israel as a Zionist state until such time as mass Jewish conversion to Christianity would usher in the End Days, as foretold in Matthew 23. He quoted: O Jerusalem, Jerusalem, thou that killest the prophets . . . Ye shall not see me henceforth, till ye shall say, *Blessed is he that cometh in the name of the Lord.*

Aziza watched this from her sofa. She was still in her nightgown—hadn't even gotten bothered to get dressed before Walter and Roxy's visit. During the next three days she managed to brush her teeth once or twice, and eat a few of the dates from a basket on the coffee table. She kept the TV on a 24-hour news channel. Occasionally she dozed off. Amin rarely appeared outside his room. He was in there with his computer and his own TV, so she let him work it out his own way.

Walter and Roxy left for America. The State Department rewarded Walter with full repatriation for his help in exposing the Saudi terror banking complex, and, upon Clark's death, expedited this to an emergency return. They needed to be at Arlington National Cemetery for the funeral.

Aziza rallied a bit when Aliya phoned, but now it seemed all their conversations were tearful. The good news this time—although as far as Aziza was concerned it wasn't so bloody great—was that Aliya's husband had been offered an *amazing* job there in Sao Paulo, and they'd found an *amazing* villa in some section of the city that Aziza had never heard of and couldn't pronounce. So in a few months, after they'd settled in, Aziza would *have* to come to Brazil, where the people were so laid-back and cool. Then Aziza mentioned the massive Beirut candlelight march that would follow the televised coverage of Clark's funeral, and they started to cry again.

Commentators predicted there would be no violence. Clark was a hometown hero. On the day after the assassination, every Beirut newspaper was printed with black bands around the front page. Someone had found an old photograph of Clark in his AUB basketball uniform and had made a small fortune printing it on t-shirts. It seemed that half the people on the street were wearing Hatling t-shirts and black arm bands. Shi'as, Sunnis, Christians, Druze—it didn't matter. They all saw him as a fair-minded candidate, and one of their own. Even Hezbollah had expressed its official outrage at his murder, and went soft on the rhetoric, mentioning that a one-state Palestine would not be a Zionist entity, and that Jews, like Christians, were protected as "people of the book."

The three groups who hated Hatling and his policies were not seen as major players in Beirut. Rejectionist Jews and Rapture Christians weren't in the picture. Al Qaeda terrorists caused a problem for the security forces, but had been defeated badly in past battles, and were under close scrutiny.

Reports on the American election showed utter confusion

as to what to do next. Federal law stipulated election day as the first Tuesday after the first Monday in November, but that was not a part of the Constitution. Congress would need to meet in emergency session in the week following Clark's funeral. They had the power to postpone an election. The Democrat's charter and bylaws sent the choice to the Democratic National Committee. Would they simply elevate Elise Torsvik to the top spot, as would have happened if Clark had been killed while in office? In the three days since his death she had said almost nothing beyond expressing her deep sorrow at her personal loss, and the loss to the nation. She said she would "withdraw to grieve" until after the funeral. The only hint that she even wanted to be included in any future consideration was a vague reference to the "common view" she had held with Congressman Hatling on the problems the next administration would face. Optimistic Arab commentators took that to mean she would follow Clark's lead, ignore the region's intransigent governments and take her message straight to the people, but that might have been an extrapolation of her comments into the realm of wishful thinking.

Other Democrats thought it best to look back to the primaries for the second highest vote winner. That would be Chris Laverty, so disgraced by his secret meeting with Abu Ali, but now at least partially rehabilitated by his active role in the Hatling campaign. Then there was good old Steve Foreman, with experience in the role of vice-president, at least, and generally liked and respected as a decent guy. Would they run him again as the bottom of the ticket, with Elise in the top spot?

Nobody knew anything; nobody said anything publicly. Officially, everybody was in silent mourning until after the election.

Between naps, she heard all that, and Clark's voice. They aired his speeches and interviews again and again. In her sleep she heard him too, only there he was talking to her. *I lost you once. I'm afraid if I miss this chance I will lose you forever. I am the former president of the United States, and you're going to dance with me. I have the best security force in the world to protect me.*

"Stay with them!" In her sleep she was trying to form the words. Her locked throat forced her awake, then forced her to remember

369

that he had breeched his protective barriers only because of her. Why hadn't she refused? Why hadn't she just let the goddamn phone flash its hellish red screen until he gave up and returned to safety? The pain in her seemed to split her chest straight down the sternum, as surgeons must when they remove a damaged heart. Her only anesthesia was sleep, but with it came his voice, and her struggle to respond, and it all started again.

The screen showed the cemetery at Arlington in its full autumn beauty. His grave was open under burning red oaks. A rim of bright leaves relieved the black rectangle, and extended to cover Jerry's grave beside him. In a week or two it would be as though a russet blanket had been thrown over both Hatling boys. She imagined their mother doing just that, as they slept through some October night long ago, when the chill crept in.

Cameras showed the horses waiting patiently, barely stamping, as the steam rose from their backs. The empty bed of the caisson seemed in no hurry either.

The station cut away for breaking news. It showed a still photograph of those three murderers, again in front of a wooden structure. Aziza started searching the background for clues, but then realized it was a grab from the original video. Only the message was new. The newsman read from the script on the screen: *On this solemn occasion we invite all the Jews of Israel to join us in the loving arms of Our Lord Jesus Christ, that we may hasten His return and join Him at the right hand of the Father. We acted as we did for the salvation of all the world. We acted on instructions from God Almighty Himself, as recorded in the Holy Book, the literal Word of God. From the standpoint of man's law, we acted alone. We had no accomplices. But we were not alone. God the Father guided our hands. God the Father pulled the trigger. His will be done. Amen.*

Aziza couldn't take this stuff any longer. She hit the mute button and left the sofa in order to take her first shower since the assassination. She put on jeans and a sweater she hadn't worn for nearly a year. She thought she could still detect the scent of the beeches of the low Pyrenees, and of Clark's cologne, in the wool. It was proper that she should wear this to tonight's commemorative march.

She tapped on Amin's door and called out, "It's almost time for the burial. Want to watch it out here with me?"

She received no answer, so she returned to the TV and put the sound back on. The rows of chairs were filling up now. The camera picked out faces as the announcer named some of the seated guests. The Warskis and their Filipina maid were honored as second row guests, as were Elise Torsvik, Chris Laverty, Steve Foreman, and their spouses. Danielle and Cole Gibson stood to hug, even to support, Toody, the great Frank Baker, who now appeared old and depleted. Wanda, front and center, all in black, black-veiled, sat as still as a monument and emitted a brave and dignified nobility. Roxy and Walter sat on one side of her, the President and First Lady on the other. Aziza knew that she should be the one in that chair, but it didn't matter. It would hurt no less there than in Beirut. It hurt where the loss was; you carried it with you.

Again she muted the sound. She suddenly realized that she was sick of announcers' voices and experts droning on, sick even of Clark's own public voice. What she wanted to hear was him being himself, talking to her as his real self. She remembered that he'd left several voice messages that she had not had the heart to erase. She got up to look for her phone, but couldn't locate it. She called out again for Amin. Where the hell had she left it? Was it even charged anyway?

She didn't know why Amin hadn't come out, so she walked back to his room and put her ear to his door. Not a sound. She rapped loudly, waited, and tried the door handle. It was locked. She called for him throughout the house, then came back to try the handle again. She peeked through the keyhole and saw that his key was on the inside. Her knees gave and she found herself leaning against a wall as the realization rushed over her that her silent son was inside this room.

She knew there was an extra set of keys somewhere around the house. Every one of the stupid doors in these old Ottoman-era homes had big skeleton-key locks, but to her knowledge nobody had used them in years. Somewhere, though . . . where was it? As she steadied herself physically, she tried to concentrate. *When* would she have seen them? Let's start there. When was the last time she'd rummaged through odd parts of the house? It must have been when Yousuf moved out. She'd taken that opportunity to sort out years' worth of junk.

She couldn't believe that while her son might be passed out in his room and her darling Clark was being buried, she was looking for a set of keys. But she was, not frantically, but . . . Yes! They were in an old equipment trunk where Yousuf had stored a ham radio set from his youth. She'd kept the radio because, who knows, it might be a valuable antique some day, and those extra keys were in there.

A solid metal ring held twenty or thirty dusty keys together. It was like carrying a dumbbell. She called through the door, "Hold on, Amin. *Maman* is right here." She tried a key at random and discovered that in order to insert it from her side she needed to dislodge the key from his side. "Amin baby if you can hear *maman*, can you take the key from your door? Just try to make it to the door and pull out the key."

There was no sound from inside the room. She got a kebab skewer from the kitchen and maneuvered it inside the lock until she heard the key bounce off the marble floor of Amin's room.

"We're making progress!" she called. "Just hang on!"

Now for the trial of one key after another. Her fingers seemed to give up hope, but her voice tried to stay steady. "Nope, not this one. Only a few more left. I'll be there quick as a flash!"

Thinking he might be lying with his head near the door, she opened it carefully and found that it opened without obstruction into an unlit room cluttered with computer parts, cables, gadgets, tools and debris, but no Amin. She switched on a light and was picking her way through the rubble toward the window when suddenly a plastic bag, a head, and then a leg, appeared through the crack in the curtains. She screamed, but turned it into a weak laugh when she realized that it was her son.

"Allah!" she said, and noticed that she was holding that bundle of keys over her head, like a weapon. "What are you doing? I was frantic."

"What are you doing in here? I thought I locked the door." Then he noticed the keys.

372

Of all the whirling emotions running through her at this second, the one that took control was embarrassment. "I was looking for my phone, and found your door . . . I thought maybe you had fallen or something."

"Why would I do that?" He put down the bag.

"Oh, there it is." She spotted her phone on his table. It came to her that this had all started as a search for Clark's voice messages, so she sat down to find them.

"Mom, let me have the phone." She looked up. "Give me the phone and please leave my room."

What was this? What gave this man the right to put her through all this nonsense and then try to take away her last memory of her lost years?

"Why do you use the window?"

"It's closer to the street."

"It's ten feet off the ground."

"There's a ladder from the balcony."

"A ladder?" She thought of his heroin trip to Israel. Was he back at that again? Had he ever really stopped? "And why is your room such a mess? What kind of hobby are you running here? What's in the bag?" She grabbed it quickly, although he made no move to stop her.

"It's a vest. I'm wearing it on the march."

She stuck her phone into her jeans pocket, in case he had notions of taking it, and looked into the bag. It was, in fact, a vest, a sturdy one like hikers use, lined with big pockets. She held it up, turned it this way and that. She was looking for a slogan or something. There was nothing to indicate why anyone would need this vest for a funeral march.

She folded it and put in back on the table, between a laptop, some gadgets that might have been gaming equipment, cables, wire cutters. There was a bundle of clay-like tubes slung together, like sausages, with copper wire. She didn't touch anything. Amin's eyes ignored her face. They were watching her hands.

Screw him. All she wanted was to hear Clark's voice. She took out her phone.

"Mom. Give me your phone."

She gripped it tight. She'd fight him for it, if it came to that. She punched through the menu. She didn't actually know how to locate undeleted audio files, and the person who usually got her through these technical thickets had somehow become the enemy. She located Voice Files and pressed OK. Her own voice came out with surprising clarity. *Clark's hotel in Tiberias is the Galilee. Three nights.*

She tried to prevent her mind from making all the links, those compelling bonds of unreason. She looked at the clay sausages, and at her son. She spoke softly, as before a sick and dying person. "I made that recording for myself, so I wouldn't forget the name of the hotel. What did you do with it?"

"I destroyed his hotel."

"Do you really believe that?"

"Absolutely. I told an Israeli agent. I don't really know the details of what followed."

"And the assassination?"

"Same thing. I'm responsible for his death. Thanks be to God."

"Let's forget about the march for now. Sit down and let's talk. We can get you some help."

He sat, but didn't take his eyes off her phone. She stroked the keys with her thumb, lovingly, as though touching the repository of her last grains of happiness, and watched Amin's eyes grow frantic. She looked at her speed dial list and saw that Clark's number one was now labeled *Allahu Akhbar.*

She fought against the way the pieces seemed to fit, against the simple geometry of understanding. Gently, she stroked the key with her thumb, looked at the string of plastic explosives, then at Amin. He was watching her eyes.

"You might as well know," he told her, "that you also got Abu Ali for me. Or had you figured that out on your own?"

"What do you mean?"

"I copied the photo from your phone."

"You little fool."

"He sold his soul to the Syrian Shi'a, and had to go."

"It wasn't even the real Abu Ali. It was a double, an imposter." She threw her head back and had her first real laugh in days.

374

"No matter. He had to go."

"Yeah, well, we all gotta go, Amin. Surely you figured that one out."

"Tell me, *maman*, was he my real father?"

He hadn't called her *maman* since he was little, except sometimes, as a teenager, when he was sick. How had she got this one so wrong?

"Clark? Of course he wasn't your father. But I can tell you this—he should have been. I wish he had been. You would wish so too, if you felt better."

"I feel great."

"That's my point. But we both know you didn't kill him. Those Christian lunatics killed him. I heard them myself."

"Ibn Burak killed him!"

"What do you mean by that?"

"Whenever you were on the phone early in the morning, I knew he was outside his security. I contacted an Israeli agent, and finally we got lucky."

"Lucky? You and the Israelis got *lucky?* He was the best hope our people ever had! How can you talk such rubbish?"

"I don't want to share Palestine. They don't want to share Palestine. The enemy of my enemy is my friend. Don't you know that rule of warfare?"

She ignored the question. She had studied thousands of years of warfare. They never disappeared, these ligatures of hatred. She repeated, "We can get you some help."

"You don't think I could pull it off, do you?"

"I mean, come on, son. You and Mossad teaming up against the U.S.?"

"I'll show you!" He pulled his laptop around. "I'll bloody well prove that I did it. He and I have an email address that only the two of us know about. With regular emails, if you write a message and send it, there's a transit record created. But if you just save it as a draft, there's no record of it. Anyone else with access to the address just goes in, reads your saved draft, writes a reply and saves it. It's as simple as that. I'll show you." He logged on to shakebadboy@ hotmail.il. "What you'll see is my last message, which just says

NOW! and gives a time. I think it was 06:06. Meaning you'd just started talking to him then."

She put her phone securely down in her jeans pocket as he turned the screen to where she could see it. Big red letters came up: INCORRECT ADDRESS.

"Wait a second." He tried again, then shouted, "That bastard! He's cancelled the account! ASSHOLE! I swear to you that's how we did it. Mom, I swear!"

"It's okay, Amin. I believe you. And you must believe me, we can find you some help. We can get through this."

"Get this through your head: I don't want to get through this. I'm proud of what I did. I am a *mujahideen*! He was trying to take away my God!"

Aziza sat back down, bent well over, put her hands in her hair, and said, "This is all my fault. I could have stopped this. Do you see that? I've killed the Palestinian dream, and my darling Clark."

"No! I killed him! He was trying to take my God from me, and now he will burn forever!"

She stood, walked to where he now sat slumped, and put her arms around him. "I should have told you, baby. This heaven-hell-God-Satan thing, it's all a big fantasy. It's Harry Potter, the Lord of the Rings. It's Superman and Père Noël. It's all made up because it helps people get through life."

"*Mulhad!* You're one of them. I knew you were. My real father told me."

"I'm so sorry. I could have prevented this. I just let things . . . I don't know why. The easiest way, I guess."

"Stop it. You're one of them!"

"And so you will kill me too? Is that a brave act of *jihad*, killing your mother? Do you get instantly cleansed for that, and go straight to heaven? Such silliness you people believe."

"It's all true. You'll soon know it's true, when the fires lick at you."

"I've killed the dream of my people, and killed my only love, because I didn't have the courage to explain to you that it was all a fantasy."

"Not fantasy!"

376

"And you were going to stuff that plastic explosive into this new vest, walk with me by candlelight, and use my phone to blow yourself up, along with your mother and as many other mourners as you could?"

"Those were my orders."

"And then you believe you'll instantly be in paradise with gardens and endless bowls of fruit and great sex and all that nonsense?"

"I *know* it's true."

"And I'll join Clark as eternal mutton *shawarma* on a spit?" She had to laugh at it all. Life had crossed over into farce. She'd had about all she wanted of it.

"It's the truth. You don't have to believe it."

"I certainly don't believe it. But I'll tell you what, Amin . . ." She fished her phone from her rear pocket, pressed speed dial one. As the mocking red screen flashed *Allahu Akhbar*, she said, "Let's find out."

377

www.ingramcontent.com/pod-product-compliance
Lightning Source LLC
Chambersburg PA
CBHW071647260626
47170CB00001B/276